Cruz only had Trinity's eyes **before his mouth crasheu uown onto hers.**

For a long moment nothing existed except this pure, spiking shard of lust—so strong that he had no option but to move his mouth and haul her even closer, until he could feel every luscious curve pressed against him.

And it was only in that moment, when their mouths were fused and he could feel her heart clamouring against his chest, that he could finally recognise the truth: he'd been aching for this moment since the night he'd kissed her for the first time.

Wedlocked!

Conveniently wedded, passionately bedded!

Whether there's a debt to be paid,
a will to be obeyed or a business to be saved…
She's got no choice but to say, 'I do!'

But these billionaire bridegrooms have got another
think coming if they think marriage will be that easy…

Soon their convenient brides become the object
of an *inconvenient* desire!

Find out what happens after the vows in

The Billionaire's Defiant Acquisition
by Sharon Kendrick

One Night to Wedding Vows
by Kim Lawrence

Wedded, Bedded, Betrayed
by Michelle Smart

Expecting a Royal Scandal
by Caitlin Crews

Trapped by Vialli's Vows
by Chantelle Shaw

A Diamond for Del Rio's Housekeeper
by Susan Stephens

Baby of His Revenge
by Jennie Lucas

Bound by His Desert Diamond
by Andie Brock

Bride by Royal Decree
by Caitlin Crews

Look out for more **Wedlocked!** stories
coming soon!

CLAIMED FOR THE DE CARRILLO TWINS

BY
ABBY GREEN

First Published in Great Britain 2017
By Mills & Boon, an imprint of HarperCollins*Publishers*
1 London Bridge Street, London, SE1 9GF

ISBN: 978-0-263-92512-8

Our policy is to use papers that are natural, renewable and recyclable
products and made from wood grown in sustainable forests. The logging
and manufacturing processes conform to the legal environmental
regulations of the country of origin.

Printed and bound in Spain
by CPI, Barcelona

Irish author **Abby Green** threw in a very glamorous career in film and TV—which really consisted of a lot of standing in the rain outside actors' trailers—to pursue her love of romance. After she'd bombarded Mills & Boon with manuscripts they kindly accepted one, and an author was born. She lives in Dublin, Ireland, and loves any excuse for distraction. Visit abby-green.com or e-mail abbygreenauthor@gmail.com.

Books by Abby Green

Mills & Boon Modern Romance

Awakened by Her Desert Captor
Forgiven but not Forgotten?
Exquisite Revenge
One Night With The Enemy
The Legend of De Marco
The Call of the Desert
The Sultan's Choice
Secrets of the Oasis
In Christofides' Keeping

Brides for Billionaires

Married for the Tycoon's Empire

One Night With Consequences

An Heir Fit for a King
An Heir to Make a Marriage

Billionaire Brothers

Fonseca's Fury
The Bride Fonseca Needs

Blood Brothers

When Falcone's World Stops Turning
When Christakos Meets His Match
When Da Silva Breaks the Rules

Visit the Author Profile page at millsandboon.co.uk for more titles.

I'd like to thank Heidi Rice, Sharon Kendrick and Iona Grey for all their cheerleading, Kate Meader, who provided counsel over cocktails in the Shelbourne, and Annie West, who always provides serene and insightful advice. And of course my editor, Sheila, who has proved beyond doubt that she believes me capable of anything, apart from perhaps AWAVMOT!

Thank you all!

PROLOGUE

CRUZ DE CARRILLO SURVEYED the thronged reception room in his London home, filled with a veritable who's who of London's most powerful players and beautiful people, all there to celebrate his return to Europe.

He felt no sense of accomplishment, though, to be riding high on the crest of his stratospheric success in North America, having tripled his eponymous bank's fortunes in less than a year, because he knew his zealous focus on work had more to do with avoiding *this* than the burning ambition he'd harboured for years to turn his family bank's fortune and reputation around.

And it killed him to admit it.

This was standing just feet away from him now—tall and slender, yet with generous curves. Pale skin. Too much pale skin. Exposed in a dress that left far too little to the imagination. Cruz's mouth compressed with distaste even as his blood ran hot, mocking him for the desire which time hadn't diminished—much to his intense irritation. It was unwelcome and completely inappropriate. Now more than ever. She was his sister-in-law.

Her blonde hair was up in a sleek chignon and a chain of glittering gold trailed tantalisingly down her naked back, bared in a daring royal blue backless dress. She turned slightly in Cruz's direction and he had to tense every muscle to stave off the surge of fresh desire when he saw the provocative curves of her high full breasts, barely disguised by the thin draped satin.

She looked almost vulnerable, set apart from the crowd slightly, but he knew that was just a mirage.

He cursed her. And he cursed himself. If he hadn't been

so weak he wouldn't know how incendiary it felt to have those curves pressed against his body. He wouldn't remember the way her eyes had turned a stormy dark blue as he'd plundered the sweetness she'd offered up to him that fateful night almost eighteen months ago, in this very house, when she'd worked for him as a housemaid.

He wouldn't still hear her soft, breathy moans in his dreams, forcing him awake, sweating, with his hand wrapped around himself and every part of him straining for release…aching to know the intimate clasp of her body, milking him into sweet oblivion.

Sweet. That was just it. There was nothing sweet about this woman. He might have thought so at one time—she'd used to blush if he so much as glanced at her—but it had all been an elaborate artifice. Because his younger half-brother, Rio, had told him the truth about what she really was, and she was no innocent.

Her seduction of Cruz had obviously been far more calculated than he'd believed, and when that hadn't worked she'd diverted her sights onto Rio, his illegitimate half-brother, with whom Cruz had a complicated relationship—to put it mildly.

A chasm had been forged between the brothers when they were children—when Cruz had been afforded every privilege as the legitimate heir to the De Carrillo fortune, and Rio, who had been born to a housemaid of the family *castillo*, had been afforded nothing. Not even the De Carrillo name.

But Cruz had never felt that Rio should be punished for their charismatic and far too handsome father's inability to control his base appetites. So he had done everything in his power after their father had died some ten years previously to make amends—going against their father's will, which had left Rio nothing, by becoming his guardian, giving him his rightful paternalistic name and paying for him to complete his education.

Then, when he had come of age, Cruz had given him a fair share of his inheritance *and* a job—first in the De Carrillo bank in Madrid, and now in London, much to the conservative board's displeasure.

At the age of twenty-one Rio had become one of Europe's newest millionaires, the centre of feverish media attention with his dark good looks and mysterious past. And he had lapped it up, displaying an appetite for the kind of playboy lifestyle Cruz had never indulged in, quickly marrying one of the world's top supermodels in a lavish wedding that had gone on for days—only for it to end in tragedy nearly a year later, when she'd died in an accident shortly after giving birth to twin boys.

And yet, much as Rio's full-throttle existence had unnerved Cruz, could he begrudge him that after being denied his heritage?

Cruz's conscience pricked. By giving Rio his due inheritance and his rightful name perhaps he'd made his brother a target for gold-diggers? Rio's first wife had certainly revelled in her husband's luxurious lifestyle, and it would appear as if nothing had changed with his second wife.

As if sensing his intense regard, his sister-in-law turned now and saw him. Her eyes widened and her cheeks flushed. Cruz's anger spiked. She could still turn it on. Even now. When he knew her real capabilities.

She faced him in that provocative dress and her luscious body filled his vision and made his blood thrum with need. He hated her for it. She moved towards him almost hesitantly, the slippery satin material moving sinuously around her long legs.

He called on every atom of control he had and schooled his body not to respond to her proximity even as her tantalising scent tickled his nostrils, threatening to weaken him all over again. It was all at once innocent, yet seductive. As if he needed reminding that she presented one face to the world while hiding another, far more mercenary one.

'Trinity.' His voice sounded unbearably curt to his ears, and he tried to ignore the striking light blue eyes. To ignore how lush her mouth was, adding a distinctly sensual edge to her pale blonde innocence.

An innocence that was skin-deep.

'Cruz…it's nice to see you again.'

Her voice was husky, reminding him vividly of how it had sounded in his ear that night. *'Please…'*

His dry tone disguised his banked rage. 'You've come up in the world since we last met.'

She swallowed, the long, delicate column of her pale throat moving. 'Wh-what do you mean?'

Cruz's jaw tightened at the faux innocence. 'I'm talking about your rapid ascent from the position of nanny to wife and stepmother to my nephews.'

That brought back the unwelcome reminder that he'd only been informed about the low-key wedding in a text from Rio.

I have you to thank for sending this beautiful woman into my life. I hope you'll be very happy for us, brother.

The news had precipitated shock, and something much darker into Cruz's gut. And yet he hadn't had any reason at that point not to believe it was a good idea—in spite of his own previous experience with Trinity, which he'd blamed himself for. Rio had been a widower, and he and Trinity had obviously forged a bond based on caring for his nephews. Cruz had believed that she was a million light years away from Rio's glamorous hedonistic first wife. *Then.*

The fact that he'd had dreams for weeks afterwards,

of being held back and forced to watch a faceless blonde woman making love to countless men, was something that made him burn inwardly with shame even now.

Trinity looked pale. Hesitant. 'I was looking for you, actually. Could we have a private word?'

Cruz crushed the unwelcome memory and arched a brow. 'A private word?'

He flicked a glance at the crowd behind her and then looked back to her, wondering what the hell she was up to. Surely she wouldn't have the gall to try and seduce him under the same roof she had before, with her husband just feet away?

'We're private enough here. No one is listening.'

She flushed and then glanced behind her and back, clearly reluctant. 'Perhaps this isn't the best time or place...'

So he'd been right. Disgust settled in his belly. 'Spit it out, Trinity. Unless it's not *talking* you're interested in.'

She blanched, and that delicate flush disappeared. Once her ability to display emotions had intrigued him. Now it incensed him.

'What do you mean?'

'You know very well what I mean. You tried to seduce me in this very house, and when it didn't work you transferred your attentions to my brother. He obviously proved to be more susceptible to your wiles.'

She shook her head and frowned, a visibly trembling hand coming up to her chest as if to contain shock, disbelief. 'I don't know what you're talking about...'

Disgust filled Cruz that she could stand here and so blatantly lie while her enormous rock of an engagement ring glinted at him mockingly. All he could see was her and her treachery. But he had to crush the recriminations that rose up inside him—it was too late for them now.

Rio had revealed to Cruz on his return to the UK a

few days before that he was on the verge of bankruptcy—
his huge inheritance all but wiped out. And Trinity De
Carrillo's name was all over nearly every receipt and
docket that had led his brother further and further into
the mire. The extent of how badly Cruz had misread her
was galling.

An insidious thought occurred to him and it made his
blood boil. 'Your innocent act is past its sell-by date. I
might not have realised what you were up to—more fool
me—but I know now. Rio has told me how you've single-
handedly run through almost every cent he has to his name
in a bid to satisfy your greedy nature. Now you're realising
his fortune isn't a bottomless pit, perhaps you're looking
for a way out, or even a new benefactor?'

Before she could respond he continued in a low, bitter voice.

'I underestimated your capacity to play the long game,
Trinity. You lulled Rio into a false sense of trust by manipulating his biggest vulnerability—his sons. I'm very
well aware of how my actions pushed you in the direction of my brother, and that is not something I will ever
forgive myself for. Needless to say if he requires financial help he will receive it, but your days of bankrupting
him are over. If you're hoping to bargain your way out
of this predicament then think again. You'll get no sympathy from me.'

Trinity was so white now Cruz fancied he could see the
blood vessels under her skin. A part of him wished she
would break out of character and get angry with him for
confronting her with who she really was.

Her hand dropped back to her side and she shook her
head. 'You have it all wrong.'

'That's the best you can come up with?' he sneered. 'I
have it *all wrong*? If I "have it all wrong" then, please, tell
me what you want to discuss.'

Cruz could see the pulse at the base of her neck beating hectically. His own pulse-rate doubled.

'I wanted to talk to you about Rio…about his behaviour. It's been growing more and more erratic… I'm worried about the boys.'

Cruz let out a short, incredulous laugh. 'Worried about the boys? You're really trying to play the concerned stepmother card in a bid to deflect attention from the fact that you're more concerned about your lavish lifestyle coming to an end?'

Bitterness filled Cruz. He knew better than most how the biological bond of a parent and child didn't guarantee love and security. Far from it.

'You're not even related to them—you've just used them as pawns to manipulate your way into my brother's bed and get a ring on your finger.'

Trinity took a step back, her eyes wide with feigned shock. He had to hand it to her. She was a good actress.

Almost as if she was talking to herself now, she said, 'I should have known he'd protect himself somehow…of course you'd believe him over me.'

A sliver of unease pierced Cruz's anger but he pushed it aside. 'I've known Rio all of his twenty-five years. I think it's safe to say I'd trust my own flesh and blood over a conniving gold-digger any day of the week.'

Heated colour came back into Trinity's cheeks. She looked at him, big blue eyes beseeching him with commendable authenticity.

'I'm not a gold-digger. You don't understand. Everything you're saying is all wrong—my marriage with Rio is not what you—'

'*There* you are, darling. I've been looking for you. Charlotte Lacey wants to talk to you about next week's charity function.'

Cruz blanched. He hadn't even noticed Rio joining

them. He'd been consumed with the woman in front of him, whose arm was now being taken firmly in her husband's hand. Rio's dark brown eyes met Cruz's over Trinity's head. They were hard. Trinity had gone even paler, if that was possible.

'If you don't mind, brother, I need to steal my wife away.'

Cruz could see it in Rio's eyes then—a familiar resentment. And shame and anger. Futility choked him. There was nothing he could do. He knew Rio would already be despising the fact that he'd allowed Cruz to see him brought so low at this woman's greedy hands.

He watched as they walked back into the crowd, and it wasn't long before they left for the evening—without saying goodbye. Rio might have shown Cruz a chink of vulnerability by revealing his financial problems, but if anything that only demonstrated how much Trinity had got to him—because he'd never before allowed his brother to see a moment's weakness. Cruz's sense that his determination to see Rio treated fairly had been futile rose up again—he had never truly bridged the gap between them.

Cruz stood at the window in his drawing room and watched his brother handing Trinity into the passenger seat of a dark Jeep in the forecourt outside the house, before he got into the driver's seat himself.

He felt grim. All he could do now was be there to pick up the pieces of Rio's financial meltdown and do his best to ensure that Rio got a chance to start again—and that his wife didn't get her grasping hands on another cent.

At the last second, as if hearing his thoughts, Trinity turned her head to look at Cruz through the ground-floor window. For a fleeting moment their eyes met, and he could have sworn he saw hers shimmer with moisture, even from this distance.

He told himself they had to be tears of anger now that

she knew she'd been found out. She was trapped in a situation of her own making. It should have filled Cruz with a sense of satisfaction, but instead all he felt was a heavy weight in his chest.

Rio's Jeep took off with a spurt of gravel.

Cruz didn't realise it then, but it would be the last time he saw his brother alive.

CHAPTER ONE

Three months later. Solicitor's office.

TRINITY'S HEART STOPPED and her mouth dried. 'Mr De Carrillo is joining us?'

The solicitor glanced at her distractedly, looking for a paper on his overcrowded desktop. 'Yes—he is the executor of his brother's will, and we *are* in his building,' he pointed out redundantly.

She'd been acutely aware that she was in the impressive De Carrillo building in London's bustling financial zone, but it hadn't actually occurred to her that Cruz himself would be here.

To her shame, her first instinct was to check her appearance—which of course she couldn't do, but she was glad of the choice of clothing she'd made: dark loose trousers and a grey silk shirt. She'd tied her long hair back in a braid, as much out of habit when dealing with small energetic boys than for any other reason. She hadn't put on any make-up and regretted that now, fearing she must look about eighteen.

Just then there was a light knock on the door and it opened. She heard Mr Drew's assistant saying in a suspiciously breathless and awestruck voice, 'Mr De Carrillo, sir.'

The solicitor stood up, immediately obsequious, greeting Cruz De Carrillo effusively and leading him to a seat beside Trinity's on the other side of his desk.

Every nerve came to immediate and tingling life. The tiny hairs on her arms stood up, quivering. She lamented her uncontrollable reaction—would she ever *not* react to him?

She sensed him come to stand near her, tall and effort-lessly intimidating. Childishly, she wanted to avoid look-ing at him. His scent was a tantalising mix of musk and something earthy and masculine. It was his scent now that sent her hurtling back to that cataclysmic evening in his house three months ago, when she'd realised just how badly Rio had betrayed her.

The shock of knowing that Rio obviously hadn't told him the truth about their marriage was still palpable, even now. And the fact that Cruz had so readily believed the worst of her hurt far worse than it should.

It had hurt almost as much as when he'd looked at her with dawning horror and self-disgust after kissing her to within an inch of her life. It was an experience still seared onto her brain, so deeply embedded inside her that she sometimes woke from X-rated dreams, tangled amongst her sheets and sweating. Almost two years later it was be-yond humiliating.

Trinity dragged her mind away from that disturbing labyrinth of memories. She had more important things to deal with now. Because three months ago, while she and Rio had been driving home from Cruz's house, they'd been involved in a car crash and Rio had tragically died.

Since that day she'd become lone step-parent to Mateo and Sancho, Rio's two-and-a-half-year-old twins. Miracu-lously, she'd escaped from the accident with only cuts and bruises and a badly sprained ankle. She had no memory of the actual accident—only recalled waking in the hospi-tal feeling battered all over and learning of her husband's death from a grim and ashen-faced Cruz.

Gathering her composure, she stood up to face him, steeling herself against his effect. Which was useless. As soon as she looked at him it was like a blow to her solar plexus.

She'd seen him since the night of the accident—at the

funeral, of course, and then when he'd called at the house for brief perfunctory visits to check that she and his nephews had everything they needed. He hadn't engaged with her beyond that. Her skin prickled now with foreboding. She had a sense that he'd merely been biding his time.

She forced herself to say, as calmly as she could, 'Cruz.'

'Trinity.'

His voice reverberated deep inside her, even as he oozed his habitual icy control.

The solicitor had gone back around his desk and said now, 'Espresso, wasn't it, Mr De Carrillo?'

Trinity blinked and looked to see the older gentleman holding out a small cup and saucer. Instinctively, because she was closer and because it was good manners, she reached for it to hand it to Cruz, only belatedly realising that her hand was trembling.

She prayed he wouldn't notice the tremor as she held out the delicate china to him. His hand was masculine and square. Strong. Long fingers…short, functional nails. At that moment she had a flash of remembering how his hand had felt between her legs, stroking her intimately…

Just before he took the cup and saucer there was a tiny clatter of porcelain on porcelain, evidence of her frayed nerves. *Damn.*

When he had the cup she sat down again quickly, before she made a complete fool of herself, and took a quick fortifying sip of her own cup of tea. He sat down too, and she was aware of his powerful body taking up a lot of space.

While Mr. Drew engaged Cruz De Carrillo in light conversation, before they started discussing the terms of Rio's will, Trinity risked another glance at the man just a couple of feet to her left.

Short dark blond hair gave more than a hint of his supremely controlled nature. Controlled except for that momentary lapse…an undoubtedly rare moment of heated insanity with someone he'd seen as far beneath him.

Trinity crushed the spike of emotion. She couldn't afford it.

Despite the urbane uniform of a three-piece suit, his impressive build was apparent. Muscles pushed at the fabric in a way that said he couldn't be contained, no matter how civilised he might look.

His face was a stunning portrait of masculine beauty, all hard lines and an aquiline profile that spoke of a pure and powerful bloodline. He had deep-set eyes and a mouth that on anyone else would have looked ridiculously sensual. Right now though, it looked stern. Disapproving.

Trinity realised that she was staring at him, and when he turned to look at her she went puce. She quickly turned back to the solicitor, who had stopped talking and was now looking from her to Cruz nervously, as if he could sense the tension in the room.

He cleared his throat. 'As you're both here now, I see no reason not to start.'

'If you would be so kind.'

Trinity shivered at the barely veiled impatience in Cruz's voice. She could recall only too well how this man had reduced grown men and women to quivering wrecks with just a disdainful look from those glittering dark amber eyes.

The half-brothers hadn't been very alike—where Rio had been dark, with obsidian eyes and dark hair, Cruz possessed a cold, tawny beauty that had always made Trinity think of dark ice over simmering heat. She shivered… she'd felt that heat.

'Mrs De Carrillo…?'

Trinity blinked and flushed at being caught out again. The solicitor's impatient expression came into focus. He was holding out a sheaf of papers and she reached for them.

'I'm sorry.' It still felt weird to be called Mrs De Carrillo—it wasn't as if she'd ever *really* been Rio's wife.

She quickly read the heading: *Last will and testament of Rio De Carrillo*. Her heart squeezed as she thought of the fact that Mateo and Sancho had now lost both their parents, too prematurely.

As bitter as her experience had been with Rio in the end, after Trinity had been sickened to realise just how manipulative he'd been, and how naive she'd been, she'd never in a million years have wished him gone.

She'd felt a level of grief that had surprised her, considering the fact that their marriage had been in name only— for the convenience of having a steady mother figure for the boys and because Rio had wanted to promote a more settled image to further his own ambitions.

Trinity had agreed to the union for those and myriad other reasons—the most compelling of which had to do with her bond with the twins, which had been forged almost as soon as she'd seen them. Two one-year-old cherubs, with dark hair, dark mischievous eyes and heart-stopping smiles.

Her heart had gone out to them because they were motherless, as she had been since she was a baby, and they'd latched on to her with a ferocity that she hadn't been able to resist, even though she'd known it would be more professional to try and keep some distance.

She'd also agreed because Rio's sad personal story— he had been all but abandoned by his own parents—had again chimed with echoes of her own. And because he'd agreed to help her fulfil her deepest ambitions—to go to university and get a degree, thereby putting her in a position to forge her own future, free of the stain of her ignominious past.

Rio hadn't revealed the full extent of *his* ambitions until shortly before the accident—and that was when she'd realised why he'd taken such perverse pleasure in marrying her. It had had far more to do with his long-held simmering resentment towards his older half-brother than any real desire to forge a sense of security for his sons, or to shake off his playboy moniker…

The solicitor was speaking. 'As you'll see, it's a relatively short document. There's really no need to read through it all now. Suffice to say that Mr De Carrillo bequeathed everything to his sons, Mateo and Sancho, and he named you their legal guardian, Trinity.'

She looked up. She'd known that Rio had named her guardian. Any concerns she'd had at the time, contemplating such a huge responsibility had been eclipsed by the overwhelmingly protective instinct she'd felt for the twins. And in all honesty the prospect of one day becoming their guardian hadn't felt remotely possible.

She realised that she hadn't really considered what this meant for her own future now. It was something she'd been good at blocking out in the last three months, after the shock of the accident and Rio's death, not to mention getting over her own injuries and caring for two highly precocious and energetic boys. It was as if she was afraid to let the enormity of it all sink in.

The solicitor looked at Cruz for a moment, and then he looked back to Trinity with something distinctly *uncomfortable* in his expression. She tensed.

'I'm not sure how aware you are of the state of Mr De Carrillo's finances when he died?'

Trinity immediately felt the scrutiny of the man to her left, as if his gaze was boring into her. His accusatory words came back to her: *'You've single-handedly run through almost every cent my brother has to his name in a bid to satisfy your greedy nature. Now you're realising Rio's fortune isn't a bottomless pit…'*

She felt breathless, as if a vice was squeezing her chest.

Until the evening of Cruz's party she hadn't been aware of any such financial difficulty. She'd only been aware that Rio was growing more and more irrational and erratic. When she'd confronted him about his behviour, they'd had a huge argument, in which the truth of exactly why he'd married her had been made very apparent. Along with his *real* agenda.

That was why Trinity had wanted to talk to Cruz—to share her concerns. However, he'd comprehensively shut that down.

She said carefully now, 'I was aware that things weren't…good. But I didn't know that it was linked to his financial situation.'

Mr. Drew looked grim. 'Well, it most probably was. The truth is that Rio was bankrupt. In these last three months the sheer extent and scale of his financial collapse has become evident, and it's comprehensive. I'm afraid that all he left behind him are debts. There is nothing to bequeath to his children. Or you.'

Trinity hadn't married Rio for his money, so this news didn't have any great impact on her. What did impact her, though, was the realisation that Cruz must have been putting money into the account that she used for day-to-day necessities for her and the boys and Mrs Jordan—the nanny Rio had hired once Trinity had married him, when her job had changed and she'd been expected to accompany him to social functions. Something she'd never felt comfortable doing…

The solicitor said, 'I'm sorry to deliver this news, Mrs De Carrillo, but even the house will have to be sold to cover his debts.'

Before she could absorb that, Cruz was standing up and saying, in a coolly authoritative tone, 'If you could leave us now, Mr. Drew, I'll go over the rest with my sister-in-law.'

The solicitor clearly had no issue with being summarily

dismissed from his own office. He gathered some papers and left, shutting the door softly behind him.

Trinity's mind was reeling, as she tried to take everything in, and revolving with a sickening sense of growing panic as to how she was going to manage caring for the boys when she didn't have a job. How could she afford to keep Mrs Jordan on?

Cruz walked over to the floor-to-ceiling windows behind the large desk, showcasing an impressive view of London's skyline.

For a long moment he said nothing, and she could only look helplessly at his broad shoulders and back. Then he turned around and a sense of déjà-vu nearly knocked her off her chair. It was so reminiscent of when she'd first met him—when she'd gone to his house in Holland Park for an interview, applying for the position of maid in his household.

She'd never met such an intimidating man in her life. Nor such a blatantly masculine man. Based on his reputation as one of the world's wealthiest bankers, she had assumed him to be older, somewhat soft… But he'd been young. And gorgeous. His tall, powerful body had looked as if it was hewn from pure granite and steel. His eyes had been disconcertingly unreadable…

'Miss Adams...did you hear my question?'

She was back in time, caught in the glare of those mesmerising eyes, his brows drawn into a frown of impatience. His Spanish accent had been barely noticeable, just the slightest intriguing inflection. She'd felt light-headed, even though she was sitting down.

'I'm sorry…what?'

Those eyes had flashed with irritation. 'I asked how old you are?'

She'd swallowed. 'I'm twenty-two. Since last week.'

Then she'd felt silly for mentioning that detail—as if

one of the richest men in the world cared when her birthday was! Not that she even knew when her birthday was for sure…

But she'd survived four rounds of intense interviews to be there to meet the man himself—evidence of how he oversaw every tiny detail of his life—so Trinity had gathered her fraying wits, drawn her shoulders back and reminded herself that she had hopes and dreams, and that if she got this job she'd be well on her way to achieving a life for herself…

'I have to hand it to you—you're as good an actress as you were three months ago when you first feigned ignorance of Rio's financial situation. But you must have known what was coming down the tracks. After all, you helped divest my brother of a small fortune.'

The past and present meshed for a moment, and then Trinity realised what Cruz had just said.

She clasped her hands tight together on her lap. 'But I didn't know.'

'Did the accident affect your memory, Trinity?' His voice held more than a note of disdain. 'Do you not recall that illuminating conversation we had before you left my house on that fateful night?'

She flushed, remembering it all too well. 'I don't have any memory of the accident, but, yes, I do recall what you said to me. You're referring to your accusation that I was responsible for Rio's financial problems.'

Cruz's mouth compressed. 'I think *ruin* would be a more accurate word.'

Trinity stood up, too agitated to stay seated. 'You're wrong. It's true that Rio spent money on me, yes, but it was for the purposes of—'

Cruz held up a hand, a distinct sneer on his face now. 'Spare me the details. I looked into Rio's accounts after he died. I know all about the personal stylist, the VIP seats to every fashion show, the haute couture dresses, private jet travel, the best hotels in the world… The list is endless. I curse the day that I hired you to work for me—because, believe me, I blame myself as much as you for ruining my brother.'

At that damning pronouncement Trinity felt something deep inside her shrivel up to protect itself. She had not been prepared for Cruz's vitriolic attack.

But then, this was the man who had wiped her taste off his mouth and looked at her with disgust when he'd realised that he'd lowered himself to the level of kissing his own maid.

Trinity bitterly recalled the intimate dinner party he'd hosted the following evening—when the gaping chasm between them had been all too apparent.

Cruz had welcomed a tall and stunningly beautiful brunette, kissing her warmly on both cheeks. As the woman had passed her fur coat to Trinity, not even glancing in her direction, Trinity had caught an expressive look from Cruz that had spoken volumes—telling her to forget what had happened. Telling her that this woman was the kind of woman he consorted with, and whatever had happened between them must be consigned to some sordid memory box, never to be taken out and examined again.

That was when she'd been unable to hold her emotions in, utterly ashamed that she'd let her crush grow to such gargantuan proportions that she'd let him actually *hurt* her. And that was when Rio, Cruz's half-brother, who had also been a guest that night, had found her outside, in a hidden corner of the garden, weeping pathetically.

He'd come outside to smoke and had sat down beside her, telling her to relax when she'd tried to rush back inside, mortified. And somehow…she still wasn't sure how… he'd managed to get her to open up, to reveal what had happened. She hadn't told him of her burgeoning feelings for

Cruz, but she probably hadn't had to. It must have been emblazoned all over her tearstained face.

'Tell me what your price is for signing away your guardianship of my nephews?'

Trinity blinked and the painful memory faded.

As she focused on his words she went cold all over. 'What did you just say?'

Cruz snapped his fingers, displeasure oozing from his tall, hard body. 'You heard me—how much will it take, Trinity, for you to get out of my nephews' lives, because I don't doubt you have a price.'

Horror curdled her insides at the thought of being removed from Mateo and Sancho. Only that morning Sancho had thrown his arms around her and said, *'I love you, Mummy...'*

She shook her head now, something much hotter replacing the horror. 'There is no price you could pay me to leave the boys.'

'I am their blood relation.'

'You've only met them a handful of times!'

Cruz snorted. 'Are you trying to tell me that you could care for them more than their own flesh and blood? You've just been using them as a meal ticket. And now that Rio's left nothing behind they're your only hope of keeping your nest feathered—presumably by extorting money out of me.'

Trinity gasped. 'I would never—'

Cruz lifted a hand. 'Spare me.'

Trinity's mouth closed as she struggled to process this. All her protective hackles were raised high now, at the suggestion that she would use her stepchildren for her own ends. She would never leave them at the mercy of a coldhearted billionaire who didn't even really know them, in spite of that flesh and blood relationship.

Impulsively she asked, 'What qualifications could you

possibly have for taking on two toddlers? Have you ever even held a baby? Changed a nappy?'

Cruz's jaw clenched. 'I do not need qualifications. I'm their uncle. I will hire the best possible staff to attend to their every need.'

His gaze narrowed on her so intently she fought against squirming under it.

'What possible qualifications could *you* have? When you came to work for me you'd left school after your A-levels with not much work experience.'

His remark went right to the heart of her and stung— badly. It stung because of the way she'd longed to impress this man at one time, and had yearned to catch his attention. It stung because of the very private dreams she'd harboured to further her education. And it stung because in all the foster homes where she'd lived through her formative years she'd instinctively found herself mothering any younger foster children, as if drawn to create what she didn't have: a family.

She pushed down the hurt at Cruz's sneering disdain now, cursing her naivety, and lifted her chin. 'I've been caring for them since they were a year old. No one is qualified to be a parent until they become one. From the moment I married Rio I became their step-parent, and I would never turn my back on them.'

'Very noble indeed. But forgive me if I don't believe you. Now, we can continue to go around in these tiresome circles, or you can just tell me how much it'll take.'

He gestured to the table and she looked down to see a chequebook.

'I will write a cheque for whatever you want, Trinity, so let's stop playing games. You've done it. Your impressive act of caring for children that aren't your own is over. You can get on with your life.'

The sheer ease with which Cruz revealed his astounding cynicism angered Trinity as much as it shocked her.

She balled her hands into fists by her sides. 'I am not playing games. And those boys are as much mine as if I'd given birth to them myself.' It hit her then—the enormity of the love she felt for them. She'd always known she loved them, but right now she'd lay her life down for them.

The thought of Cruz taking the boys and washing his hands of them the way Rio had done—abdicating all responsibility to some faceless nanny—made her feel desperate. She had to try and make him believe her.

She took a deep breath. 'Please listen to me, Cruz. The marriage wasn't what you think... The truth is that it was a marriage of convenience. The twins were primarily the reason I agreed to it. I wanted to protect them.'

Trinity could feel her heart thumping. Tension snapped between them.

Then, showing not a hint of expression, Cruz said, 'Oh, I can imagine that it was very convenient. For you. And I have no doubt that my nephews were front and centre of your machinations. I know my brother was no saint—believe me, I'm under no illusions about that. But, based on his first choice of wife, it stretches the bounds of my credulity that he would turn around and marry a mere nanny, for convenience's sake. He was a passionate man, Trinity. You are a beautiful woman. I can only imagine that you used every trick in the book to take it beyond an affair between boss and employee. After all, I have personal experience of your methods. But, believe me, the only "convenience" I see here is the way you so *conveniently* seduced your way into his bed and then into a registry office, making sure you'd be set for life.'

Trinity ignored Cruz's *'you're a beautiful woman'* because it hadn't sounded remotely complimentary. She longed to reveal that no such affair had taken place, but she felt suddenly vulnerable under that blistering gaze, all her anger draining away to be replaced with the humiliation she'd felt after that *'personal experience'* he'd spoken of.

She found the words to inform him that Rio hadn't been remotely interested in her lodging in her throat. The reality was that one brother had rejected her and another had used her for his own ends. And the fact that she was letting this get to her now was even more galling. She should be thinking of Mateo and Sancho, not her own deep insecurities.

She stood tall against the biggest threat she'd ever faced. 'I'm not going anywhere. I am their legal guardian.'

Cruz folded his arms. 'I won't hesitate to take you to court to fight for their custody if I have to. Do you really want that to happen? Who do you think the courts will favour? Their flesh-and-blood uncle, who has nothing but their best interests at heart and the means to set them up for life, or their opportunistic stepmother who systematically spent her way through her husband's wealth? Needless to say if you force this route then you will receive nothing.'

Trinity felt her blood rush south so quickly that she swayed on her feet, but she sucked in a quick breath to regain her composure before he could see it. 'You can't threaten me like this,' she said, as firmly as she could. 'I'm their legal guardian, as per Rio's wishes.'

Cruz bit out, 'I told you before—I'm not interested in playing games.'

'Neither am I!' Trinity almost wailed. 'But I'm not letting you bully me into handing over custody of Matty and Sancho.'

Cruz looked disgusted. '*Matty?* What on earth is that?'

Trinity put her hands on her hips. 'It's what Sancho has called him ever since he started talking.'

Cruz waved a hand dismissively. 'It's a ridiculous name for an heir to the De Carrillo fortune.'

Trinity went still. 'What do you mean, heir? Surely any children *you* have will be the heirs…'

Cruz was close to reaching boiling point—which wasn't helped by the fact that his libido seemed to be reaching boiling point too. He was uncomfortably aware of how Trinity's breasts pushed against the fabric of her seemingly demure silk shirt. It was buttoned to her neck, but it was the most provocative thing he'd ever seen. It made him want to push aside the desk and rip it open so he could feast his gaze on those firm swells…

Which was an unwelcome reminder of how he'd reacted that night when he'd found her in his study—*supposedly* looking for a book—testing the very limits of his control in not much more than a vest and sleep shorts, with a flimsy robe belted around her tiny waist.

It *had* broken the limits of his control, proving that he wasn't so far removed from his father after all, in spite of his best efforts.

Cruz had had her backed up against the wall of shelves, grinding his achingly hard arousal into her quivering body, his fingers buried deep in slick heat and his mouth latched around a hard nipple, before he'd come to his senses…

Cursing her silently, and reining in his thundering arousal, Cruz said, with a coolness that belied the heat under the surface, '*Mateo* and Sancho will be my heirs, as I have no intention of having any children.'

Trinity shook her head. 'Why would you say such a thing?'

Already aware that he'd said too much, Cruz clamped down on the curious urge to explain that as soon as he'd heard Rio was having children he'd felt a weight lift off his shoulders, not having been really aware until then that he'd never relished the burden of producing an heir for the sake of the family business.

He'd learnt from a young age what it was to have to stand by helplessly and watch his own half-brother being treated as nothing just because he was the result of an affair. He'd experienced the way parents—the people who were meant to love you the most—sometimes had scant regard for their offspring. Cruz might have been the privileged legitimate heir, but he'd been treated more like an employee than a loved son.

He'd never felt that he had the necessary skills to be a father, and he'd never felt a desire to test that assertion. However, his nephews had changed things. And the fact that Rio was no longer alive *really* changed things now. And the fact that this woman believed she could control their fate was abominable.

Cruz was aware that he barely knew his nephews—every time he saw them they hid behind Trinity's legs, or their nanny's skirts. And until Rio had died he hadn't felt any great desire to connect with them...not knowing *how* to, in all honesty. But now an overwhelming instinct to protect them rose up in him and surprised him with its force. It reminded him of when he'd felt so protective of Rio when he'd been much smaller, and the reminder was poignant. And pertinent. He hadn't been able to protect Rio, but he could protect his nephews.

Perhaps Trinity thought she'd get more out of him like this. He rued the day she'd ever appeared in his life.

Curtly he said, 'I'll give you tonight to think it over. Tomorrow, midday, I'll come to the house—and trust me when I say that if you don't have your price ready by then, you'll have to prepare yourself for a legal battle after which you'll wish that you'd taken what I'm offering.'

CHAPTER TWO

ON THE BUS back to Rio's house near Regent's Park—Trinity had never considered it hers—she was still reeling. She felt as if someone had physically punched her. Cruz had…except without using fists…and the reminder that she'd once fancied herself almost in love with him was utterly mortifying now.

The full enormity of his distrust in her was shocking—as was his threat that he would take her to court to get the boys if he had to.

She didn't need Cruz to tell her that she wouldn't fare well up against one of the world's wealthiest and most powerful men. As soon as his lawyers looked into her background and saw that she'd grown up in foster homes, with no family stability to her name, she'd be out of Matty and Sancho's lives.

It didn't even occur to her to consider Cruz's offer—the thought of leaving the twins in his cold and autocratic care was anathema to her.

Being in such close proximity to him again had left her feeling on edge and jittery. Too aware of her body. Sometimes the memory of that cataclysmic night in Cruz's study came back like a taunt. And, no matter how much she tried to resist it, it was too powerful for her to push down. It was as vivid as if it had just happened. The scene of her spectacular humiliation.

The fact that Cruz obviously hated himself for what had happened was like the lash of a whip every time she saw him. As if she needed to be reminded of his disgust! As if he needed another reason to hate her now! Because that much was crystal-clear. He'd judged her and condemned her—he hadn't even wanted to hear her defence.

Trinity tried to resist thinking about the past, but the rain beating relentlessly against the bus windows didn't help. She felt as if she was in a cocoon...

She'd been working as Cruz's housemaid for approximately six months, and one night, unable to sleep, she'd gone down to the study to find a new book. Cruz had told her to feel welcome to read his books after he'd found her curled up in a chair reading one day.

Trinity had been very aware that she was developing a monumentally pathetic crush on her enigmatic boss—she'd even read about him in one of his discarded copies of the *Financial Times*.

She'd loved to read the papers, even though she hadn't understood half of what they talked about, and it had been her ambition to understand it all some day. She'd finally felt as if she was breaking away from her past, and that she could possibly prove that she didn't have to be limited by the fact that her own parents had abandoned her.

Cruz had epitomised success and keen intelligence, and Trinity had been helplessly impressed and inspired. Needless to say he was the kind of man who would never notice someone like her in a million years, no matter how polite to her he was. Except sometimes she'd look up and find him watching her with a curious expression on his face, and it would make her feel hot and flustered. Self-conscious...

When she'd entered the study that night, she'd done so cautiously, even though she'd known Cruz was out at a function. She'd turned on a dim light and gone straight to the bookshelves, and had spent a happy few minutes looking for something to read among the very broad range he had. She'd been intrigued by the fact that alongside serious tomes on economics there were battered copies of John Le Carré and Agatha Christie. They humanised a very intimidating man.

She'd almost jumped out of her skin when a deep voice had said, with a touch of humour, 'Good to know it's not a burglar rifling through my desk.'

Trinity had immediately dropped the book she was looking at and turned to see Cruz in the doorway, breathtakingly gorgeous in a classic tuxedo, his bow tie rakishly undone. And her brain had just…melted.

Eventually, when her wits had returned, she'd bent down to pick up the book, acutely aware of her state of undress, and started gabbling. 'I'm sorry… I just wanted to get a book…couldn't sleep…'

She'd held the book in front of her like a shield. As if it might hide her braless breasts, covered only by the flimsiest material. But something in Cruz's lazy stance changed as his eyes had raked over her, and the air had suddenly been charged. Electric.

Her eyes had widened as he'd closed the distance between them. She'd been mesmerised. Glued to the spot. Glued to his face as it was revealed in the shadows of the room, all stark lines and angles. He'd taken the book she was holding out of her hand and looked at it, before putting it back on the shelf. He'd been so close she'd been able to smell his scent, and had wanted to close her eyes to breathe it in even deeper. She'd felt dizzy.

Then he'd reached out and touched her hair, taking a strand between two fingers and letting it run between them. The fact that he'd come so close…was touching her…had been so unlikely that she hadn't been able to move.

Her lower body had tightened with a kind of need she'd never felt before. She'd cursed her inexperience in that moment—cursed the fact that living in foster homes all her life had made her put up high walls of defence because she'd never been settled anywhere long enough to forge any kind of meaningful relationship.

She'd known she should have moved…that this was ridiculous. That the longer she stood there, in thrall to her gorgeous boss, the sooner he'd step back and she'd be totally exposed. She'd never let anyone affect her like this before, but somehow, without even trying, he'd just slipped under her skin…

But then he'd looked at her with a molten light in his eyes and said, 'I want you, Trinity Adams. I know I shouldn't, but I do.'

He'd let her hair go.

His words had shocked her so much that even though she'd known that was the moment to turn and walk out, her bare feet had stayed glued to the floor.

A reckless desire had rushed through her, heady and dangerous, borne out of the impossible reality that Cruz De Carrillo was looking at her like this…saying he wanted her. She was a nobody. She came from nothing. And yet at that moment she'd felt seen in a way she'd never experienced before.

It had come out of her, unbidden, from the deepest part of her. One word. *'Please…'*

Cruz had looked at her for a long moment, and then he'd muttered something in Spanish as he'd taken her arms in his hands and walked her backwards until she'd hit the bookshelves with a soft *thunk*.

And then he'd kissed her.

But it had been more like a beautifully brutal awakening than a kiss. She'd gone on fire in seconds, and discovered that she was capable of sudden voracious desires and needs.

His kiss had drugged her, taking her deep into herself

and a world of new and amazing sensations. The feel of his rough tongue stroking hers had been so intimate and wicked, and yet more addictive than anything she'd ever known. She'd understood it in that moment—what the power of a drug might be.

Then his big hands had touched her waist, belly, breasts, cupping their full weight. They'd been a little rough, unsteady, and she hadn't expected that of someone who was always so cool. In control.

The thought that she might be doing this to him had been unbelievable.

He'd pulled open her robe so that he could pull down her vest top and take her nipple into his mouth, making Trinity moan and writhe like a wanton under his hands. She remembered panting, opening her legs, sighing with ecstasy when he'd found the naked moist heat of her body and touched her there, rubbing back and forth, exploring with his fingers, making her gasp and twist higher and higher in an inexorable climb as he'd spoken low Spanish words into her ear until she'd broken apart, into a million shards of pleasure so intense that she'd felt emotion leak out of her eyes.

And that was when a cold breeze had skated over her skin. Some foreboding. Cruz had pulled back, but he'd still had one hand between her legs and the other on her bared breast. He'd been breathing as harshly as her, and they'd looked at each other for a long moment.

He'd blinked, as if waking from the sensual spell that had come over them, and at the same time he'd taken his hands off her and said, 'What the hell…?'

He'd stepped away from her so fast she'd lurched forward and had to steady herself, acutely aware of her clothes in disarray. She'd pulled her robe around herself with shaking hands.

Cruz had wiped the back of his hand across his mouth

and Trinity had wanted to disappear—to curl up in a ball and hide away from the dawning realisation and horror on his face.

'I'm sorry… I—' Her voice had felt scratchy. She hadn't even been sure why she was apologising.

He'd cut her off. '*No*. This was *my* fault. It should never have happened.'

He'd turned icy and distant so quickly that if her body hadn't still been throbbing with the after-effects of her first orgasm she might have doubted it had even happened—that he'd lost his control for a brief moment and shown her the fire burning under that cool surface.

'It was an unforgivable breach of trust.'

Miserable, Trinity had said, 'It was my fault too.'

He'd said nothing, and then, slightly accusingly, 'Do you usually walk around the house dressed like that?'

Trinity had gone cold again. 'What exactly are you saying?'

Cruz had dragged his gaze back up. His cheeks had been flushed, hair a little mussed. She'd never seen anyone sexier or more undone and not happy about it.

'Nothing,' he'd bitten out. 'Just…get out of here and forget this ever happened. It was completely inappropriate. I *never* mix business with pleasure, and I'm not about to start.' He'd looked away from her, a muscle pulsing in his jaw.

Right then Trinity had never felt so cheap in her life. He obviously couldn't bear to look at her a moment longer. She'd felt herself closing inwards, aghast that she'd let herself fall into a dream of feeling special so easily. She should have known better. Cruz De Carrillo took beautiful, sophisticated and intelligent women to his bed. He didn't have sordid fumbles with staff in his library.

The divide between them had yawned open like a huge dark chasm. Her naivety had slapped her across the face.

Without saying another word, she'd fled from the room.

Trinity forcibly pushed the memory back down deep, where it belonged. Her stop came into view and she got up and waited for the bus to come to a halt.

As she walked back to the huge and ostentatious house by Regent's Park she spied Mrs Jordan in the distance with the double buggy.

Her heart lifted and she half ran, half walked to meet them. The boys jumped up and down in their seats with arms outstretched when they spotted her. She hugged each of them close, revelling in their unique babyish smell, which was already changing as they grew more quickly than she knew how to keep up with them.

Something fierce gripped her inside as she held them tight. She was the only mother they'd ever really known, and she would not abandon them for anything.

When she stood up, Mrs Jordan looked at her with concern. 'Are you all right, dear? You look very pale.'

Trinity forced a brittle smile. She couldn't really answer—because what could she say? That Cruz was going to come the next day and turn their world upside down? That lovely Mrs Jordan might be out of a job? That Trinity would be consigned to a scrap heap somewhere?

The boys would be upset and bewildered, facing a whole new world...

A sob made its way up her throat, but she forced it down and said the only thing she could. 'We need to talk.'

The following day, at midday on the dot, the doorbell rang. Trinity looked nervously at Mrs Jordan, who was as pale as she had been yesterday. They each held a twin in their arms, and Matty and Sancho were unusually quiet, as if sensing the tension in the air. Trinity had hated worrying the older woman, but it wouldn't have been fair not to warn her about what Cruz had said...

Mrs Jordan went to open the door, and even though Trinity had steeled herself she still wasn't prepared to see Cruz's broad, tall frame filling the doorway, a sleek black chauffeur-driven car just visible in the background. He wore a three-piece suit and an overcoat against the English spring chill. He looked vital and intimidating and gorgeous.

He stepped inside and the boys curled into Trinity and Mrs Jordan. They were always shy around their uncle, whom Matty called *'the big man'*.

'Mr De Carrillo, how nice to see you,' Mrs Jordan said, ever the diplomat.

Cruz looked away from Trinity to the older woman. There was only the slightest softening on his face. 'You too, Mrs Jordan.'

They exchanged pleasantries, and Mrs Jordan asked if he wanted tea or coffee before bustling off to the kitchen with Sancho. Trinity noticed that he'd looked at his nephews warily.

Then he looked at her with narrowed eyes. 'I presume we can talk alone?'

She wanted to say no, and run with the boys and Mrs Jordan somewhere safe. But she couldn't.

She nodded jerkily and said, 'Just let me get the boys set up for lunch and then I'll be with you.'

Cruz just inclined his head slightly, but he said *sotto voce*, as she passed him to follow Mrs Jordan to the kitchen, 'Don't make me wait, Trinity.'

Once they were out of earshot, Matty said in an awe-struck voice. 'Tha's the big man!'

Trinity replied as butterflies jumped around her belly. 'Yes, sweetie. He's your uncle, remember...?'

'Unk-*el*...' Matty repeated carefully, as if testing out the word.

Trinity delayed as much as she dared, making sure the

boys were strapped securely into their high chairs, but then she had to leave.

Mrs Jordan handed her a tray containing the tea and coffee, and looked at her expressively. 'I'm sure he'll do what's right for the boys and you, dear. Don't worry.'

Trinity felt shame curl through her as she walked to the drawing room with the tray. She'd been too cowardly to tell Mrs Jordan the truth of Cruz's opinion of her. The woman believed that he only wanted custody of his nephews because he was their last remaining blood relative.

Stopping at the door for a second, she took a breath and wondered if she should have worn something smarter than jeans and a plain long-sleeved jumper. But it was too late. She balanced the tray on her raised knee, then opened the door and went in. Her heart thumped as she saw Cruz, with his overcoat off, standing at the main window that looked out over the opulent gardens at the back of the house.

She avoided looking at him and went over to where a low table sat between two couches. She put the tray down and glanced up. 'Coffee, wasn't it?'

Cruz came and sat down on the couch opposite hers. 'Yes.'

No *please*. No niceties.

Trinity was very aware of how the fabric of his trousers pulled taut over his powerful thighs. She handed over the coffee in a cup, grateful that this time her hands were fairly steady. She sipped at her own tea, as if that might fortify her, and wished it was something slightly stronger.

After a strained moment Trinity knew she couldn't avoid him for ever. She looked at him and blurted out, 'Why are you doing this now? If you're so sure I'm... what you say I am...why didn't you just step in after Rio's death?'

Cruz took a lazy sip of his coffee and put the cup down,

for all the world as if this was a cordial visit. He looked at her. 'I, unlike you, grieved my brother's death—'

'That's not fair,' Trinity breathed.

Okay, so Rio had made her angry—especially at the end—and theirs hadn't been a real marriage, but she had felt a certain kinship with him. They hadn't been so different, as he'd told her—both abandoned by their parents. But then he'd betrayed her trust and her loyalty.

Cruz continued as if she'd said nothing. 'Once the state of Rio's finances became apparent, there was a lot of fire-fighting to be done. Deals he'd been involved in had to be tied up. I had to search for his mother to let her know what had happened—'

'Did you find her?' Trinity's heart squeezed as she thought of the impossible dream she never let herself indulge in: that some day she'd find *her* mother.

Cruz shook his head. 'No—and yes. She died some years ago, of a drug overdose.'

'Oh,' she said, feeling sad.

'I knew when the reading of the will would be taking place, and I wanted to see your face when you realised that there was nothing for you. And I'd been keeping an eye on you, so I knew what you were up to and how my nephews were.'

Trinity gasped. 'You had us followed?'

Cruz shrugged minutely. 'I couldn't be sure you wouldn't try to disappear. And you're the very public widow of a man most people still believe was a millionaire, with two small vulnerable children in your care. It was for your protection as much as my surveillance.'

Before she could fully absorb that, he went on, with palpable impatience.

'Look, I really don't have time for small talk, Trinity. Tell me how much you want so that I can get on with making the necessary arrangements to have my custody of my nephews legalised.'

His words were like a red rag to a bull—having it confirmed that he'd just been biding his time. That she'd never really registered on his radar as anyone worth giving the benefit of the doubt to.

She put her cup down with a clatter on the tray and glared at him. 'How dare you? Do you really think it's that simple? They are not pawns, Cruz. They are two small human beings who depend on structure and routine, who have lost both their parents at a very vulnerable age. Mrs Jordan and I are the most consistent people in their lives and you want to rip them away from that?'

She stood up then, too agitated to keep sitting down. Cruz stood too, and Trinity immediately felt intimidated.

He bit out, 'I want to take them away from a malignant influence. *You*. Are you seriously telling me you're prepared to go up against me? You know what'll happen if you do. You'll lose.'

'*No!*' Trinity cried passionately. 'The twins will lose. Do you know they've only just stopped asking for their *papa* every night? Because that's usually when he came to see them, to say goodnight. Their world has been turned upside down and you want to do it again. Who will be their primary carer? Don't tell me it's going to be *you*.' Trinity would never normally be so blunt or so cruel, but she felt desperate. 'Have you noticed how they look at you? They're intimidated by you. They hardly know who you are.'

Clearly unaccustomed to having anyone speak to him like this, Cruz flashed his eyes in disapproval. 'If anyone has been these boys' primary carer, I'd wager it's been Mrs Jordan. There's no reason why she can't remain as their nanny. But you have no claim on these boys beyond the legal guardianship you seduced out of Rio in a bid to protect your own future.'

Trinity's hands balled into fists. Her nails cut into her palms but she barely noticed. She wondered how she'd ever felt remotely tender about this man. 'That is *not* true. I love these boys as if they were my own.'

Cruz let out a curt laugh. 'I *know* that's not true.'

His smile faded, and his face became sterner than she'd ever seen it.

'And do you know why? Because Rio and I both learned that the people who are meant to love you the most *don't*. There's no such thing as an unbreakable bond.'

The fire left Trinity's belly. She felt shaky after the rush of adrenalin. Rio had told her about the way he'd been treated like an unwelcome guest in his own father's home. How his mother had abandoned him. It had played on all her sympathies. Now she wondered about Cruz's experience, and hated herself for this evidence that he still got to her.

'Not all parents were like yours or Rio's.'

Cruz arched a brow. 'And you know this from personal experience, when you grew up in a series of foster homes? Your experience wasn't too far removed from ours, was it, Trinity? So tell me how you know something I don't.'

Trinity went very still. 'How do you know that?'

He watched her assessingly. 'I run background checks on all my staff.' His lip curled. 'To think I actually felt some admiration for you—abandoned by your parents, brought up in care, but clearly ambitious and determined to make something of yourself. I seriously underestimated how little you were actually prepared to work to that end.'

The unfairness of his assessment winded her when she thought of the back-breaking work she'd done, first as a chambermaid in a hotel, then as a maid in his house, before becoming nanny to two demanding babies. And then Rio's *wife*.

Feeling seriously vulnerable upon finding out that Cruz

had known about her past all this time and had mentioned it so casually, she said, 'My experience has nothing to do with this.'

Liar, said a voice. It did, but not in the way Cruz believed.

'I love Matty and Sancho and I will do anything to protect them.'

Cruz was like an immovable force. 'You have some nerve to mention love. Are you seriously trying to tell me you loved Rio?'

Feeling desperate, she said, 'I told you—it wasn't like that.'

He glared at her. 'No, it wasn't. At least you're being honest about that.'

Trinity shivered under his look. His anger was palpable now. She said then, 'I did care for him.'

Before Cruz could respond to that there was a commotion outside, and Mrs Jordan appeared in the doorway with a wailing Sancho, who was leaning out of her arms towards Trinity, saying pitifully, *'Mummy...'*

Everything suddenly forgotten, she rushed forward and took him into her arms, rubbing his back and soothing him.

Mrs Jordan said apologetically, 'Matty hit him over the head with his plastic cup. It's nothing serious, but he's fractious after not sleeping well again last night.'

Trinity nodded and Mrs Jordan left to go back to Matty. She was walking up and down, soothing a now hiccupping Sancho, when she realised Cruz was staring at her with an angry look on his face.

He said almost accusingly, 'What's wrong with him?'

Suddenly Trinity was incredibly weary. 'Nothing much. He had a bug and he hasn't been sleeping, so he's in bad form. Matty just wound him up.' When Cruz didn't look appeased she said, 'Really, it's nothing.' She felt exposed under Cruz's judgemental look. 'Let me settle him down for a nap. That's all he needs.'

* * *

Cruz watched Trinity walk out of the room with Sancho in her arms, his nephew's small, chubby ones wrapped tight around her neck, his flushed face buried in her neck as if it was a habitual reflex for seeking comfort. He had stopped crying almost as soon as he'd gone into her arms.

Cruz had felt a totally uncharacteristic sense of helplessness seeing his nephew like that. It reminded him uncomfortably of his own childhood, hearing Rio cry but being unable to do anything to help him—either because Rio would glare at him with simmering resentment or his father would hold him back with a cruel hand.

Sancho's cries hadn't fazed Trinity, though. In fact she'd looked remarkably capable.

Feeling angry all over again, and this time for a reason he couldn't really pinpoint, Cruz turned back to the window. He ran a hand through his hair and then loosened his tie, feeling constricted. And he felt even more constricted in another area of his anatomy when he recalled how his gaze had immediately dropped to take in the provocative swell of Trinity's bottom as she'd walked away, her long legs encased in those faded jeans that clung like a second skin.

Damn her.

Witnessing this little incident was forcing Cruz to stop and think about what he was doing here. It was obvious that not only had Trinity seduced Rio for her own ends, she'd also ensured that the boys would depend on her...in case of this very scenario?

Cruz thought of pursuing his plans to take Trinity to court to fight her for custody, but he'd already seen what a good actress she was. If someone were to come to the house and see her interacting with his nephews they wouldn't be able to help being swayed by her *apparent* love and concern. As he had just been.

And did he really want to court a PR frenzy by pitting himself against the grieving widow of his brother? He knew she wasn't grieving—she wasn't even pretending. But no one else would see that. They'd only see him, a ruthless billionaire, protecting his family fortune.

It had taken him since his father's death to change the perception his father had left behind of a failing and archaic bank, blighted by his father's numerous high-profile affairs. Did he really want to jeopardise all that hard work?

Something hardened inside him as he had to acknowledge how neatly Trinity had protected herself. She was potentially even worse than he'd thought—using his nephews like this, manipulating them to need her.

She'd lived a quiet life since Rio's death—she'd only moved between the house, the local shops and the nearby park. No shopping on Bond Street or high-profile social events.

When she'd been with Rio, Cruz had seen countless pictures of them at parties and premieres, so she had to be approaching the end of her boredom threshold.

He thought again of her assertion that she loved the boys... He couldn't countenance for a second that she loved these children who weren't even her own flesh and blood.

A memory of his own mother came back with startling clarity—he'd been a young teenager and he'd confronted her one day, incensed on her behalf that his father had been photographed in the papers with his latest mistress.

She'd just looked at him and said witheringly, 'The only mistake he made, Cruz, was getting caught. This is how our world works.' She'd laughed then—nastily. '*Dios mio*, please tell me you're not so naive as to believe we married because we actually had *feelings* for one another?'

He'd looked at his mother in shock. No, he'd never laboured under the misapprehension that any such thing as *affection* existed between his parents, but he'd realised in that moment that some tiny part of him that hadn't been obliterated after years of only the most perfunctory parenting had still harboured a kernel of hope that something meaningful existed… Shame had engulfed him for being so naive.

She'd said then, with evident bitterness, 'I was all but packaged up and sent to your father, because our two families belong to great dynasties and it was a strategic match. I did my duty and bore him a son, and I put up with his bastard son living under this very roof, and his mistresses—because, no matter what he does, this family's legacy is safe with you, and *I* have ensured that. That is all that matters in this life Cruz. Cultivating our great name and protecting it. One of these days your father will die, and as far as I'm concerned it can't come soon enough. Because then *you* will restore this family's reputation and fortune. That is your duty and your destiny, above all else.'

She'd died not long after that speech. The memory of her had faded but her words hadn't. *Duty and destiny.* There was no room for emotion, and he'd had to acknowledge the enormity of what he stood to inherit. He'd become a man that day, in more ways than one, leaving behind any childish vulnerabilities and misconceptions.

And because he'd stepped up to that responsibility he now had something solid to pass on to his nephews. They aroused something in him that he'd only felt before for Rio—an urge to protect and forge a bond. He'd become Rio's guardian while he'd still been underage, and he wanted to do the same for his vulnerable nephews. He vowed now that they would not go the way of their father. By the time they came of age they would know how to handle their legacy…he would make sure of it.

When Cruz had realised that he hadn't been named as guardian after Rio's death he'd felt inexplicably hurt, even though he'd known that he was hardly in a position to take on two small children he barely knew. It had been like a slap from beyond the grave, and he'd had to wonder if the rapprochement he'd believed to be present in his relationship with Rio had actually been real.

Or, as he'd come to suspect, was it more likely to have been someone else's influence?

Cruz had looked at Trinity, dressed in black on the other side of Rio's grave at the funeral, as his brother had been lowered into the ground. Her face had been covered in a gauzy veil, her body encased in a snug-fitting black suit. And that was when he'd vowed to do whatever it took to make sure her influence over his nephews was thwarted. He wanted them under his protection—away from a gold-digging manipulator.

Suddenly an audacious idea occurred to him. He immediately thrust it aside—appalled that he'd even thought it. But it wouldn't go away. It took root, and as he looked at it analytically it held a kind of horrific appeal.

He stared out over the gardens without really seeing them, and finally had to acknowledge grimly that there was really only one option where Trinity was concerned—but was he prepared to go to those lengths?

His gut answered him. *Yes.*

As if fate was contriving to make sure he didn't have time to change his mind he heard a noise and turned around to see Trinity coming back into the room. Her hair was pulled back into a low ponytail, but loose tendrils curled around her face. He noticed for the first time that there were delicate smudges of colour under her cornflower-blue eyes. Evidence of fatigue.

He ruthlessly pushed down a very curious sensation he'd never felt in relation to a woman before—and certainly not one he welcomed for this one: *concern.*

He faced her and saw how she tensed as she came towards him, folding her arms in a defensive gesture. Her chin tilting towards him mutinously.

With not a little relish, Cruz said, 'I have a solution which I think will work for both of us, my nephews and Mrs Jordan.'

He could see Trinity's arms tighten fractionally over her chest and he focused on her treacherously beautiful face. Even now she looked as innocent as the naive twenty-two-year-old who had come to work for him. Except, of course, she hadn't been naive. Or innocent. And she was about to face the repercussions of her actions.

'What solution?'

Cruz waited a beat and then said, very deliberately, 'Marriage, Trinity. You're going to marry me.'

CHAPTER THREE

For a moment all Trinity heard was a roaring in her ears. She shook her head but Cruz was still looking at her with that expression on his face. Determined.

She asked weakly, 'Did you just say marriage?'

'Yes, I did.'

Trinity's arms were so tight across her chest she was almost cutting off her air supply. 'That is the most ridiculous thing I've ever heard.' And yet why was there an illicit shiver deep in her belly at the thought of being married to this man?

Cruz started to stroll towards her and Trinity had a very keen sense that he was a predator, closing in on his prey.

'Even though I know I'd win in a courtroom battle for the twins, I don't really have the inclination to invite unnecessarily adverse PR in my direction by pitting myself against my brother's widow. And from what I've seen it's evident to me that Mateo and Sancho are clearly attached to you.'

'Of course they are,' she said shakily. 'I'm all they've known as a mother since they were one.'

He stopped within touching distance and Trinity's breath hitched at his sheer charisma. She forced herself to fill her lungs. She couldn't afford to let him distract her.

'Why on earth would you suggest marriage?'

He grimaced, 'You are legally my nephews' guardian, and I don't trust you not to exert your right to do something drastic. Marriage will make me their legal guardian too, and I'm not prepared to settle for anything less to ensure their protection.'

Trinity shook her head and took a step back, hating

herself for it but needing some space. 'You're crazy if you think I'll agree.'

With lethal softness he said now, 'Who do you think has been funding your existence these past few months?'

'You,' she said miserably.

'If you were to walk out of this house with my two nephews that allowance would be stopped immediately. How on earth do you think you would cope without a nanny?'

Desperation clawed upwards. 'I could get a job.'

Cruz was scathing. 'You'd be happy to lower yourself to Mrs Jordan's status again? Because that's all you're qualified for—either working as a maid or as a nanny.'

Trinity refused to let him intimidate her. 'Of course—if I had to.' A voice screamed at her—how on earth could she work with two small children in tow?

Cruz was obdurate, and Trinity knew with a sinking feeling that one way or the other he wasn't leaving until he'd got what he wanted. Her. And his nephews.

'It's very simple. I don't trust you not to take advantage of your position. And you seem to be forgetting a very pertinent fact.' He looked at her.

Eventually, with extreme reluctance and the sensation of a net closing around her, she said, 'What fact?'

'Since Rio's death those boys have had nothing but their name. The only way they will receive their inheritance now is through me, and I'm not going to let that happen unless you marry me.'

The net closed around Trinity as the full significance of that sank in. She would be responsible for not letting Matty and Sancho receive their inheritance?

'That's blackmail,' she breathed, astounded at his ruthlessness.

Cruz all but shrugged, supremely unperturbed. 'Their legacy is considerable, and as such I have a responsibility to see that it, and they, are protected.'

Affront coursed through her. 'I would never touch what's theirs.'

Cruz's lip curled. 'And yet you managed to divest Rio of a small fortune within less than a year of marriage?'

Trinity opened her mouth to defend herself again but from the look on Cruz's face she knew it would be pointless to say anything. Not in this emotive atmosphere.

She whirled away from that mocking look in his eyes and took refuge by a solid object—the couch. When she felt relatively composed again, she turned back to face him.

'There has to be some other way.' She seized on an idea. 'I can sign something. A contract that says I have no claim to their inheritance.'

Cruz shook his head and moved, coming closer. 'No. Marriage is the only option I'm prepared to consider. I've decided to move back to the De Carrillo ancestral home in Spain, near Seville. The bank is flourishing here in the UK, and in America. Its reputation has been restored. It's time to build on that, and presenting a united family front will only strengthen the business and in turn my nephews' legacy.'

Rendered speechless, Trinity could only listen as Cruz went on.

'Locking you into a marriage with me is the only way they'll get their inheritance and I'll be satisfied that you're not going to prove to be a threat to my nephews. And as it happens a convenient wife will suit my needs very well. But I'm afraid I can't offer you the bling of married life with Rio. You might have been keeping a low profile since my brother died, but I would estimate that once the reality of living in a remote *castillo* hits you'll be climbing the walls and looking for a divorce before the year is out…which I'll be only too happy to grant once I've got full custody of my nephews.'

The extent of his cynicism shocked her anew. She'd

surmised from Rio's account of his early life that things probably hadn't been idyllic for Cruz either, but she'd never imagined that he carried such a deep-rooted seam of distrust.

Trinity hated it that it aroused her empathy and curiosity—again. She cursed herself. She'd felt empathy for Rio and she'd let him manipulate her. If it hadn't been for Mateo and Sancho she'd tell Cruz where to shove his autocratic orders and storm out.

But how could she? He was threatening to withhold their very legacy if she didn't comply. And there was no way she was leaving her boys in his cold and cynical care alone. She was all they had now.

Surely, she thought quickly, if she said yes he'd realise what he was doing—marrying someone he hated himself for kissing—and agree to make some kind of compromise? Trinity shoved down the betraying hurt that Cruz would never even be suggesting such a thing if she didn't have something he wanted. His nephews.

She called his bluff. 'You leave me no choice. Yes, I'll marry you.'

She waited for Cruz to blanch, or for realisation to hit and for him to tell her that he'd only been testing her commitment, but he showed no emotion. Nor triumph. After a beat he just looked at his watch, and then back at her, as cold as ice.

'Good. I'll have my team draw up a pre-nuptial agreement and organise a fast and discreet civil wedding within the next few weeks, after which we'll leave directly for Spain.'

He had turned and was walking out of the room before the shock reverberating through Trinity subsided enough for her to scramble after him—clearly he was not a man who was easily bluffed. He was deadly serious about this.

His hand was on the doorknob when she came to a

stumbling halt behind him, breathless. 'Wait a minute—you don't really want to marry me. What about falling in love?'

Cruz turned around with an incredulous look on his face, and then threw his head back and laughed so abruptly that Trinity flinched. When he looked at her again his eyes glittered like dark golden sapphires.

'*Love?* Now you really are over-acting. Choice in marriage and falling in love are best left to the deluded. Look where infatuation got my brother—driven to fatal destruction. I have no time for such emotions or weaknesses. This marriage will be one in name only, purely to protect my nephews from your grasping hands, and you will fulfil your role as my wife to the best of your ability.'

Trinity tried one more time. 'You don't have to do this. I would never harm my stepsons, or take their inheritance from them.'

Cruz's eyes gleamed with stark intent. 'I don't believe you, and I don't trust you. So, yes, we *are* doing this. You'll need to see if Mrs Jordan is happy to stay in my employment and come to Spain. If not, we'll have to hire another nanny. The sooner you come to terms with this new reality and start preparing the boys for the move the easier it will be for me to make the necessary arrangements.'

For long minutes after he'd walked out Trinity stood there in shock. What had she just done?

True to his word, just over two weeks later Trinity stood beside Cruz De Carrillo in a register office. He was dressed in a sleek dark grey suit, white shirt and matching tie. She wore an understated cream silk knee-length sheath dress with matching jacket. Her hair was up in a smooth chignon, her make-up light.

In the end resistance had been futile. No matter which way she'd looked at it, she'd kept coming back to the fact that she wasn't prepared to walk away from Mateo and Sancho after all they'd been through—as well as the fact that the thought of leaving them made her feel as if someone was carving her heart out of her chest.

By agreeing to marry Rio she'd at least felt that she could offer them some permanence, which she'd never had. She hadn't wanted them to go through the same insecurity…and now she was in exactly the same position. So it had come down to this: she had nowhere to go, and no one to turn to.

When she'd put Cruz's plan to Mrs Jordan, the woman had thought about it, consulted with her son who was at university in Scotland, and then agreed to stay with them as long as she could be guaranteed regular visits home. Trinity had felt emotional, knowing that at least she'd have Mrs Jordan's quiet and calm support.

She was acutely conscious now of Cruz's tall, hard body beside her as the registrar spoke the closing words of the ceremony. She was all but a prisoner to this man now. The perfect chattel. She looked at the simple gold band on her finger that marked her as married for the second time in her life. This time, though, she thought a little hysterically, at least she wasn't remotely deluded about her husband's intentions.

'I now pronounce you husband and wife. Congratulations. You may kiss your wife, Mr De Carrillo.'

Slowly, reluctantly, Trinity turned to face Cruz. She looked up. Even though she wore high heels, he still towered over her.

Cruz just looked at her for a long moment. Trinity's breath was trapped in her throat like a bird. Was he going to humiliate her in front of their small crowd of witnesses—largely made up of his legal team—by refusing to kiss her?

But then, just when she expected him to turn away

dismissively, he lowered his head and his mouth touched hers. Firm. Cool. His lips weren't tightly shut, and neither were hers, so for a second their breaths mingled, and in that moment a flame of pure heat licked through her with such force that she was hurled back in time to that incendiary kiss in his study.

Before she could control her reaction, though, Cruz was pulling back to look down at her again with those hard, glittering eyes. They transmitted a silent but unmistakable message: he would do the bare minimum in public to promote an image of unity, but that was as far as it would go.

Trinity was humiliated by her reaction, by the fact that he still had such a devastating effect on her. And terrified at the prospect of him realising it. She tried to pull her hand free of his but he only tightened his grip, reminding her of how trapped she was.

She glared up at him.

'Smile for the photos, *querida*.'

Trinity followed Cruz's look to see a photographer waiting. Of course. This was all part of his plan, wasn't it? To send out a message of a family united.

Aware that she must look more like someone about to be tipped over the edge of a plank than a besotted bride, Trinity forced a smile and flinched only slightly when the flash went off.

Cruz could hear his nephews chattering happily as they were fed at the back of the plane. Then he heard softer, lower tones… Trinity's… He tensed. Any sense of satisfaction at the fact that he'd achieved what he'd set out to achieve was gone. He cursed silently. Who was he kidding? He'd been tense since he'd left her standing in that room in Rio's house, with her eyes like two huge pools of blue, and a face leached of all colour.

It should have given him an immense sense of accomplishment to know he'd pulled the rug from under her feet, but he'd walked away that day with far more complicated emotions in his gut—and a very unwelcome reminder of when he'd seen a similar look of stunned shock on her face...the night he'd kissed her.

She'd been the last person he'd expected to see when he'd walked into his study that night, weary from a round of engaging in mind-numbingly boring small-talk. And fending off women who, up until a few months before, would have tempted him. His mind had been full of...*her*. And then to find her there, stretching up, long legs bare and exposed, the lush curve of her bottom visible under the short robe and the even more provocative curve of her unbound breasts... It was as if she'd walked straight out of his deepest fantasy...

He could still recall the second he'd come to his senses, when he'd realised he was moments away from lifting her up against his shelves and finding explosive release in her willing body, all soft and hot and *wet*. No other woman had ever caused him to lose it like that. But she'd been his *employee*. Someone he'd been in a position of power over.

The stark realisation that he was following in his father's footsteps in spite of every effort he'd made to remove the shadow of that man's reputation had been sickening. He was no better after all.

He'd been harsh afterwards...angry at his reaction... demanding to know what she was doing there as if it had been her fault. He'd felt like a boor. Little had he known then that she'd obviously been waiting until he got home and had made sure he found her...

It was galling. A sign of weakness. Cruz scowled. Trinity had no power over his emotions. She represented a very fleeting moment in time when he'd forgotten who he was.

The reality of his situation hit him then—in marrying Trinity he was consigning himself to a life with a woman he would never trust. But the sacrifice would be worth it for his nephews' sake.

At least now she was under his control and his watchful eye.

He'd felt anything *but* watchful earlier, though, when she'd turned to face him in that sterile register office and everyone had waited for their kiss. He'd had no intention of kissing her—it would show her how it would be between them. And prove that he could control himself around her... But for a split second his gaze had dropped to that lush mouth and every cool, logical intention had scattered, to be replaced with an all too familiar desire just to take one sip, one taste...

So he'd bent his head, seeing the flash of surprise in her eyes, and touched his mouth to hers. And he'd felt her breath whisper over his mouth. It had taken more effort than he liked to admit to pull back and deny himself the need he'd had to take her face in his hands, angle her mouth for better access so he could explore her with a thoroughness that would have made him look a complete fool...

Cruz only became aware that he was being watched when the hairs went up on the back of his neck, and he turned his head from brooding out of the small window. He had to adjust his gaze down to see that one of his nephews—he couldn't tell which—was standing by his chair with small pudgy hands clutching the armrest.

For a second time was suspended, and his mind went blank. Two huge dark eyes stared up at him guilelessly. Thick, dark tousled hair fell onto a smooth forehead and the child's cheeks were flushed. Something that looked like mashed carrot was smeared around his mouth. And then he smiled, showing a neat row of baby teeth. Something gripped Cruz tight in his chest, throwing him back in time to when he'd looked at an almost identical child, six years his junior.

'*Matty*, don't disturb your uncle.'

That low, husky voice. Gently chiding. Two slender pale hands came around his nephew to lift him up and away. Trinity held him easily with one arm, against her body. The small face showed surprise, and then started to contort alarmingly just before an ear-splitting screech emerged.

Cruz noted that she looked slightly frayed at the edges. Her hair was coming loose and she had smears of food on her jacket. He looked down and saw pale bare feet, nails painted a delicate shade of coral, and he felt a surge of blood to his groin. Immediately he scowled at his rampant reaction and Trinity backed away.

'Sorry, I didn't realise he'd slipped out of his chair.'

She was turning to walk back down the plane when Cruz heard himself calling out, 'Wait.'

She stopped in her tracks and Cruz saw Mrs Jordan hurrying up the aisle, reaching for Mateo to take him from Trinity. The indignant shouting stopped as the older woman hushed him with soothing tones.

Trinity turned around and Cruz felt something pierce him as he acknowledged that, *in*convenient wedding or not, most brides were at least given a meal before being whisked away after their nuptials.

They'd gone straight from his solicitor's office, where Trinity had signed the pre-nuptial agreement, to the register office and then to the plane. He'd expected her to pore over the pre-nuptial agreement, but she'd just glanced through it and then looked at him and said, 'If we divorce then I lose all custody of the boys, is that it?'

He'd nodded. Aware of his body humming for her even while they were surrounded by his legal team. She'd just muttered something under her breath like, *Never going to happen*, and signed. Cruz had had to include some kind of a severance deal for her if they divorced, so Trinity would always be a wealthy woman, but he knew she could have fought him for a better deal.

So why hadn't she? asked a voice, and Cruz didn't like the way his conscience smarted. He wasn't used to being aware of his conscience, never doubting himself in anything—and he wasn't about to start, he told himself ruthlessly. For all he knew Trinity's actions thus far were all an act to lull him into a false sense of security.

'Have you eaten yet?' he asked abruptly, irritated that she was making him doubt himself.

She looked at him warily and shook her head as she tucked some hair behind her ear. 'I'll eat when the boys have eaten.'

Cruz gestured to the seat across the aisle from him. 'Sit down. I'll get one of the staff to take your order.' He pressed the call button.

Trinity looked towards the back of the plane for a moment. Her visible reluctance was not a reaction he was used to where women were concerned.

'Sit before you fall. They're fine. And we have some things to discuss.'

She finally sat down, just as an attentive air steward appeared and handed her a menu. Trinity's head was down-bent for a moment as she read, and Cruz found it hard to look away from that bright silky hair.

When the air steward had left Trinity felt uncomfortable under Cruz's intense gaze. It was as if he was trying to get into her head and read her every thought. Just the prospect of that made her go clammy—that he might see the effect his very chaste kiss had had on her.

In a bid to defuse the strange tension, she prompted, 'You said we have things to discuss…?'

Cruz blinked and the intensity diminished. Trinity

sucked in a breath to acknowledge how attuned she felt to this man. It was disconcerting—and unwelcome.

'As soon as you're settled at the *castillo* I'll organise interviews for another nanny to help Mrs Jordan. You're going to be busy as my wife.'

The castillo. It even sounded intimidating. She said, as coolly as she could, as if this was all completely normal, 'Maybe this would be a good time for you to let me know exactly what you expect of me as your wife.'

Maybe, crowed a snide voice, *it would have been a good idea for you not to get so attached to two babies that aren't yours in a bid to create the family you never had.*

Trinity gritted her jaw.

Cruz said, 'My calendar is already full for the next three months, and I should warn you that my social events are more corporate-orientated than celebrity-based... I'll expect you on my arm, looking the part, and not scowling because you're bored.'

Trinity boiled inside. Clearly he was expecting her to last for about two weeks before she ran for the hills. And he was obviously referring to Rio's predilection for film premieres or events like the Monte Carlo Grand Prix, which Trinity had found excruciating—all she could remember of that particular event was the overwhelming diesel fumes and the constant seasickness she'd felt while on some Russian oligarch's yacht.

Rio had invariably paraded her in public and then promptly dropped her once the paparazzi had left—which had suited her fine. She'd usually been in her own bed, in her own separate room, by the time he'd finished partying around dawn. But she could just imagine telling Cruz that, and how he'd merely shut her down again.

Then she thought of something. 'What do you mean, "looking the part"?'

He swept an expressive look over her, and at that moment she was aware of every second of sleep she hadn't got in the past couple of years. *And* the fact that today was probably the first day she'd worn smart clothes and actually put on make-up in months.

Compounding her insecurity, Cruz said, 'As *my* wife you'll need to project a more…classic image. I've already arranged for you to be taken shopping to buy new clothes.'

Trinity tensed at the barb. 'But I have clothes.'

His lip curled. 'The kind of clothes you wore around my brother will not be suitable and they've been donated to charity.'

Her face grew hot when she recalled seeing Cruz again, for the first time since her marriage to Rio, three months ago. His effect on her had been instantaneous—a rush of liquid heat. And then he'd looked at her as if she was a call girl. How could she blame him? She'd felt like one.

Rio's sense of style for women had definitely favoured the 'less is more' variety. He'd handed her a dress to wear for that party that had been little more than a piece of silk. Skimpier than anything she'd ever worn.

She'd protested, but he'd said curtly, 'You're working for me, Trinity. Consider this your uniform.'

It hadn't been long after their row and her finding out exactly why he'd married her. Rio had been acting more edgily than usual, so Trinity hadn't fought him on the dress and had assured herself that she'd talk to Cruz that night—seek his help. Except it hadn't turned out as she'd expected. She'd been a fool to think she could turn to him.

The memory left her feeling raw. She averted her eyes from Cruz's now and said stiffly, 'It's your money—you can spend it as you wish.'

The air steward came back with Trinity's lunch, and she focused on the food to try and distract herself from a feeling of mounting futile anger and impotence. But the fact that she was destined to dance to the tune of another autocratic De Carrillo man left the food in her mouth tasting of dust.

She gave up trying to pretend she had an appetite and pushed her plate away. Cruz looked up from the small laptop he'd switched his attention to. He frowned with disapproval at how little she'd eaten—it was an expression that was becoming very familiar to Trinity, and one she guessed was likely to become even more familiar.

Her anger rose. 'Was this marriage really necessary?' she blurted out, before she could censor her tongue.

A bit late now, whispered that annoying voice.

As if privy to that voice, Cruz mocked, 'It really is futile to discuss something that's already done. But by all means, Trinity, feel free to seek a divorce whenever you want.'

And leave Matty and Sancho at this man's mercy? Never, vowed Trinity.

Just then a plaintive wail came from the back of the plane.

'Mummy!'

She recognised the overtired tone. Seizing her opportunity to escape, Trinity stood up and tried not to feel self-conscious in her creased dress and bare feet.

'Excuse me. I should help Mrs Jordan.'

She walked away with as much grace as she could muster and tried her best not to feel as though her whole world was shrinking down to the size of a prison cell—even if it was to be the most luxurious prison cell in the world.

A few hours later Trinity shivered, in spite of the warm Spanish breeze. They'd driven into a massive circular courtyard and she was holding a silent and wide-eyed Sancho in her arms, thumb stuck firmly in his mouth. Mrs Jordan was holding a similarly quiet Matty. They were still a little groggy after the naps they'd had on the plane.

Her instinct about the *castillo* being intimidating had

been right. It was massive and imposing. A mixture of architecture, with the most dominant influence being distinctly Moorish. Cruz had explained that they were about midway between Seville and a small historic town called El Rocio, which sat on the edge of a national park. But there was nothing around them now except for rolling countryside; he hadn't been lying about that.

Cruz was greeting some staff who had appeared in the imposing porch area. They were all dressed in black. Trinity caught Mrs Jordan's eye and was relieved to see that the older woman looked as intimidated as she felt.

Mrs Jordan said brightly, 'Well, my word, I don't think I've ever seen anything so grand. I'm sure it's bright and airy on the inside.'

But when they went in, after a whirlwind of introductions to several staff whose complicated names Trinity struggled to imprint on her brain, it wasn't bright and airy. It was dark and cool—and not in a refreshing way.

The stone walls were covered with ancient tapestries that all seemed to depict different gruesome battles. Then there were portraits of what had to be Cruz's ancestors. She could see where he got his austere expression. They all looked fearsome. There was one in particular whose resemblance to Cruz was uncanny.

She hadn't even noticed that she'd stopped to stare at it for so long until a cool voice from behind her said, 'That's Juan Sanchez De Carrillo—my great-great-grandfather.'

Unnerved, in case he might guess why she'd been momentarily captivated by the huge portrait, Trinity desisted from saying that she thought it looked like him. Instead she asked, 'So is this where you and Rio grew up?'

For a moment he said nothing, and Trinity looked at him. She caught a fleeting expression on his face that she couldn't read, but then it was gone.

He led her forward, away from the portrait, as he said

smoothly, 'Yes, we were both born in this *castillo*. But our circumstances couldn't have been more different.'

'I know,' Trinity said cautiously. 'Rio told me that his mother was a maid here, and that she blackmailed your father for money after their affair and then left Rio behind.'

In spite of everything that had happened, she *still* felt sympathy. These dark corridors and austere pictures only confirmed that Cruz's experience couldn't have been much happier here. That treacherous curiosity to know more rose up again, much to her disgust. She was a soft touch.

But Cruz was clearly not up for conversation. He was moving again, leaving the long corridor, and she had to follow or be left behind. He opened a door to reveal an enclosed open-air courtyard and Trinity automatically sucked in a deep breath, only realising then how truly oppressive the *castillo* had felt.

They'd lost Mrs Jordan and the other staff somewhere along the way. Afraid that Cruz suspected she was angling for a personal tour, she shifted Sancho's heavy and now sleeping weight on her shoulder and hurried after his long strides.

'You don't have to show me around—there'll be plenty of time for that.'

A whole lifetime, whispered that wicked voice.

Cruz just said brusquely, 'This isn't a tour. We're just taking another route to your quarters.'

Trinity felt a childish urge to poke her tongue out at his back. *Your quarters.* She shivered a little.

He led them back into the *castillo* on the other side of the surprisingly pretty courtyard. The sensation of the walls closing around her again made her realise that this was *it*. Hers and the boys' home for the foreseeable future. The prospect was intimidating, to say the least.

Trinity vowed then and there to do everything she could to ensure Matty and Sancho's happiness and security in such a dark and oppressive atmosphere. After all, she'd chosen to be their protector and she had no regrets.

Cruz helped himself to a shot of whisky from the sideboard in his study on the other side of the *castillo*. He took a healthy sip, relishing the burn which distracted him from the uncomfortable feeling that lingered after walking away from Trinity, Mrs Jordan and the boys, all looking at him with wide eyes, as if they'd just been transported to Outer Mongolia.

He didn't like the way his nephews fell silent whenever he approached them, looking at him so warily, clinging on to Trinity. His urge to protect them had grown exponentially since he'd decided marriage was the only option—thanks to which he was now their legal guardian too.

While the jury was still very much out on Trinity—her easy signing of the pre-nup had thrown up questions he wasn't eager to investigate—he had to admit grudgingly that so far it didn't look as if his nephews were being adversely affected by her.

Cruz had been surprised to discover that Rio had told her the full extent of his mother's treachery.

When he and Rio had been younger they'd never been allowed to play together, and on the few occasions Cruz had managed to sneak away from his nanny to find Rio his younger half-brother had always looked at him suspiciously.

One day they had been found together. Cruz's father had taken Rio into his study, and he could still remember the shouts of humiliation as his father had beaten him. Rio had eventually emerged with tears streaking his red face, holding his behind, glaring at Cruz with a hatred that had been vivid.

Their father had appeared in the doorway and said to Cruz, 'That's what'll happen if you seek him out again. His is *not* your real brother.'

Cruz had felt so angry, and yet so impotent. That was the moment he'd vowed to ensure that Rio was never denied what was rightfully his...much good it had done his brother in the end.

He realised now for the first time that the knowledge that he was his nephews' legal guardian had soothed something inside him. Something he never could have acknowledged before, while Rio had held him at arm's length. It was the part of him that had failed in being able to protect his brother when they were younger. He was able to do this now for his nephews in the most profound way. It made emotion rise up, and with it futile anger at Rio's death.

Cruz's mind deviated then, with irritating predictability, back to his new wife. He'd expected something more from her by now—some show or hint of defiance that would reveal her irritation at having her wings clipped. But there was nothing. Just those big blue eyes, looking at him suspiciously. As if he might take a bite out of her... That thought immediately made him think of sinking his teeth into soft pale flesh.

What the hell was wrong with him? He would not fall into that pit of fire again. She disgusted him.

A little voice jeered at him. *She disgusts you so much that your blood simmers every time she's close?*

Cruz shut it down ruthlessly.

Trinity would not tempt him again. This situation was all about containment and control and ensuring his nephews were in his care and safe. That was all that mattered—their legacy. As soon as she realised how limited her life would be she'd be begging for a divorce, and that day couldn't come soon enough.

CHAPTER FOUR

A WEEK LATER Trinity felt as if she were on a slightly more even keel. She and the boys and Mrs Jordan had finally settled, somewhat, into their palatial rooms. Decorated in light greys and soft pinks and blues, with contemporary furniture and a modern media centre, they made for a more soothing environment than the rest of the dark and brooding *castillo*, which was not unlike its owner.

Mrs Jordan had an entire apartment to herself, as did Trinity, and they were both connected by the boys' room, which was light and bright but other than that showed no indication that it was home to two small boys with more energy than a bag of long-life batteries.

They took their meals in a large sunny dining room, not far from their rooms, that led out to a landscaped garden. Trinity and Mrs Jordan spent most of their time running after Matty and Sancho, trying to stop them pulling the very exotic-looking flowers out of the pristine beds.

Trinity sighed now, and pushed some hair behind her ear as she contemplated the two napping toddlers who looked as exhausted as she felt. She'd have to talk to Cruz about modifying their bedroom and installing something more practical outside that would occupy their vast energy and satisfy their need to be stimulated. Otherwise the head gardener was going to be very upset, and the boys were going to grow more and more frustrated.

The staff they'd seen so far—a taciturn housekeeper who spoke no English and a young girl who looked terrified— hardly inspired confidence in it being a happy household where she could get to know people and let the boys run free. It was very obvious that Cruz believed he had corralled them exactly where he wanted them and had now all but washed his hands of her, in spite of his decree that she be available as his social escort.

Mrs Jordan had had the morning off, and was going to keep an eye on the boys this afternoon when they woke, so Trinity took the opportunity to go and see if Cruz had returned from his trip to Madrid yet—she'd managed to ascertain that he'd gone from the shy maid.

She refused to give in to a growing feeling of helplessness but while making her way from their wing of the *castillo*, back through the pretty courtyard, she could feel her heart-rate increasing. She told herself it was not in anticipation of seeing Cruz after a few days. What was wrong with her? Was she a complete masochist?

As she walked past the stern portraits of the ancestors she didn't look up, not wanting to see if their eyes would be following her censoriously, judging her silently.

Just at that moment a door opened and a tall hard body stepped out—right in front of Trinity. She found herself slamming straight into the man who so easily dominated her thoughts.

Big hands caught her upper arms to stop her lurching backwards. All her breath seemed to have left her lungs with the impact as she stared up into those tawny eyes.

Somehow she managed to get out the words, 'You're back.'

Cruz's hands tightened almost painfully on Trinity's arms. 'I got back late last night.'

Tension was instant between them, and something else much more ambiguous and electric. She tried to move back but she couldn't.

Panic that he might see her reaction to him spiked. 'You can let me go.'

Cruz's eyes widened a fraction, as if he'd been unaware he was holding her, and then suddenly he dropped his hands as if burnt. Trinity stepped back, feeling sick at the expression crossing his face—something between disgust and horror. She'd seen that look before, after he'd kissed her.

She said quickly, 'I was looking for you, actually.'

After a silent moment Cruz stepped aside and gestured for her to go into the room he'd just left. She stepped inside, still feeling shaky after that sudden physical impact.

Cruz closed the door and walked to his desk, turning around to face her. 'I'll call for some coffee—or would you prefer tea?'

'Tea would be lovely, thank you.'

So polite. As if he *hadn't* just dumped her and her stepsons in his remote intimidating home and left them to their own devices. Maybe he thought she would have run screaming by now?

When Cruz turned away to lean over his desk and pick up the phone Trinity had to consciously drag her gaze away from where his thin shirt stretched enticingly over flexed and taut muscles. She looked around the room, which was huge and obviously his home office.

Dark wood panelling and big antique furniture gave it a serious air. Floor-to-ceiling shelves dominated one whole wall, and Trinity felt a wave of heat scorch her from the inside out as the memory of another wall of shelves flashed back, of how it had felt to have Cruz press her against it so passionately.

'Do you still read?'

Trinity's head snapped back to Cruz. She hadn't even noticed that he'd finished the call. She was mortified, and crushed the memory, hoping her cheeks weren't flaming.

She shook her head, saying with a slightly strangled voice, 'I haven't had much time lately.' She was usually so exhausted when she went to bed now that her love of reading was a thing of the past. A rare luxury.

'Well? You said you were looking for me?'

He was looking at her expectantly, one hip resting on his desk, arms folded. Formidable. Remote. Her ex-employer, now her husband, but a stranger. It struck her then that even though they'd shared that brief intimacy, and she'd had a glimpse of what lay under the surface, he was still a total enigma.

She shoved down her trepidation. 'Yes. I wanted to talk to you about the boys.'

A light knock came on the door, and he called for whoever it was to come in as he frowned and said, 'What's wrong? Are they okay?'

The maid, Julia, appeared with a tray of tea and coffee, distracting Trinity. She noticed how the girl blushed when Cruz bestowed a polite smile on her and said thank you. Trinity felt humiliation curl inside her. She'd used to blush like that when she'd worked for him. It felt like a lifetime ago.

When the girl had left Cruz was still looking at Trinity, waiting for her answer. Feeling exposed under that laser-like intensity, she said, 'Nothing is wrong with them—they're fine. Settling in better than I'd expected, actually.'

Some of the tension left Cruz's shoulders and she felt a dart of unexpected emotion—what if he really did care about the boys?

He deftly poured tea for her and coffee for him and handed her a cup. 'Sit down.'

She chose a chair near the desk and cradled her cup, watching warily as he took a seat on the other side of his desk. He took a sip of his coffee and arched one dark golden brow, clearly waiting for her to elaborate.

She put the cup down on the table in front of her and sat up straight. 'The rooms…our rooms…are lovely. And very comfortable. But the boys' room isn't exactly tailored for children their age. It could do with brightening up, being made more cheerful—somewhere they can play and where they'll want to go to sleep. Also, they've been playing in the gardens—which they love—but again it's not exactly suitable for them. Your head gardener has already had to replant some of his flowerbeds.'

Cruz's conscience pricked as he acknowledged that he'd not even had the courtesy to stick around for one day and make sure that Trinity and his nephews and their nanny were comfortable.

He knew that the *castillo* was dated in parts, but the rooms he'd given to them had been those used by his mother before her death, so they were the most up-to-date. But evidently not up-to-date enough.

It hadn't even occurred to him to make the space child-friendly, and that stung now. What also stung was the fact that he had to acknowledge that his trip to Madrid had been less about business and more about putting some space between him and this new domestic world he'd brought back to Spain with him.

He was distracted by Trinity's very earthy clean-faced appeal. A look he had thought she'd eschewed as soon as she'd married Rio. Certainly any pictures he'd seen of them together had shown her to have morphed into someone who favoured heavy make-up and skimpy clothes.

And yet where was the evidence of that now? Her hair was pulled back into a low, messy bun. She was wearing soft jeans and a loose shirt, with a stain that looked sus-piciously like dried food on her shoulder—as unalluring as any woman who had ever appeared in front of him, and yet it didn't matter. Cruz's blood sizzled over a low-banked fire of lust.

'So, what are you suggesting?' he asked, irritated at this reminder of how much she affected him.

Trinity swallowed, making Cruz notice the long slim column of her throat. Even that had an effect on him. *Damn it.*

'I'd like to make the boy's room more colourful and fun. And with regards to the garden… I'm not saying that that's not enough for them—your grounds are stunning—but they're bright, inquisitive boys and they're already becoming frustrated with being told they can't roam freely and touch what they want. Perhaps if they had something that would occupy their energy, like swings… They loved the children's playground in Regent's Park.'

All of what she'd just said was eminently reasonable, yet Cruz felt a tide of tension rising up through his body.

'Anything else?'

As if she could sense his tension, something flashed in her eyes. Fire. It sent a jolt of adrenalin through Cruz. She certainly wasn't the shy girl who'd come for that job interview a couple of years ago. More evidence of her duality, if he'd needed it.

She lifted her chin. 'Yes, actually. I don't know how the school systems work here, but if it's anything like in the UK I'll—' She stopped herself and flushed slightly. 'That is, *we'll* have to think about enrolling them in a local school. Also, I'd like to investigate playschools in the area—they should be around other children their own age. Surely you weren't expecting to them to never go beyond the *castillo* gates?'

He'd never been allowed beyond the *castillo* gates until he'd gone to boarding school in England.

He reacted testily to the fact that she was showing a level of consideration for his nephews that he'd never expected to see. 'Are you sure you're not just looking for opportunities to spread your own wings beyond these walls? You're not a prisoner, Trinity, you can leave any time you want. But if you do the boys remain here.'

She paled dramatically, any bravado gone, but seconds later a wash of bright pink came into her cheeks. Cruz was momentarily mesmerised by this display of emotion—he was used to people disguising their natural reactions around him. It had intrigued him before and he was surprised that she still had the ability.

She stood up. 'I'm well aware that I am here because I have little or no choice—not if I want to see my stepsons flourish and be secure—but I will never walk away from them. Not while they need me. I will do whatever it takes to ensure their happiness and wellbeing.'

Her blue eyes blazed. *Dios*, but she was stunning.

'So if you're hoping to see the back of me it won't be any time soon, I can assure you.'

With that, she turned on her heel and stalked out of the room, the heavy door closing with a solid *thunk* behind her. Cruz cursed volubly and stood up, muscles poised to go after her. But then he stopped.

He turned to face the window, which took in the breathtaking vista of the expanse of his estate. He couldn't allow Trinity to distract him by fooling him into thinking she'd changed. Because the moment he dropped his guard she'd have won.

'What on earth did you say to him?'

Trinity was too shocked to respond to Mrs Jordan's question as she took in the scene before her. Building was underway on a playground for the boys…an exact replica of the playground in Regent's Park.

At that moment the atmosphere became charged with a kind of awareness that only happened around one person. *Cruz*.

Mrs Jordan reacted to his presence before Trinity did. 'Mr De Carrillo, this really is spectacular—the boys will love it.'

He came to stand beside Trinity and his scent tickled her nostrils, earthy and masculine. Her belly tightened and she flushed. Superstitiously she didn't want to look at him, as if that might make his impact less.

He answered smoothly, 'Please, Mrs Jordan, call me Cruz… Trinity was right—the boys need somewhere they can expend their energy safely.'

Matty and Sancho were currently playing with big toy building bricks in an area that had been cordoned off for them by the builders. They were wearing small hard hats and jeans and T-shirts and they looked adorable, faces intent, trying to keep up with the real builders just a few feet away.

Mrs Jordan turned to Cruz more directly and said, with an innocent tone in her voice, 'We were just about to bring the boys in for lunch—won't you join us?'

Trinity glanced at the woman, aghast, but Mrs Jordan was ignoring her. Fully expecting Cruz to refuse, she couldn't believe it when, after a long moment, he said consideringly, 'Thank you. That would be lovely.'

Mrs Jordan smiled. 'I'll ask Julia to add another place.'

She disappeared with a suspicious twinkle in her eye before Trinity could say anything. She supposed she couldn't really blame the woman for taking the opportunity to meddle gently when it arose.

When Trinity glanced up at Cruz she almost expected him to look irritated at the thought of spending lunch with them, but he was staring at the boys with an enigmatic expression on his face. Uncertainty?

Then, as if he sensed her watching him, the expression was gone and he looked down at her. 'You haven't said anything—are the plans all right?'

Against her best intentions to remain impervious to this man's pull, something inside her melted a little at his thoughtfulness. She forced a smile. 'They're perfect. I didn't expect you to take my words so literally.'

He frowned. 'But you said they loved that playground, so naturally I would try to recreate it for them.'

Trinity desisted from pointing out that only a billionaire would think along such lavish lines and just said dryly, 'It's extremely generous, and they will love it. Thank you.'

Cruz looked away from her to the boys and another curious expression crossed his face. She'd seen it before when he looked at them: something between fear and longing. Trinity cursed herself for not reading it properly till now. This man scrambled her brain cells too easily.

She said, 'They won't bite, you know. They're as curious about you as you are about them.'

Without taking his eyes off them Cruz said gruffly, 'They always seem to look at me as if they don't know what I am.'

Trinity felt something weaken inside her at this evidence of rare vulnerability. 'They don't really know you yet, that's all. Once they become more used to you they'll relax. Why don't you help me get them in for lunch?'

She moved forward before he could see how easily he affected her.

'Matty! Sancho!' she called out when she came near to where they were playing so happily. 'Time to go in for lunch.'

Two identical faces looked up with predictable mulishness—and then they spied Cruz and immediately put down what they were playing with to come to Trinity. She bent down to their level and took their hats off, ruffling their heads, feeling the heat from their small, sturdy bodies. Even though they were in the shade the Spanish spring was getting warmer every day.

Cruz was towering over them in one of his trademark pristine suits. No wonder he intimidated the boys. He intimidated her. Softly she said, 'It might help if you come down to their level.'

He squatted down beside her and the movement made her uncomfortably aware of his very potent masculinity. She closed her eyes for a second. What was wrong with her? Until she'd shared that incendiary moment with him in his study she'd had no great interest in sex. And yet a couple of days in Cruz's company again and all her hormones seemed to have come back to life.

She focused her attention on her boys, who were huddled close, brown eyes huge. 'Matty, Sancho...you know this is your Uncle Cruz's house, where we're going to live from now on?' She ignored the pang inside her when she said that, and the thought of a life stretching ahead of her as a wife of inconvenience.

'Man. The big man,' Matty observed.

Trinity bit back a smile at the innocent nickname. 'Yes, sweetie—but he's also your uncle and he wants to get to know you better.'

Sancho said nothing, just regarded his uncle. Then he said imperiously, 'Play with us.'

Matty jumped up and down. 'Yes! Play!'

Sensing things starting to unravel, Trinity said firmly, 'First lunch, and then you can play again for a little while.'

She scooped up Matty and handed him to Cruz, who took him awkwardly and rose to his feet. She then picked up Sancho and started to walk inside, almost afraid to look behind her and see how Matty must be tarnishing Cruz's sartorial perfection.

He was saying excitedly, 'Higher, Unkel Cooz...higher!'

Seeing his brother in the arms of the tall, scary man who now wasn't so scary was making Sancho squirm to get free from Trinity's arms. 'I want higher too!'

They walked into the bright dining room where Mrs Jordan was waiting for them. Trinity didn't miss the gleam of approval in the woman's eyes when she saw Cruz carrying one of his nephews.

Trinity thought again of that rare chink of vulnerability Cruz had revealed outside. She realised belatedly that this had to be hard for him—coming from such a dark and dour place with only a half-brother he'd never been allowed to connect with properly. And yet he was making a real effort.

A rush of tenderness flooded her before she could stop it.

She tried to hide her tumultuous emotions as she strapped Sancho into his high seat. When she felt composed again she looked up to see Mrs Jordan showing Cruz how to strap Mateo into his. He looked flummoxed by such engineering, and it should have emasculated the man but it didn't. It only made that tenderness surge again. Pathetic.

Cruz sat down at the head of the table. The boys were seated one on each side beside Trinity and Mrs Jordan. Staff scurried in and out, presenting a buffet of salads and cold meats, cheese and bread. The boys were having chopped up pasta and meatballs. They ate with their habitual gusto, insisting on feeding themselves and invariably spraying anyone in close proximity with tiny bits of pasta and meat.

Trinity sneaked another glance at Cruz to see if this domestic milieu was boring him, but he was watching his nephews, fascinated.

'How do you tell them apart?' he asked, during a lull when small mouths were full.

Trinity nodded her head towards Mateo on the other side of the table. 'Matty is a tiny bit taller and leaner. He's also a little more gregarious than Sancho. Where he leads, Sancho follows. She scooped some of Sancho's food back onto his plate and said with a fond smile, 'Sancho is more watchful and quiet. He's also got a slightly different coloured right eye—a tiny discolouration.'

Cruz leaned forward to look and Sancho grinned at the attention, showing tiny teeth and a mouth full of masticated food.

When he pulled back, Cruz said a little faintly, 'Rio had the same thing…one eye was slightly lighter in colour.'

'He did…?' Trinity had never noticed that detail.

Cruz sent her a sharp glance and she coloured and busied herself cleaning up Sancho's tray, feeling absurdly guilty when she had no reason to. It wasn't as if she'd spent any time looking deep into Rio's eyes. Not that Cruz would believe that. She wondered if he ever would.

It didn't escape her notice that Mrs Jordan had excused herself on some flimsy pretext. Trinity sighed inwardly. She wouldn't put it past the woman, who subsisted on a diet of romance novels, to try and matchmake her and Cruz into a real marriage.

The thought of that was so absurd that she coloured even more for a moment, as if Cruz might see inside her head.

The very notion of this man looking at her with anything other than suspicious disdain was utterly inconceivable.

But he looked at you differently once before, said a little voice.

Trinity blocked it out. Cruz wouldn't touch her again if his life depended on it—of that she was sure. And that suited her just fine. If he ever discovered how susceptible she still was—*and* how innocent she still was, in spite of his belief that her marriage to Rio had been a real one… The thought sent a wave of acute vulnerability through her.

Cruz's comprehensive rejection of her had left a wound in a deeply private feminine space. The thought of opening herself up to that rejection again was terrifying.

Cruz cleared his throat then, and said, 'I've arranged

for you to be taken to a local boutique tomorrow morning, where a stylist will help you choose a wardrobe of clothes. Think of it as a trousseau.'

Trinity put down the napkin and looked at him. She felt raw after her recent line of thinking. She hated to be so beholden to him. It made her feel helpless and she didn't like that. She saw the look in his eye, as if he was just waiting for her to show her true avaricious nature.

'There's not just me to think of,' she said testily. 'I need to get the boys some new clothes too, more suitable for this warmer climate. They're growing so fast at the moment that they've almost outgrown everything.'

Cruz inclined his head, only the merest glint in his eye showing any reaction to her spiky response. 'Of course. I should have thought of that. I'll see to it that the stylist takes you to a suitable establishment for children also.'

The boys were starting to get bored now, having eaten enough and grown tired of the lack of attention and activity. Sancho was already manoeuvring himself to try and slip out of his chair and Trinity caught him deftly.

She took advantage of the distraction. 'I'll let them play some more while their lunch digests and then it'll be time for their afternoon nap.'

Without asking for help, Cruz stood and plucked a clearly delighted Matty, little arms outstretched, out of his seat. It irked her no end that Cruz was already holding him with an ease that belied the fact that it was only the second time he'd held one of his nephews in his arms.

It suited him. Matty looked incredibly protected in those strong arms and a sharp poignancy gripped her for a moment as she realised that he was already charming them. They'd gone from looking at him as if he was about to devour them whole, to looking at him with something close to awe and adoration. Their tiny minds were obviously cottoning onto the fact that this tall person might become an important ally and be able to do things that Trinity and Mrs Jordan couldn't.

Sancho was whingeing—he wanted to be in the big man's arms too.

Cruz held out his other arm, 'I can take him.'

After a moment's hesitation Trinity handed him over, to see Cruz expertly balance Sancho in his other arm. And then he walked out of the room, two glossy brown heads lifted high against his chest. The twins were delighted with themselves, grinning at her over those broad shoulders.

And just like that Trinity knew she'd started to lose them to Cruz... And, as wrong as it was, she couldn't but help feel a tiny bit jealous at how easily he accepted the innocence of his nephews when he would never ever accept the possibility of Trinity's. Not while he was so blinded by his loyalty to his deceased brother.

The next few days passed in a blur for Trinity. She was taken to cosmopolitan and beautiful Seville by Cruz's driver, to a scarily exclusive boutique where she lost track of the outfits she tried on. Then she was taken to a department store that stocked children's clothes, where she picked up everything she needed for the boys.

Their bedroom had been refurbished, and once again Cruz's efficiency had been impressive. An interior designer had taken her ideas on board and now, with murals of animals and tractors and trains on the walls, it was a bright and inviting space for two small boys. And they each had a bed, built in the shape of a car.

For a moment, when she'd seen it transformed and the way the boys had stood there in wide-eyed awe, she'd felt ridiculously emotional. They would have so much more than she'd ever had...or even their father.

She would have thanked Cruz, but he hadn't been

around much in the last few days. He hadn't joined them for lunch again, and the boys had been asking for him plaintively.

Trinity folded up the last of Sancho and Matty's new clothes and put them in the colourful set of drawers, chastising herself for the constant loop in her head that seemed to veer back to Cruz no matter how hard she tried to change it.

She was about to push the drawer closed when a deep voice came from behind her. 'Where are the boys?'

She jumped and whirled around to see Cruz filling the doorway, dressed in jeans and a shirt open at the neck. Irritation at the way she'd just been wondering about him, and the effortless effect he had on her, made her say waspishly, 'They're outside, playing with Mrs Jordan.'

Her irritation only increased when she found herself noticing how gorgeous he looked.

'They've been asking for you, you know. If you're going to be in their lives you need to be more consistent. They don't understand why you're there one day but not the next…it confuses them.'

Her conscience pricked. What she really meant was that it put *her* on edge, not knowing where or when he was likely to turn up…

His gaze narrowed on her and he slowly raised one brow. Clearly the man wasn't used to having anyone speak to him like this. Well, tough, she told herself stoutly. She was no longer in awe of her scarily sexy stern boss. She folded her arms.

'I understand that you've had your wardrobe replenished, as well as my nephews'?' Cruz drawled.

Trinity flushed. She immediately felt churlish and unfolded her arms. 'I wanted to say thank you for the bedroom—it worked out beautifully, and the boys love it. And, yes, we got clothes… But more clothes were delivered from the boutique than I ever looked at or tried on…it's too much.'

Cruz shook his head slowly, a hard light in his eye. 'Still with the act? I'm impressed. I thought you would have cracked by now and shown your true colours—but perhaps you're saving yourself for a more appreciative audience.'

She just looked at him. This evidence of his continued mistrust hurt her and, terrified to look at why that was, and not wanting him to see her emotions, she focused on the last thing he'd said. 'What do you mean, *audience?*'

'I have a function to attend in Seville tomorrow night. It'll be our first public outing as husband and wife.'

Panic gripped her. 'But Mrs Jordan—'

Cruz cut her off. 'Has already agreed to babysit. And we're rectifying that situation next week. I've organised with a local recruitment agency for them to send us their best candidates for another nanny. It'll free you up to spend more time with me, and Mrs Jordan will have more of her own free time.'

'Is that really necessary?' she asked, feeling weak at the thought of more time with him.

'Yes.' Cruz sounded impatient now. 'I'll have social functions to attend and I expect you to be by my side. As discussed.'

Trinity's irritation flared again. and she welcomed it. 'As I recall it was more of a decree than a discussion.'

Cruz's jaw clenched. 'You can call it what you want. We both know that, thanks to Rio's dire financial state when he died, you had no way of offering independent support to my nephews without me. The sooner you accept this as your new reality, the easier it will be for all of us.'

And evidently Cruz still believed that state of financial affairs to be *her* fault, based on her alleged profligate spending of her husband's money.

For a moment Trinity wanted to blurt out the truth—that

Rio had hated Cruz so much he'd wanted to ruin him—but Cruz wouldn't believe her, and she found that the impulse faded quickly. First of all, it wasn't in her to lash out like that, just to score a point. And she also realised she didn't want to see the effect that truth would have on him, when he clearly believed that his brother had been flawed, yes, but inherently decent.

And that shook her to the core—knowing that she resisted wanting to hurt him. Even as he hurt her.

She had to take responsibility for the fact that she'd agreed to the marriage of convenience with Rio. She really had no one to blame but herself.

And, as much as she hated this situation and being financially dependent, she couldn't deny the immutable fact that Matty and Sancho were in the privileged position of being heirs to this great family legacy and fortune. She didn't have the right to decide on their behalf, even as their legal guardian, that she was going to fight to take them away from all this and turn their lives into something it didn't have to be.

The silence grew between them almost to breaking point, a battle of wills, until eventually Trinity said, 'Fine. What time do I need to be ready?'

There was an unmistakable gleam of triumph in Cruz's eyes now and he said, 'We'll leave at six. It's a formal event, so wear a long gown. I'll have Julia show you to the vaults so you can pick out some jewellery.'

Jewellery...vaults... Not wanting him to see how intimidated she was, or how easily he affected her emotions, she just said coolly, 'Fine. I'll be ready by six.'

CHAPTER FIVE

THE FOLLOWING EVENING Cruz paced back and forth in the entrance hall of the *castillo* and looked at his watch again impatiently. He forced himself to take a breath. It was only just six o'clock so Trinity wasn't actually late *yet*. Just then he heard a sound and looked to where she stood at the top of the main stairs.

For a long second he could only stare, struck dumb by the glittering beauty of the woman in front of him. She was refined…elegant. Classic. Stunning.

Her dress was long—as he'd instructed—and a deep blue almost navy colour. It shone and glistened and clung to those impossibly long legs, curving out to her hips and back in to a small waist. It shimmered as she came down the stairs. It clung everywhere—up over her torso to where the material lovingly cupped full, perfectly shaped breasts. All the way to the tantalising hollow at the base of her throat.

Cruz was dimly aware that he'd possibly never seen less flesh revealed on a woman, and yet this dress was sexier than anything he'd ever seen in his life. Her hair was pulled back at the nape of her neck, highlighting the delicate slim column of her throat and her bone structure.

She gestured to herself and he could see that she was nervous.

'What is it? Is the dress not suitable?'

Cruz realised he was ogling. He felt a very uncharacteristic urge to snap, *No, the dress is entirely unsuitable*. And yet that would be ridiculous. The dress effectively covered her from head to toe and he was reacting like an animal in heat—how the hell would he react when he saw some flesh? As it was, all the blood in his body was migrating from his brain to between his legs with alarming speed.

Any delusion he'd been under that he could successfully block out his awareness of this woman was laughable. She was under his skin, in his blood, and he couldn't deny it. His intellect hated this desire for her but his body thrummed with need.

Calling on all the control and civility he possessed, Cruz locked eyes with Trinity's—not that that helped. The colour of the dress only made her bright blue eyes stand out even more. They were like light sapphires, stunning and unusual.

'It's fine,' he said tightly. And then, goaded by thoughts of how she'd dressed for Rio, he said provocatively, 'Or perhaps you'd feel more comfortable in less material?'

To his surprise he saw the faintest shudder pass through her body. 'No. I never felt comfortable in the clothes Rio wanted me to wear.'

He looked at her. For some reason that admission only made him feel more conflicted.

Tersely he said, 'The driver is waiting—we should go.'

He indicated for her to precede him out of the *castillo* and his gaze tracked down her back and snagged on the enticing curves of her buttocks. He cursed himself. He was behaving as if he'd never seen a beautiful woman before in his life.

The driver helped her into the back of the luxury Jeep and Cruz got in the other side. As they were pulling out of the *castillo* courtyard his gaze swept over her again and he noticed something. 'You're not wearing any jewellery. Didn't you go to the vaults?'

She looked at him and Cruz saw a flush stain her cheeks. 'I did, but everything was so valuable-looking I was afraid to take anything.'

Something dark pierced him—was this finally evidence of her avaricious methods? Was this how she angled for more?

'Perhaps you'd have preferred something from Cartier or Tiffany's?'

She shook her head, eyes flashing. 'No, I wouldn't prefer that.' She held out her hand. 'I'm wearing the wedding band—isn't that enough? Or maybe you'd prefer if I wore a diamond-studded collar with a lead attached so no one is mistaken as to whom I belong?'

Irritation vied with frustration that she was so consistently refusing to conform to what he expected. He curtly instructed his driver to turn around and go back to the *castillo*.

'Why are we going back?' Trinity asked.

Cruz looked straight ahead. 'We're going back to get you an engagement ring.'

'I don't need one,' she said stubbornly.

He looked at her. 'It's not a choice. People will expect you to have a ring.'

She rounded on him, tense and visibly angry. 'Oh, and we can't have anyone suspecting that this isn't a real marriage, can we? Do you really think an engagement ring will convince people that you fell in love with your brother's widow?'

Cruz wanted to laugh at her suggestion of anyone in his circle ever being convinced that people married for love, but for some reason the laugh snagged in his chest.

'Don't be ridiculous,' he breathed, his awareness of her rising in an unstoppable wave in the confined space. 'No one would expect that. They'll know I'm protecting what's mine—my heirs.'

'And I'm just the unlucky pawn who got in your way.'

The bitterness in Tiffany's voice surprised him. Anger spiked at the way his control was starting seriously to fray at the edges. 'You put yourself in the way—by seducing my brother. By inserting yourself into my nephews' lives so they'd come to depend on you.'

She went pale and looked impossibly wounded. 'I've told you—that's not—'

Before she could issue another lie Cruz's control snapped and he acted on blind instinct and need. He reached for Trinity, clamping his hands around her waist, and pulled her towards him, vaguely registering how slender and light she felt under his hands.

He only had a second of seeing her eyes widen with shock before his mouth crashed down onto hers, and for a long second nothing existed except this pure, spiking shard of lust, so strong that he had no option but to move his mouth and haul Trinity even closer, until he could feel every luscious curve pressed against him.

And it was only in that moment, when their mouths were fused and he could feel her heart clamouring against his chest, that he could finally recognise the truth: he'd been aching for this since the night he'd kissed her for the first time.

Trinity wasn't even sure what had happened. A minute ago she'd been blisteringly angry with Cruz and now she was drowning and burning up at the same time. The desire she'd hoped she could keep buried deep inside her was shaming her with its instant resurrection. Brought back to life by a white-hot inferno scorching along every artery and vein in her body.

Cruz's mouth was hot and hard, moving over hers with such precision that Trinity couldn't deny him access, and when his tongue stroked hers with an explicitness that made heat rush between her legs her hands tightened around his arms, where they'd gone instinctively to hang on to something…anything…so she wouldn't float away.

His hands were still on her waist and one started moving up her torso, until it came tantalisingly close to the side of her breast, where her nipple peaked with need, stiffening against the sheer material of her underwear and her dress. She remembered what it was like to have his mouth on her there...the hot sucking heat...the excruciating pleasure of his touch.

A voice from the past whispered through the clamour of her blood—his voice. *'It should never have happened.'* It was like a slap across the face.

Trinity jerked backwards away from Cruz. She was panting as if she'd just run a race. Mortification was swift and all-consuming. He'd barely had to touch her before she'd gone up in flames. Any hope of convincing him she didn't want him was comprehensively annihilated. It wasn't even a comfort to see that his hair was dishevelled and his cheeks were flushed.

Those amber eyes glittered darkly. He muttered, 'I told myself I wouldn't touch you ever again, but I can't *not* touch you.'

She took her hands off him, but he caught them and held them tightly. The recrimination on his face was far too painfully familiar. She was angry and hurt.

'So now it's justifiable for you to kiss me, even if you still hate yourself for it? Because I'm your wife and not just a lowly maid?'

She pulled her hands free and balled them into fists in her lap.

Cruz frowned, 'What the hell are you talking about— justifiable?'

Trinity tried not to sound as emotional as she felt. 'You rejected me that night because you couldn't bear the thought that you'd kissed your maid. I saw the kind of women you took as lovers, and you don't need to tell me that I was nowhere near their level—socially, economically or intellectually.'

Cruz clamped his hands around her arms, his face flushing. He was livid. 'You think I stopped making love to you because I was a snob? *Dios* Trinity, that was *not* the case. I had to stop because you were my employee and I had a duty of care towards you. I put you in a compromising situation where you might have felt too scared to say no.'

His mouth twisted.

'My father was renowned for his affairs—some of which were with willing and impressionable staff members at the *castillo*. I vowed that I would never follow his footsteps—not least because I'd seen the destruction one of his affairs cost us all. He slept with Rio's mother, who took advantage of the situation, only to then abandon her son.'

Trinity was speechless for a moment as she absorbed this. 'You think,' she framed shakily, 'that I'm like Rio's mother, then? That I'm no better…?'

Cruz's wide, sensual mouth compressed. 'I didn't think so at first—not that night. I hated myself for losing control like that, but I didn't blame you. Since then…let's just say any illusions about your innocence I may have had have been well and truly shattered.'

An awful poignancy gripped Trinity at the thought that for a short while Cruz *had* seen the real her…and respected her. But even the memory of her naivety and humiliation couldn't stop her saying bitterly, 'It would only have ever been a mistake, though, wouldn't it? I mean, let's not fool ourselves that it would have developed into anything… more…'

More. Like the kind of more that Cruz had once hoped existed until any such notion was drummed out of him by his mother and her bitter words? Since then he'd never been proved wrong—any woman he'd been with had only confirmed his cynicism. Not least this one. And yet… when he'd first laid eyes on her he'd never seen anyone who looked so untouched and innocent.

And she was looking at him now with those huge eyes, taunting him for his flight of fancy. It was as if she was reaching inside him to touch a raw wound.

He was unaware of his hands tightening on her arms, knew only that he needed to push her back.

'More...like what?' he all but sneered. 'Hearts and flowers? Tender lovemaking and declarations of undying love? I don't *do* tender lovemaking, Trinity, I would have taken you until we were both sated and then moved on. I have no time for relationships—my life isn't about that. It never was and it never will be. I have a duty of care to my nephews now, and you're here only because I'm legally bound to have you here.' His mouth twisted. 'The fact that I want you is a weakness I'm apparently not capable of overcoming.'

A veritable cavalcade of emotions crossed Trinity's face, and then a look of almost unbelievable hurt—it had to be unbelievable—superseded them all. She shrank back, pulling herself free, and he only realised then how hard he'd been holding her. He curled his hands into fists and cursed himself. What was it about this woman that made his brain fuse and cease functioning?

In a low voice that scraped along all of Cruz's raw edges she said, 'I wasn't looking for anything more than a book that night, no matter what you choose to believe.'

Cruz still felt volatile, and even more so now at this protestation of innocence and her stubborn refusal to reveal her true nature. He ground out, 'Maybe if I'd taken you as I'd wanted to, there against the bookshelves, we wouldn't be here now and Rio would still be alive.'

Trinity had thought he couldn't hurt her much more than he already had, but he just had—even as a lurid image blasted into her head of exactly the scenario he mentioned...his powerful body holding her captive against a wall of books while he thrust up, deep into her body.

She held herself rigid, denying that hurt, and blasted back, 'So you would have thrown over that elegant brunette beauty for me? Am I supposed to be flattered that you would have been happy to conduct an affair on your terms, only to discard me by the wayside when you were done with me?'

A muscle ticked in Cruz's jaw but he just said tersely, 'We're back at the *castillo*, we should get the ring. We've wasted enough time.'

Wasted enough time.

Trinity was still reeling as she followed Cruz's broad tuxedoed form down stone steps to the vaults, holding her dress up in one hand. The depth of his cynicism astounded her all over again, and she hated it that he'd hurt her so easily.

She blamed his interaction with Matty and Sancho. It had made her lower her guard against him and he'd punished her for it, reminding her that he was not remotely someone to pin her hopes and dreams on... She scowled at herself. Since when had she ever entertained those notions herself? It wasn't as if she'd ever been under any delusions of *more*.

More existed for people who weren't her or Cruz. Who had grown up with normal, functioning, loving families. And yet she couldn't deny that when she'd worked for him for a brief moment she'd entertained daydreams of him noticing her...wanting her...smiling at her—

Trinity slammed a lid on that humiliating Pandora's box.

She wasn't sure what was worse—finding out that Cruz hadn't dismissed her because she was a nobody all those years ago, or believing that if he'd taken her *until they were both sated* he could have averted Rio's destruction. Right now, she hated Cruz with a passion that scared her.

But not far under her hatred was something much more

treacherous. A very illicit racing excitement at the knowledge that he still wanted her. And that he'd rejected her because he'd felt he'd taken advantage of his position, not because he'd been horrified to find himself attracted to her...

Once in the vault, Trinity welcomed the change of scenery from the heightened and heated intensity of the back of the Jeep even as she shivered in the cold, dank air.

She hated herself for it, but found herself instinctively moving closer to Cruz's tall, lean form because the place gave her the creeps. She could imagine it being used as a location for the Spanish Inquisition, with its dark stone walls and shadowy cavernous corridors.

She thought, not a little hysterically, that if they'd been back in medieval times Cruz might have just incarcerated her down here in a cell.

He had pulled out a velvet tray of rings from a box in the wall and stood back. 'Choose one.'

Trinity reluctantly stepped forward. Almost immediately one ring in the centre of the tray caught her eye. It was one of the smallest rings, with an ornate gold setting and a small square ruby in the middle.

Cruz followed her gaze and picked it up. 'This one?'

She nodded. He took her hand and held it up and slid the ring onto her finger. It was a perfunctory gesture, so it shouldn't feel in any way momentous but it did. The ring fitted like a glove and, bizarrely, Trinity felt emotion rising when emotion had no place there—especially not after what had just passed between them.

Swallowing the emotion with effort, Trinity was unprepared when Cruz took her chin in his thumb and forefinger, tipping it up. The look in his eyes burned.

'As much as I'd like to be able to resist you, I don't think I can.'

Her heart thumped—hard. The thought of Cruz touching her again and seeing right through to where she was most vulnerable was anathema.

She jerked her chin out of his hand. 'Well, I can resist you enough for both of us.'

He smiled urbanely and stood back, putting out a hand to let her go ahead of him up the stairs and out of the vaults. 'We'll see,' he said with infuriating arrogance as she passed him, and she had to stop herself from running up the stairs, away from his silky threat.

This was Cruz's first social appearance back in Seville. His return was triumphant, now he had tripled his family's fortune and restored the reputation of the once great bank. Now no one would dare say to his face or behind his back the things they'd used to say when his father had been alive.

And yet he could not indulge in a sense of satisfaction. He was too keyed-up after that white-hot explosion of lust in the back of the Jeep, which had proved to him that where Trinity was concerned he had no control over his desires.

His body still throbbed with sexual frustration. And he was distracted by their exchange, and how it had felt to see her with that ring on her finger down in the vaults. It had affected him in a place he hadn't welcomed. As if it was somehow *right* that she should wear one of his family's heirlooms.

Down in that vault it had suddenly been very clear to him that he couldn't fight his desire for her—so why should he? He might not like himself for his weakness but she was his wife, and the prospect of trying to resist her for the duration of their marriage was patently ridiculous.

But something niggled at him—why wasn't she using his desire for her as a means to negotiate or manipulate? Instead she'd looked almost haunted when she'd fled up the steps from the vault. She was still pale now, her eyes huge. Irritation prickled across Cruz's skin. Maybe now that she knew he wanted her she was going to play him in a different way, drive him mad…

'What is it?' he asked abruptly. 'You look paler than a wraith.'

She swallowed, the movement drawing Cruz's gaze to that long, slender column. Delicate. Vulnerable. Damn her. She *was* just playing him. He was giving in to his base desires again and—

'I'm fine. I just… Events like this are intimidating. I never get used to it. I don't know what to say to these people.'

Cruz's recriminations stopped dead. If she was acting then she was worthy of an award. He had a vivid flashback to seeing her standing alone in the crowd at that party in his house, the night of the accident, her stunning body barely decent in that scrap of a dress.

Cruz had been too distracted by the rush of blood to his extremities to notice properly. He'd hated her for making him feel as if he was betraying his brother by still feeling attracted to her. But the memory jarred now. Not sitting so well with what he knew of her.

Almost without registering the urge, Cruz took his hand off her elbow and snaked it around her waist, tugging her into his side. It had the effect of muting his desire to a dull roar. She looked up at him, tense under his arm. Something feral within him longed for her to admit to this attraction between them.

'What are you doing?'

'We're married, *querida*, we need to look it. Just follow my lead. most of the people here are committed egotists, so once you satisfy their urge to talk about themselves they're happy.'

'You don't count yourself in that category?'

Her quick comeback caused Cruz's mouth to tip up.

Suddenly the dry, sterile event wasn't so…boring. And she had a flush in her face now, which aroused him as much as it sent a tendril of relief to somewhere she shouldn't be affecting him.

He replied dryly, 'I find it far more fruitful to allow others to run their mouths off.'

Cruz's hand rested low on Trinity's hip and he squeezed it gently.

She tensed again, as someone approached them, and he said, 'Relax.'

Relax…

It had been the easiest thing and the hardest thing in the world to melt into his side, as if she was meant to be there. It was a cruel irony that she seemed to fit there so well, her softer body curving into his harder form as if especially made for that purpose.

Cruz hadn't let her out of his orbit all night. Even when she'd gone to the bathroom as soon as she'd walked back in to the function room his eyes had been the first thing she'd seen, compelling her back to his side like burning beacons.

It had been both disconcerting and exhilarating. In social situations before she'd invariably been left to fend for herself, Rio being done with her once their initial entrance had been made.

Trinity sighed now and finished tucking Matty and Sancho into their beds—she'd come straight here upon their return from the function, all but running away from Cruz, who had been lazily undoing his bow tie and looking utterly sinful.

The boys were spreadeagled, covers askew, pyjamas twisted around their bodies. Overcome with tenderness for these two small orphaned boys, she smoothed back a lock of Sancho's hair and sat on the side of Matty's bed, careful not to disturb him. Resolve filled her anew not to bow under Cruz's increasingly down-and-dirty methods to disturb her—that incendiary kiss in the back of his Jeep, his words of silky promise in the vault...

After this evening things had changed. Cruz had obviously given himself licence to seduce her. And she knew if he touched her again her ability to resist would be shamefully weak.

She looked at the ring on her finger—heavy, golden. A brand. And an unwelcome reminder of the emotion she'd felt when Cruz had pushed it onto her finger.

She hated it that he believed whatever lies Rio had told him about her so easily. She wasn't remotely mercenary or avaricious. She had remonstrated with Rio countless times over the amounts of money he was spending on her. But he hadn't wanted to know. He'd told her that they had a certain standard to maintain, and that she needed to educate herself about fashion, art, et cetera.

The prospect of a future in which Cruz refused to listen to her and wore down her defences until he found out about her innocence in the most exposing way possible filled Trinity with horror.

She stood up and left the room decisively. She had to at least try to make Cruz see that she wasn't who he thought she was. She would appeal to him rationally, without emotion and physical desire blurring the lines between them.

Above all, she had to make him see that the twins were and always had been her priority.

It was time to talk to her husband and make him listen to her.

'Come in.'

Trinity nearly lost her nerve at the sound of that deeply authoritative voice, but she refused to give in to it and pushed the door open. Cruz was sitting behind his desk, jacket off, shirtsleeves rolled up and the top of his shirt undone. There was a glass of something in his hand. He epitomised louche masculine sensuality.

He looked up from the papers he'd been perusing and immediately sat up straight and frowned when he saw it was her. 'What's wrong? Is it the boys?'

His instant concern for his nephews heartened something inside her. Some fledgling and delicate hope that perhaps she *could* appeal to him. In spite of all the evidence so far to the contrary.

She shook her head. 'No, they're fine. I just checked on them.'

'Well, is it something else?'

Trinity came further into the room, suddenly aware that Cruz was looking at her with a very narrow-eyed assessing gaze and that she was still in the dress. She cursed herself for not having changed into something less…dramatic.

Cruz stood up. 'Would you like a drink?'

She shook her head, thinking that the last thing she needed was to cloud her brain. 'No, thank you.'

He gestured to a seat on the other side of the table and as she sat down he said, 'I noticed you didn't drink much earlier—you don't like it?'

She shook her head. 'Not really. I never acquired the taste.' As soon as she said that, though, she regretted not asking for some brandy—she could do with the Dutch courage.

'So? To what do I owe the pleasure of this late-night visit?'

Trinity looked at Cruz suspiciously. Something about the tone of his voice scraped across her jumping nerves. Was he mocking her for having exposed herself so easily earlier, when he'd kissed her? His expression was unreadable, though, and she told herself she was imagining things.

She took a breath. 'I just…wanted to talk to you about

this arrangement. About going forward, making a practical life together.'

Cruz took a sip of his drink and lowered the glass slowly again. 'Practical? I seem to recall events earlier which would turn the "practical" aspects of this relationship into far more pleasurable ones.'

Trinity immediately stood up, agitated. He *was* mocking her. 'I did not come here to talk about that.'

Totally unperturbed, and like a lazy jungle cat eyeing its prey, Cruz just sat back and said, 'Pity. What did you want to talk about, then?'

She ploughed on before this far more disturbing and *flirty* Cruz could make her lose her nerve.

'I know that I won't be able to continue with this sham marriage while you believe the worst of me and don't trust me. It'll start to affect the boys. They're too young to pick up on the tension now, but they're intelligent and inquisitive and it'll soon become apparent. That kiss earlier…it was unacceptable and disrespectful of my boundaries. This is meant to be a marriage in name only. You will either need to learn to deal with your antipathy for me or…' she took a breath '…we can move on from the past.'

Cruz went very still and then he put his glass down. He stood up and put his hands on the table, his eyes intense. A muscle ticked in his jaw. 'You think that kiss was a demonstration of my antipathy? That kiss was the inevitable result of our explosive mutual desire and proof that you want me as much as I want you.'

Trinity sucked in a breath, mortification rushing through her, and in a desperate bid to deny such a thing she blurted out, 'You gave me no time to respond. I was in shock.'

He arched a brow. 'So your response was down to shock?'

He stood up straight and started to move towards her.

Trinity panicked, stepping away from the chair. She should never have come in here. This had been a terrible idea.

'Yes,' she said desperately. 'Of course it was shock. And you can't do that… Just…manhandle me when you feel like it.'

Cruz stopped in his tracks. Trinity's words hung starkly in the air between them. Anger raced up his spine. No, *fury*. He had to control himself, because he was very close to *manhandling* her into admitting that their kiss had been very mutual.

But she was looking at him with wide eyes, as if he was some kind of wild mountain lion. He felt wild, and he was *not* wild. He was civilised.

He bit out, 'For someone being *manhandled* your response was very passionate.'

He saw her throat move as she swallowed and the pulse beating frantically at the base of her neck. Right now he knew with every cell in his body that if he was to touch her they would combust. But something held him back— some sense of self-preservation. He couldn't trust that she wasn't just baiting him on purpose.

When they did come together it would be on his terms, and he wouldn't be feeling these raw, uncontrolled urges pushing him to the limits of his control.

'Look,' she said, 'I'm here because there are things I want to talk to you about. Important things.'

Cruz kept his gaze up, away from her tantalising curves in that amazing dress. He would put nothing past her. One thing was for sure, though. She wasn't going to see how his blood throbbed just under the surface of his skin. He wouldn't lose it twice in one evening.

He leant back against his desk and folded his arms, as if that might stop him from reaching for her. 'Well, no one is stopping you from talking now, Trinity. I'm all ears.'

She swallowed visibly, and Cruz saw that she was nervous. Once again she could be taking advantage of this situation, seducing him, but she wasn't. It irritated him.

'All that stuff Rio told you about me being a gold-digger…none of it is true. He lied to you.'

Cruz went cold. She didn't have to come here and seduce him—she was smarter than that. She just had to come and mess with his head.

He stood and closed the distance between them and her eyes widened. He stopped just short of touching her. 'How dare you use the fact that my brother is silenced for ever as an excuse to further your own cause?'

'I'm not,' she said fiercely, tipping up her chin. 'You need to listen to me. You need to know the real truth of my marriage to Rio…'

A dark emotion was snapping and boiling inside Cruz at the thought of *the truth* of her marriage to Rio. Sharing his bed. The thought that his brother had got to fully taste what she'd offered up to Cruz so enticingly before he'd stopped her.

Did he want to hear about that? *No.* He wished that thoughts of her with Rio would make him turn from her in disgust, but the fire inside him only burnt brighter as he battled a primal urge to stake a claim that reduced him to an animal state.

He caught her arms in his hands and hauled her into his body, so he could remind her of where she was and with whom. *Him.*

He ground out, 'When will you get it that I will never trust a word you say? From now on if you want to try to manipulate me I'd prefer if you used the currency you use best…your body. At least that way we'll both get pleasure out of the interaction and it'll be a lot more honest.'

'Cruz…'

That was all he heard before he stopped Trinity's poisonous words with his mouth.

The kiss was an intense battle of wills. Cruz's anger was red-hot, thundering in his veins. But then she managed to break free, pulling back, her hands on his chest, breathing heavily. If Cruz had been able to call on any rationality he would have been horrified. No woman had ever driven him to such base urges. To want to stamp his brand on her.

They stared at each other, tension crackling. But then, as he looked down into those blue eyes, swirling with something he couldn't fathom, the intense anger dissipated to be replaced by something far less angry and more carnal.

He curled an arm around her waist, drawing her right in, close to his body, until he saw her cheeks flush with the awareness of his erection against her soft flesh. It was torture and pleasure all at once. With his other hand he reached around to the back of her head and undid her hair, so that it fell around her shoulders in a golden cloud.

He could feel her resistance melting. Even though she said, 'Cruz…don't…'

'Don't what?' he asked silkily. 'Do this?' And he touched her jaw, tracing its delicate line, then cupped her cheek, angling her head up.

She spread her hands on his chest and he thought she was going to push him away, but she didn't. Something inside him exulted. This time when he bent his head and kissed her there was an infinitesimal moment of hesitation and then her mouth opened to him and his blood roared. There was just *this,* and this was all that mattered right now.

CHAPTER SIX

TRINITY WAS RUNNING down the long, dark corridors of the *Castillo*. The stern faces of all those ancestors were staring down at her, each one silently judging her. The footsteps behind her were getting closer…her heart was in her throat, thumping so hard she could hardly breathe…

There was an open door on the left. She ducked in and slammed the door shut, chest heaving, sweat prickling on her skin. And then she heard it. The sound of breathing in the room…

Terror kept her frozen in place, her back to the door as the breathing got closer and closer. And then out of the gloom appeared a face. A very familiar, starkly beautiful face. Amber eyes hard. Stern. Angry. *Hot.*

Hands reached for her and Trinity knew she should try to escape. But suddenly she wasn't scared any more. She was excited… And instead of running she threw herself into Cruz's arms…

The disturbing dream still lingered, and Trinity shivered in the bright morning sunlight of another beautiful day. She didn't have to be a psychologist to figure out where it had come from. When Cruz had kissed her after that angry exchange in his study at first she'd resisted, but then something had changed…and when he'd touched her again she'd responded against her best intentions.

All the man had to do was touch her, look at her, and she wanted him. And with each touch and kiss it was getting harder to resist… She'd finally had the sense to pull back and step away last night, but it had taken every last shred of control she had.

Shakily she'd said, 'I didn't come here for this.'

'So you say,' Cruz had answered, with infuriating insouciance, looking as if he hadn't just kissed her so hard she could barely see straight. It had been particularly galling, because just moments before he'd demonstrated that once again any attempt to defend herself or tell the truth would be met with stubborn resistance.

A sense of futility made her ache inside. How could she continue like this? With Cruz blatantly refusing to listen to her? Maybe this was how he'd drive her away...by stonewalling her at every turn...

Matty shouted, 'Mummy, look! Unkel Cooz!'

Sancho jumped up, clapping his hands. 'Play, play!'

Trinity tensed all over as a long shadow fell over where she was sitting cross-legged in the grass; the boys were playing nearby. With the utmost reluctance she looked up, shading her eyes against Cruz's sheer masculine beauty as much as against the sun. Matty and Sancho—not scared of him at all any more—had grabbed a leg each, looking up at their new hero.

He lifted both boys up into his arms with an easy grace that annoyed her intensely. The fact that he was dressed down, in faded jeans and a dark polo shirt that strained across his chest muscles, was something she tried desperately not to notice. But it was hard when his biceps were bulging enticingly, reminding her of how it felt when they were wrapped around her.

She stood up, feeling at a disadvantage.

Cruz said, 'I came to tell you that I've been invited to another function this evening. We'll leave at seven.'

His autocratic tone sliced right into her, as did the scary prospect of countless more evenings like the previous one, when she'd reveal herself more and more. When he might *touch* her again.

She folded her arms and said coolly, 'I'm not going out this evening.'

The boys were squirming in Cruz's arms, growing bored already, and when he put them down they scampered off to the nearby sandpit. Trinity saw how his eyes followed them for a moment, making sure they were all right, and his concern made her feel warm inside until she clamped down on the sensation. This man evoked too much within her.

He looked back at her. 'I don't recall you being offered a choice.'

Irritation spiked at her reaction as much as to his tone. 'I'm not just some employee you can order around. It would be nice if you could pretend you're polite enough to *ask* if I'd like to come.'

'You're my wife,' Cruz offered tersely.

Something poignant gripped Trinity—if she was his wife for *real* then presumably they'd have a discussion about this sort of thing... She might agree to go because he'd tell her he'd be bored, or that he'd miss her if she didn't. The thought of that kind of domesticity made a treacherous shard of longing go through her before she could stop it.

Where had that illicit fantasy come from? One of the reasons she'd agreed to marry Rio—apart from her concern for the boys—was because after years of being an outsider in other people's homes as a foster child it had been easier to contemplate a marriage of convenience than to dare dream that she might one day have a real family of her own...

The prospect of Cruz ever seeing that deeply inside her made her go clammy all over.

Her arms tightened. 'I'm not going out this evening because I think the boys are coming down with something and I want to observe them for twenty-four hours to make sure they're okay. Sancho still isn't over his bug completely.'

Cruz glanced at the boys and back to her. 'They look fine to me.'

'They were off their food at breakfast, which isn't like them.'

'Mrs Jordan can watch them, and call us if she's worried.'

Exasperated, Trinity unfolded her arms and put her hands on her hips. 'You don't get it, do you? I'm worried about them, and even if it's only a niggle then I will put them first. *I* am the one they need if they're not feeling well.'

Scathingly, Cruz said, 'So you're not above using my nephews as an excuse?'

Hurt that he should think her capable of such a thing she said, 'Their welfare comes first, so I don't really care what you think.'

Cruz's jaw clenched, and then he just said, 'Seven p.m., Trinity. Be ready.' And then he turned and walked away.

To her shame she couldn't stop her gaze from dropping down his broad back to where his worn jeans showed off his powerful buttocks. Disgusted with herself, she whirled around and went over to the boys who, she had to admit, would look fine to most observers but not to her, who knew all their little habits and foibles.

Something wasn't quite right and she wasn't going to let Cruz bully her.

Later that evening Cruz's blood was boiling. No one had ever stood him up. Certainly not a woman. But Trinity had. Julia, looking terrified—*was he really that scary?*—had come with a note when he'd been waiting for Trinity in the hall.

Sorry, Cruz, but I'm just not certain the boys aren't coming down with something. I'm not coming. T.

The note was crumpled in his palm now, as he strode along the dark corridors to the wing Trinity and the boys occupied. Something about the oppressiveness of the *castillo* scraped along his nerves, when it never really had before. It was as if having Trinity and the boys here was throwing everything into sharp relief…

When he was near the boys' bedroom he could hear fractious cries and Trinity's tones, soothing. He stopped in the doorway to see her changing a clearly cranky Sancho into his pyjamas.

Mateo was running around in his nappy. As soon as he saw Cruz he sped over. 'Come play, Unkel Cooz!'

Cruz's chest felt tight. He bent down. 'Not now, *chiquito*. Tomorrow.'

He put his hand to Mateo's head and it felt warm. He looked up to see Trinity standing in front of him, still wearing the jeans and shirt she'd had on earlier. She really wasn't coming.

He straightened up and a determined expression came over her face. 'I meant it, Cruz, I'm worried about the boys. They've been off their food all day and they're both running slight temperatures. They also didn't nap today, so they're overtired now. It's probably nothing serious, but I'm not leaving them. I've given Mrs Jordan the evening off so she can take over in the morning.'

Cruz was slightly stunned yet again to think that she wasn't even their mother. Right now, with the boys in the room behind her, he had the distinct impression of a mother bear guarding her cubs from danger. He couldn't figure out what she could possibly be gaining from this if she *was* playing some game.

To his surprise something dark gripped his gut, and it took him a moment to acknowledge uncomfortably that it was jealousy—and something else…something more ambiguous that went deeper.

Jealousy of his nephews, who were being afforded such care and protection—the kind of protection he'd vowed to give them but which now he realised he was too woefully inexperienced to give.

The something deeper was a sharp sense of poignancy that his own mother had never cared for him like this. *Dios*, even his nanny hadn't shown this much concern.

Feeling very uncharacteristically at a momentary loss, he recognised that for the first time in his life he would have to back down.

'Call me if they get worse, or if you need anything. Maria the housekeeper has the number of my doctor.'

Trinity nodded, shocked that Cruz was conceding. She'd half expected him to insist on dressing her himself and dragging her out of the *castillo*.

He stepped away and said, 'I'll check on you when I get back.'

The thought of him coming in later, with his bow tie undone and looking far too sexy, made her say quickly, 'There's no—'

He looked at her warningly. 'I'll check on you.'

'Okay.'

For a moment something seemed to shimmer between them—something fragile. Then Cruz turned and left and she breathed out an unsteady breath. She turned around to focus on the boys and told herself that she'd just been imagining that moment of softening between them. Wishful thinking.

When Cruz returned later that night he went straight to the boys' room, where a low light leaked from under the door. He ruminated that he hadn't enjoyed one minute of the function—not that he usually did, because he considered these events work—and he realised now with some irritation that he'd missed having Trinity at his side. Seeing her reaction to everything. Having her close enough to touch.

He opened the door softly and stepped in. His eyes immediately tracked to the two small figures in their beds and he went over, finding himself pulling their covers back over their bodies from where they'd kicked them off. Something turned over in his chest at seeing them sprawled across their beds, dark lashes long on plump cheeks, hair tousled. They looked so innocent, defenceless. Once again he was overcome with a sense of protectiveness.

Then he looked up and saw another figure, curled in the armchair near the beds. Trinity. She was asleep, her head resting on her shoulder. A book lay open on her thigh and he looked at it: *The A-Z of Toddlers*.

For a moment he felt blindsided at this evidence of her dedication. That sense of poignancy he'd felt earlier gripped him again, and it was deeply disturbing and exposing.

Something else prickled under his skin now. If she was playing a game then it was a very elaborate one.

He recalled her coming into his office last night and her words: *'All that stuff that Rio told you about me being a gold-digger...none of it is true.'*

Cruz's rational mind reminded him that there was evidence of her treachery. Her name on receipts. Demands she'd made. Rio's humiliation. Maybe this was her game— she was trying to convince him she was something she wasn't and would wriggle under his skin like she had with Rio until he too felt compelled to give her everything...

'Cruz?'

She was awake now, blinking up at him. She sat up, looking deliciously dishevelled, compounding the myriad conflicting emotions she evoked.

His voice was gruff when he spoke. 'Go to bed, Trinity. I'll sit up with them.'

She looked flustered. 'No!' She lowered her voice. 'You don't have to do that. It's fine… I think they're okay now, anyway. Their temperatures were normal last time I checked.'

'Go to bed. I'll let you know if anything happens.'

She looked up at him helplessly and he offered ruefully, 'I'm going to have to get used to doing this kind of thing. I'm their uncle, and I don't intend to treat them like guests in my home.'

For the first time since Rio had died it struck Cruz forcibly that he hadn't really thought about how taking responsibility for his nephews would affect him until now. And this was what it meant, he realised with a kind of belated wonder. Being concerned. Sitting up all night to watch over them if need be.

Trinity eyes were wide, and even in this light Cruz could see the smudges of fatigue under them. From this angle he could also see down her shirt to the bountiful swells of her breasts. His body reacted.

He gritted out, 'Just go.'

She stood up jerkily, as if her muscles were protesting. 'You'll let me know if they wake?' She sounded uncertain.

Cruz nodded and took her place on the chair, stretching out his long legs and picking up the book. He gestured with it for her to go.

Feeling more than a little discombobulated at having woken to find Cruz standing over her, looking exactly like the sexy fantasy she'd envisaged earlier, Trinity eventually moved towards her own room, glancing back to see Cruz tipping his head back and closing his eyes, hands linked loosely across his flat abdomen.

Her footsteps faltered, though, as she was momentarily transfixed by the fact that he had insisted on staying. Emotion expanded in her chest at the domestic scene—dangerous emotion—as she thought how incongruous he looked here, yet how *right*.

His willingness to forge a bond with his nephews made that emotion turn awfully poignant... She had a vision of going over to him, smoothing his hair back...of him looking up at her and reaching for her, smiling sexily as he pulled her down onto his lap...

Shock at the vividness of this fantasy made her breathless. And at how much she yearned for it. When it was only his nephews he cared about. Not her.

Without opening his eyes, Cruz said softly, 'Go to bed, Trinity.'

And she fled before he might see any vestige of that momentary fantasy on her face.

When Trinity woke the following morning it was later than she'd ever slept since she'd started looking after the twins. And they were her first thought.

She shot out of bed and went into their room, to see that their beds were empty and their pyjamas were neatly folded on their pillows.

She washed quickly and got dressed in jeans and a T-shirt, pulling her hair back into a low ponytail as she went down to the dining room, where she found Mrs Jordan and the twins.

'*Mummy!*' they both screeched in unison when they saw her, and her heart swelled.

She went over and kissed them both. She looked at the older woman. 'You should have woken me.'

Mrs Jordan waved a hand. 'Cruz wouldn't hear of it. He insisted that you sleep in and I agreed. You've been looking tired lately.'

Trinity's heart skipped. She still felt raw after that moment of insanity when she'd wished for a domestic idyll that would never exist.

'He was still there this morning?'

She sat down and helped herself to coffee, noting with relief that the boys seemed to be making up for their lack of appetite the previous day, with their mouths full of mushy cereal.

Mrs Jordan nodded and a look of unmistakable awe came over her face. 'He was changing them when I went in this morning, and apart from putting Sancho's nappy on back to front he didn't do a bad job at all...'

Trinity choked on her coffee, spraying some out of her mouth inelegantly, and the boys went into paroxysms of giggles.

'Funny, Mummy...do it again!'

She distracted them for a minute, playing aeroplanes with their spoons as she fed them, and avoided Mrs Jordan's far too shrewd gaze. She almost felt angry with Cruz for blurring the boundaries like this and inducing disturbing fantasies. And then she felt awful—she should be happy that he was intent on connecting with his nephews in a real and meaningful way.

After the boys had finished their breakfast, and Mrs Jordan had taken them outside to play, Trinity sipped her coffee, recalling again how dangerously intimate it had felt to share that space with Cruz last night. And how seductive.

Just then a sound made her look up and her heart stopped at the sight of the object of her thoughts standing in the doorway, dressed in a three-piece suit, looking so gorgeous it hurt.

He came in and Trinity still felt a little raw, unprepared to see him. It made her voice stiff. 'Thank you for watching the boys last night.'

Cruz poured himself a cup of coffee and took a seat opposite her. He shook his head minutely. 'Like I said, I'm going to be in their lives in a meaningful way.'

Feeling absurdly shy, she said, 'Mrs Jordan told me you changed them.'

Cruz's eyes gleamed with wry humour and it took Trinity's breath away. 'I won't ever again underestimate the ability of a two-and-a-half-year-old to create a toxic smell to rival the effluent of a chemical plant. Or the skill it takes to change one of those things.'

Cruz took a sip of his coffee and put down the cup. 'I've arranged for some potential nannies to come later today, for you and Mrs Jordan to interview.'

'Do you really think that's necessary?'

'Yes.' The wry gleam was gone from his eyes now. 'I've been invited to an event at the newly refurbished opera house in Madrid this Friday night, and I have meetings to attend in the afternoon. Barring any unforeseen events, I am asking you to attend the function with me in Madrid. We'll be gone until Saturday. It'll be a good opportunity for the new nanny to start and get used to the boys under Mrs Jordan's supervision.'

Two things were bombarding Trinity at once. Namely he fact that he was *asking* her, even if it was slightly mocking, and that she'd be away for a whole night with Cruz.

'But I've never left the boys for that long before.'

His tone was dry. 'I think they'll survive less than twenty-four hours without you, and with two nannies in attendance. I spoke with Mrs Jordan about it earlier—she's fine.'

Of course she was, thought Trinity churlishly. Mrs Jordan was his number one fan.

'Tell me, Trinity,' Cruz asked silkily, 'is the reason you're reluctant because you fear maintaining the lie that you don't want me? Are you afraid that you won't be able to control your urges if we're alone? I don't think it's out of concern for the boys at all—I think it's much more personal.'

She felt shamed. He was right. She *was* scared—scared of her reactions around this man. Scared of what might happen if he touched her again. Scared to have him see underneath to where her real vulnerabilities lay. Scared of what he would do if he were faced with the ultimate truth of just how deeply Rio had loathed him. Her guts twisted at the thought in a way that told her she was far more invested in this man than she liked to admit.

But as Cruz looked at her, waiting for her response, she knew she couldn't keep running. She could resist him. She had to.

Coolly she ignored what he'd said and replied, 'Friday should be fine. What time do we leave?'

A few days later Trinity risked looking at Cruz from where she sat in the back of the chauffeur-driven limousine that had picked them up at Madrid airport, but he was engrossed in his palm tablet on the other side of the car, seemingly oblivious to her. She'd just had a conversation on her mobile phone with Mrs Jordan, to check on her and the boys and the new nanny, who were all fine.

As if reading her mind, Cruz put down his tablet and looked at her, that golden amber gaze sweeping down her body and taking in the very elegant and classic sheath dress and matching jacket she'd put on that day in a bid to look presentable.

His gaze narrowed on her assessingly, and she had to fight not to squirm self-consciously. 'What is it?'

She was half raising a hand to check her hair when Cruz answered simply, 'You're a good mother to them.'

If there'd been a grudging tone in his voice Trinity would have hated him, but there hadn't. He'd sounded… reluctantly impressed. She desperately tried to ignore the rush of warmth inside her that signified how much she wanted his approval.

'I love them, Cruz, even though they're not mine.' Impulsively she asked, 'Why is that so hard for you to believe? Is it because of your upbringing?'

He smiled, but it wasn't a nice smile. 'You could say that. Rio wasn't the only one neglected in the *castillo*. Once she'd had me, my mother considered her maternal duty taken care of. She didn't love me, and she didn't love my father either. Their marriage was a purely strategic one, bringing two powerful families together as was the tradition in my family for centuries.'

Cruz's eyeline shifted over Trinity's shoulder just as the car came to a smooth halt on a wide tree-lined street.

'We're here,' he said, leaving Trinity's brain buzzing with what he'd just shared.

She looked out of the window on her side, saw a scrum of men with cameras waiting for them and instantly felt nervous. She'd always hated the way Rio had wanted to court as much media attention as possible.

Cruz said tersely, 'Wait in the car. I'll come round to get you.'

Trinity would have been quite happy if the car had turned around and taken them straight back to the airport.

When Cruz appeared outside the car the scrum had become a sea of flashing lights and shouting. Her door was opened and his hand reached in for her. She took it like a lifeline. He hustled her into the foyer of the gleaming building and within seconds they were in the elevator and ascending with a soft *whoosh*.

It was the hushed silence after the cacophony of sound that registered first, and then Trinity became burningly aware that she was pressed from thigh to breast into Cruz's body. His free arm was around her shoulder and her other hand was still in his, held over his taut belly.

She couldn't be any closer to him if she climbed into his very skin.

She scrambled apart from him, dislodging his arm and taking her hand from his. She couldn't look at him. For a split second before she'd come to her senses she'd loved the sensation of his strength surrounding her, and for someone who'd long ago learnt to depend on herself it was scary how easy it had felt just to…give in.

Thankfully the lift doors opened at that moment, and the sight that greeted Trinity took her breath away. She stepped out into a huge open space dominated on all sides by massive glass windows which showcased the breath-taking view of one of Europe's most beautiful and stately cities.

She walked over to one of the windows and could see a huge cathedral soaring into the blue sky.

'That's the Almudena Cathedral, infamous for taking five hundred years to complete.'

Cruz's voice was far too close, but Trinity fought the urge to move away and instead turned around to take in the penthouse apartment. It was unmistakably a bachelor pad, every inch of every surface gleaming and pristine. But it was also cultured—low tables held massive coffee table books on photography and art. Bookshelves lined one entire interior wall. Huge modern art canvases sat in the centre of the few walls not showcasing the view.

'Let me show you around.'

Trinity followed Cruz as he guided her through a stunning modern kitchen that led into a formal dining room, and then to where a series of rooms off a long corridor revealed themselves to be sumptuous en-suite bedrooms and an office.

When they were back in the main open-plan living and dining area, she felt a little dazed. 'Your apartment is stunning.'

'But not exactly toddler-proof.'

She looked at Cruz, surprised that he'd articulated the

very thing she'd just been thinking in her head: it was beautiful apartment but a potential death trap for small energetic boys.

He glanced at her and she quickly closed her open mouth, looking around again. 'No. Not exactly.'

'I will ensure this place is made child-friendly for when the boys come to visit. I intend on my nephews becoming familiar with their capital city. This is where the seat of the main De Carrillo bank has been since the Middle Ages. This is where their legacy resides, as much as it does in Seville.'

Their capital city. It had been said with such effortless arrogance. But the truth was that Cruz was right—he was undoubtedly a titan of this city. Probably owned a huge swathe of it. And the twins would one day inherit all this.

It was mind-boggling to contemplate, and for the first time Trinity felt a sense of fear for the boys and this huge responsibility they'd have one day.

She rounded on Cruz. 'What happens if Matty and Sancho don't want any of this?'

His gaze narrowed on her and something flashed across his face before she could decipher it. Something almost pained.

'Believe me, I will do what's best for my nephews. They will not be forced to take on anything they can't handle or don't want. I won't let that happen to them.'

Trinity's anger deflated. She'd heard the emotion in Cruz's voice. Almost as if he was referring to someone who *had* taken on something they couldn't handle. Was he thinking of Rio and the irresponsible and lavish way he'd lived?

Cruz looked at his watch. 'I have to go to meetings now, but I'll be back to get ready for the function this evening. We'll leave at six p.m.'

Before he left he took something out of his inner pocket. He handed her a black credit card.

She took it warily. 'What is this? A test?'

His face was unreadable, but she wasn't fooled. She knew he'd be assessing her every reaction.

'You'll need access to funds. Do what you want for the afternoon—a driver will be at your disposal downstairs.'

He left then, and for a long minute Trinity found herself wondering if he *had* been talking about Rio not being able to handle things...

Then, disgusted with herself for obsessing like this, she threw the credit card down on a nearby table and paced over to a window. When she looked down to the street far below she could see Cruz disappearing into the back of another sleek Jeep.

It pulled into the flow of traffic and she shivered slightly, as if he could somehow still see her. He was so all-encompassing that it was hard to believe he wasn't omnipresent.

She sighed and leaned forward, placing her hot forehead against the cool glass. It felt as if every time they took a step forward they then took three backwards. Clearly the credit card was some kind of a test, and he expected her to revert to type when given half a chance.

Cruz was standing with his back to the recently emptied boardroom on the top floor of the De Carrillo bank, loosening his tie and opening a top button on his shirt. Madrid was laid out before him, with the lowering sun leaving long shadows over the streets below where people were leaving their offices.

He hated himself for it, but as soon as the last person had left the room he'd pulled out his phone to make a call, too impatient to wait.

'*Where* did she go?' he asked incredulously, his hand dropping from his shirt.

His driver answered. 'She went to the Plaza Mayor, where she had a coffee, and then she spent the afternoon in the Museo Del Prado. She's just returned to the apartment.'

'And she walked,' Cruz repeated flatly, not liking the way the thought of her sightseeing around Madrid on her own made him feel a twinge of conscience. As if he'd neglected her. 'No shopping?'

'No, sir, apart from two cuddly toys in the museum shop.'

Cruz terminated the call. So Trinity hadn't spent the day shopping in Calle de Serrano, home to the most lavish boutiques. He had to admit that the credit card *had* been a test, and a pretty crude one at that. But once again either she was playing a longer game than he'd given her credit for…or he had to acknowledge that she had changed. Fundamentally. And in Cruz's experience of human nature that just wasn't possible.

Cruz didn't deal in unknowns. It was one of the driving motives behind his marrying Trinity—to make sure she was kept very much within his sphere of *knowns*.

Suddenly he wasn't so sure of anything any more.

But *how* could he trust her over his own brother?

He could still see the humiliation on Rio's face when he'd had to explain to Cruz that that his own wife had tipped him over the edge. Cruz knew that Rio's lavish lifestyle and his first wife had undoubtedly started the process of his ultimate destruction, but Trinity had finished it off. And, worse, used his nephews to gain privileged access.

But then he thought of her, standing between him and his nephews the other night, so adamant that they came first. And he thought of how he'd found her, curled up asleep in the chair… He shook his head angrily and turned away from the window. *Merda*, she was messing with his head.

Cruz blocked out the niggles of his conscience. He would be the biggest fool on earth if he was to believe in this newly minted Trinity De Carrillo without further evidence. She was playing a game—she had to be. It was that simple. And he had no choice but to go along with it for now…

Because eventually she would reveal her true self, and when she did Cruz would be waiting.

CHAPTER SEVEN

A COUPLE OF hours later Cruz's mind was no less tangled. The woman beside him was drawing every single eye in the extravagantly designed and decorated open-air court-yard of the new opera house. When he'd arrived back at the apartment she'd been in her room getting ready, so he'd been showered and changed before he'd seen her, waiting for him in the living area of the apartment.

The shock of that first glimpse of her still ran through his system, constricting his breath and pumping blood to tender places. She wore a strapless black dress that was moulded to every curve. Over one shoulder was a sliver of chiffon tied in a bow.

She wore no jewellery apart from the engagement ring and her wedding band. Her nails were unpainted. Minimal make-up. And yet people couldn't stop looking at her. *He* couldn't stop looking at her.

Very uncharacteristically, Cruz wanted to snarl at them all to look at their own partners. But he couldn't, because he could see what they saw—a glowing diamond amidst the dross. She appealed to this jaded crowd because she had an unfashionable air of wonder about her as she looked around, which only reinforced the shadow of doubt in his mind...

Just then her arm tightened in his and he looked down to see a flush on her cheeks. She was biting her lip. Irri-tated at the effect she had on him, he said more curtly than he'd intended, 'What is it?'

She sounded hesitant. 'I shouldn't have put my hair up like this. I look ridiculous.'

Cruz looked at her hair, which was in a sleek high ponytail. He didn't consider himself an expert on women's hair-styles, but he could see that the other women had more complicated things going on. Another reason why Trinity stood out so effortlessly. She looked unfussy—simple and yet sexy as sin all at once.

'Someone left a fashion magazine on the table in the café earlier and I saw pictures of models with their hair up like this. I thought it was a thing...'

The shadow of doubt loomed larger. He thought of how she'd shrunk back from the paparazzi earlier. She certainly hadn't been flaunting herself, looking for attention. Anything but. She'd clung to him as if terrified.

He took her arm above the elbow and she looked up at him. He could see the uncertainty and embarrassment in her eyes. It was getting harder and harder to see her as the cold-hearted mercenary gold-digger who had willingly fleeced his brother.

His voice was gruff. 'Your hair is absolutely fine. They're looking because you're the most beautiful woman here.'

Trinity was disorientated by Cruz's compliment. He'd barely said two words to her since he'd got back to the apartment and they'd left to go out again, and he'd just looked at her suspiciously when he'd asked her what she'd done for the afternoon.

Cruz was staring at her now, in a way that made her heart thump unevenly. But then a low, melodic gong sounded, breaking the weird moment.

He looked away from her and up. 'It's time for the banquet.'

Breathing a sigh of relief at being released from that intensity, and not really sure what it meant, she followed Cruz into a huge ballroom that had the longest dining table she'd ever seen in her life. Opulent flowers overflowed from vases and twined all along the table in artful disarray. A thousand candles flickered, and low lights glinted off the solid gold cutlery. She sighed in pure wonder at the scene—it was like a movie set.

And then she spotted Lexie Anderson, the famous actress, and her gorgeous husband, Cesar Da Silva, and felt as if she'd really been transported into a movie. The stunning petite blonde and her tall husband were completely engrossed in each other, and it made something poignant ache inside her.

'Trinity?'

She blushed, hating it that Cruz might have caught her staring at the other couple, and sat down in the chair he was holding out for her.

When she was seated, Trinity saw Cruz walking away and she whispered after him. 'Wait, where are you going?'

He stopped. 'I've been seated opposite you—beside the president of the Spanish Central Bank.'

'Oh, okay.' Trinity feigned nonchalance, even though she was taking in the vast size of the table and realising he might as well be sitting in another room.

Of course he couldn't resist the opportunity to mock her. He came back and bent down, saying close to her ear, 'Don't tell me you'll miss me, *querida*?'

'Don't be ridiculous,' she snapped, angry that she'd shown how gauche she was. She turned away, but hated it that her stomach lurched at the thought of being left alone to fend for herself in an environment where she'd never felt comfortable.

She couldn't take her eyes off him as he walked around to the other side of the table, being stopped and adored by several people on his way. One of them was Cesar Da Silva, who got up to shake Cruz's hand, and the two tall and ridiculously handsome men drew lots of lingering looks. He even bent down to kiss Lexie Anderson on both cheeks, and it caused a funny twisting sensation in Trinity's stomach, seeing him bestow affection so easily on anyone but her.

No, what he'd bestow on *her* was much darker and full of anger and mistrust.

Determined not to be intimidated, Trinity tried talking to the person on her left, but he couldn't speak English and she had no Spanish so that went nowhere. She had more luck with an attractive older gentleman on her right, who turned out to be a diplomat and did speak English, and who put her at ease as only a diplomat could.

Finally she felt herself relax for the first time in weeks, chuckling at her companion's funny stories of various diplomatic disasters. With Cruz on the other side of the very large and lavishly decorated table she relished a reprieve from the constant tension she felt around him, even if she fancied she could feel his golden gaze boring into her through the elaborate foliage. She resisted the urge to look in his direction. She'd already given far too much away.

After the coffee cups had been cleared away her dinner partner's attention was taken by the person on his other side. Trinity risked a look across the table and saw that Cruz's seat was empty. And then she spotted him—because it would be impossible to miss him. He was walking towards her with that lean animal grace, eyes narrowed on her, this time oblivious to people's attempts to get his attention.

The tension was back instantly. Making her feel tingly and alive as much as wary. When he reached her he didn't even have to touch her for a shiver to run through her body.

'Cold?' The tone of his voice was innocuous, but the expression on his face was hard.

Trinity shook her head, feeling a sense of vertigo as she looked up, even though she was sitting down. 'No, not cold.'

'Enjoying yourself?'

Now his words had definite bite in them, and she saw his eyeline shift over her head. 'Nice to see you, Lopez,' he drawled. 'Thank you for keeping my wife amused.'

The man's smoothly cultured voice floated over Trinity's shoulder.

'The pleasure was all mine, De Carrillo. Trinity is a charming, beautiful woman. A breath of fresh air.'

Trinity watched, fascinated, as Cruz's face darkened and a muscle ticked in his jaw. 'Then I'm sorry that I must deprive you of her presence. I believe the dancing has started.'

She barely had time to get a word out to say goodbye to the other man before Cruz was all but hauling her out of her chair and onto the dance floor, where a band was playing slow, sexy jazz songs. His arm was like steel around her back and her other hand was clasped in his, high against his chest.

He moved around the floor with such effortless expertise that Trinity didn't have time to worry about her two left feet. To her horror, though, she felt absurdly vulnerable, reminded of how lonely she'd felt during the day even while she'd appreciated the beautiful majesty of Madrid.

She'd missed Matty and Sancho and she'd felt a very rare surge of self-pity, wondering if this would be her life now—forever on the periphery of Cruz's antipathy.

It was a long time since she'd indulged in such a weak emotion and it made her voice sharp. 'What do you think you're doing?'

Cruz's mouth was a thin line. 'I'm not sure. Maybe you want to tell me? Sebastian Lopez is a millionaire and renowned for his penchant for beautiful young women— maybe you knew that and saw an opportunity to seek a more benevolent benefactor?'

Trinity fought to control her breathing and her temper, and hated it that she was so aware of every inch of her body, which seemed to be welded against his.

'Don't be ridiculous,' she hissed. 'He's old enough to be my father and there was nothing remotely flirtatious about our conversation.' She tilted her head back as much as she could so she could look Cruz dead in the eye. 'But do you know what? It was nice to talk to someone who doesn't think I'm one step above a common thief.'

Terrified that Cruz would see emotion she shouldn't be feeling, she managed to pull herself out of his embrace and stalked off the dance floor, apologising as she bumped into another couple. She walked blindly, half expecting a heavy hand on her shoulder at any moment, but of course Cruz wouldn't appreciate that public display of discord.

She made it out to the marbled foyer area, where a few people milled around, and walked out to the entrance. She sucked in a breath to try and steady her heart. Night was enfolding Madrid in a glorious velvet glow but it couldn't soothe her ragged nerves.

It wasn't long before she felt Cruz's presence. The little hairs all over her body seemed to stand up and quiver in his direction. She refused to feel foolish for storming off. He'd insulted her.

He came to stand beside her, but said nothing as his car arrived at the front of the building with a soft sleek purr. Trinity cursed the fact that she hadn't been quicker to call a cab. Cruz held open the back door and she avoided his eye as she got in, not wanting to see the undoubtedly volcanic expression on his face.

As the driver pulled into the light evening traffic Trinity said frigidly, 'You don't have to leave. You should stay. Your brother soon learned that it made more sense to let me leave early.'

* * *

Cruz was in the act of yanking at his bow tie and opening his top button, wanting to feel less constricted. But now his hand stilled and the red haze of anger that had descended over his vision during the course of the evening as he'd watched Trinity talking and laughing with that man finally started to dissipate.

'What did you just say?' he asked.

Trinity was staring straight ahead, her profile perfect. But she was tense—her full lips pursed, jaw rigid.

It slammed into him then—the truth he'd been trying to deny. He was insanely jealous. He'd been jealous since the day she'd walked out of his house and got into Rio's car to go and work for him.

At that moment she looked at him, and he could feel himself tipping over the edge of an abyss. Those huge blue eyes were full of such...*injury*.

Her voice was tight. 'I said that your brother soon learned that I don't fit into those events well. I'm not from that world, and I don't know what to do or say.'

She clamped her mouth shut then, as if she'd said enough already.

Cruz reeled. His impression had been that Rio had taken her everywhere and that she'd loved it and milked it, but something in the tightness of her voice told him she wasn't lying, and that revelation only added to the doubts clamouring for attention in his head.

He tried and failed to block out the fact that when she'd pulled free of his arms on the dance floor and stalked away he'd thought he'd seen the glitter of tears in her eyes.

She turned her head away again and he saw the column of her throat working. His gaze took in an expanse of pale skin, slim shoulders, delicate clavicle, the enticing curve of her breasts under the material of the dress, and heat engulfed him along with something much more nebulous:

an urge to comfort, which was as bewildering as it was impossible to resist.

He reached across and touched Trinity's chin, turning her face towards him again. 'I'm sorry,' he said. 'You didn't deserve that. The truth is that I didn't like seeing you with that man.'

The shock on her face might have insulted Cruz if he hadn't been so distracted by those huge eyes.

Her mouth opened and the tense line of her jaw relaxed slightly. 'I...okay. Apology accepted.'

That simple. Another woman would have made the most of Cruz's uncharacteristic apology.

His thumb moved back and forth across Trinity's jaw, the softness of her delicate skin an enticement to touch and keep touching.

'What are you doing?'

He dragged his gaze up over high cheekbones, perfect bone structure. 'I can't *not* touch you.' The admission seemed to fall out of him before he could stop it.

Trinity put a hand up over his. The car came to a smooth stop. Cruz knew that he had to keep touching her or die. And he assured himself that it had nothing to do with the emotion that had clouded his judgement and his vision as he'd watched her at ease with another man, and everything to do with pure, unadulterated lust.

Trinity was locked into Cruz's eyes and the intensity of his gaze. One minute she'd been hurt and angry, and then he'd apologised...once again demonstrating a level of humility that she just wouldn't have expected from him. And now... Now she was burning up under his explicit look that told her that whatever they'd just been talking about was forgotten, that things had taken a far more carnal turn.

She felt a breeze touch her back. She blinked and looked

around to see the driver standing at the door, waiting for her to get out. They'd arrived back at the apartment building and she hadn't even noticed.

She scrambled out inelegantly, feeling seriously jittery. It was as if some kind of silent communication had passed between them, and she wasn't sure what she'd agreed to.

The journey up to the apartment passed in a blur. The lift doors opened and they stepped into the hushed interior of Cruz's apartment. He threw off his jacket and Trinity's mouth dried as she watched the play of muscles under the thin silk of his shirt.

He glanced back at her over his shoulder. 'I know you don't really drink, but would you like something?'

Trinity was about to refuse, but something in the air made her feel uncharacteristically reckless. She moved forward. 'Okay.'

'What would you like?'

She stopped, her mind a blank. Embarrassment engulfed her—she was no sophisticate.

Cruz looked at her. 'I've got all the spirits. What do you like?'

Trinity shrugged one shoulder. 'I'm not sure...'

He looked at her for a long moment and then turned back to the drinks table, doing something she couldn't see. Then he turned and came towards her with two glasses. One was large and bulbous, filled with what looked like brandy or whisky. The other glass was smaller, with an orange liquid over a couple of ice cubes.

He handed her the second glass. 'Try this—see what you think.'

After a moment's hesitation she reached for the glass and bent her head, taking a sniff. Cruz was waiting for her reaction, so she took a sip of the cool liquid and it slid down her throat, leaving a sweet aftertaste. She wrinkled her nose, because she'd been expecting something tart or strong.

She looked at him. 'It's sweet. I like it—what is it?'

A small smile played around the corner of Cruz's mouth. 'It's Pacharán—a Spanish liqueur from Navarre. Very distinctive. It tastes sweet, but it packs quite the alcoholic punch. Hence the small amount.'

Before he could suck her under and scramble her brain cells with just a look Trinity went and sat down at the end of one couch, bemused by this very fragile cessation in hostilities. Cruz sat too, choosing the end of a couch at right angles to hers. He effortlessly filled the space with his muscled bulk, long legs stretched out, almost touching hers.

Trinity felt unaccountably nervous, and a little bewildered. She was so used to Cruz coming at her with his judgement and mistrust that she wasn't sure how to navigate these waters. He sat forward, hands loose around his glass, drawing her attention to long fingers.

'Tell me something about yourself—like your name. How did you get it?'

She tensed all over. Every instinct within her was screaming to resist this far more dangerous Cruz. 'What are you doing? You're not interested in who I am...you don't have to ask me these things.'

'You were the one,' he pointed out reasonably, 'who said we need to learn to get along.'

And look how that had ended up—with him kissing her and demonstrating just how weak she was. What could she say, though? He was right.

Hating it that she was exposing her agitation, but needing space from his focus on her, Trinity stood up and walked over to one of the windows, holding her glass to her chest like some kind of ineffectual armour.

Looking out at the view, she said as lightly as she could,

'I was called Trinity after the church where I was found abandoned on the steps. The Holy Trinity Church in Islington.'

She heard movement and sensed Cruz coming to stand near her. She could feel his eyes on her.

'Go on,' he said.

Night had descended over Madrid, and the skyline was lit up spectacularly against the inky blackness.

'They think I was just a few hours old, but they can't be sure, and it wasn't long after midnight, so they nominated that date as my birthday. I was wrapped in a blanket. The priest found me.'

'What happened then?'

Trinity swallowed. 'The authorities waited as long as they could for my biological parent, or parents, to come and claim me. By the time I was a toddler I was in foster care, and there was still no sign of anyone claiming me, so they put me forward for adoption.'

'But your file said you grew up in foster homes.'

Trinity was still astounded that he'd looked into her past. She glanced at him, but looked away again quickly. 'I did grow up in foster homes. But I was adopted for about a year, until the couple's marriage broke up and they decided they didn't want to keep me if they weren't staying together.'

She shouldn't be feeling emotion—not after all these years. But it was still there...the raw, jagged edges of hurt at the knowledge that she'd been abandoned by her own mother and then hadn't even managed to persuade her adoptive parents to keep her.

'Apparently,' she said, as dispassionately as she could, 'I was traumatised, so they decided it might be best not to put me through that experience again. That's how I ended up in the foster home system.'

'Were you moved around much?'

'Not at the start. But when I came into my teens, yes. I was in about six different foster homes before I turned eighteen.'

'Your affinity with Mateo and Sancho... You have no qualification in childcare, and yet you obviously know what to do with small children.'

Trinity felt as if Cruz was peeling back layers of skin. It was almost physically painful to talk about this. 'For some reason the small children in the foster homes used to latch on to me... I felt protective, and I liked mothering them, watching over them...'

But then the inevitable always happened—the babies and toddlers would be taken away to another home, or put up for adoption, and Trinity would be bereft. And yet each time it had happened she'd been helpless to resist the instinct to nurture. Of course, she surmised grimly now, a psychologist would undoubtedly tell her she'd been desperately trying to fulfil the need in herself to be loved and cared for.

And the twins were evidence that she hadn't learned to fill that gap on her own yet.

'Did you ever go looking for your parents?'

Trinity fought to control her emotions. 'Where would I start? It wasn't as if they'd logged their names anywhere. I could have investigated pregnant women on record in the local area, who had never returned to give birth, but to be honest I decided a long time ago that perhaps it was best to just leave it alone.'

The truth was that she didn't think she could survive the inevitable rejection of her parents if she ever found either one of them.

She felt her glass being lifted out of her hands, and looked to see Cruz putting it down on a side table beside his. He turned back and took her hand in his, turning it over, looking at it as if it held some answer he was looking for. The air between them was charged.

'What are you doing?' Trinity asked shakily.

Their eyes met and she desperately wanted to move back, out of Cruz's magnetic orbit, but she couldn't.

'You're an enigma,' he said, meeting her eyes. 'I can't figure you out and it bothers me.'

Feeling even shakier now, she said, 'There's nothing to figure out. What you see is what you get.'

Cruz gripped her hand tighter and pulled her closer, saying gruffly, 'I'm beginning to wonder if that isn't the case.'

It took a second for his words to sink in, and when they did Trinity's belly went into freefall. Was he...could he really listen to her now? And believe her?

But Cruz didn't seem to be interested in talking. His hand was trailing up her arm now, all the way to where the chiffon was tied at her shoulder.

With slow, sure movements, and not taking his eyes off hers, Cruz undid the bow, letting the material fall down. He caressed her shoulder, moving his hand around to the back of her neck and then up, finding the band in her hair and tugging it free so that her hair fell down around her shoulders.

Trinity was feeling incredibly vulnerable after revealing far more than she'd intended, but Cruz was looking at her and touching her as if he was burning up inside, just as she was, making her forget everything. Almost.

She couldn't let him expose her even more...

It was the hardest thing in the world, but she caught his hand, pulling it away. 'We shouldn't do this...'

He turned her hand in his, so he was holding it again, pulling her even closer so she could feel every inch of her body against his much harder one.

'Oh, yes, we should, *querida*. It's inevitable. The truth is that it's been inevitable since we first kissed.'

Cruz wrapped both hands around her upper arms. Trinity's world was reduced down to the beats of her heart and the heat prickling all over her skin. Surely his mention of that cataclysmic night should be breaking them out of this spell? But it wasn't...

A dangerous lassitude seeped into her blood, draining her will to resist. Cruz bent his head close to hers, his breath feathering over her mouth.

'Tell me you want this, Trinity. At least this is true between us—you can't deny it.'

She was in a very dangerous place—feeling exposed after her confession and the tantalising suggestion that Cruz might be prepared to admit that he was wrong about her... All her defences were snapping and falling to pieces.

As if sensing her inner vacillation, Cruz touched her bare shoulder with his mouth and moved up to where her neck met her shoulder. He whispered against her skin. 'Tell me...'

Unable to stop herself, she heard the words falling out of her mouth. 'I want you...'

He pulled back, a fierce expression on his face. Triumph. It made her dizzy. She didn't even have time to think of the repercussions before Cruz's mouth was on hers and suddenly everything was slotting into place. She didn't have to think...she only had to feel. It was heady, and too seductive to resist.

The intimacy of his tongue stroking roughly along hers made blood pool between her legs, hot and urgent. Pulsing in time with her heart.

Time slowed down as Cruz stole her very soul right out from inside her. A fire was taking root and incinerating everything in its path.

His hands landed on her waist, hauling her right into him, where she could feel the solid thrust of his arousal just above the juncture of her legs. Any warning bells were lost in the rush of blood as her own hands went to Cruz's wide chest and then higher, until she was arching into him and winding her arms around his neck.

When his mouth left hers she gasped for air, light-headed, shivering as he transferred his attention to her neck, tugging at her skin gently with his teeth before soothing with his tongue.

Air touched her back as the zip of her dress was lowered. The bodice loosened around her breasts and she finally managed to open her eyes. Cruz's short hair was dishevelled, his eyes burning, as he pulled the top of her dress down, exposing her bare breasts to his gaze. The cut of the dress hadn't allowed for a bra.

'So beautiful,' he said thickly, bringing a hand up to cup the weight of one breast in his palm.

Trinity felt drunk…dazed. She looked down and saw her own pale flesh surrounded by his much darker hand. Her nipple jutted out, hard and stark, as if begging for his touch. When he brushed it with his thumb she let out a low moan and her head fell back.

Her arms were weakening around his neck and her legs were shaking. There was so much sensation on top of sensation. It was almost painful. And then suddenly the ground beneath her feet disappeared altogether and she gasped when she realised that Cruz had picked her up and was now laying her down on the nearby couch.

Her dress was gaping open and she felt disorientated yet hyper-alert. Cruz came down on his knees beside her supine body and pulled her dress all the way down to her waist, baring her completely.

She couldn't suck in enough air, and when he lowered that dark golden head and surrounded the taut peak of her breast with sucking heat her back arched and she gasped out loud, funnelling her hands through his hair…

She ignored the part of her whispering to stop this

now…she couldn't stop. She wasn't strong enough. She'd never felt so wanted and connected as she did right in that moment, and for Trinity that was where her darkest weakness lay. Still…

Cruz was drowning…in the sweetest, softest skin he'd ever felt or tasted in his life. The blood thundering through his veins and arteries made what he'd felt for any other woman a total mockery. It was as if he'd been existing in limbo and now he was alive again.

One hand was filled with the flesh of Trinity's breast, the hard nipple stabbing his palm, and he tugged the sharp point of her other breast into his mouth, his tongue laving the hard flesh, making it even harder. She tasted of sweet musky female and roses, and she felt like silk.

He wasn't even aware of her fingers clawing into his head so painfully. He was only aware of this pure decadent heaven, and the way she was arching her body at him so needily.

He finally let go of the fleshy mound of her breast and found her dress, pulling it up over her legs. He needed to feel her now, feel how ready for him she was. He wanted to taste her… His erection hardened even more at that thought.

He found her heat, palpable through the thin silk of her panties, and lifted his head, feeling animalistic at way she throbbed so hotly into his palm.

Trinity stopped moving. Her eyes opened and Cruz wanted to groan when he saw how sensually slumberous she looked, golden hair spread around her, breasts moving up and down, nipples moist from his touch. Mouth swollen from his kisses.

Giving in to his base needs, he moved down, pulling her dress up higher. Her panties were white and lacy and he pulled them off, heedless of the ripping sound, dropping them to the floor.

'Cruz…what are you doing…?'

She sounded breathless, rough. Needy. And there was some other quality to her voice that Cruz didn't want to investigate. Something like uncertainty.

'I need to taste you, *querida.*'

Her eyes widened. 'Taste me…? You mean like…?'

Cruz touched her with his finger, sliding it between soft silken folds. She gasped and tried to put her hand down, but he caught it and stopped her. He explored the hot damp seam of her body, pressing into the fevered channel of her body and exerting pressure against her clitoris.

He took his finger away, even though he wanted to thrust it all the way inside, and brought it to his mouth, taking the wet tip into his mouth. His eyes closed…his erection jumped. For the first time since he was a teenager Cruz was afraid he'd spill before he even got inside her.

The taste of her musky heat on his tongue…

He opened his eyes and she was looking at him, shocked. Two spots of red in her cheeks. A thought drifted across the heat haze in his brain… Why was she looking so shocked? Surely she'd…? But he batted the thought away, not wanting images of what she'd done with previous lovers—*his brother*—to intrude.

There would only be one lover now. Him. She was here and she was *his.*

He said in a rough voice, 'I need to taste you…like that.'

She said nothing. He saw her bite her lip. She looked feverish, and then she gave an almost imperceptible nod. Cruz pushed her legs apart, exposing the blonde curls covering her slick pink folds…slick for him.

There was none of his usual finesse when he touched her. He licked her, sucked and tasted, until he was dizzy and drunk. He thrust two fingers inside her heat, moving them in and out. He felt her hips jerk, her back arch. Heard soft moans and gasps, felt hands in his hair.

Her thighs drew up beside his head and her whole body tensed like a taut bow, just seconds before powerful muscles clamped down tight on his fingers and her body shuddered against his mouth.

She was *his*.

CHAPTER EIGHT

TRINITY WAS BARELY CONSCIOUS, floating on an ocean of such satisfaction that she wondered if she might be dead. Surely this wasn't even possible? This much pleasure? For her body to feel so weighted down and yet light as a feather? She could feel the minor contractions of her deepest muscles, still pulsing like little quivering heartbeats...

She finally came back to some level of consciousness when she felt a soft surface under her back and opened her eyes. She was on a bed, and Cruz was standing before her, pulling off his shirt and putting his hands on his trousers, undoing them, taking them down.

She saw the way his erection tented his underwear, and watched with avid fascination as he pulled that off too, exposing the thick stiff column of flesh, moisture beading at the tip.

'If you keep looking at me like that—' He broke off with a curse and bent down, hands on the sides of her dress, tugging it free of her body.

Trinity was naked now, and yet she felt no sense of self-consciousness. She was so wrapped in lingering pleasure and so caught up in this bubble of sensuality that she ignored the persistent but faint knocking of something trying to get through to her...

Cruz reached beside the bed for a condom and rolled it onto his erection, the latex stretched taut. Incredibly, as he came down onto the bed and moved over her, she felt her flesh quiver back to life. Her pulse picked up again and she no longer felt like floating...she wanted to fly again.

Cruz's hips pushed her legs apart and he took himself in his own hand, touching the head of his sex against hers, teasing her by pushing it in slightly before drawing it out again, her juices making them both slick. She felt as if she should be embarrassed, but she wasn't.

Between her legs she could feel her flesh aching for Cruz, aching for more than his mouth and tongue and fingers…aching for more.

She arched up. 'Please, Cruz…'

Was that ragged voice hers? She didn't have time to wonder, because with one feral growl and a sinuous move of his lean hips he thrust deep inside her. His whole body went taut over hers, and the expression on his face was one of pure masculine appreciation.

But Trinity wasn't seeing that. It had taken only a second for the intense need and pleasure to transform into blinding hot pain. She couldn't breathe, couldn't make sense of what she was feeling, when seconds ago she'd craved for him to do exactly this…

'*Dios,* Trinity…' he breathed. 'You're so tight…'

Cruz started to pull back, and Trinity's muscles protested. She put her hands on his hips and said, as panic mounted through her body along with the pain, 'Get off me! I can't…breathe…'

Cruz stopped moving instantly, shock in his voice. 'I'm hurting you?'

Her eyes were stinging now, as she sobbed while trying to push him off, '*Yes*, it hurts!'

He pulled away and Trinity let out a sound of pain. Cruz reared back, staring at her, and then down at something on the bed between them.

'What the hell—?'

She was starting to shiver in reaction and she looked down. The cover on the bed was cream, but even in the dim light she could see the spots of red—blood.

Her head started to whirl sickeningly as what had just happened sank in and she scrambled to move, almost falling off the bed in her bid to escape. She got to the bathroom and slammed the door behind her.

Cruz paced up and down after pulling on his trousers. There was nothing but ominous silence from the bathroom. His mind was fused with recrimination. He simply could not believe what her tight body and the evidence of blood told him. That she was innocent. That she was a virgin. It was like trying to compute the reality of seeing a unicorn, or a pig flying across the sky.

It simply wasn't possible. But then his conscience blasted him… He'd never been so lost in a haze of lust— he'd thought she was there with him, as ready as he was.

He wanted to go after her, but the sick realisation hit him that he was probably the last person she wanted to see right now. Nevertheless, he went and knocked softly on the door. 'Trinity?'

Silence.

Just when Cruz was about to try and open the door she said, 'I'm fine. I just need a minute.'

Cruz's hand clenched into a fist at the way her voice sounded so rough. He took a step back from the door and then he heard the sound of the shower being turned on. His guts curdled. Was she trying to wash him off her?

He'd never been in this situation before. He'd never slept with a virgin before…

And then his mind went on that disbelieving loop again— how was it even possible? She'd been his brother's *wife*!

Cruz sat down on the end of the bed and a grim expression settled over his features as he waited for Trinity to come out of the bathroom and explain what the hell was going on.

Trinity sat on the floor of the shower stall, knees pulled into her chest, arms wrapped around them and her head resting on the wall behind her, eyes closed as the hot water sluiced down over her skin. She couldn't stop shivering, and all she could see was the shock on Cruz's face.

Between her legs it still stung slightly, but the red-hot pain had gone. And yet along with that pain Trinity had felt something else—something on the edges of the pain, promising more—but the shock of realising that Cruz was witnessing her ultimate exposure had eclipsed any desire to keep going.

She opened her eyes and saw nothing but steam. In the heated rush of more pleasure and sensations than she'd ever known, maybe she'd hoped that Cruz wouldn't realise…

But he had. And what she'd experienced before when he'd rejected her was nothing compared to the prospect of how he would look at her now.

When Trinity emerged a short time later, wrapped in a thick towelling robe, Cruz stood up from where he'd been sitting on the end of the bed. He looked as pale as she felt, and something quivered inside her.

His chest was bare, and it was if she hadn't really seen it the first time he'd bared it. She'd been so consumed with desire. It was wide, with defined musculature and dark golden hair covering his pectorals, leading down in a line between an impressive six-pack to arrow under his trousers. A glorious example of a masculine male in his prime.

'Trinity…?'

She looked at his face and saw an expression she'd never seen before—something between contrition and bewilderment.

'I'm sorry,' she said, her voice husky.

Now something more familiar crossed his face—irritation. 'Why the hell didn't you tell me that you were still a virgin?'

She wanted to curl up in a corner, but she stood tall. 'I didn't think you'd notice.'

He frowned. 'How could I not have noticed?'

He seemed to go even paler for a second, as if he was remembering what it had been like to breach that secret and intimate defence. And that only made Trinity remember it too—the pain and then that other tantalising promise of pleasure…hovering on the edges. How amazing it had felt up to that point. How lost she'd been, dizzy with need and lust. Forgetting everything. Forgetting that she needed to protect herself from this…

She went to move past him. 'I don't really want to talk about this now.'

He caught her arm as she was passing. 'Wait just a second—'

'Look, I *really* don't want to talk about this right now.' She felt flayed all over, and way too vulnerable.

Cruz's hand tightened on her arm. 'I deserve an explanation. *Dios*, Trinity, I *hurt* you. And you were married to my brother—how the hell are you still a virgin?'

Her heart slammed against her ribs. This was it. The moment when Cruz would *have* to listen to her. Because of the irrefutable physical humiliation she'd just handed him on a plate.

She turned to face him and looked up. Her voice was husky with emotion. 'I've been trying to explain to you all along that it wasn't a real marriage, Cruz, but you didn't want to hear it. It was a marriage of convenience.'

There was silence for a long moment. The lines of Cruz's face were incredibly stark and grim. He said, 'I'm listening now.'

Trinity's legs felt wobbly and she sat down on the edge of the bed, seeing the stain of her innocence on the sheets in her peripheral vision.

Her cheeks burning, she gestured with her hand. 'I should do something with the sheet—the stain—'

'Can wait,' Cruz said with steel in his tone. 'Talk, Trinity, you owe me an explanation.'

Anger surged up, because if he'd been prepared to listen to her weeks ago they could have avoided this scene, but it dissipated under his stern look. In truth, how hard had she really tried to talk to him? Had she been happy just to let him think the worst so she could avoid him seeing how pathetic she really was? Contriving to make a home out of a fake marriage with children who weren't even her own?

'Okay,' Cruz said, when the words still wouldn't come. 'Why don't we start with this: why did you go to work for Rio? I hadn't fired you.'

She looked up at him. 'How could I have stayed working for you after what had happened? I was embarrassed.' Realising that she'd reached peak humiliation, she said bitterly, 'I had a crush on you, Cruz. I was the worst kind of cliché. A lowly maid lusting after her gorgeous and unattainable boss. When you rejected me that night—'

'I told you,' he interrupted. 'I did not reject you. I hated myself for crossing a line and taking advantage of you.'

Trinity stood up, incensed. 'You asked me if I regularly walked around the house in my nightclothes, as if I'd done it on purpose!'

A dull flush scored along Cruz's cheekbones. 'I didn't handle the situation well. I was angry... But it was with myself. Not you—no matter how it sounded.'

Refusing to be mollified, Trinity said, 'The following night you gave me that look as you greeted the beautiful brunette... You were sending me a message not to get any ideas. Not to forget that what had happened was a huge mistake.'

Cruz ran his hands through his hair impatiently, all his

muscles taut. 'I don't even remember who that was. All I could see was you and that hurt look on your face.'

Trinity's cheeks burned even hotter. She'd been so obvious.

She continued, 'At one point during the evening I went outside. Rio was there, smoking a cigarette. He saw that I was upset and he asked me why...so I told him. He seemed nice. Kind. And then...then he told me that he was looking for a new nanny. He asked me if I'd be interested... and I said yes. I couldn't imagine staying in your house knowing that every time you looked at me it would be with pity and regret.'

Cruz's eyes burned. 'And yet after six months you were his wife?'

Trinity sat down again on the bed. 'Yes.'

Cruz was pacing back and forth now, sleek muscles moving sinuously under olive skin. Distracting.

He stopped. 'So do you want to tell me how you went from nanny to convenient wife?'

She'd wanted this moment to come, hadn't she? And yet she felt reluctant. Because she knew she'd be revealing something of Rio to Cruz that would tarnish him in his eyes, and even after everything she was loath to do that.

But she didn't have a choice now.

She took a breath. 'I'd gone out to the cinema one night. Rio had assured me he had no plans and that he'd be home all evening. When I got back the twins were awake in their room and hysterical. Their nappies were soaking and I don't think they'd been fed. It took me a couple of hours to calm them down, feed them and put them down again. Frankly, it terrified me that they'd been in that state. I went downstairs and found Rio passed out over his desk, drunk. I managed to wake him up and get some coffee into him... but it was clear then that he was in no fit shape to be left alone with his sons—ever.'

Cruz looked shocked. 'I know Rio liked to indulge, but I never would have thought he'd do it while looking after his sons.'

Trinity sucked in a breath. 'I threatened to tell the police…even call you…but Rio begged me not to. He said it was a one-off. I told him I couldn't stand by and let him neglect his children and he begged me to listen to him before I did anything. He told me what had happened to him as a child. He told me he wasn't a perfect father but that he didn't want his boys to be taken into care.'

Trinity looked at Cruz.

'He knew about my past…where I'd come from. I'd told him not long after I started working for him.' Her mouth compressed at the memory of her naivety. 'He seemed to have an ability to unearth people's secrets. And he used that to make me feel guilty for even suggesting that I'd report him. That I would risk subjecting his sons to the same experience I'd had.'

Cruz interjected. 'I would never have let that happen.'

'You were on the other side of the world,' Trinity pointed out. 'And Rio didn't want me to tell you what had happened. I knew you weren't close, so how could I go behind his back?'

She stood up, feeling agitated. Pacing back and forth, aware of Cruz's preternatural stillness.

'But then suddenly he was offering me a solution—to marry him. It was crazy, ridiculous, but somehow he made it seem…logical.'

She stopped and faced Cruz.

'He promised that it would be strictly in name only. He told me he'd hire a nanny to help. He said he wanted to appear more settled, to prove to people that he wasn't just a useless playboy. He said that in return for taking care of the boys and going to some social functions with him I could name my price. Whatever I wanted…'

Something gleamed in Cruz's eyes. 'What was it, Trinity? What did you want?'

She hated it that even now Cruz seemed to be waiting for her to expose herself. She lifted her chin. 'I told him I'd always wanted to go to college. To get a degree. And so he promised to fund my course once the boys were a little older and in a more settled routine.'

Cruz looked at her for a long moment and then shook his head. 'I don't get it. Even with the promise of fulfilling your college dream, why would you agree to a marriage like that unless you were going to get a lot more out of it? Evidently you didn't sleep with Rio, but did you want to? Did you plan on seducing him? Making the marriage real?'

Disappointment vied with anger. 'You will never believe me, will you? Even when you have to admit that I'm not a gold-digger, your cynicism just won't let you…'

She went to walk out of the room, but Cruz caught her arm. She stopped and gritted her jaw against the reaction in her body.

Cruz pulled her around to face him, but before he could say anything, she inserted defensively, 'Of course I wasn't planning on seducing Rio. I had no interest in him like that, and he had no interest in me.'

She looked down for a moment, her damp hair slipping over one shoulder, but Cruz caught her chin between his thumb and forefinger, tipping it back up. Not letting her escape. There was something different in his eyes now—something that made her heart flip-flop.

He just said, '*Why*, Trinity?'

She felt as if he could see right down into the deepest part of her, where she had nothing left to hide.

She pulled her chin away from his hand and said, 'I felt a sense of affinity with him…with the fact that in spite of our differences we had a lot in common.' Her voice turned husky. 'But the largest part of why I agreed was because I'd come to love Matty and Sancho. They needed me.' Afraid that the next thing she'd see on Cruz's face would be pity, Trinity said, 'I'm well aware that my motivations had a lot to do with my own experiences, but I'm not afraid to admit that. They had no one else to look out for them, and I believed I was doing the right thing by them.'

She tried to pull her arm free of Cruz's grip but it only tightened.

She glared at him, hating him for making her reveal so much. 'Just let me go, Cruz. Now you know everything… and I know that after what just happened you won't want a repeat performance…so can we just put it behind us? *Please?*'

He frowned. 'Won't want a repeat performance?'

He pulled her closer. Her breath hitched and her heart started pounding.

'I hurt you, Trinity. If I'd known it was your first time I would have been much more gentle.'

She looked away, humiliation curdling her insides. 'You really don't have to pity me, Cruz. You came to your senses after kissing me that first time. I was unsuitable before and now I'm *really* unsuitable.'

Trinity had managed to pull her arm free and take a couple of steps towards the door when Cruz acted on blind instinct and grabbed her waist and hauled her back, trapping her against him with his arms around her body.

He was reeling from everything that had just transpired—the sheer fact of Trinity's physical innocence was like a bomb whose aftershocks were still being felt. He didn't like to admit it, but the knowledge that her marriage to Rio hadn't been real… It eclipsed everything else at that moment, making a ragged and torn part of him feel whole again.

Trinity put her hands on his arms and tried to push,

but he wouldn't let her go. *Not now. Not ever*, whispered a voice. Base desires were overwhelming his need to analyse everything she'd just said. *Later*. When his brain had cleared.

She said in a frigid voice, 'Let me go, Cruz.'

He turned her so she was facing him. Her face was flushed, eyes huge. He felt feral as he said, 'Believe me when I say that the last thing I feel for you is pity, Trinity. Or that you're unsuitable. And you're wrong, you know...'

'Wrong about what?' She sounded shaky.

Looking down at her now, some of the cravening need Cruz was feeling dissipated as his chest tightened with an emotion he'd never expected, nor welcomed. But this woman evoked it effortlessly, especially after the shattering revelations of her innocence, and in more ways than one.

He shook his head, honesty compelling him to say, 'I haven't come to my senses since that night. You've bewitched me, Trinity.'

'What do you mean?'

Cruz knew that he'd never before willingly stepped into a moment of emotional intimacy like this. No other woman had ever come close enough to precipitate it. After everything that had just happened he felt exposed and raw, in a way that should have been making him feel seriously claustrophobic, but what he *was* feeling was...a kind of liberation.

'What I mean is that I haven't looked at another woman since that night.' His voice turned rough as he admitted, 'I haven't *wanted* another woman since I touched you.'

Her eyes widened. Her mouth closed and then opened again. Finally she said, 'You're not just saying this?'

Her vulnerability was laid bare, and Cruz wondered bleakly how he'd blocked it out before now.

Because he'd wanted to. Because it had been easier to believe the worst rather than let himself think for a second that she could possibly be as pure as he'd believed from the start. Because then he'd have had to acknowledge how she made him feel.

He shook his head. 'No, I'm not just saying this. You're all I want, Trinity. I hated thinking of you and Rio together... I was jealous of my own brother.'

Trinity felt breathless at Cruz's admission. She could see how hard it was for him to open up like this, even as it soothed a raw hurt inside her. And with that came the heavy knowledge that he was beating himself up now over feeling jealous of Rio—and that was exactly the result Rio had wanted to achieve. To mess with Cruz's head.

Loath to shatter this fragile moment, Trinity pushed that knowledge down deep, like a coward, and said, 'We were never together...not like that.' Feeling absurdly shy, she said, 'No other man has ever made me feel like you did. After...that night... I couldn't stop thinking about you... about how it would have been...'

'If we hadn't stopped?'

She nodded jerkily.

He gathered her closer and a tremor ran through her body. The air shifted around them, tension tightening again. 'We don't have to stop now...'

Trinity couldn't battle the desire rising inside her—not after what he'd just told her. She was already laid bare. Nowhere to hide any more. And she wanted this—wanted to fulfil this fantasy more than she wanted to take her next breath.

She looked up at him and fell into molten amber heat. 'Then don't stop, Cruz. Please.'

He waited for an infinitesimal moment and then lowered his head, touching his firm mouth to her softer one with a kind of reverence that made emotion bloom in her chest. To counteract it, because she wasn't remotely ready to deal with what it meant, she reached up and twined her arms around his neck, pressing closer, telling him with her body what she wanted...

He deepened the kiss, stroking into her mouth with an explicitness that made her groan softly, excitement mounting again. His hands moved around to her front, unknotting her robe. He pushed it apart and spread his hands on her hips, tracing her curves, before she broke away from the kiss, breathing raggedly.

He pulled back and looked at her, before pushing her robe off completely. Without looking away, he opened his trousers and pushed them down, kicking them off. Now they were both naked. Trinity looked down and her eyes widened. That stiff column of flesh jerked under her look, and a sense of very feminine wonder and sensuality filled her at the thought that she could have an effect on him like this.

He took her hand and brought it to his hard flesh, wrapping her fingers around him. Slowly, gently, he guided her, moving her hand up and down... It was heady, the way her skin glided over steely strength...

Cruz felt beads of perspiration pop out on his forehead as Trinity's untutored touch drove him to the edge of any reason he had left. It was a special kind of torture...and before she could reduce him to rubble he took her hand from him and led her to the bed.

He wanted to consume her until she was boneless and pliant and *his*.

When he laid her down on the bed and came down alongside her she reached out a tentative hand and touched his chest.

He sucked in a breath. 'Yes...touch me.'

His eyes devoured her perfect curves, slender and yet lush all at once. An intoxicating mix. Innocent and siren.

Innocent.

She laid her hand flat on his pectoral, and then bent her head and put her tongue to the blunt nub of his nipple. Cruz tensed. He'd never even known he was sensitive there. Small teeth nibbled gently at his flesh and his erection grew even harder at the certainty that she would be a quick study…that she would send him to orbit and back all too easily.

A fleeting moment of vulnerability was gone as she explored further and took him in her hand again, moving over his flesh with more confidence.

He groaned and put his hand over hers. She looked at him—suddenly unsure—and it made his chest squeeze. 'If you keep touching me like that I won't last…and I need to.'

'Oh,' she said, a blush staining her cheeks.

Cruz cupped her chin and said roughly, 'Come here.'

She moved up and his arm came around her. He hauled her into him so that she half lay on him, breasts pressed against his side. Her nipples scraped against his chest. Cruz pressed a hot kiss to her mouth, his tongue tangling lazily with hers, revelling in the lush feel of her body against his and the taste of her.

When he could feel her moving against him subtly, he gently pushed her back so that he was looking down at her. Her sheer beauty reached out and grabbed him deep inside, transcending the physical for a moment. Her eyes were wide and her pupils dilated. Her cheeks were flushed and her hair was spread around her head like a golden halo.

She was perfection. And everything she'd told him, if it was true— Cruz shut his mind down. He couldn't go there now.

He explored her body with a thoroughness that made her writhe against him, begging and pleading. But there was no way he wasn't going to make sure she was so ready for him that when they came together there would be no pain. Only pleasure.

He smoothed his hand over her belly, down to where her legs were shut tight. He bent his head again, kissing her deeply, and as he did so he gently pushed them apart and felt her moist heat against his palm.

He cupped her sex, letting her get used to him touching her there, and explored along the seam of her body, releasing her heat, opening her to him with his fingers. He moved his fingers in and out. He could feel her body grow taut, and then he lifted his head to look down at her.

'Come for me, Trinity...'

And as if primed to do his bidding, she did, tipping over the edge with a low, keening cry. He had to exert extreme control to stop himself from spilling at the stunning beauty of her response.

Her hand was gripping his arm, and he could feel her body pulsating around his fingers. He looked at her for a long moment and said, 'If you don't want to go any further now, that's okay.'

Her eyes opened and it seemed to take her a second to focus on him. She shook her head. 'No, I'm okay. Keep going...'

Cruz sent up a prayer of thanks to some god he'd never consulted before. He reached over her to get protection from the drawer. When he was sheathed, he came up on his knees between her legs, pushing them apart, hands huge on her thighs.

Cruz came forward, bracing himself on one hand on the bed beside her, and with his other hand notched the head of his erection against her body, using her arousal to ease his passage into her. He teased her like this until she started panting a little, and arching herself towards him.

Unable to wait a second longer, slowly, inch by inch, he sank into her body, watching her face. She stared up at him, focused, and something inside him turned over even as all he could think about was how perfect it felt to have his body filling hers.

And then, when Cruz was so deep inside her that he could barely breathe, he started to move in and out, with achingly slow precision. She wrapped one of her legs around his waist and he had to clench his jaw as it deepened his penetration.

'I'm okay…' she breathed. 'It feels…good.'

He couldn't hold back. The movements of his body became faster, more urgent. Trinity was biting her lip, her pale skin dewed with perspiration. Cruz reached under her and hitched her hips up towards him, deepening his thrusts even more. Trinity groaned.

'That's it, *querida*, come with me.'

When she shattered this time it was so powerful that he shattered with her, deep inside her, his whole body curving over hers as they rode out the storm together.

Trinity woke slowly from a delicious dream, in which she had arms wrapped tight around her and she was imbued with an incredible sense of acceptance, belonging, safety, home.

Trust.

As soon as that little word reverberated in her head, though, she woke up. She was in Cruz's bedroom, amongst tangled sheets, and her whole body was one big pleasurable ache.

And she was alone.

When that registered it *all* came back.

Trinity's sense of euphoria and well-being faded as she recalled telling Cruz *everything*.

She'd trusted him with her deepest vulnerabilities.

Trust. Trinity went even colder as the magnitude of that

sank in. She'd let Cruz into a space inside her that had been locked up for as long as she could remember.

Trust was not her friend. Trust had got her where she was today. First of all she'd trusted herself to follow her instincts and allow Cruz to kiss her that night. Then she'd trusted Rio, believing his motives for hiring her and marrying her were transparent and benign. Instead he'd manipulated her into becoming a tool of destruction against Cruz.

And now that urge was whispering to her again…to trust Cruz just because he'd made her body weep with more pleasure than she'd ever known could be possible. And because he'd admitted that he hadn't been with another woman since that night in his study. Since he'd kissed her.

Just remembering that now made her chest grow tight all over again. She'd never expected him to say that. What if it had just been a line, though? To get her back into bed? And she, like the fool, had believed him…

Feeling panicky now, at the thought of Cruz suddenly appearing and finding her when she felt so raw, she got out of bed and slipped on a robe. She picked up her severely crumpled dress, her face burning.

There was no sign of him as she went back to her room, and after a quick shower and changing into clean clothes she went into the main part of the apartment. She was very conscious of her body—still tender in private places—and it only made her feel more vulnerable. As if Cruz had branded her.

She knew he wasn't there even before she saw that it was empty and an acute sense of disappointment vied with relief. What had she wanted? To wake up with his arms around him? *Yes*, whispered a voice, and Trinity castigated herself. Men like Cruz didn't indulge in such displays of affection.

Her phone pinged from her bag nearby just then, and Trinity took it out to see a text from Cruz. Instantly her heart skipped a beat. Scowling at herself she read it.

I had an early-morning meeting and some things have come up so I'm going to stay in Madrid for another day/night. My driver is downstairs and he will take you to the airport where the plane is waiting whenever you are ready. Cruz.

Trinity dithered for a few minutes before writing back.

Okay.

She almost put an automatic *x* in the text, but stopped herself just in time.

A couple of minutes later there was another ping from her phone. She put down the coffee she'd just poured to read the text.

Just okay?

Feeling irritated at the mocking tone she could almost hear, she wrote back.

Okay. Fine.

Ping.

How are you feeling this morning?

Trinity's face was burning now. She would bet that Cruz didn't text his other lovers like this. They'd know how to play the game and be cool.

She wrote back.

Totally fine. Same as yesterday.

Ping.

Liar.

She responded.

I thought you had meetings to go to?

Ping.

I'm in one. It's boring.

Trinity was smiling before she stopped herself and wrote back.

Okay, if you must know I'm a little tender, but it feels nice.

She sent it before she had time to change her mind, feeling giddy.
Ping.

Good.

Not knowing how to respond to that smug response, Trinity put the phone down and took a deep breath. Her phone pinged again and she jumped.
Cursing Cruz, she picked it up.

We'll talk when I get back to the castillo.

The giddiness Trinity had been feeling dissipated like a burst balloon. She went cold. Of course they would talk. He'd had a chance to process what she'd told him now, and she could imagine that he didn't appreciate her telling him those less than savoury things about Rio.

That wasn't even the half of it. He didn't know the full extent of just how much Rio had despised him.

Trinity wrote back.

Okay.

Cruz didn't respond. She left the coffee untouched and put her arms around herself as the full enormity of what had happened the previous night sank in. She walked to the huge window in the living room and stared out, unseeing.

The prospect of Cruz going over what she'd told him and digging any deeper than he'd already done, finding out the true depth of hatred that Rio had harboured for him, made her go icy all over. She couldn't do that to him.

And that was the scariest revelation of all. The intensity of the emotion swelling in her chest told her she was in deep trouble. The walls she'd erected around herself from a young age to protect herself in uncaring environments were no longer standing—they were dust.

First two small brown-eyed imps had burrowed their way in, stealing her heart, and now—

She put a hand to her chest and sucked in a pained breath. She could no longer claim to hate Cruz for what he'd done in forcing her into this marriage—if she ever truly had.

From the start she'd been infatuated with him, even after what she'd perceived to be his rejection of her. And then she'd seen a side to him that had mocked her for feeling tender towards him. But hadn't he shown her last night that he could be tender? Achingly so.

And, as much as she was scared that he'd just spun her a line about there being no women since he'd kissed her, just to get her into bed, she realised that she *did* trust him. He was too full of integrity to lie about something like that. He didn't need to.

And that left her teetering on the edge of a very scary precipice—although if she was brutally honest with herself she'd fallen over the edge a long time ago. Right about the time when Cruz had insisted on her going to bed so that he could sit up with the twins and she'd found herself yearning to be part of that tableau. *A family*...

She whirled away from the window, suddenly needing to leave and get back to the *castillo*—put some physical space between her and Cruz. One thing was uppermost in her mind—there couldn't be a repeat of last night. She wasn't strong enough to withstand Cruz's singular devastating focus and then survive when he got bored or decided to move on—which he would undoubtedly do.

For the first time, shamefully, Trinity had to admit to feeling unsure of her ability to sacrifice her own desires for the sake of Matty and Sancho. And she hated Cruz for doing this to her. Except...she didn't.

She loved them all and it might just kill her.

CHAPTER NINE

TRINITY HATED FEELING so nervous. She smoothed her hand down over the linen material of her buttoned shirt-dress. She'd changed after Julia had come to tell her that Cruz was back and wanted to see her.

She hated that she wondered if it was a bad omen that Cruz hadn't come looking for her himself. If not for her, then for the boys, who'd been asking for him constantly.

Cursing her vacillation, she lifted her hand and knocked on his study door, feeling a sense of déjà-vu when she heard him say, 'Come in.'

She went in and saw Cruz was behind the desk. He stood up, his gaze raking her up and down, making her skin tingle. She was conscious of her bare legs. Plain sandals. Hair tied back.

She closed the door behind her.

Cruz gestured to a chair. 'Come in…sit down.'

His voice sounded rough and it impacted on her.

She walked over and took the seat, feeling awkward. Not knowing where to look but unable to look away from those spectacular eyes and that tall, broad body. Remembering how it had felt when he'd surged between her legs, filling her—

Cruz sat down too. 'How are the boys?'

Trinity fought against the blush she could feel spreading across her chest and up into her face. Sometimes she really hated her colouring.

'They're fine… They were asking for you, wondering where you were.'

An expression that was curiously vulnerable flashed

across Cruz's face. 'I'll go and see them later,' he said. 'How are you?' he asked then.

Trinity fought not to squirm. 'I'm fine.'

An altogether more carnal look came across his face now. 'No...soreness?'

Trinity couldn't stop the blush this time. 'No.'

The carnal look faded and suddenly Cruz stood up again, running a hand through his hair. Trinity's gaze drank him in, registering that he must have changed when he got back as he was wearing soft jeans and a polo shirt.

When he didn't say anything for a moment she dragged her gaze up to his face and went still. He looked tortured.

She stood up, immediately concerned. 'What is it?'

He looked at her. 'I owe you an apology...on behalf of me *and* my brother.'

She went very still, almost afraid to say the words. 'You believe me, then...?'

Cruz paced for a moment, and then stopped and faced her again. He looked angry, but she could recognise that it wasn't with her.

'Of course I do.'

She sat down again on the chair behind her, her legs suddenly feeling weak. She waited for a feeling of vindication but it didn't come. She just felt a little numb.

Cruz shook his head. 'After Rio died I took everything his solicitor told me for granted. The truth was that I was in shock...grieving. Based on what he'd told me, I believed you deserved to be the focus of my anger and resentment, so I didn't do what I should have done—which was to investigate his finances with a fine-tooth comb. I've started to do that now,' he said heavily, 'and I had my own legal team haul in his solicitor for questioning yesterday. That's why I stayed behind in Madrid.'

Trinity's throat moved as she swallowed. 'What did you find?'

'Did you know he was a chronic gambler?'

She shook her head, shocked. 'No, of course not... He was away a lot. And worked odd hours. He never really explained himself.'

Cruz was grim. 'He hid it very well. It seems that as soon as he knew what was happening he spent even more money, and he started putting your name on things—like authorising the redecoration of the house, ordering credit cards in your name but using them himself...'

Trinity breathed in, feeling sick. 'So *that* was the trail directly back to me?'

Cruz nodded. 'He made sure you were seen out and about, at fashion shows and events, so if anyone ever questioned him he could point to you and say that you'd been instrumental in his downfall.' Cruz continued, 'You shouldn't feel like he duped you too easily—he did it to countless others along the way. Including me. If I hadn't been so blinkered where Rio was concerned, and had looked into his affairs before now—'

'Then you wouldn't have felt obliged to marry me because you'd have known I wasn't a threat,' Trinity said quickly.

She was avoiding his eye now and Cruz came over.

'Look at me,' he commanded.

After an infinitesimal moment she did, hoping her emotions weren't showing.

'I'm Matty and Sancho's uncle, and I'm going to be in their lives. You are the only mother my nephews have known and I was always going to come back here. Marriage was the best option.'

Trinity felt herself flinch minutely. *Marriage was the best option.* Suddenly feeling exposed under that amber gaze, she stood up and stepped around the chair in a bid to put some space between them. He was too close.

'We haven't finished this conversation,' he said warningly.

Her need to self-protect was huge. 'I think we have. You've said sorry and I accept your apology.'

'There's more, though, isn't there?' he asked now, folding his arms. 'That night—the night of the party at my house—you wanted to tell me something but I shut you down. What was it, exactly?'

Trinity felt panicky and took a step back towards the door. 'It was just my concerns about Rio—he'd been acting irrationally and I was worried, and we'd had that row—' She stopped suddenly and Cruz seized on it.

'You had a row? What about?'

She cursed her mouth and recognised the intractability in Cruz. He wouldn't let this go. He'd physically stopped her leaving before, and if he touched her now...

Reluctantly she said, 'I'd confronted him about being so...erratic. He was spending no time with the boys. He was drinking. And I'm sure he was doing drugs. I threatened to call you and tell you I was worried.'

Rio had sneered at her. *Go on, run to lover boy and cry on his shoulder and you'll see how interested he still is. Cruz doesn't care about you, or me. He only cares about the precious De Carrillo legacy. The legacy that's mine!'*

'What did he say?'

Trinity forced herself out of the past. 'He said that if I did anything of the sort he'd divorce me and never let me see Matty or Sancho again, and that he'd ruin any chances for my future employment, not to mention my chances of going to college.'

Cruz said, 'That must have been just after I'd returned to London. I'd asked to meet him—I'd been alerted by our accountants that he was haemorrhaging money. That's when he told me those lies about you and blamed you for pretty much everything. I had no reason not to believe him when there were all those receipts and the evidence of your social lifestyle...'

Trinity felt unaccountably bitter to hear Cruz confirming all this. She was also shocked at one person's ability to be so cruel. Without thinking, she said, 'He used me because he wanted to get back at you. He wanted to make you jealous because he—' She stopped suddenly, eyes fixed guiltily on Cruz.

What was wrong with her? It was as if she physically couldn't keep the truth back.

'Because he *what*?' Cruz asked, eyes narrowed on her flaming face.

She backed away, feeling sick. 'Nothing.'

Cruz was grim as he effortlessly reached for her, caught her by the hands and pulled her back, forcing her back down into the chair and keeping her hands in one of his.

'Tell me, Trinity. I know there's more to it than just the fact that Rio was going off the rails. He'd been going off the rails ever since he got his inheritance and, believe me, I know that's my fault.'

She looked up at him, momentarily distracted. Anger rushed through her because Cruz felt such irrational guilt over someone who didn't deserve it. Especially when that guilt had blinkered him to Rio's true nature and crimes.

She pulled her hands back, resting them on her lap. 'That wasn't your fault, Cruz. I lived with him for a year and a half, so I should know. Rio was selfish and self-absorbed, and all that inheritance did was highlight his flaws.'

Cruz looked at her carefully. 'There's still more.'

She shook her head, desperately wishing he'd drop it. 'No, there's not.'

He grabbed a nearby chair and pulled it over to sit down right in front of her, all but trapping her. Their knees were touching and she was very conscious of her bare legs under the dress. It didn't help when his gaze dropped momentarily to her chest.

He looked up again and arched a brow. She scowled at him. 'You can't force me to talk.'

'You'll talk, Trinity, and if you don't want to talk then we'll find other ways to occupy our time until you do.'

He put a hand on her bare knee, sliding it up her thigh until she slapped her hand down on his. He gripped her thigh and she felt a betraying pulse throb between her legs.

'Your choice. Either way, you're talking.'

She was between a rock and a hard place. If Cruz touched her she'd go up in flames and might not be able to hold back her emotions. But if she told him the truth about Rio, and he realised why she'd been so reluctant to tell him...

But he deserved to know—however hard it was. However much she wished she didn't have to.

She blurted out, 'I don't want to tell you because I don't want to hurt you.'

Cruz looked at her. Trinity couldn't have said anything more shocking. No one had ever said such a thing to him because no one had ever cared about hurting him before. Certainly not a lover, because he was always very careful not to give them that power.

But right now he could feel his insides contracting, as if to ward off a blow. Instinctively he wanted to move back, but he didn't. 'What are you talking about?'

Her eyes were like two blue bruises.

'Rio set me up way before he needed to use me to blame for his money problems.' She felt her face grow hot as she admitted, 'He offered me the job because he saw an opportunity to distract you, to make you jealous. He told me when we had the row that he'd hated you for as long as he could remember, but that he'd managed to make you believe he was grateful for the hand-outs he said you gave him.'

Cruz forced himself to say, 'Go on.'

'His ultimate ambition was to take you over—to use the marriage and his sons as evidence that he was the more stable heir. That he could be trusted. He wanted to see you humiliated, punished for being the legitimate heir. He never got over his resentment of you, Cruz.'

He realised dimly that he should be feeling hurt, exactly as Trinity had said. But it wasn't hurt he was feeling. It was a sense of loss—the loss of something he'd never had. And that realisation was stark and painful.

Trinity was looking at him and he couldn't breathe. He took his hand off her thigh and moved back, standing up. A sense of inarticulate anger rushed up...that awful futility.

Trinity stood too, and she was pale, and it made his anger snap even more. An irrational urge to lash out gripped him. A need to push her back to a safe distance, where it wouldn't feel as if her eyes could see right down to the depths of his very soul.

'You have to admit,' he said now, 'things worked out for you remarkably well, considering. You still managed to elevate yourself from humble maid to nanny to wife. You may have proved your physical innocence, but can I really trust that you weren't the one who saw your opportunity that night when you spoke to Rio? Maybe you followed him into the garden?'

'No!'

She shook her head, and now there was fire in her eyes as well as something far more disturbing. Something that twisted Cruz's guts.

'*No.* I was hurt, and I was naive enough to let him see it...and he took advantage of that.'

All Cruz could see was her. Beautiful. Injured. *His*

fault. The desire to push her back faded as quickly as it had come on.

Acting on instinct, he went over to her, chest tight. The desk was behind her—she couldn't move. Cruz took her face in his hands, lifting it up. 'Who are you, Trinity Adams? Is it really possible that you're that wide-eyed naive girl who turned up in my office looking for a chance? Full of zeal and a kind of innocence I've never seen before?'

Cruz's character assessment of her chafed unbearably, and Trinity balled her hands into fists at her sides.

'Yes,' she said, in a low voice throbbing with pain. 'I was that stupidly naive girl who was so starved for a sense of belonging that at the first sign of it she toppled right over the edge.'

She hated it that his proximity was making her melt even as hurt and anger twisted and roiled in her gut.

She took his hands down off her face. 'Just let me go, Cruz... There's nothing more to discuss. There's nothing between us.'

She felt his body go rigid and saw his eyes burn.

'You're wrong. There isn't nothing—there's this.'

His mouth was over hers before she could take another breath and Trinity went up in flames. Panic surged. She couldn't let this happen.

She tore her mouth away. 'Stop, Cruz, this isn't enough.'

'It's more than enough, *querida,* and it's enough for now.'

He started undoing the buttons of her shirt-dress, exposing her breasts in her lacy bra, dragging one cup down and thumbing her nipple. She wanted to tell him to *stop* again, but it was too late. She was tipping over the edge of not caring and into wanting this more. Anything to assuage the ache in her heart.

He lifted her with awesome ease onto the side of his

desk. She heard something fall to the floor and smash, but it was lost in the inferno consuming them. He was yanking open her dress completely now...buttons were popping and landing on the floor.

He captured her mouth again as he pushed the dress off her shoulders and down her arms, pulling her bra down completely so her breasts were upthrust by the wire and exposed. The belt was still around her waist—the only thing keeping her dress attached to her body.

He palmed her breast as he stroked his tongue along hers, thrusting, mimicking a more intimate form of penetration. Trinity groaned into his mouth, instinctively arching her back to push her breast into his palm more fully, gasping when he trapped a hard nipple between his fingers before squeezing tightly.

She blindly felt for his T-shirt, pushing it up until they had to break apart so he could lift it off. He dropped it to the floor and Trinity reached for his jeans, snapping open the top button, aware of the bulge pressing against the zip. Heat flooded her—and urgency.

She was hampered when Cruz bent down and tongued a nipple, his hand going between her legs, spreading her thighs and pushing aside her panties to explore along her cleft. He pulled her forward slightly, so that she was on the edge of the desk, feet just touching the ground.

He slowly thrust one finger in and out, while torturing her breasts with his mouth and tongue. She was throbbing all over, slick and ready. The previous emotional whirlwind was blissfully forgotten in this moment of heated insanity.

'Please, Cruz...'

He looked up, his face stark with need. He undid his jeans and pushed them down and his erection sprang fee. Trinity took it in her hand, the moisture at the tip wetting her palm.

Cruz settled himself between her legs, the head of his

erection sliding against her sex, and it was too much. She was ready to beg when he tipped her back and notched himself into her heat. They both groaned, and he rested his forehead on hers for a moment.

Then he said, 'Wrap your legs around my waist.'

She did, barely aware that her sandals had fallen off. Cruz pulled her panties to one side and with one earth-shattering movement thrust into her, deep enough to steal her breath and her soul for ever.

He put an arm around her and hauled her even closer as he slowly thrust in and out, each glide of his body in-side hers driving them higher and higher to the peak. She wrapped one arm around his neck, the other around his waist, struggling to stay rooted.

'Look at me,' he commanded roughly.

She opened her eyes and tipped back her head. The look on his face made a spasm of pure lust rush through her. It was feral. Desperate. Hungry. *Raw.*

Their movements became rougher...something else fell to the floor.

Cruz pushed her back onto the table, lying her flat, and took her hands in one of his, holding them above her head as he kept up the relentless rhythm of their bodies. She dug her heels into his buttocks, biting her lip to stop from screaming as the coil of tension wound so tight she thought she couldn't bear it any longer. But just at that moment he drew her nipple into his mouth, sucking fiercely, and the tension shattered to pieces and Trinity soared free of the bond that had been holding her so tight.

Cruz's body tensed over hers and she felt the hot burst of his release inside her.

Cruz took her to his room in his arms, because her legs were too wobbly to hold her up. She'd buried her face in his shoulder, eyes closed, weakly trying to block out the storm that had just passed but had left her reeling and trembling.

Her head hurt after too many confessions and an overload of pleasure. And too many questions that she didn't want to answer now. Or ever, maybe.

His room was dark and austere. There was a four-poster bed with elaborate drapes. This was very evidently the old part of the *castillo*.

He put her down on the side of his bed and she felt shell-shocked when he disappeared into what she presumed to be the bathroom. She heard the sound of running water and a few minutes later he appeared again and took her into the en-suite.

The bath smelled amazing. Like Cruz. Musky and exotic. He helped her out of her dishevelled clothes and into the hot water. She sank down and looked at him warily. He wore nothing but his jeans, slung low on his hips. She wished she had the nerve to ask him to join her, but she also wanted time to herself, to try and take in everything without him scrambling her brain to pieces.

As if reading her mind, he said, 'I'll be waiting outside,' and walked out, leaving her alone with thoughts she suddenly didn't want to think about.

Coward. She wanted to sink down under the water and block everything out, but she couldn't.

She let out a long, shuddering breath. It really was as if a storm had taken place down in Cruz's study, whipping everything up and then incinerating it in the fire that had blown up between them, white-hot and devastating. But a very fragile sense of peace stole over her as she lay there, even as she had to acknowledge that she wasn't sure where she stood now. And wasn't sure if she wanted to find out.

Aware that the water was cooling rapidly, and Cruz was waiting, she washed perfunctorily, stiffening as a jolt of sensation went through her when she touched the tenderness between her legs.

When she finally emerged, in a voluminous towelling robe with the sleeves rolled up her arms, Cruz was standing at the window. He turned around and she could see that he'd changed into dark trousers and a long-sleeved top and his hair was damp. So he'd gone to another room to shower. Because he'd wanted to give her space, or because he couldn't bear to spend more time with her?

Trinity gritted her jaw against the sudden onset of paranoia.

He came forward. 'How are you?'

She nodded. 'I'm okay.'

He was looking at her with a strange expression on his face, as if he'd never seen her before. In spite of the explosive intimacies they'd just shared Trinity felt as if a chasm yawned between them now.

'I'm sorry,' she said impulsively, thinking of the look on his face when she'd revealed the depth of Rio's hatred.

A muscle ticked in Cruz's jaw. 'You're sorry? For what? It's me who should be apologising to you for all but forcing you into this marriage, and for what my brother put you through to get back at me.'

His belief in her innocence didn't make her feel peaceful now—it made her feel sick. If he really believed that she had just been a pawn in Rio's game what future was there for them? Her heart lurched. *None*. Because he had to be regretting this marriage, which had been born out of an erroneous belief that he couldn't trust her and that he needed to protect his nephews.

It was the last question she wanted to ask, but she had to. 'What happens now?'

He smiled, but it was mirthless. 'What happens now? What happens now is that you could be pregnant. We didn't use protection.' He cursed volubly. 'I didn't even think of it.'

Trinity sank down onto the side of the bed nearest to her as her legs gave way. 'Neither did I,' she said faintly. She'd felt it…the hot rush of his release inside her…and she'd conveniently blocked it out.

She stared at Cruz's grim countenance as the significance of this sank in. The full, horrifying significance.

If she was pregnant then he wouldn't be able to disentangle himself from this marriage—and she didn't need to be psychic to intuit that that was exactly what he wanted. He was angry.

'There was two of us there,' she pointed out, feeling sick. 'It wasn't just your oversight.'

His mouth twisted. 'As much as I appreciate your sentiment, I was the one who should have protected you.'

You. Not *us.*

Panic galvanised Trinity at the prospect of Cruz resenting her for ever for a moment of weakness.

She calculated swiftly and stood up. 'I'm sure I'm not pregnant. It's a safe time for me. And even if it happened, by some miracle, it doesn't mean anything. We don't have to stay married—we could work something out.'

'That,' Cruz said coolly, fixing his amber gaze on her, 'would never be an option in a million years. If you are pregnant then we stay married.'

'But if I'm not…?'

'Then we will discuss what happens. But for now we wait. I have to go to Madrid again in two weeks. I'll set up an appointment with my doctor and we'll go together. That should be enough time for a pregnancy test to show up positive or negative…'

Feeling numb, Trinity said, 'We could just wait. I'll know for sure in about three weeks.'

Cruz shook his head. 'No, we'll find out as soon as possible.'

Trinity really hated the deeply secret part of her that hoped that she might be pregnant, because that was the only way she knew she'd get to stay in Cruz's life. But if she wasn't... The sense of desolation that swept over her was so acute that she gabbled something incoherent and all but ran out of the room to return to hers.

Cruz didn't come after her, or try to stop her, which told her more eloquently than words ever could how he really felt about her.

Cruz stood in the same spot for a long time, looking at the door. He'd had to let Trinity go, even though it had taken nearly everything he possessed not to grab her back. But he couldn't—not now. Not after the most monumental lapse in control he'd ever experienced.

He started to pace back and forth. He'd fallen on her in his study like a caveman. Wild. Insatiable. Filled with such a maelstrom of emotions that the only way he'd known how to avoid analysing them was to sink inside her and let oblivion sweep them away. But he couldn't avoid it now.

He'd been angry with her for revealing the extent of Rio's antipathy—but hadn't he known all along, really? And she'd just been the reluctant messenger.

He'd felt anger at himself for indulging in that delusion in a bid to forge some meagre connection with his only family. And he'd felt anger that Trinity had been so abused by Rio *and* him. He hadn't deserved her purity and innocence after all he'd put her through, and yet she'd given it to him with a sensuality and abandon that still took his breath away.

He stopped. Went cold. He'd actually had a tiny moment of awareness just before he'd come that there was no protection. But he'd been so far gone by then that to have pulled away from Trinity's clasping heat would have killed him… Cruz knew that there was no other woman on this earth who would have had that effect on him.

The insidious suspicion took root… Had he subconsciously wanted to risk getting her pregnant? Because he was aware that after what she'd told him he could no longer insist they stay married if she was innocent of everything he'd thrown at her?

Cruz sank down heavily on the end of the bed. If that was what had happened then he was an even sicker bastard than Rio.

When he thought of how he'd treated Trinity…how he'd shoved the past down her throat at every opportunity without giving her a chance to defend herself or explain…he deserved for her to walk away without a second glance.

But if she was pregnant then she would stay. And Cruz would be aware every day of his life that he had trapped her for ever.

That moment when she'd said so emotionally, *'I don't want to tell you because I don't want to hurt you,'* came back to him. Its full impact.

The fact that she'd actually been willing to keep it from him—the full extent of Rio's ambition and hatred—made him feel even worse. At best she pitied him. At worst she would come to resent him, just as Rio had, if she was pregnant and had no choice but to stay…

By the time Trinity came down for breakfast with the boys the following morning, feeling hollow and tired, she knew that Cruz was no longer in the *castillo*. And sure enough Julia appeared with a note for her.

I have to go to Madrid for a couple of days and then New York. I'll return in time for the doctor's appointment. Cruz.

It couldn't be more obvious that he didn't want to have anything to do with her until they knew if she was pregnant and then he would *deal* with it.

Even Mrs Jordan seemed to sense that something was going on, because she kept shooting Trinity concerned looks. She did her best to project as happy a façade as possible, and suggested that Mrs Jordan take the opportunity to go to Scotland for a few days to see her son, telling her that she'd just need her back for when she would be going to Madrid.

She also, if she was honest, wanted time alone with the boys to lick her wounds.

She filled their days with activities, wearing herself and the boys out so comprehensively that she could sleep. But that didn't stop the dreams, which now featured her running through the *castillo*, going into every room, endlessly searching for Cruz.

And each night before she went to sleep she forced herself to remember what he'd said in London, when she'd asked him about marrying for love: *'I have no time for such emotions or weaknesses...'*

Two weeks later...

Trinity was standing on Harley Street, having just come out of the doctor's office, in the bright spring sunshine. Cruz had brought her to London instead of Madrid at the last minute, because there had been something urgent he had to attend to at the UK bank.

She felt raw now, being back here. Where it had all started. And she felt even more raw after her appointment with the doctor...

A sleek car pulled up just then, and stopped. Trinity saw a tall figure uncoil from the driver's seat. *Cruz*. He'd timed his meeting so that he could meet her after the doctor's appointment.

He held the passenger door open for her to get in, saying nothing as she did so, just looking at her carefully. When he was behind the wheel he looked at her again.

Feeling too brittle at that moment, Trinity said, 'I'll tell you when we get to the house.'

They were staying overnight.

A muscle pulsed in Cruz's jaw, but he said nothing and just drove off. Trinity felt a little numb as she watched the streets go by outside, teeming with people engrossed in their daily lives.

When they got to the Holland Park house her sense of déjà-vu was overwhelming. The door closed behind them, echoing in the cavernous hall. Trinity's heart was thumping and she could feel clammy sweat breaking out on her skin. She sensed Cruz behind her, watching her, waiting, and slowly turned around.

She knew she had to say the words. She opened her mouth and prayed to sound cool and in control. Not as if she was breaking apart inside. She looked at him.

'I'm not pregnant, Cruz.'

He said nothing for a long moment. Trinity was expecting to see relaxation in the tense lines of his body. Eventually he said, 'We should talk, then.'

She recoiled at the thought of doing it right now. 'Can we do it later, please? I'm quite tired.'

Cruz nodded once. 'Of course. Whenever you're ready. I'll be in my study.'

'Okay,' Trinity said faintly, and turned to go up the stairs to the bedrooms. Calling herself a coward as she did so. She was just staying the execution. That was all.

CHAPTER TEN

AFTERNOON PASSED INTO dusk and evening outside Cruz's study, but he was oblivious. Two words echoed in his head: *not pregnant...not pregnant.* He'd felt an unaccountably shocking sense of loss. When he had no right.

Trinity would get pregnant one day, and create the family she'd always wanted. And she deserved that. There was no reason for him not to let her go now. If anything, *he had to.* It was time for him to make reparation.

It had come far too belatedly—the realisation that Rio's deep hatred of Cruz hadn't irreparably damaged his ability to care. That his mother's even deeper cynicism hadn't decimated the tiny seed of hope he'd believed to have been crushed long ago—hope for a different kind of life, one of emotional fulfilment and happiness. One not bound by duty and destiny and a desire to protect himself from emotional vulnerability at all costs.

He'd never wanted more because he'd never really known what that was. Until he'd seen Trinity interact so lovingly and selflessly with his nephews and had found himself sitting up in their room all night, watching them sleep and vowing to slay dragons if he had to, to keep them safe.

The thought of family had always been anathema to him, but now—

He heard a sound and looked up to see his door open. *Trinity.* She'd changed and was wearing soft faded jeans and a long cardigan, which she'd pulled around herself. Her hair was down and a little mussed, and her face was bare of make-up. Her feet were bare too.

For a second Cruz thought he might be hallucinating... even though she wasn't wearing the same clothes as that night... Past and present were meshing painfully right now. Mocking him with the brief illusory fantasy that perhaps there could be such a thing as a second chance.

He stood up as she came in and shut the door behind her.

Her voice was husky. 'I'm sorry. I slept far later than I wanted to.'

On automatic pilot, Cruz asked, 'Are you hungry? Do you want to eat?'

She shook her head and smiled, but it was tight. 'No, thanks—no appetite.'

A bleakness filled Cruz. No doubt she just wanted to sort this out and be gone. Back to the life he'd snatched out of her hands.

'Please, sit down.'

Again, so polite. Trinity came in and sat down. The weight of their history in this room was oppressive. She'd told a white lie about sleeping—she hadn't slept a wink all afternoon, was too churned up. She'd spent most of her time pacing up and down.

After an initial acute sense of loss that she wasn't pregnant she'd felt a sense of resolve fill her. She wasn't going to give up without a fight. She knew Cruz had an innate sense of honour and decency, so even if that was all she had to work with she would.

Cruz sat down. His shirt was open at the top and his shirtsleeves were rolled up.

'You said that part of the deal with Rio was that he would pay for you to do a degree?'

Trinity blinked, taken by surprise that he'd remembered that. 'Yes, he did.'

'Do you still want to do it?'

She felt as if she was in an interview. 'Well, I haven't had much time to think about it lately, but yes...at some point I think I'd like to.'

Cruz nodded. 'I'll make sure you get a chance to do your degree, Trinity, wherever you want to do it.'

'Cruz…' She trailed off, bewildered. 'I presumed we were going to talk about what happens next—not my further education and career options.'

His voice was harsh. 'That is what happens next. You get to get on with your life—the life you would have had if you hadn't had the misfortune to meet me and my brother.'

He stood up then, and walked to the window which overlooked the park. It was still light outside—just.

Trinity stood up too, anger starting to sizzle. 'You do not get to do this, Cruz—blame yourself for what happened. Even Rio can't be apportioned blame either…not really.'

She came around the desk and stood a few feet away from him.

'I was just as much to blame. I shouldn't have been so hurt after what had happened between us that I spilled my guts to Rio with the slightest encouragement. You might not have handled it very well, but you didn't take any liberty I wasn't willing to give. It was the most thrilling moment of my life up to that point.'

Cruz turned around. Trinity saw his gaze drop and widen, and colour darken his cheeks. She didn't have to look down to know that her cardigan had fallen open, revealing her flimsy vest top and braless breasts underneath. She could feel her nipples peak under his gaze, and her heart thumped hard. She couldn't deny that she'd hoped to provoke a reaction from him.

'And there's this, Cruz.' She gestured between them, where tension crackled. 'This hasn't gone away…has it?'

His gaze rose and his jaw clenched. 'It's not about that any more. It's about you getting a divorce and moving on.'

Divorce.

Trinity's heart started thumping. She pulled the cardi-

gan around herself again, feeling exposed. 'I told you before that I won't abandon Matty and Sancho—that hasn't
changed.'

Cruz's voice was tight. 'The fact that you stepped in
and protected and nurtured my nephews went above and
beyond the call of duty.'

Trinity felt even more exposed now. 'I told you—I explained why—'

'I know,' Cruz said, and the sudden softness in his voice
nearly killed her. 'But they're not really your responsibility. You have a life to live. And I won't be responsible for
stopping you. We can work out a custody arrangement. I
wouldn't stop you from being in their lives. But they're in
good hands now.'

For a second Trinity wondered how she was still standing…how she wasn't in a broken heap at Cruz's feet. Whatever pain she'd experienced in her life didn't come close
to the excruciating agony she felt right now.

Yet something dogged deep within her forced her to ask
hoarsely, 'Do *you* want a divorce, Cruz?'

His eyes were burning. 'I want you to have your life
back, Trinity. And I will support you and your relationship with the boys however you want.'

She folded her arms across her chest and Cruz's gaze
dropped again to where the swells of her breasts were
pushed up. Something came to life in her blood and belly.
The tiniest kernel of *hope*.

'You didn't answer me. Do *you* want a divorce?'

His eyes met hers and she saw something spark deep in
their golden depths before it faded. Something cold skated
across her skin. A sense of foreboding.

'What I want,' Cruz bit out, 'is for my life to return to
where it was before I ever met you.'

Trinity looked at him blankly for a long moment. And
then, as his words impacted like physical blows, she sucked

in a pained breath. Her fight drained away and her arms dropped heavily to her sides.

She might have fought Cruz if she'd thought there was half a chance. But there wasn't. He wanted her to have her life back. But he wanted his back too. She'd been a fool to think they had a chance. To think that she could persuade him by seducing him...

She whirled around to leave, terrified he'd see how badly he'd hurt her. The door was a blur in her vision as she reached for the knob, just wanting to escape.

She heard a movement behind her and then Cruz said hoarsely, 'Stop. Do not walk out through that door, Trinity.'

Her hand was on the knob. Her throat was tight, her vision blurring. She wouldn't turn around. 'Why?' she asked rawly.

His voice came from much closer. He sounded broken. 'Because I let you go through it once before and it was the worst mistake of my life.'

He put his hands on her shoulders and turned her around. She didn't want him to see the emotion on her face. But this was Cruz, who demanded and took, so he tipped her face up and cursed.

She looked at him and her heart flip-flopped. The stark mask was gone and he was all emotion. Raw emotion. And it awed her—because she realised now how adept he'd been at holding it all back for so long.

He'd been so controlled. But no more.

'I'm sorry,' he said, cupping her face, thumbs wiping at tears she hadn't even realised were falling. 'I didn't mean what I just said. It was cruel and unforgivable. I only said it because in that split second I thought going back to the life I had before I knew you was preferable to the pain of opening up. I thought I was doing the right thing...forcing you out of my life...'

Trinity whispered brokenly, 'I don't want you to force me out of your life.'

Cruz's whole body tensed. 'Do you mean that?'

She nodded, heart thumping. She put her hands on his and repeated her question. 'What do you want, Cruz?'

His eyes glowed with a new light. He said roughly, 'I want you. For ever. Because I know there can never be anyone else for me. I want to stay married to you and I want a chance to show you how sorry I am—for everything.'

Trinity just stared at him. Wondering if she was hallucinating.

He went on. 'I want to create a family with you—the kind of family neither of us had. Nor Rio. Maybe through his sons we can give him that finally. But,' he said, 'if you want a divorce…if you want to walk away…then I won't stop you. As much as I wanted you to be pregnant, I'm happy you aren't because I couldn't have borne knowing that you'd never had a choice… Now you do have a choice.'

Trinity's vision blurred again. 'I choose you, Cruz. I would always choose you.'

'I love you,' Cruz said fervently.

Trinity blinked back her tears and sucked in a shuddering breath. 'I came down here this evening prepared to fight and make you see, and then you said—'

Cruz stopped her mouth with his in a long soulful kiss. When they broke apart they were both breathing heavily, and Trinity realised that her back was against the wall of shelves. Cruz's body was pressed against hers, the unmistakable thrust of his arousal turning her limbs to jelly and her blood into fire. With an intent look on his starkly beautiful face he pushed her cardigan off her shoulders and pulled it off.

Euphoria made Trinity's heart soar. 'What are you doing?'

But Cruz was busy pulling down the straps of her vest top and exposing her breasts to his hungry gaze. Hoarsely he said, 'I'm taking care of unfinished business—if that's all right?'

As he made short work of undoing her jeans and pulling them down excitement mounted, and she said breathily, 'I have no objections.' She kicked her jeans off completely.

Cruz stopped for a moment and looked at her, all teasing and sexy seductiveness gone as the significance of the moment impacted on them. 'I love you.'

Trinity nodded, biting her lip to stave off more emotion. 'I love you too…'

But then their urgency to connect on a deeper level took over again.

Cruz stepped out of his clothes. She reached up and wound her arms around his neck, revelling in the friction of her body against his, and when Cruz picked her up she wrapped her legs tight around his hips and together they finished what they'd started, soaring high enough to finally leave the past behind and start again.

EPILOGUE

'CAREFUL, BOYS, YOUR little sister is not a doll,' Cruz admonished Matty and Sancho, who were tickling their four-month-old sister where she lay in her pram in the shade. The fact that she was their cousin and not really their sister was something they could wrap their heads around when they were older.

The boys giggled and ran away, chasing each other down the lawn, dark heads gleaming in the sunlight.

Cruz watched them go. They'd grown so much in the two years since he and Trinity had officially adopted them—turning their legal guardianship into something much more permanent and binding.

One day, not long after the adoption had come through, they'd both suddenly started calling him Papa. As if they'd taken a private mutual consultation to do so. The day it had happened he'd looked at Trinity, unable to keep the emotion from filling his eyes and chest. She'd reached out and taken his hand, her eyes welling up too as they'd realised what had just happened.

They were a family.

He shook his head now, marvelling that he couldn't even remember a time before these two small boys existed. He would die for them. It was that simple. It was bittersweet to know that he was finally able to show his love for Rio by protecting and nurturing his nephews like this.

A happy gurgle made Cruz look down again to see his daughter, Olivia—who was already being called Livvy—smiling gummily and waving her arms and legs. She had the bright blue eyes of her mother and a tuft of golden curls on her head, and she had Cruz so wrapped around her tiny finger that he could only grin like a loon and bend down to pick her up.

'Hey,' protested a sleepy voice, 'you're meant to be getting her to sleep.'

Cruz looked to where Trinity was lying in a gently rocking hammock between two trees. Her hair was loose and long around her shoulders and she was wearing short shorts and a halterneck top that showed off her lightly golden skin and luscious curves. An indulgent smile made her mouth curve up, telling Cruz that he was *so* busted where his baby daughter was concerned.

Whatever he felt for his children expanded tenfold every time he looked at this woman, who filled his heart and soul with such profound grace and love he was constantly awed by it.

In spite of their busy lives she was already one year into a three-year degree in business and economics at the University of Seville, and loving it.

The *castillo* was almost unrecognisable too, having undergone a massive renovation and redecoration. Now it was bright and airy, with none of the darkness of its tainted past left behind.

Cruz devoured her with his eyes as he walked over, holding his precious bundle close. Trinity's cheeks flushed as their eyes met and desire zinged between them. Everpresent. Everlasting.

She made room for him on the family-sized hammock and then settled under the arm he put behind her, her hand over Livvy where she was now sleeping on his chest, legs and arms sprawled in happy abandon.

The boys were shouting in the distance—happy sounds. Cruz could hear Mrs Jordan's voice, so he knew they were being watched. He took advantage of the brief respite and tugged Trinity closer into his chest. She looked up at him, her mouth still turned up in a smile that was halfway between innocent and devilishly sexy.

Emotion gripped him, as it so often did now, but instead of avoiding it he dived in. 'Thank you,' he said, with a wealth of meaning in his words.

Thank you for giving him back his heart and an emotional satisfaction he would never have known if he hadn't met her and fallen in love.

And even though he didn't say those words he didn't have to, because he could see from the sudden brightness in her eyes that she knew exactly what he meant.

She reached up and touched her lips to his—a chaste kiss, but with a promise of so much more. And she whispered emotionally against his mouth, 'I love you, Cruz. Always.'

'Always,' he whispered back, twining his fingers with hers where they rested over their daughter.

Trinity rested her head in the spot made for her, between his chin and his shoulder, and the future stretched out before them, full of love and endless days just like this one.

* * * * *

Alice brought her gaze back up to Cristiano's glittering one. 'You're surely not going to go through with this…are you?'

A smile that wasn't quite a smile courted the edges of his mouth. 'But of course. It is what Nonna wanted. Who am I to disregard her last wishes?'

Alice frowned so hard she might have frightened off twenty ampoules of Botox. 'What happens if I don't agree?'

'To me?' He gave a careless shrug. 'Nothing—other than losing a few shares in the company, which will pass to a relative if I don't comply with the terms of the will.'

Alice wondered how important those shares were to him. Was his easy-come-easy-go shrug disguising deeper, far more urgent motivations? Enough to marry someone he now hated?

She sent her tongue out over lips so dry it felt as if she was licking talcum powder. 'So…why would you want to marry someone who clearly doesn't want to marry you?'

His dark-as-night gaze gleamed, making the floor of Alice's belly shudder.

'You know why.'

Alice arched one of her brows, trying to ignore the pulsing heat his words evoked deep in her feminine core. 'Revenge, Cristiano? I thought you were a civilised man.'

Melanie Milburne read her first Mills & Boon at the age of seventeen, in between studying for her final exams. After completing a Master's Degree in Education she decided to write a novel, and thus her career as a romance author was born. Melanie is an ambassador for the Australian Childhood Foundation and a keen dog lover and trainer. She enjoys long walks in the Tasmanian bush. In 2015 Melanie won the HOLT Medallion—a prestigious award honouring outstanding literary talent.

Books by Melanie Milburne

Mills & Boon Modern Romance

Unwrapping His Convenient Fiancée
His Mistress for a Week
At No Man's Command
His Final Bargain
Uncovering the Silveri Secret

The Ravensdale Scandals

Ravensdale's Defiant Captive
Awakening the Ravensdale Heiress
Engaged to Her Ravensdale Enemy
The Most Scandalous Ravensdale

The Playboys of Argentina

The Valquez Bride
The Valquez Seduction

Those Scandalous Caffarellis

Never Say No to a Caffarelli
Never Underestimate a Caffarelli
Never Gamble with a Caffarelli

Visit the Author Profile page at millsandboon.co.uk for more titles.

THE TEMPORARY
MRS MARCHETTI

BY
MELANIE MILBURNE

MILLS &
BOON

First Published in Great Britain 2017
By Mills & Boon, an imprint of HarperCollins*Publishers*
1 London Bridge Street, London, SE1 9GF

© 2017 Melanie Milburne

ISBN: 978-0-263-92512-8

Our policy is to use papers that are natural, renewable and recyclable
products and made from wood grown in sustainable forests. The logging
and manufacturing processes conform to the legal environmental
regulations of the country of origin.

Printed and bound in Spain
by CPI, Barcelona

THE TEMPORARY
MRS MARCHETTI

To Sarah Lewer.

Thanks for the inspiration for this novel and thanks also for being such a wonderful beauty therapist and gorgeous person.

XXXX

CHAPTER ONE

THE FIRST THING Alice noticed when she came to work that morning was the letter on her desk. Something about the officious-looking envelope with its gold embossed insignia made her skin shrink against her skeleton. Letters from lawyers always made her feel a little uneasy. But then she looked closer at the name of the firm. Why would a firm of Italian lawyers be contacting her?

She picked the letter up and her breath came to a juddering halt when she saw it was postmarked Milan.

Cristiano Marchetti lived in Milan.

Alice's fingers shook as if she had some sort of movement disorder. Surely he hadn't...*died*? A sharp pain sliced through her, her breath coming in short, erratic bursts, making not just her fingers tremble but her whole body.

Oh, no. Oh, no. Oh, no.

How had she missed that in the press? Surely there would have been an announcement for someone with Cristiano's public profile? They reported every other thing he did. The glamorous women he dated. The fading hotels he bought and rebuilt into stunning boutique accommodation all over the Mediterranean. The charity events he attended. The parties. The nightclubs. Cristiano couldn't change his shirt or shoes or socks without someone reporting it in the press.

Alice peeled open the envelope, her eyes scanning the brief cover letter, but she couldn't make any sense of it...or maybe that was because her brain was scrambled with a host of unbidden memories. Memories she had locked away for the last seven years. Memories she refused to acknowledge—even in a weak moment—because that was the pathway to regret and that was one journey she was determined never to travel. Her legs were so unsteady she reached blindly for her chair and sat down, holding the document in front of her blurry gaze.

But wait...

It wasn't Cristiano who had died. It was his grandmother, Volante Marchetti, the woman who, along with his late grandfather Enzo, had raised him since he was orphaned at the age of eleven when his parents and older brother had been killed in an accident.

Alice frowned and cast her gaze over the thick document that had come with the cover letter that named her as a beneficiary of the old woman's will. But why had his grandmother mentioned *her* in her will? Why on earth would the old lady do that? Alice had only met Cristiano's grandmother a handful of times. Volante Marchetti had been a feisty old bird with black raisins for eyes and a sharp intellect and an even sharper sense of humour. She had instantly warmed to the old lady, thinking at the time of how lucky Cristiano was to have a grandmother so spritely and fun, and had often thought of her since.

Maybe his grandmother had left her a trinket or

two—a keepsake to mark their brief friendship. A piece of jewellery or one of the small watercolour paintings Alice remembered admiring at the old lady's villa in Stresa. She began to read through the legalese with her heart doing funny little skips. So many words... Why did lawyers have to sound as if they'd swallowed a dictionary?

'Someone here to see you, Alice,' Meghan, her junior beauty therapist, said from the door.

Alice glanced at the time on her computer screen next to her appointment diary and frowned. 'But my first client isn't until ten. Clara Overton cancelled her facial. One of her kids is sick.'

Meghan waggled her eyebrows meaningfully and, lowering her voice to a stage whisper, said, 'It's a man.'

Alice had several male clients who came to her for waxing and other treatments but something told her the man waiting to see her wasn't one of them. She could feel it in her body. In her bones. In her blood. In her heartbeat. The awareness of imminent danger making a prickling sensation pass all over her flesh, as if her nerves were radar picking up a faint but unmistakable signal. A signal she had forced herself to forget. To wipe from her memory in case it caused her to regret the decision she had made back then. She pushed back her chair and stood but then decided it was better to remain seated. She didn't trust her legs. Not if she was going to come face to face with Cristiano Marchetti after all this time. 'Tell him I'll be ten minutes.'

'You can tell me yourself.'

Alice looked up to see Cristiano framed in the door, his chocolate-brown eyes as hard as two black bolts. All she could think of was how different it was seeing him in the flesh instead of a photograph in a gossip magazine or newspaper. Shockingly different. Heart-stoppingly different. *I'm-not-sure-I-can-handle-this* different.

For a moment she couldn't locate her voice. With him standing there, with his towering frame and command-ing air, her office seemed to shrink to the size of a tis-sue box. Shoulders so broad he looked as if he'd been bench-pressing bulldozers—two at a time. An abdo-men so hard and toned you could tap dance on it wear-ing stilettos and not leave a dent. Jet-black hair, thick and currently brushed back from his forehead in loose finger-groomed waves.

'Hello, Cristiano, what brings you to Alice's Won-derland of Beauty? An eyebrow-shape? Back and leg wax? Personality makeover?'

Alice knew it was crazy of her to goad him but she did it anyway. It was her defence mechanism. Sarcasm instead of emotion. Better to be cutting and mocking than to show how much his brooding presence disturbed her. It more than disturbed her. It unbalanced her. Her neatly controlled world felt as if it had been picked up and rattled like a maraca held by a maniac. The walls of her office were closing in on her. The floor was shift-ing beneath her feet like a sailboat pitching in a wild squall. The air was pulsing with crackling electricity that made her aware of every inch of her skin and every hit-and-miss beat of her heart.

His bottomless eyes roved her face as if he was look-ing for something he had lost and never thought to find again. His brow was etched in a deep frown that gave him a much more intimidating air than the way he had looked at her in the past. Back then he had looked at her with tenderness, with gentleness. With love.

A love she had thrown back in his face.

'Did you put her up to it?' he asked with a searing look that made the backs of her knees fizz as if sand were being trickled through her veins.

Alice placed her hands on the tops of her thighs below her desk so he wouldn't see their traitorous shaking. 'I presume you're referring to your grandmother?'

Something flashed in his gaze. Bitterness. Anger. Something else she wasn't ready to acknowledge, but she felt it all the same. It breathed scorching hot fire all over her body, stirring up memories. Erotic memories that made the blood in her veins pick up speed. 'Have you been in contact with her over the last seven years?' he asked in that same terse *don't-mess-with-me* tone.

'No. Why would I?' Alice gave him a pointed look. 'I rejected your proposal, remember?'

His jaw tensed so hard she could see the white tips of his clenched muscles showing through his olive tan. 'Then why has she mentioned you in her will?'

So he hadn't known about the terms of his grandmother's will until recently? Had the old lady not told him of her plans? *Interesting.* 'No idea,' Alice said. 'I only met her a couple of times when we were…back then. I've had zero contact since.'

He glanced at the will lying in front of her on her desk. 'Have you read it?'

Alice gave him another speaking look. 'I was getting to that when you rudely barged into my office.'

His eyes nailed hers. Hard eyes. Eyes that could melt a month's supply of salon wax with a single glare. 'Let me summarise it for you. You stand to inherit a half share of my grandmother's villa in Stresa in Italy if you agree to be my wife and live with me for a minimum of six months. You will also receive a lump sum on the announcement of our engagement, which is to last no longer than one month.'

Shock hit Alice like a blow to the chest. *His...wife?*

She fumbled for the document, the sound of the pages rustling overly loud in the silence.

Engaged to him for a month? Married for six?

She cast her gaze over the words again, her breath coming in such short spark bursts it felt as if she were having an asthma attack. Her heart was beating so heavily it felt as if someone were punching it from behind. She hadn't seen any mention of marriage in her quick appraisal earlier. She'd barely had time to read any of it before he had gatecrashed into her day. Why hadn't she put on her make-up before work? Why hadn't she worn her brand-new uniform instead of this one with the eyebrow-tint stain on the right breast? Why hadn't she done her own eyebrows, for God's sake?

But there it was in black and white.

Alice was to co-inherit Volante Marchetti's summer retreat on the shores of Lake Maggiore if, and only if, she married and stayed married to Cristiano for six months. *Six months?* Six seconds would be too long. And there was the other clause. They must be engaged for no more than a month before the wedding. What sort of weird time frame was that? It shamed her that Cristiano saw the pages of the document shaking before she put it back down on the desk. But at least he couldn't see the tumult going on inside her stomach.

His wife?
Live with him?

She had been to his grandmother's villa one memorable weekend with Cristiano. Memorable because it was the first time he'd told her he loved her. Apart from her mother, no one had ever said that to her before. She hadn't said the words back because she hadn't trusted her feelings. But then, she had always been a step behind him in their relationship. She'd thought they were having a fling while she was on a brief working holiday in Europe. He'd decided it was a relationship. She'd thought it was temporary because she'd planned to go back to England and set up her own beauty spa, but he had wanted it to be permanent.

Permanent as in marriage and kids.

For as long as she could remember Alice had been against marriage—or at least for herself. After witnessing her mother go through three of them with exactly the same result: misery, subjugation, humiliation and financial ruin. She had told Cristiano a little about her background, not much, but more than she had told anyone, which made her all the more annoyed he had still gone ahead and asked her to marry him. In a crowded public place to boot, which had added a whole other layer of pressure she resented him for.

His arrogance made her furiously angry. Had he really thought she would fall upon him with a grateful squeal of *Yes!* just because he was super-rich and said he loved her and wanted to spend the rest of his life with her? How long would that love have lasted? They'd had a passionate if a little volatile relationship. How could she be sure his desire/love for her wouldn't burn out as fast as it had been ignited?

If he had truly loved her he would have accepted her no as final and settled for a less formal arrangement. People lived together for years and years without needing the formality of marriage. Why be so damn nineteen-fifties about it? A marriage certificate didn't make a relationship any more secure. In fact, it could do the very opposite, forcing women into a subservient role once kids came along from which they could never escape.

But Cristiano at heart was a traditionalist. For all of his modern male sophistication, deep down he wanted a wife and family to come home to while he built his empire. So he had given her an ultimatum. Tried to control her. Tried to manipulate her into doing what he wanted.

Marriage or nothing.

Alice had called his bluff and ended their relationship then and there, and flown back to England, never expecting to hear from him again. Well, maybe that wasn't quite true. She *had* expected to hear from him with a big apology and 'let's try again' but it hadn't happened. Showed how much he'd 'loved' her. Not enough to fight for her. Not enough to compromise.

Not that she had offered to compromise, but still.

Alice brought her gaze back up to his glittering one. 'You're surely not going to go through with this…are you?'

A smile that wasn't quite a smile courted with the edges of his mouth. 'But of course. It is what Nonna wanted. Who am I to disregard her last wishes?'

Alice frowned so hard she could have frightened off fifty units of Botox. 'What happens if I don't agree?'

'To me?' He gave a careless shrug. 'Nothing other than a few shares in the company which will pass to a relative if I don't comply with the terms of the will.'

Alice wondered how important those shares were

to him. Was his easy-come, easy-go shrug disguising deeper, far more urgent motivations? Enough to marry someone he now hated? What about the villa? It was his grandmother's home, the place where he had spent much of his childhood being raised by his grandparents. Wouldn't he want to contest such an outrageous will? Surely he wouldn't want to share it with anyone, much less her? Why would he agree to such unusual conditions? She sent her tongue out over lips so dry it felt as if she were licking talcum powder. 'So…why would you want to marry someone who clearly doesn't want to marry you?'

His dark as night gaze gleamed, making the floor of Alice's belly shudder. 'You know why.'

Alice arched one of her brows, trying to ignore the pulsing heat his words evoked deep in her feminine core. 'Revenge, Cristiano? I thought you were a civilised man.'

'I am prepared to be reasonable.'

Alice affected a laugh. That was not a word she readily associated with him. He saw the world in black and white. He didn't know the meaning of the word compromise. What he wanted he got and woe betide anyone who got in his way. Not that she could talk. Compromise wasn't her favourite word in the dictionary, either. 'Reasonable in what way?'

He held her look with one she couldn't read. 'The marriage won't be consummated.'

Not…? Alice hoped she wasn't showing any sign of the numb shock she was feeling. Not just shock. Hurt. Humiliation. Their affair had been so wildly passionate. She had never had a lover before or since who made her feel the things he had made her feel. She had all but given up dating because of it. His touch was indelibly branded on her body. No one else's touch made her flesh sing—the opposite, in fact. Her flesh crawled when someone else touched her. The last time she slept with a date, well over a year ago, she came home and showered for an hour.

'You speak as if this…this preposterous marriage is a fait accompli,' she said. 'I said it seven years ago and I'll say it again now. I am not going to marry you.'

'Six months is not a long time. At the end of it you get joint ownership of a luxury villa to do with as you please. You can sell your half or keep it. The choice is yours.'

The choice wasn't hers. How could it be? She was being forced into a marriage with a man who no longer loved her—if he ever had. What he had wanted to do back then was control her. It was what he wanted to do now. What better way to punish her for having the gall to say no to him than to chain her to him in a loveless union?

Alice wouldn't do it. *No. No. No.*

She wouldn't subject herself to the humiliation of being his trophy wife while he continued to sleep with whomever he liked. He knew…*he knew* how much she'd hated seeing her mother cheated on by each of her husbands. It had been one of the things that had impressed her about him. He believed in monogamy—or so he'd said.

But what about your business plan?

Alice had somehow become the go-to girl for wedding make-up. The girl who had sworn against marriage was preparing brides all over London for theirs. *Go figure.* Her appointment diary was booked out for months ahead for the wedding season. It was becoming the biggest source of her income, especially high-profile weddings. She had plans to buy another salon—a larger place so she could extend her business because her Chelsea salon was getting too small to handle the burgeoning wedding market.

It had been a dream of hers for months. Years, actually. The only thing holding her back was the thought of taking on a load of property debt. Debt was something that terrified her. The mere thought of it kept her awake at night. She remembered too well how it had felt as a child to have not enough money for food, for clothes, for electricity when her mother had been between relationships.

She knew she could always rent another property like this one in Chelsea, but that left her at the mercy of landlords, something she had seen too many times during her childhood. Rents could be put up and buildings suddenly sold. The business she had worked so hard to establish would be jeopardised if she didn't own the property herself.

You could sell the villa after six months and be debt-free for the rest of your life.

Alice allowed the thought a little traction. The business she had sacrificed so much for was her baby, her mission, her purpose in life. Seeing it grow and develop over the last few years had been enormously satisfying. She had built it up from just a handful of clients to now one of the busiest salons in the area. She had celebrities and minor royalty on her books. People came to her because of the standards of excellence she maintained. To achieve her dream of setting up a luxury wedding spa would finally prove she had made it.

Failing wasn't an option.

Not after using her career as the excuse for not wanting to marry Cristiano. The career she put before everything else. Relationships. Holidays. Fun. Even friendships. All of it had been sacrificed for work.

But she couldn't marry Cristiano to solve that problem for it would throw her in the middle of an even bigger one.

Alice rose from her chair with her spine steeled with resolve. 'I've made my choice. Now, if you've finished catching up on old times, I have a business to run.'

His eyes continued to tether hers as if he were waiting for her cool composure to crack. 'Are you involved with someone? Is that why you're saying no?'

Was he *still* so arrogant? *Yes.* Arrogance was hardwired into his DNA. A man in his privileged position had no concept of why a woman wouldn't want to thrust her hand out for him to put a ring on it. He had it all: the money, the looks, the luxury lifestyle, the fast cars and exotic holiday destinations. Alice wished she had a lover to fling in his face. She considered inventing one but knew it wouldn't take him long to call her out on her lie. He wouldn't have to hunt around too far to find her social life was practically non-existent. Her work was her social life.

'I know you find it hard to believe you're irresistible because of your wealth and other…erm…assets, but I am not going to prostitute myself for the sake of an inheritance I neither asked for nor need.'

His expression gave nothing away. 'I meant what I said, Alice. It will be a marriage in name only.'

No one said her name quite the way he did. His Italian accent gave it a completely different emphasis. *Aleece.* The sound of it was like an erotic caress. It made the base of her spine shiver as if he had touched her with a brush of his warm male hand. Thinking of his hands made her want to look at them.

Don't. Don't. Don't.

But in spite of her rational brain's pleas, she looked. Those broad-spanned hands had travelled over every inch of her flesh. Those long tanned fingers had coaxed her into her first proper orgasm. They had discovered all of her erogenous zones, tortured them with such intense pleasure it had shaken her to the core of her being. She could feel the echo of it even now, as if just being in the same room as him, breathing the same air as him, made her body recognise him as her only pleasure giver.

Alice dragged her gaze upwards and collided with his. He knew. Damn it, he knew how much sensual power he had over her. She could see it in the knowing glint in his pitch-black eyes. She felt it when he sent his gaze over her body as if he too were remembering what it had felt like to hold her in his arms as she splintered into a thousand pieces of shivering, quivering ecstasy.

He lifted a hand to his jacket pocket and took out a business card and placed it on the desk next to the copy of his grandmother's will. 'My contact details should you change your mind. I'll be in London for the next week while I sort out some business affairs.'

Alice wilfully ignored the card. 'I'm not going to change my mind, Cristiano.'

I'm not. I'm not. I'm not.

A cynical smile lifted one side of his mouth. 'We'll see.'

We'll see?

What did he mean, 'We'll see'? Alice didn't get the

chance to ask him for he turned and left her office, leaving her with the lingering fragrance of his aftershave, the lemon and lime with a base note of leather that made her nostrils tingle…not to mention the rest of her body.

Meghan was bug-eyed when she came back. 'Oh, my God! You didn't tell me you knew Cristiano Marchetti. I didn't recognise him at first. He's much more gorgeous in the flesh than he is in photographs in the press. I nearly fainted when he walked past me just then and smiled at me. What did he want? Is he going to come here for treatments? Please let me do him. Can I do him? Please, please, please?'

Alice wasn't going to explain her past relationship with her employee even if Meghan was turning out to be one of the best she'd ever had. And as for Meghan 'doing him', if anyone was going to 'do him' it was going to be her. She would like nothing better than to get a pot of hot wax and strip that supercilious smile off his too-handsome face. 'He's not a client. I met him a few years ago. He just dropped in to say hi.'

'Met him as in met him and dated him?'

Alice didn't respond other than to purse her mouth. Meghan blushed and bit her lower lip. 'Sorry. I shouldn't have asked that. I know you insist on absolute confidentiality with celebrity clients. It's just he's so handsome and you never seem to date anyone and I wondered if it was because—'

'Can you get my treatment room ready for my next client?' Alice said. 'I have some urgent paperwork to see to.'

Alice blew out a breath once Meghan scuttled away. For seven years she had told herself she'd made the right decision. She had chosen her career over commitment.

Freedom over having a family. She had stood firm on her decision, not once wavering on it. Now, within her grasp was a way to finally achieve the success and financial security she had thus far only dreamt about.

Six months of marriage.

In name only.

She glanced at his business card. It seemed to taunt her with its presence.

Do it. Do it. Do it.

Alice snatched it up and tore it into as many pieces as she could and tossed them in the bin. It was kind of weird how they floated down just like a handful of confetti.

She hoped to God it wasn't an omen.

Cristiano would have had a stiff drink if he'd been a drinking man, but the death of his parents and his older brother to a drunk driver when he was eleven made him wary of using alcohol other than in strict moderation. Seeing Alice Piper again was like having his guts slashed wide open. And stomped on. The mere sight of her reopened the wound of his bitterness until he wondered how he had stood there without showing it.

He'd felt it, though. God in heaven, how he'd felt it. The blood rush. The pulse race. The adrenalin surge. The kick and punch of lust.

He had stood there and drunk in her features like a dehydrated man standing in front of a long cool glass of water. Her indifferent poise, her cornflower-blue gaze that could freeze mercury, the way she looked down her aristocratic nose at him as if he had crept in from a primeval swamp with his knuckles dragging. Her body was as lissom and gorgeous as ever—perhaps even more so. Her unusual silver-blonde hair with her naturally dark eyebrows and the creamy, ageless perfection of her skin gave her a striking appearance that never failed to snatch his breath.

Her rejection of him stung and burned and churned even after all this time. He had thought what they'd had was for ever. A once in a lifetime love. Their passionate affair had been unlike anything he'd experienced before. He'd wanted to build a future with her. A family. He'd believed it to be like the love his parents had had for each other. Like the love his grandparents had before his grandfather died. The death of his grandfather a couple of months before he met Alice had made him acutely aware of how important family was. It had been all he had thought about—having a family to replace the one he had lost so young. He'd felt ready. More than ready. He'd been twenty-seven and well established in the hotel business he had inherited from his parents. He was ready for the next phase of his life.

But Alice hadn't loved him. She had never said the words but he'd fooled himself into thinking she'd been showing it instead. How gullible he had been. How stupid to be so naively romantic when all she'd wanted was a quick fling with a foreigner to boast about with her friends.

What had his *nonna* been thinking? She had only met Alice a couple of times. Why bequeath her a share in a property worth millions and with such odd conditions attached? Six months of marriage? What sort of nonsense was this?

He hoped to God it wasn't some sneaky match-making ploy from the grave. His grandmother knew he had changed his mind about settling down. He had laughed off the suggestion every time she asked him when he was going to provide her with a great-grand-child. Nonna had expressed her disapproval of his play-boy lifestyle on numerous occasions but he had always dismissed her concerns because no one was going to tell him how to run his life.

No one.

His grandmother had been disappointed when his relationship with Alice broke down. Terribly disap-pointed. But he had refused to talk about it. He'd had enough trouble managing his own disappointment with-out having to handle his grandmother's. Over the years she had stopped mentioning Alice's name knowing it would get zero response from him. Why then had she done this? Forced him back into Alice's life when it was the last thing he wanted?

The way the will was written meant if he didn't con-vince Alice to marry him then he would lose valuable shares in the family company to a cousin he had no time for. He wasn't going to hand over those shares only to have his cousin Rocco sell them to another party when he ran a little low on cash after playing the tables in a casino. Cristiano would rather marry his worst enemy before seeing that day dawn. He blamed himself for not telling his grandmother of Rocco's disturbing spend-ing habits of late. But he hadn't wanted to burden her in the last months of her terminal illness.

Now it was too late.

The will had been written and now he had to con-vince Alice Piper to marry him.

Not that Alice was an enemy in the true sense of the word. She was a mistake he had made. A failure he wasn't particularly fond of being reminded about. He had wiped her from his memory. Every time a thought of her would enter his mind he would ruthlessly erase it like someone cleaning a whiteboard. He had lived his life since as if she had never been a part of it. As if he had never had such amazing sex with her it had made his body tingle for hours afterwards. As if he had never kissed that sensually supple mouth. As if he had never felt that mouth around him while she blew the top of his head off.

Cristiano wasn't going to let Alice think he was anything but delighted with the way his grandmother had orchestrated things. It suited him to let Alice think he was eager to put that ring on her finger and tie her to him for six months. Besides, maybe avoidance wasn't the way to handle the lingering sting of her rejection. Maybe some immersion therapy would finally end his torment.

Alice might have given him that haughty look and said no as if it were her last word on it, but this time he wasn't taking no for an answer.

CHAPTER TWO

ALICE NEITHER HEARD nor saw anything of Cristiano for the next couple of days. She had been expecting him to show up at work again, knowing him to be implacably determined when he set his mind to something. She had received a call from the lawyer handling the execution of the will, who explained some of the finer points. There was a time limit on accepting the terms. If she didn't marry Cristiano by the end of a month-long engagement the villa would be sold outside the Marchetti family. Alice wondered what Cristiano would think about that—his childhood home sold to strangers. Was that why he was pushing for this marriage? Or was it purely revenge?

On the third day without sight or sound of Cristiano, Alice got a call from her salon building's landlord, Ray Gormley. 'I know this will come as a bit of a surprise, Alice, but I've sold the building,' he said. 'The new owner is taking possession immediately. You have a few months left on your current three-year lease so it shouldn't disrupt—'

'Sold?' Alice gasped. 'I didn't even realise you had it on the market.'

'I didn't, but I got an offer I'd be a fool to refuse,'

he said. 'I'm consolidating some of my interests. This guy's bought the building next door as well. Says he's going to make them both into a luxury hotel.'

Suspicion made every hair on the back of Alice's neck stand up and fizz at the roots. 'A…a hotel?'

'Yes,' Ray said. 'You ever heard of Cristiano Marchetti? He has boutique hotels all over Europe.'

Alice's jaw was so tight she felt the tension in her neck as if someone had a noose around it—which they did. *Damn it.*

'So…let me get this straight… Marchetti approached you completely out of the blue?'

'Yes,' Ray said. 'He's been looking for suitable property in London. The UK is the only place he doesn't have a hotel. This is stage one of his British expansion.'

Alice was still trying to get her heart out of her mouth and back in her chest where it belonged. Cristiano was her new landlord? What did he plan to do? Hike up her rent so she had no choice but to marry him? She had three months left on her three-year lease. It had always worried her having such a short-term lease, which was one of the reasons she wanted to buy her own property. But Ray had always assured her he wasn't selling any time soon. His wife and three daughters were clients of hers. She had thought—stupidly thought—she was safe.

But what would happen once Cristiano took possession?

Alice ended the call and started pacing her office so hard she thought she'd go right through the floorboards to the subway below. This was absolutely outrageous. Cristiano was going to such devious lengths to bend her to his will. She wished now she hadn't torn up his card.

Not that she had forgotten his number—no matter how hard she tried to erase it, for some reason, it remained fixed in her brain. But he might well have changed it. After all, she had changed hers.

She sat back at her desk and dialled his number. She listened to it ringing and ringing, her courage just about deserting her when finally it was answered by a husky female voice. 'Hello?'

Alice's stomach dropped. 'Erm… I'm not sure if I have the right number—'

'Are you looking for Cristiano?' the young woman said.

'Erm…yes, but if he's busy I can—'

'He's right here beside me,' the woman said. 'Who will I say is calling?'

Right here beside her doing what?

Alice clenched her teeth so hard she could have bitten through a pair of tweezers. It was the middle of the day, for pity's sake. Why wasn't he at work instead of in bed with some gorgeous nymphet?

'It's Alice Piper.'

She heard the sound of the phone being handed over and couldn't stop an image forming of him lying amongst the rumpled bed linen of a hotel with a naked woman's body draped over his. 'I've been expecting you to call,' Cristiano said. 'Changed your mind yet?'

Alice gripped her phone so hard she thought her knuckles were going to burst through her skin. 'No, I have not.'

'That's a pity.' There was a note of casual amusement in his tone. 'I didn't want to have to play dirty but needs must.'

Alice's spine tightened as if someone were turning a

wrench on each and every vertebra. 'I know what you're trying to do but—'

'Come to my hotel and we'll discuss this over a drink.'

Alice wasn't going anywhere near his hotel. A hotel room was way too intimate. If she and Cristiano were alone together with a bed nearby, who knew what might happen? It wasn't him she didn't trust. It was her. Her body remembered him like a language she thought she'd long forgotten. Even now it was responding to the deep gravelly cadence of his voice, making her senses reel as if she had ingested some sort of mind-altering drug. 'I'd rather meet somewhere less...'

'Dangerous?'

The silky tone of his voice loosened the bolts on her vertebrae.

Alice pressed her lips together, trying to garner her defences. He wasn't the same man as seven years ago. He had changed. He was harder. More ruthless. More calculating and brutally tactical. She was going to have to be careful dealing with him. He wasn't in love with her now. He hated her. He wanted revenge. 'I'm not scared of you, Cristiano.'

'Perhaps not, but you're scared of how I make you feel. It's always been that way between us, has it not?'

'I felt lust for you back then. Nothing else.'

'You still feel it, don't you, *cara mia*?' His voice was a teasing feather stroking over the nerve-sensitive base of her spine.

'You're mistaken,' she said, injecting her voice with icy hauteur. 'I feel nothing for you but contempt.'

'That's a strong word for someone who once shared their body with me.'

'You know something? I didn't break your heart,' Alice said. 'I bruised your ego. That's what all this is about, isn't it? You hadn't had a woman say no to you before. You weren't in love with me. If you were you would have accepted and respected my decision not to get married.'

'That is an argument for another time,' he said with a thread of steel entering his tone. 'I want to see you tonight to discuss the rent on your salon going forward.'

Alice stiffened. It was all right for him with the millions he'd inherited when his parents were killed. She didn't have any rich relatives to hand her an empire or to give her a financial leg up when things turned ugly. Everything she had worked for had been out of her own blood, sweat and tears—and occasional tantrum. If he turned the financial screws on her now, everything she'd worked for could be compromised. Or— God forbid—even lost. 'Sometimes I wonder how you speak so fluently with all those silver spoons hanging out of your mouth.'

A pulsing silence passed.

Alice wondered if this was going to turn into one of their massive arguments. With hindsight she could see a large part of their relationship had been a power struggle. They had constantly bickered over things without anything being resolved other than in bed. Neither of them had wanted to compromise or back down from a stance. Making love had diffused the battle temporarily, but it hadn't solved the underlying issue.

He had wanted control of her and she wouldn't give it.

Cristiano released a long breath. 'I would give each and every one of those silver spoons back if I could have my parents and brother back for a day, let alone for the last twenty-three years.'

Alice suddenly felt ashamed of herself. He couldn't help his background any more than she could help hers. It was a cheap shot, similar to the ones she'd tossed at him in the past. Their verbal sparring had been a sort of foreplay. The battle of two strong wills, combined with a fierce lust for each other, had created some combustible arguments on occasion. Too many occasions. When had they ever sat down and had a discussion without one or both of them flying off in a temper? Had either of them actually listened to what the other said? Or were they too busy trying to think of a cutting comeback? 'I'm sorry. That was…unfair of me.'

'I have to go. Natalia is waiting for me.'

A dagger went to Alice's belly. She'd forgotten all about his gorgeous little bed buddy lying right beside him while he spoke to her on the phone. Jealousy rose in her like a beast that had been woken too abruptly. Giant paws of jealousy clawing at her insides, making her feel strangely hollow. Why was she feeling like this? She had no right to feel this way. She had ended their affair. She'd been the one to walk away, not him. She didn't have any rights over him now. He was a free agent to sleep with whomever he pleased. There should be no reason why the thought of him talking to her on the phone while a woman was in bed beside him should… *hurt* her so much.

'I'm sorry to force you to talk business in the middle of pleasure,' she said. 'Maybe next time turn your phone to silent so you don't get interrupted during one of your marathon sex sessions.'

There was another little silence.

Alice wished she hadn't spoken with such crisp venom. Every word she had spoken sounded as if it were painted bright green. What was wrong with her? It was crazy to give him ammunition he could use against her. If he thought for a picosecond she was jealous he would exploit it every opportunity he could.

'I'll pick you up for dinner at seven,' Cristiano said as if she hadn't spoken. 'What's your address?'

'I'm not having dinner with—'

'You will have dinner with me or I'll cancel your lease as of now.'

Alice's heart banged against her breastbone. 'You can't do that!'

'Can't I?'

She swallowed a rush of panic. She had to get control of her tongue. It wouldn't help her cause to challenge him all the time. It would only make him all the harder to manage. She could handle dinner. Sure she could. It would be a test for her. It would be proof she could spend an hour or two in his company without wanting to tear his clothes off his hot body.

Yikes. Do not even think about that body.

It was probably still naked and sweaty from bed-wrecking sex. 'Won't Natalia mind you taking out another woman for dinner?'

'No.'

Alice was frustrated by his one-word answer so went digging for more. 'She must have a very laid-back attitude to relationships to allow you to entertain other women while she's involved with you.'

'Natalia knows her place.'

'Are you going to marry her?'

'She's already married.'

Shock rendered Alice speechless for a moment. What had happened to Cristiano's conservative old-fashioned values? The Cristiano of the past would never have slept with a married woman. He'd had no time for men and women who betrayed their marital vows. He'd spoken at length about the commitment his parents had made and how he admired and respected them for staying true to it until their untimely deaths. Until death do us part had been something he had believed in to the letter.

What had changed him?

You changed him.

The thought was an uncomfortable weight in the pit of her stomach. Had she been the one to destroy his faith in relationships? But she hadn't been ready to settle down back then. Rejecting a proposal wasn't a crime, was it? Surely she'd had the right to decide whether she wanted to be married or not. It wasn't the Dark Ages, for God's sake. But the thought continued to niggle at her. Had she turned him into a casual-living playboy who had no time for commitment? These days he used women to suit his needs. He was in and out of relationships faster than a racing driver changed gears. Was he really no longer a man who longed for a wife and family of his own? And why should that make her feel so…so sad? 'Well then, I'd better get off the phone so you can get back to your grubby little affair, hadn't I?'

'I'll see you tonight,' he said and before she could think of a comeback, or tell him she wasn't going, he ended the call.

Alice dressed for dinner as if she were dressing for combat. Each layer of clothing was like putting on a suit of armour. The armour of sophistication she had been so sadly lacking seven years ago.

She sometimes wondered what Cristiano had seen in her back then. She had been twenty-one years old and newly qualified as a beauty therapist. It had been her first trip abroad without friends accompanying her. She had been on a shoestring budget while she back-packed around Europe but she'd only got as far as Italy when she'd met him in a crowded street in Milan when a sharp catch on her backpack had become caught on his clothing, as she'd brushed past.

They'd stood in the middle of the street, comically locked together by their clothes. He'd made a comment about it bringing a whole new meaning to 'hooking up with someone' and she'd laughed. Once he had untangled himself he'd insisted on buying her a coffee.

One coffee had turned into two coffees and then dinner. Instead of going back to the backpackers' centre she'd found herself accepting his offer of accommodation for the night or two she'd planned to spend in his home city. At no time had she felt any pressure to sleep with him. She was not unaware of his interest in her and she hadn't been all that good at hiding hers in him. But his respectful handling of her had impressed her. Not many healthy and virile young men of twenty-seven, as he was at that time, would have asked a woman back to his place and not expected something in return.

In the end it had been Alice who made the first move. She still remembered their first kiss. Sometimes when she closed her eyes she could still feel those firm lips moving with such urgency against hers, making every cell in her body vibrate. One kiss hadn't been enough.

Next minute she was tearing his clothes off him and all but throwing herself at him.

Her mind drifted… The drugging kisses. The phenomenal foreplay. The earth-rocking sex. The mind-bending orgasms. The electric tingling of her flesh for hours afterwards.

How had she gone so long without it?

Alice sighed and picked up her lipstick. She had never found anyone else who made her feel desire quite like that, as if she would literally die if she didn't have him. Which meant she would have to be super careful around him now. She didn't want to betray herself, to give him any hint she hadn't managed to move on with her life. Of course she had moved on with her life. She was a successful businesswoman with money in the bank…most of it borrowed, but still.

What else did she need?

The doorbell sounded and she put her lipstick in her purse and picked up her evening wrap and went to the door. Even though she was in four-inch heels Cristiano towered over her. 'You're late,' she said. 'I thought you said seven. It's half-past.'

He gave a shrug of one broad shoulder as if punctuality and common politeness were no longer of any interest to him. 'I knew you'd wait for me.'

The way he said it made it sound as if she had spent the last seven years doing exactly that. She raised her chin and sent him a look that would have soured long-life milk. 'How did you find out where I lived?'

'Your very helpful *previous* landlord.'

The slight emphasis on the word 'previous' made Alice's nerves jangle.

She wound her wrap around her shoulders, wishing she could wind it around Cristiano's neck instead. 'Where are we going to dinner?'

'Aren't you going to show me around your house first?'

Alice pinched her lips together. 'My home is hardly on a league with yours.'

He glanced around her foyer with an appraising eye. 'Nice. How long have you lived here?'

'Two years.'

'Alone?'

Alice forced herself to hold that piercing gaze even though it made every atom in her body protest. 'At the moment.'

He gave a slight nod as if her answer satisfied him on some level. 'Big place for a single girl. How many bedrooms?'

'Four.'

His ink-black brows lifted in an arc. 'Are you renting?'

Alice threw him a black look. 'Why? Are you thinking of buying it too, and jacking up the rent? Sorry to spoil your fun but I own it.' *Or at least the bank does.*

His mouth curved at one corner in a half-smile that should not have caused her heart to stumble. 'You could pay this mortgage off and have money to spare if you agree to the terms of my grandmother's will. You could expand your business as well.'

Alice's brows snapped together in a frown. How did he know she wanted to expand her business? Who on earth had he been talking to? He had an unnerving ability to gain information about her. And read her mind. Not to mention her body.

Oh, dear God, why wasn't her body ignoring him? Damn it.

Her body was a traitor. It remembered him too well. It only had to be within touching distance and it went haywire. It was as if the last seven years hadn't happened. All her nerves were screaming out for his touch like starstruck teenage fans at a boy-band concert. 'My business plans are absolutely no concern of yours. Nor indeed are my private ones.'

His eyes moved over her body in an assessing sweep that made her insides coil with lust. She knew that look. The look that said, *I want you and I know you want me. And I can prove it.*

'It must get a bit lonely at times, living in this big old house by yourself, *si*?'

'I'm not one bit lonely.'

He released a small puff of air that had cynicism riding on its backdraft. 'Sure you're not.' He was suddenly standing closer than she'd realised. Had she been so mesmerised by his gaze she hadn't detected him closing the distance between them? He reached out and picked up a tendril of her hair and wound it around the length of his index finger. It was too late to step back.

Why the hell hadn't she stepped back?

Every nerve root on her scalp was tingling from the tether of his touch.

'Have you missed me, *cara*?' His voice was a deep, seductive burr of sound that sucker-punched her self-control.

Alice had to swallow three times to locate her voice. *Three times!* As it was she only just stopped herself from giving a betraying whimper. 'If you don't let go of me this instant I'll file my nails on your cheek. Got it?'

His mouth curved in an indolent smile and he wound

her hair a little tighter. 'I'd much rather you'd rake them down my back.'

His incendiary words sent a shockwave of lust through her body. She swore she could feel the echo of where he had been in the past—the thickened length of him driving into her until they both lost control. Her blood simmered in her veins, rushing through her system as if it were on fire.

Get control. Get control. Get control.

The words were sounding an alarm in her brain but her body was blatantly ignoring it. Her body swayed towards his...or maybe his moved closer. His muscle-packed thighs brushed hers, reminding her of all the times they had trapped hers beneath their sensual power and superior strength. Sex with Cristiano had always had an element of danger to it. The dark unknowable power of it. The uncontrollable force of it had thrilled and frightened her in equal measure. Her body felt things with him it had never felt before or since. Not even close. She was spoilt now for anyone else.

Another good reason to hate him.

Alice pushed back against his chest even though it tugged cruelly on her hair. 'In your dreams, buddy.'

Cristiano's gaze had a mocking glint to it. 'I could have you in a heartbeat and you damn well know it.'

'Ah, but you don't want me, remember?' Alice said with an arch look. 'A marriage in name only, wasn't it?'

A whip-quick flicker of tension moved across his mouth. He stepped back and held open the door. 'We'll lose the booking if we don't make a move. I had to pull strings to secure it.'

'You're good at that, aren't you, Cristiano? Pulling strings to get people to do what you want?' Alice gave him a sugar-sweet smile on her way past him in the doorway. 'What a pity you can't get *me* to toe the line.'

He captured her forearm in the steel bracelet of his long, strong fingers, tugging her around so his gaze clashed with hers. His eyes were onyx-dark and brooding with indomitable purpose. 'I haven't finished with you yet. But once I am, I swear to God you'll be on your knees begging me to marry you.'

Alice flashed him a look of pure defiance and wrenched out of his hold, rubbing her arm as if it had been scorched. Which it had. Why, oh, why was it so damn exciting sparring with him? She hadn't felt like this in years. Alive. Switched on after a long time on pause. Running at breathtaking speed instead of idling. It was nothing short of exhilarating. 'You think you can bully me into doing what you want? Try it and see what happens.'

His eyes dipped to her mouth, setting off a feverish chain of reaction in her body. Only he could do that. Make her hot for him by looking at her. 'You'd be a fool to throw away this chance to build your asset base,' he said. 'Don't let emotion get in the way of a good business deal.'

'Who are you to lecture me about emotion?' Alice said. 'You're the one who was in love with me, not me with you, and now you're punishing me because I'm about the only person on this planet who has the backbone to stand up to you and—'

'I wasn't in love with you.'

The words stung like a hail of rubber bullets. Alice blinked. Swallowed. Blinked again. *Not in love with her?* Not even a little bit? Why that should bother her she didn't want to examine too closely. 'Right, well then, that's good to know. At least I did you a favour then in rejecting your proposal. We would've been divorced by now otherwise and think how much that would've cost you.'

He opened the passenger door for her, jerking his head towards the vacant seat like a police officer taking in a suspect for interrogation. 'Get in.'

Alice straightened her shoulders, throwing him a glare that could have stripped ten years of graffiti off a council estate wall. 'Ask nicely.'

A muscle flicked in his jaw and his eyes smouldered like black coals. 'You know what will happen if you push me too far.' His tone was silk wrapped around a will of steel.

Alice did know and it was perverse of her to keep doing it. But she couldn't seem to help herself. It was an urge she couldn't control. She wanted to push him. She wanted to bait him. To break him. To reduce him to his most primal. A spurt of excitement lit like a wick inside her, sending a radiant heat coursing through her body. Her breasts tingled as if they were preparing themselves for the possessive cup of his hands. Her thighs trembled with the memory of his intimate invasion, her blood stirring into a frenzied whirlpool that made her aware of every feminine muscle contracting and releasing in her groin.

Oh, how she had missed this!

No one made her feel so...so energised. So vital. So...*aroused*.

She kept her gaze locked on his. The air was so charged with static she could hear it like a fizzing roar in her ears. 'What are you going to do, Cristiano? Lug me over your shoulder and carry me off like the caveman you really are underneath that smart Armani suit?'

Another ripple of tension passed over his rigidly set mouth, his eyes blazing as they tussled with hers. His hand left the top of his car door and snared one of hers before she could do anything to counter it—if she had wanted to, that was—ruthlessly tugging her towards him so there was barely a breath of air between their bodies. Alice could feel the slight protrusion of his belt buckle digging her in the stomach, a shockingly erotic reminder of the latent male power stirring just below it.

'Been a long time between drinks, has it, *cara*?' he asked in that dangerously smooth tone.

Alice huffed out a laugh but it didn't come out quite as convincing as she would have liked. It sounded breathless. Uncertain. Out of its depth. 'You don't get to hear about my love-life. It's none of your business.'

His fingers subtly tightened around her wrist, his touch a band of fire that sent lightning-fast currents of hot electricity straight to her core. 'It will become my business once we're married next month.'

Next month? Eek!

Alice elevated her chin, sending him a look of undiluted disdain. 'You seem to have a big problem understanding the concept of the word no. I'm. Not. Marrying. You.'

His top lip lifted in a sardonic curl. 'You want me so bad I can smell it.'

Alice disguised a quick swallow. She could smell it too. The musk and salt of arousal coming off both of them like a black magic potion. A swirling wicked spell. Its dangerous tentacles were wrapping around her body, coiling like a serpent, strangling her resolve until it was gasping for air.

Only he could do this to her. Make her so wild with need she forgot everything but the greedy hunger in her body clamouring for satiation.

His thighs were flush against hers, the swell of his erection so powerfully male—so blatantly, unashamedly male—it made every feminine cell in her body roll over and beg. Somehow—miraculously—she managed to conjure up a mocking smile. 'That ego of yours is so big it deserves its own postcode. Or its own government.'

A spark of amusement lit his gaze and his fingers around her wrist loosened slightly, his thumb stroking in a fainéant movement over the hummingbird leap of her pulse. 'Did you miss what we had together?'

Alice schooled her features into a mask of cool indifference. 'Not a bit.'

His probing gaze kept hers captive. 'So why haven't you had a serious relationship since?'

How on God's sweet earth did he know that?

Alice arched a brow. 'None that *you* know about. Unlike you, I don't live my life followed by paparazzi documenting every time I sneeze.'

'When was your last relationship?'

She flicked her eyelids upwards. 'Oh, for God's sake, what is this? Twenty questions?'

His gaze didn't waver. 'A long time, then.'

Alice pursed her lips and then released them with a rush of air. 'Are we having dinner or are we going to stand here and swap dating histories? I can get you a list of name and numbers if you'd like? I could even do a printout of some of their messages and emails if that gives you a hard-on.'

Cristiano put his hand back on top of the rim of the car door. 'That won't be necessary.'

Alice brushed past him to get in the car, shooting him a glare through the windscreen when he strode in front of the car to take his place behind the wheel. He started the engine with a powerful roar and entered the traffic with a quick glance over his shoulder, the G-force sending her back against the butter-soft leather seat.

Why did his driving always remind her of sex?

The thunderous growl of his engine, the thrusting of the gears, the press on the brakes and the push down on the throttle made her think of all the times he had taken her to bed—or other places—and driven them both to paradise.

Alice's gaze went to his hands holding the steering wheel with such indolent confidence, the long, tanned fingers with their dusting of dark hair doing all sorts of strange things to her insides. What was it about those hands that made her squirm with need? How was she to get through an evening with him? Sitting across the table with him at a restaurant, for God's sake?

How the hell had he got her to agree to dinner?

That was one of the scariest things about Cristiano Marchetti. He had an unnerving ability to get her to do things she had no intention of doing.

But...

That tricky little 'but' kept gnawing at the wainscoting of her mind. But what if she did agree to it? Six months was nothing. It would flash past. And at the end of it she would be set up financially. For life. She could build her wedding spa with money to spare. She could buy the best equipment, lavishly decorate the place without the limitations of a budget. She could take a holiday—something she hadn't done in years.

Alice chewed it over… He was expecting her to say no. But wait a minute… What if he didn't *want* her to say yes? What if he was only making all this fuss to make her think he was keen to get that ring on her finger?

She smiled a secret smile. She would string him along for a while longer and then she would call his bluff and expose his true motivations.

Married for six months to her mortal enemy?

Game on.

CHAPTER THREE

CRISTIANO OPENED AND closed the fingers of his right hand where they were gripping the steering wheel. He could still feel the hot tingle of Alice's skin against his fingertips. His lust for her was pounding like a jungle drum deep in his body. He ached with it. Burned with it. Vibrated with it. No one but her could reduce him to this. To stir in him such primitive, out of control longings. Longings he had never felt for anyone else. Longings that made a mockery of the sex he'd had before her and since.

Not that he hadn't had great sex over the years. He had. Many times. He'd made a point of it—using every sexual encounter to drive home the point to himself he could live without her.

It was just that in comparison to what he'd shared with Alice…well, it wasn't in the same league. Her body, her touch, her wildcat-on-heat response to him triggered something in him. Something indefinable. Something that made his flesh shudder in reaction when she came near. Something that, even now, with her sitting less than a half a metre away, he could feel moving through his body like the aftershocks of an earthquake.

He had to get her out of his system.

He had to.

He could no longer tolerate the rush of adrenalin every time he saw a silver-blonde head in the crowd and the savage drop of his gut afterwards when he realised it wasn't her. He had to prove to himself he was over her.

Was this why his *nonna* had set her will up this way? To help him move past the five-foot-six blonde road-block in his life? To force him to confront the failure he would give anything to forget?

Cristiano had made a promise to himself not to sleep with Alice. *Look, but don't touch.* But how long was that going to last? He was barely keeping his hands off her now. All he had to do was reach over and stroke his hand down the slim flank of her thigh peeping out from above the knee-high hem of her little black dress.

His fingers twitched against the steering wheel. His groin growled when she crossed one long leg over the other, her racehorse-slim ankle moving up and down as if she were feeling the same restless agitation he was feeling.

Of course she was.

Cristiano allowed himself an internal smile. His ego had nothing to do with it. He could see the struggle she was having controlling her desire for him. He had felt it from the moment he'd stepped into her office and seen her sitting like a starchy schoolmistress behind that desk. She'd used the desk as a barrier. She hadn't trusted herself to get too close to him. She knew her body would betray her as his was doing to him. It was the way they were together. Match and tinder. Spark and flame. Trigger and explosion.

It was only a matter of time before he had her where he wanted her. Begging him. Clawing at him with those little wildcat claws. Gasping his name between panting breaths as he showed her what she'd been missing. What *he'd* been missing. Dear God, how he'd missed it! Missed her. The feistiness of her. The razor-sharp wit of her tongue. The flashpoint temper and the come-and-get-me teasing that had made him feel as if he were living on the edge of a vertiginous cliff.

The way her body felt around him when he drove in to the hilt.

Getting her to marry him was his goal, not sleeping with her…although if what he had seen from her so far was any indication, sleeping with her might happen sooner rather than later. A little financial blackmail was not his usual modus operandi, but he had to get her married to him otherwise his shares would be lost.

Not to mention the villa.

He couldn't lose that. It was the place where his father had grown up. It was where Cristiano had spent numerous happy family holidays before his parents' and brother's death. It was his home for the rest of his childhood and adolescence, the place where overnight he had grown from boy to man. Losing the villa would be like losing even more of his family than he had lost already.

Why had his grandmother done such an outrageous thing as to force him to share it with Alice?

He didn't need a conscience right now. Six months would pass before he knew it. He would insist on Alice living with him because he wasn't going to let the press get wind of there being anything amiss with his 'marriage'. No way was Alice Piper going to make a laughing stock out of him in the daily tabloids. He would enjoy making her act the role of devoted wife. It would be amusing to see her push against the boundaries he laid down.

'So, we'll have a nice dinner and discuss this situation we find ourselves in,' Cristiano said after a time.

'Discuss?' Alice's voice held a generous note of scorn. 'You don't discuss. You command.'

He sent her a smiling glance. 'And as my wife you will obey.'

Even from the other side of the car he could feel the heat coming off her livid blue glare. 'They have rewritten the marriage ceremony since the nineteen-fifties, you know. Women no longer have to obey their husbands. Not that you're going to be my hus—'

'We'll have a month-long engagement as the will specifies,' Cristiano said. 'You either marry me at the end of it or find yourself paying a rent you can ill afford.'

Her face was a picture of impotent outrage, almost puce instead of her natural creamy colour. 'You…you *bastard*.' Her hands curled into tight little balls as if she was tempted to fly at his face and was only just stopping herself. 'You scheming bastard.'

He gave a careless shrug. 'Sticks and stones.'

It was a while before she said anything. Cristiano wondered if she were thinking things over, running her mind over the figures, so to speak. She ran a good business, he had to give her that, but it would not survive a big hike in rent. And to get her to do what he wanted, he was prepared to go as high as it took.

Whatever it took.

'Why engaged for a month?' she said. 'If you're in such a hurry to get a ring on my finger then why not frogmarch me to a register office right away?'

'I'm not having anyone speculate on why we're not having a proper wedding, that's why,' Cristiano said, wondering if she was speaking figuratively or if she was changing her mind about marrying him.

'But you can't really mean to go to such lengths? I mean, a wedding is a big expense.'

'I can afford it.'

There was another silence.

'All right.' Her breath came out in a whoosh. 'You win. I'll marry you.'

Cristiano hadn't expected such a rapid capitulation. He'd thought she would have fought it a little longer and a little harder. But then he wondered if she had a counter plan. She was clever. Whip-smart and streetwise. What devious plan had she cooked up? Did she intend to make him suffer every minute they were engaged? Did she really think she could outmanoeuvre him? He smiled another private smile.

Who knew this could be so much fun?

'I'm glad you're starting to see the positive side of our circumstances. It's a win-win for both of us, *si*?'

The look she gave him would have sent a swarm of wasps running for cover. 'Everyone's going to know this is a farce the moment we're seen out in public together.'

'Ah, but that's where you're wrong, *tesoro*,' Cristiano said. 'We're going to act like a happy and devoted couple at all times and in all public spaces.'

A spluttering noise came from her side of the car. 'Not on your life—'

'Apart from when we're alone,' he continued as if she hadn't spoken. 'Then the claws can come out. I'm quite looking forward to it, actually.' He gave her another goading smile. 'It will be like old times, yes?'

Her eyes were spitting chips of blue ice, her mouth set in such a tight line her lushly shaped lips all but disappeared. Her whole body seemed to be shaking with rage. He could feel the vibration of it from his side of the car.

'Why are you doing this? Why? Why? Why?'

Why was he?

Good question. It wasn't just the shares, although that was a big part of it. It was more the sense of wanting to rewrite the past. To be in control this time. To be in charge of his emotions and passions. To be the one who told her when it was over, not the other way around. He was not going to be that person ever again—the person left behind. He had been that person as a child of eleven.

Left behind by his family.

The shock of that loss had never left him. Sometimes he could still feel that claw of despair in his chest, dragging, tearing at his organs. That terrible day when his grandparents had delivered the devastating news of the death of his parents and brother, he had felt as if he were the only person left on the planet.

Alone.

Abandoned.

Isolated.

It was the same feeling he'd felt when Alice walked out on his proposal. He stood in the middle of that crowded restaurant feeling as if a wall of thick glass were separating him from everyone else. No one could reach him. He could not reach them. He was blocked. Imprisoned in a cage along with his frustrated hopes and shattered dreams.

'We have unfinished business, Alice.'

'No. We. Don't.' Her words came out like hard pellets. 'Our business is finished. Kaput. Over. Dead and buried.'

Cristiano parked the car before he swivelled in his seat to look at her. She was sitting with her arms stiffly folded, her legs crossed, and her ankle jerking up and down as if she had a tic. 'It's not though, is it, *cara*? It's not one little bit finished.'

Her eyes met his and her throat moved up and down over a swallow like a small creature moving under a rug. But then she lowered her gaze to a point just below the knot of his tie. He heard her take a breath that sounded more like a shudder than a breath. 'You always did play dirty.'

'I play to win,' he said. 'So do you. It's why we clash so much.'

Her eyes came back to his. Hard. Bright. Flashing with such palpable rage he could feel it throbbing in the air that separated them. 'I won't let you win this, Cristiano. You might be able to blackmail me into marrying you, but you can't make me fall in love with you. That's what you want, isn't it? You want me to fall in love with you and then throw it back in my face like I threw back yours.'

'On the contrary, falling in love with me would be most inadvisable,' Cristiano said. 'Falling into bed with me? Well, that may be worth considering.'

Her eyes went as wide as the steering wheel he was resting his arm across. 'But you said you don't—'

'A man can change his mind, can't he?'

Her mouth opened and shut a couple of times, two flags of pink riding high on her cheekbones. 'I'm not going to sleep with you. I don't care how much you blackmail me.'

'Fine. Probably better that way.' He opened his door and proceeded to get out. 'I can get my needs met elsewhere.'

She sprang out of the car before he could get round to her side. 'Oh, no, you don't,' she said, hands on hips. 'You don't get to cheat on me. No way. If you can have lovers then so can I.'

Cristiano slowly shook his head as if dealing with a small, wilfully disobedient child. 'No. I'm the one who makes the rules. You follow them.'

She came at him with a pointed finger, drilling him in the chest like a tiny outraged jackhammer. 'I'm not obeying any of your stupid rules. I'm going to do what I damn well like and you can't stop me.'

Cristiano captured her hand, every cell in his body aching to tug her flush against him and show her what she was doing to him. But he was biding his time, waiting for her to come to him, as he knew in his bones she would. Her fiery nature stirred the banked-down embers of his. The heat was rising in a wildfire of lust, thundering through him like a runaway train on a steep decline.

He wanted her.

Oh, how he *wanted* her.

It was a thirst he couldn't quench with anyone else. A hunger that refused to be satisfied with another's touch. She was in his blood. In his body. She was a fever that had lain dormant until he had walked into her beauty salon and seen her sitting there with that coolly indifferent look on her face.

She wasn't indifferent to him. Not one little bit. He could see it in her eyes, the way they kept darting to his mouth and the way her tongue swept over her lips as if recalling the taste and feel of his crushed to its softness.

Cristiano slid one hand up her warm, silky smooth thigh. 'If we weren't in a public place I would take you right here and now.'

She pushed back from him as if he had suddenly burst into scorching flames. 'Get away from me.'

'Careful, Alice,' he said. 'We're in public. It's time to behave yourself.'

Her eyes went to needle-thin slits, her body visibly quaking with fury. 'Just you wait until I get you alone.'

He smiled and gave a mock shiver of delight. 'I can hardly wait.'

Alice was so angry she could barely read the menu. A red mist was before her eyes at the way he had turned things around so deftly. So he *did* want to marry her. But why? What did he hope to achieve? A bunch of stupid old shares he probably didn't need? She didn't buy that for a second. He wanted to marry her to punish her. To humiliate her.

But the more she thought about the long-term benefits for the short-term pain, she realised she really didn't have a choice. If she wanted to reach the pinnacle of success she had always dreamed of then this was the way to do it, and far quicker than she could ever have imagined.

She remembered his grandmother's villa. That lakeside villa was not some modest little run-down holiday shack. That villa was a luxury resort complete with lush gardens and trickling fountains and marble statues and a swimming pool big enough to set an Olympic record. If she walked away from a gift like that she would be certifiable.

Besides, the old lady had liked her and Alice had

liked her. A lot. She didn't want any paranormal consequences if she didn't accept the bequest with good grace. It was the sensible, respectful thing to do.

The only trouble was Cristiano was part of the deal.

The man who could make her come on the spot by looking at her with those sinfully sexy eyes.

Alice shifted in her seat, painfully aware of the swollen excitement of her body. For a moment there she'd thought he was going to kiss her. His body had been so close to hers she'd felt his warmth, smelt his lemon and lime and hint of leather scent that wreaked such havoc on her senses. She had seen the way his eyes had dipped to her mouth, lingering there as if recalling the way her lips had responded to his in the past. The even more shocking thing was she'd wanted him to. So much her whole body had ached to feel that firm mouth come crashing down on hers. To take the choice away from her.

What was wrong with her?

But wasn't that what he wanted? To show how weak she was when it came to him? He knew her as a maestro knew a difficult instrument. He knew what chords to strike, what strings to pluck, what melodies to play.

Alice was annoyed for thinking she could outsmart him. When had calling his bluff ever worked? He wasn't the type of man to be manipulated. He enjoyed power too much to allow anyone else to control him.

The truth was she had been a little shocked when he'd let her go seven years ago. Shocked and hurt. She'd thought he'd wanted her too much to let her go without a fight. She'd thought he desired her so much he would have moved heaven and earth and planets and whole galaxies to get her back. She'd thought he would contact her within a day or two when he calmed down and apologise for pressuring her with that public proposal.

But he hadn't contacted her.

Not a single word. No phone call. No text or voice-mail message. No flowers. No cards. Days, a week, two weeks went past and still she heard nothing from him. But then she saw a press photo of him in a night-club in Milan with a bevy of beautiful women draped all over him. And a day later another photo with just the one woman—his new mistress. A gorgeous inter-national model. It had driven a stake through her chest to see him getting on with his life as if she had never been the 'only woman in the world' for him. What non-sense. He hadn't loved her at all. He had wanted to own her. To control her.

As if that was ever going to happen.

He might be able to stir her hormones into a fizzing frenzy, but no way was Alice going to let him take over her life. She would marry him to get what she wanted.

You want him.

It was an inconvenient truth but she would deal with it. She had willpower, didn't she? A month-long engage-ment was the first hurdle. It wasn't a long period of time. Anyway, she would be at work most of the time. Sep-tember was still a busy time. And he had his little thing on the side. *Grrr.* Alice wasn't going to show she was jealous about his nubile little Natalia. If he wanted to play around then why should she care? If she was going to be Cristiano's fiancée and then wife, then she would be the worst fiancée and wife in the world.

Alice smiled a *you-ain't-seen-nothing-yet* smile and picked up her wine glass and drained it in a couple of noisy swallows. She put it down on the starched white tablecloth with a distinctive thud. 'Nice drop. So, when do I get a big rock on my finger? Or have you got your old one stashed away in your pocket?'

His dark eyes pulsed like the shimmer off a heat-wave. 'I do, actually.' He reached inside his jacket and took out the ring he'd bought her seven years ago.

Alice took it from the centre of his outstretched palm and slipped it on. 'Slipped' being the operative word. It was loose and the heavy diamond slipped around her finger so it was facing downwards. Those few pounds she'd carried at twenty-one had thankfully been whit-tled off with diet and exercise. The ring hadn't suited her hand back then and it didn't now. Which was per-fectly fine because she didn't want it to suit. It wasn't going to be there long enough for her to worry about it being clumsily big.

'Lovely. I'll be the envy of all my friends.' She looked up to see a furrowed frown between his eyes and gave him a guileless blink. 'Is something wrong?'

His frown relaxed but his mouth lost none of its tight-ness. 'There are some domestic things to discuss. Like where we'll live for the next four weeks before the wed-ding.'

Alice straightened her posture. 'I'm not living with you. I have my own house and—'

'It will seem odd for us not to cohabit. You can move in with me at my hotel or I can move in with you. Your choice.'

Her choice? What a joke. Alice raised her chin to a combative height. 'What if I say no?'

His unwavering gaze made something in her belly turn over. 'How about a compromise? A few nights at your place, a few nights at mine.'

Alice snorted. 'Compromise? You mean you actually *know* what that word means?'

He ignored her taunt. 'After we're married we'll have to live under the one roof, and since my base is in—'

'I'm not moving to Italy so you can squash that thought right now. I have work commitments. I'm solidly booked till Christmas.' Not solidly, but heavily. Not that she was going to tell him that. Why should she give up her career when he wasn't giving up his?

A muscle moved in his jaw. In. Out. In. Out. 'I want you with me. Six months, that's all the will requires. I won't accept any other arrangement.'

Alice gave a mock pout and leaned forward as if she were talking to a spoilt child. 'Oh, poor baby, did you want to have it all your own way?' She sat back with a resounding thump and folded her arms. 'Sorry. No can do.'

Cristiano's eyes hardened. 'Must you always be so damn obstinate?'

'Me, obstinate?' Alice laughed. 'You win the prize for that. A mule has nothing on you. Your heels are dug so deep in the ground you could drill for oil.'

He gave her a droll look. 'I've booked a flight to Italy this Friday. We'll stay the weekend in Stresa so you can get acquainted with your new property. Think of it as a trial honeymoon.'

Honeymoon?

Alice's stomach dropped like an anchor. 'I presume you mean for the sake of appearances?'

A ghost of a smile flirted with the edges of his mouth. 'That depends.'

She disguised a lumpy swallow. 'On what?'

'On whether you have the self-discipline to say no to me.'

Alice gave him a look that would have withered poison ivy. 'Not going to happen, Italian boy. You're getting your needs met elsewhere, remember?'

'Natalia is my personal assistant.'

Alice arched her brow. 'And what, pray tell, does she personally assist you with? Your sex life?'

A smile cocked one side of his mouth, making his eyes crinkle attractively at the corners. Too attractively. So attractively she was having trouble keeping her eyes off it and remembering how sexy it had once felt against her own. 'You're jealous.'

Alice gave a honk of a laugh. 'Yes, of course I am. I'm just so in love with you I can barely stand it. I've been waiting all these years for you to show up and take me back to chain me barefoot to the kitchen sink and make me pregnant.'

His smile disappeared to be replaced by a thin line of white. 'I would've given you a good life, Alice. Better than the one you've got now.'

Alice helped herself to more wine, not caring it was going to her head. 'I love my life. I have my own business. I have my own house. Money. Friends.'

'But you're not happy.'

She stabbed a finger in his direction. 'You know what that is you're doing right there? It's projection. What you're really saying is *you're* not happy.'

'I will be happy when this six months is over,' he said, through tight lips. 'My grandmother had no right to meddle in my affairs.'

Alice toyed with her glass, wondering why his grandmother had taken it upon herself to orchestrate things the way she had. Hadn't Volante Marchetti realised how pointless it would be locking her and Cristiano together? They hated each other. They fought like cage fighters. What good would it serve? They would only end up worse enemies than before.

She realised then, she hadn't yet expressed her condolences for his loss. She knew how much he adored his grandmother. It was another thing she had liked about him—how much he respected the elderly and saw them as gatekeepers of wisdom. 'You must miss her terribly.'

He released a long sigh that sounded rough around the edges. 'Yes.'

'Was she ill for long or was it a sudden—?'

'Pancreatic cancer,' he said. 'Four months from diagnosis to death.'

'It must have been an awful shock.'

'It was, but less so than my parents' and brother's death. She was eighty-five and frail. She was ready to go.'

Alice wondered if he was close to his extended family. He hadn't spoken much about his family back in the day. She knew there were an uncle and an aunt and a few cousins scattered about. But having lost every member of his immediate family must surely be extremely painful, even now. She wasn't that close to her mother, and, while she had some contact with her father since they reconnected a couple of years ago, her extended family were not the sort of people she associated with. But even so, Alice couldn't imagine being all alone in the world.

The waiter came to take their order, and once he left, Cristiano switched the subject as if he didn't want to linger on the subject of his grandmother's passing.

'There are some legal things to see to. I presume you won't object to a prenuptial agreement?'

'No, why should I?' Alice shot him a *don't-call-me-a-gold-digger* glare. 'I want to protect my own assets.'

'Fine. I'll have the papers drawn up and make an appointment for tomorrow.'

He was moving things along so quickly Alice wondered if he was worried she would back out at the last minute and was taking measures so she couldn't. 'How are you going to handle the press on this?' she asked. 'I mean, who is going to buy this is a genuine love match?'

His expression gave nothing away. 'We have a history which makes the lie all the more believable. Everyone loves a love-wins-out-in-the-end story.'

'Well, don't expect me to get all gussied up for the wedding,' Alice said. 'Me in one of those big meringue dresses? Not my thing at all.'

There was a moment or two of silence.

The air seemed to ring with her words as if testing their veracity. Just as well Cristiano didn't know about the stash of bridal magazines she had at home. Dozens of them. It was a silly little pastime but she rationalised it by insisting it helped her follow make-up trends for her clients. And it was a tax deduction.

'You might never get married again,' he said. 'Why not go to town on this one chance to be a princess for the day?'

'You're darn right I'm not getting married again,' Alice said. 'I'm going to be drinking champagne by the bucket once our marriage is over.'

Once our marriage is over.

It was strange to say those words when most people entered marriage thinking it was going to be for ever.

Weddings had never been Alice's fantasy. She hadn't dressed up as a bride as a child or pored over bridal magazines as a teenager. She'd always seen marriage as a trap to keep women enslaved to the patriarchy. A tool to maintain male privilege in society. Women lost financial traction once they married and had kids and few ever truly regained it. She had seen her mother lose self-esteem and money with every failed relationship. Alice had lived in near poverty too often as a child to ever think of getting married herself.

But lately, Alice had dealt with a lot of brides. Happy brides. Brides who were madly in love with their men and their men with them. The excitement of building a future with a man who loved you and wanted to spend his life with you had rubbed off on her even though she'd thought it never would. Every time she prepared a bride's make-up for her big day she wondered what it would be like to be a bride herself. To dress in a beautiful gown and have her hair and make-up done. To walk into a flower-filled church and say the vows that couples for centuries had been saying to each other.

A lot of the brides she had done still came into the salon as regular clients. It might be an isolated statistic, but so far not one of them had separated or divorced. On the contrary, they seemed happier and even more radiant. Several of them had babies and young children now.

It made Alice wonder if her bias was a little unjustified.

'What will you do with your share of the villa once we get an annulment?' he asked.

An annulment? Wait, he was actually *serious* about not sleeping with her? But why the hell not? Alice knew she wasn't going to be asked to strut down a catwalk any time soon but she hadn't had any mirrors explode when she'd walked past, either. 'Of course I'll sell my share. It's the money I want, not the property. I wouldn't be able to maintain a property that size—even a half share in it—not while working and living in London. Old places like that cost a fortune in upkeep.'

Cristiano gave a single nod as if that made perfect sense. But Alice couldn't help feeling he was disappointed in her answer. What did the villa mean to him? Would he want to buy her share back once their marriage came to an end? Her conscience began to prickle her. Why should he be made to pay for something that should rightfully be his?

'Were you expecting your grandmother to leave her villa entirely to you?' Alice asked after a moment.

'Yes and no.' His expression was masked. 'I have enough property of my own without hankering after that old place. But that doesn't mean I want to see it sold to strangers.'

'It must hold a lot of memories for you.'

'It does. Both good and bad.' He reached for his water glass but he didn't drink from it. Instead, his index finger scrawled a swirly clockwise pattern on the condensation on the side of the glass. 'It was a happy place before it became a sad place. Over time it became happy again, mostly due to my grandparents' commitment to making my childhood and adolescence as normal as they could under the circumstances.'

Alice chewed at her lip. When had she ever talked to him like this? *Really* talked? She had tried asking him about his childhood seven years ago but he had always brushed the topic aside. Told her he didn't like talking about it. She had respected that and left well alone. But now she wondered if that had been a mistake. 'It must have been devastating to lose your family like that...'

'And then some.' He let out a small breath and began drawing on his glass in an anti-clockwise fashion this time. 'I still remember the day my parents and brother were killed... I was staying overnight with my grandparents as I'd caught a stomach bug and couldn't go to the party they were attending.' His mouth came up on one side in a rueful slant and his finger left the glass. 'Lucky me. Saved by a rotavirus.'

Alice swallowed against a knot of emotion for the little boy he had been. How lonely and desperate he must have felt to have his family wiped out like that. Never to see them again. Never to have the opportunity to say the words he'd wanted to say. All the questions kids ask their parents about themselves—the funny anecdotes of infancy and childhood that only a parent can relay.

Why hadn't she asked more about how he'd felt when they'd dated? Why had she let him fob her off? Had he been riddled with survivor guilt? Wondering why he had been spared and not his brother? How could it not have an effect on him even now? He had grown up without the most important people by his side. Yes, his grandparents were marvellous substitutes, but they could only ever be his grandparents. He carried the wound of loss in every fibre of his being.

'I wish I'd asked you more about your childhood in the past... You always seemed so...so reluctant to talk about it and I didn't want to pry.'

'I hardly ever talked about it, even to my grandparents.' He continued to stare at his glass, his brow creased in a slight frown. 'I thought it was my family coming back when I heard the car. But it was a police vehicle. My grandfather broke the news to me…'

The trench of his frown deepened.

'It's weird, but I never really thought about that until a few years ago. How it would have been for him to hear his only son and daughter-in-law and eldest grandson had died and then have to break that news to me in a calm and controlled and caring manner. He was so… so unbelievably strong. For me. For Nonna. I never saw him cry but I sometimes heard him. Late at night, in his study, long after Nonna and I and the staff had gone to bed. It was a terrible sound.'

Alice reached across the table and placed her hand over his large warm tanned one where it was resting on the snowy-white tablecloth. He looked up when she touched him, his gaze shadowed by memories. By sadness. Bone-deep sadness. 'I'm so sorry…' she said.

He pulled his hand away and leaned back in his chair. 'It was a long time ago. I never lacked for anything. My grandparents made sure of that.'

Alice wondered if anyone—even grandparents as loving and stable as Cristiano's—could ever make up for the loss of one's parents and only brother. Children were known to be fairly resilient, but how hard it must have been for him to know he would never see his parents and brother again. He had all the money anyone could wish for and yet he couldn't bring back his loved ones. Was that why he was so controlling? So rigid and uncompromising? Was that why he had insisted on marrying her seven years ago and wouldn't take no for an answer? He had wanted stability because he had lost it in childhood.

But Alice hadn't been in love with him back then…*or*

had she? It was a question she always shied away from. She didn't like looking back. Regrets were for people who weren't confident in their ability to make choices.

She had made her choice.

She had chosen her career over marriage.

Not because she couldn't have combined them both, but more because Cristiano wouldn't have wanted her to. He'd wanted her to have babies and stay at home to rear them as his mother had done for him and his brother. He hadn't wanted any talk of nannies or childcare. In his opinion, there was only one way to bring up a family and that was to have a wife and full-time mother running the household.

They had argued about it constantly. For a while, Alice had naively thought he was only doing it to get a rise out of her. That he didn't really think so strongly about the issue but enjoyed the way she reacted when he expressed his opinion. But when he'd dropped that proposal on her, she'd realised he was deadly serious about it. For him there was no middle ground.

Marriage or nothing.

Alice had chosen nothing. Which had been fine when she was twenty-one with her whole life ahead of her. Now, at twenty-eight, with all her peers pairing up and marrying and starting families, and her own biological clock developing a recent and rather annoying and persistent ticking, she wondered if 'nothing' was going to keep her satisfied…if she had ever been so.

They finished their meal without much further conversation. Alice tried a couple of times to talk to him about his hotel plans for London, but he seemed disinclined to talk about anything but the arrangements to do with their marriage next month. His single-minded focus was a little unnerving to say the least. She wondered if he had pulled the drawbridge up on his personal life because she had got him to talk about his childhood in a way he had never done before.

When he led her out of the restaurant she half expected him to suggest they continue the evening by taking her somewhere else for a nightcap or coffee. But he simply drove her home and barely lingered long enough to walk her to the door.

Alice stood in the frame of her front door and watched the red glow of his taillights disappear into the distance. She flatly refused to admit she was disappointed. But when she went inside and closed the door, her beautiful house with its spacious rooms and gorgeous décor had never felt so empty.

CHAPTER FOUR

THE MEETING WITH the lawyer to deal with the prenuptial agreements was held the following day. Cristiano had organised to pick Alice up from the salon but she got held up with a client who had turned up late to her appointment, so when Alice came out to Reception she found Meghan talking to Cristiano, who had been kept waiting for nigh on twenty minutes.

Meghan turned around with a beaming smile. 'Congratulations! Oh, my God, it's so romantic. It's all over social media—everyone's tweeting about it. I knew there was something cooking between you two. I just knew it. You're engaged!'

Alice had never considered herself a consummate actor, but right then and there she thought she was worthy of an Oscar *and* an Emmy.

She moved closer to Cristiano and slipped an arm around his lean waist. 'Thanks. Yes, it is exciting. We're very happy.'

His arm came around hers, his hand coming to rest on the curve of her hip, the heat of his broad palm sending a red-hot current straight to her core. 'Aren't you going to kiss me hello?' he said, smiling down at her.

Alice smiled back through mentally gritted teeth.

'Not in front of my staff. You know how I am about public displays of affection.'

'Oh, I don't mind,' Meghan said, with her hands clasped in front of her as if waiting for the penultimate kiss scene in a romantic movie.

Alice eased out of Cristiano's hold to collect her bag from behind the counter. 'I'll be out for a couple of hours,' she said to Meghan. 'I've called in Suze to help with my Saturday clients while I'm away on the weekend.'

'I'm so happy for you both,' Meghan said. 'Can I do your wedding make-up? Please, please, please? Or are you going to do it yourself?'

'Erm…we're not having that sort of wedding,' Alice said. 'We're going to do things simply—'

'Not have a proper wedding?' Meghan's pretty young face fell as if all her facial muscles had been severed. 'But you *love* weddings. You put so much time and effort into getting your brides ready. You're the best at it in the business. Everyone says so. Why wouldn't you want to be a bride your—?'

'Because I just want to be married without all the fuss,' Alice said before her young employee let slip about the bridal magazines under the counter. Yes, she had two stashes of them—one for clients and one for herself. 'Besides, we're being married next month. There's no time to do anything extravagant. Cristiano's in a hurry, aren't you, darling?'

Cristiano's glinting black gaze left no room for doubt on the subject. 'I've been waiting seven long years to have you back where I want you. I don't want to waste a second more than I have to.'

'Show me your ring!' Meghan said.

Alice took it out of the pocket of her uniform and slipped it back on her finger. 'It's a little loose but—'

'Oh…' Meghan's expression failed to conceal her disappointment. 'It's very…erm…nice.'

'It's not the official one,' Cristiano said. 'That's being designed as we speak.'

'Oh, how wonderful.' Meghan's face brightened as if a dimmer switch had been turned to full beam. 'Alice loves a good engagement ring, don't you, Alice?'

Alice wanted to slip between the polished floorboards of her salon. Why hadn't she been a little more circumspect when examining her clients' engagement rings? She had oohed and aahed over so many beautiful rings. It was the classical settings she loved the most. Simple and elegant instead of big and flashy. She stretched her mouth into a smile. 'Sure do.'

After Meghan's next client came in, Cristiano put a hand beneath Alice's elbow and led her out of the salon. 'Nice kid.'

'Yes…'

And I'm going to make her drink boiling-hot wax when I get back.

'She's very enthusiastic.'

'I should probably warn you there will be paparazzi hanging—uh oh, too late.' His hand on her elbow shifted to go around her waist when a cluster of people with cameras and recording devices surged towards them. 'Let me handle it.'

Alice stood in the circle of his arm and listened to him give a brief interview about their whirlwind romance. He was scarily good at lying. No one would ever think he wasn't in love with her. What her mother was going to say about their engagement was something that was niggling at Alice's conscience. She hadn't yet called her to give her the heads up. She'd been delaying it because she had been so preachy about her mother's multiple marriages. She hadn't attended the last one on principle. How was her mother going to react to this news?

'We'd like to hear a comment from the blushing bride,' a female journalist said, pushing the recording device towards Alice. 'Your reputation as the go-to girl for wedding make-up is on the up and up. Does this mean you'll expand the business into Italy and beyond or will you be keen to start a family?'

Alice blithely ignored the slight pressure increase from Cristiano's fingers and painted on a bright smile. Why should she let him answer for her? She wasn't a ventriloquist's puppet. He might have cornered her in private, but in public, well, that was where she could win a few points back. 'We're going to get started on the baby-making right away, aren't we, darling?'

His eyes sent her a warning. 'I'd like a little bit of time with you all to myself first.'

After the press moved on, Cristiano took her firmly by the hand and led her down the street. 'What the hell were you playing at?'

Alice threw him a glance that could have cut through plate glass. 'Why do women get asked such ridiculous questions? Why didn't that journalist ask you if you were going to give up your career to start a family? Why are women always expected to give up everything they've worked so hard for?'

His mouth was pulled tight. 'I'm not asking you to have a child, for God's sake, Alice. All I'm asking is for six months of your time.'

'I can't believe women still have to put up with this crap,' Alice said. 'It's no one's business but mine if I want a baby.'

'Presumably it would also be your partner's business.'

Alice sent him a sideways glance but his expression gave little away. 'Do you plan on having a family with… with someone else after we're—?'

'No.'

'But you were so keen—'

'It's not something I envisage for myself now.'

Why? Because I ruined your dream of happy families?

Alice didn't like the feeling she'd been the one to change his mind. He would make a wonderful father. Why would he give up that dream of having a family of his own? He had so much to offer a child. Stability. Security. Love. She stopped walking and glanced at him again. 'Did I make you change your mind?'

His eyes met hers for a brief moment before he looked away and continued walking in long purposeful strides. 'We're going to be late for the lawyer if we don't step on it.'

Alice blew out a breath and trotted alongside him. 'I'm a career woman. So shoot me.'

A career woman with a vague sense of something missing…

Cristiano led her into the lawyer's office where they dealt with the business of signing the prenuptial agreements. It was all so cold and clinical it made Alice feel uncomfortable, as if she was breaking some sort of taboo. What about, *What's yours is mine and what's mine is yours*? It was contrary of her to be feeling so piqued because she had her own financial interests to protect, but still it made her wonder, if she had married Cristiano seven years ago, whether he would have insisted on drawing up such a clinical agreement.

The lawyer brought their meeting to a close with the news that a lump sum as promised in the will would be deposited in Alice's bank account now her engagement to Cristiano was official. The money did not have to be refunded if the engagement came to an end as in the marriage not taking place, which was a surprising footnote to Alice.

It was a large sum of money, enough to pay a decent deposit on new premises plus some, if not half, of the mortgage. She found it hard to understand why Volante Marchetti had stipulated that particular clause. Or had his grandmother known Alice would think twice about walking away with such a large amount of money without seeing the whole arrangement through?

When they were leaving the lawyer's office Alice got a call from her mother. She looked at the caller ID and grimaced. 'Hi, Mum, I was about to call you—'

'Tell me I'm dreaming,' her mother said loud enough for Cristiano to hear. Possibly the whole street. 'My daughter—the daughter who swore she would never ever get married—is now getting *married*?'

Alice turned away from Cristiano's satirical expression. 'Yes, it's all happened very quickly and—'

'See?' Her mother sounded smug. 'I told you love hits you out of the blue. When you meet the right one you just know. When's the wedding? I'll have to get something flash to wear. Will you be able to help me pay for something? I don't want to look frumpish. But for God's sake don't invite your father. You'll have to get someone else to walk you down the aisle. Not that he's been a proper father to you anyway, running off with that woman when you were barely out of nappies and carrying on about paying maintenance for all those years. Why you have to have a relationship with him now after all those years of no contact, I will never know. I won't go if he's there.'

'Mum, there's not going to be a big wedding,' Alice said, mentally rolling her eyes at her mother's usual tirade about her father. Twenty-six years was a long time to be bitter, especially as her dad hadn't had an easy time of it since, bringing up a disabled child with his most recent partner. 'We're having a low-key ceremony. We don't want a lot of guests. We just want to keep things simple to make it more…meaningful.'

'Oh, well, if you're too ashamed to have your own mother at your wedding then so be it,' her mother said in a wounded tone. 'I know I'm not posh like some of your precious clients, but I'm the one who brought you into the world and made every sacrifice I could to give you a decent childhood.'

A decent childhood?

Alice wanted to scream in frustration. Nothing about her childhood had been decent. Her mother was the type of woman who didn't feel complete without a man in her life. *Any* man. It didn't matter how bad he was, as long as he fulfilled the role of male partner. During her childhood Alice hadn't known who would be at their flat when she got home from school. There had been a revolving door on her mother's bedroom in her quest to find 'The One'.

There had been numerous partners over the years,

two of whom subsequently became husbands. The second husband after Alice's father had been a financial control freak and heavy drinker who used his fists and filthy tongue when he didn't get his own way. The third had made a pass at Alice the day her mother introduced her to him, and stolen money from her purse on two other occasions. Alice refused on principle to attend their wedding as a result. And since the wedding, her mother had been subjected to constant put-downs and fault-finding, and such financial hardship she regularly called on Alice for handouts. But if ever Alice said anything about her mother's partner she would defend him as if he were Husband of the Year.

'Mum, I really can't talk now,' she said. 'I'll call you when I get back from my…holiday.' She hung up and slipped her phone back in her bag.

Cristiano was looking at her with a thoughtful expression. 'You okay?'

Alice relaxed her stiff frown but she could see he wasn't fooled for a second. She blew out a breath. 'My mother and I don't agree on some things…lots of things, actually.'

'She didn't ask to meet me?'

Alice gave him a wry twist of her mouth. 'As long as you're male you tick the box as far as she is concerned.'

His frown formed a crevasse between his dark eyes. 'But you're her only child. Why wouldn't she insist on meeting the man who's going to be your husband?'

'She's not the overprotective type. Anyway, I'm an adult. I'm old enough to make my own decisions.'

'Did you tell her about us when you came back from Italy after we broke up?'

Alice thought back to that time, how angry she had

been, and how that anger, once she had cooled down, had turned to a deeper hurt. But her mother had been in the process of separating from her second husband who had found another partner—a woman only a year older than Alice.

Alice had spent hours and hours listening to her mother lament the loss of another marriage—how she was losing the love of her life and how she wouldn't be able to survive without him, *blah, blah, blah*. Alice had suppressed her feelings about her own breakup and channelled her energies into getting her mother through the divorce process, and then on starting up her own beauty business. There hadn't been time to examine too closely how she felt about Cristiano.

Maybe that had been a mistake...

'We don't have that sort of relationship,' Alice said. 'Not all mothers and daughters are best friends.'

'What about your father? Do you ever see him?'

'I didn't use to,' Alice said. 'But he tracked me down a couple of years ago. We meet up occasionally. Mostly when he needs money.'

Why did you tell him that?

His frown deepened. 'You don't give it to him, do you?'

Alice didn't want to go into the complex details of her relationship with her father. Charles *call-me-Chas* Piper was a happy-go-lucky charmer who, in spite of everything he had done and not done as a father, she couldn't help feeling a little sorry for. He was a hobby gambler and a regular drinker, but to his credit—after years of abandoning partners once he got bored—he had stayed with the young woman he'd married a few years ago. They had a son with severe autism and money was always tight on getting little Sam the support and care he needed.

Alice was a soft touch when it came to people with special needs. She told herself the money she gave to her father was for Sam, even though deep down she knew some of it would be spent on other things. But she figured her father and his partner Tania surely deserved something for themselves after everything they had been through. 'He's my father. He's not a bad person—just an unlucky one.'

'Unlucky in what way?'

Alice shook her hair back and readjusted the strap of her bag over her shoulder. 'Are we done? I have to get back to work. I have back-to-back clients this afternoon.'

Cristiano held her gaze for a long moment. 'I'll be around tonight. I'll bring dinner.'

Alice sent him a reproachful look. 'Here's a lesson in manners for you. What you say is: Would you be free this evening? I would like to bring you dinner. See? Not that hard, is it?'

He ran a lazy hand down the length of her arm. She was wearing a cashmere-blend cardigan over her uniform but still every nerve stood up and took notice, especially when he encountered her hand. His fingers closed around it and then he brought it up to his mouth. Alice watched in a state of mesmerisation when his lips brushed against the backs of her knuckles, his eyes holding hers in a lock that made something fall off a high shelf inside her stomach. The scrape of his stubble sent a shockwave of lust straight between her thighs. The clean sharp citrus scent of his aftershave teased her senses until she felt slightly drunk. She couldn't stop staring at his mouth—the shape of it was pure male perfection. Strong and firm, and yet with a sensual curve that could unravel her self-control in a hummingbird's heartbeat.

'Are you free this evening?' he said. 'I would like to bring you dinner.'

Alice could have done with a bit of that self-control right about now. She knew saying yes would be saying yes to other things besides dinner. How long would she be able to resist that mouth? Those hands? That body? So far he hadn't kissed her. So far. But how long before he did? 'Yes, I'm free.' *Sucker.*

A smile lifted the edges of his mouth and he released her hand. 'I'll look forward to it.'

Cristiano walked back to his hotel after he left Alice at her salon. His mind ran back over their conversation. In the past she had told him a bit about her background but he hadn't realised—or been astute enough back then—to read between the lines. He had been quietly envious of her having both parents still living so hadn't been able to see how complicated her relationship was with both of her parents. Her mother sounded like a petulant child, and her father asking Alice for money now he was back in her life after years of no contact was nothing short of scandalous.

But one thing he did know was that kids—no matter how difficult they were—loved their parents. It was a fact of nature. Bonds were created in childhood and it took a lot to destroy them.

Alice had been adamant about not marrying. She had voiced her opinions on the subject volubly. Heatedly. Stridently. He had—naively, perhaps—thought she was only saying it because she hadn't wanted to come across as a gold-digger. He was well aware of how his wealth made him an attractive prospect for a woman who was looking for security. That was another fact of nature. Women had good reason to want to connect with a man who could provide for her once it came time to have children.

But Alice insisted she didn't want children. That was another thing he didn't take all that seriously back then. What young woman of twenty-one wanted children at that stage of their lives? He'd been confident—too confident—she would change her mind once they were married.

Cristiano had been too proud to go after her when she'd rejected his proposal. Proud and angry. Bitterly, blindingly angry. He'd expected her to come crawling back. That was another thing he'd been far too confident about. He'd thought she'd go home and think about what she was throwing away and call him and say she'd changed her mind. But the only thing she'd changed was her phone number.

That was the nail that finally closed the lid on his hopes.

But now he wondered what was really behind Alice's adamant stance on marriage. Lots of kids of divorced parents went on to have successful marriages themselves. Was it because she was a staunchly independent career woman? Having a career didn't mean you had to give up everything else. Did she still hold those views or had she shifted some ground over the passage of time?

Her friendly little employee gave the impression Alice was a big fan of weddings. Word on the street was she was the go-to girl for bridal make-up. Did that mean she secretly dreamed of a white wedding with all the trimmings? But she hadn't dated anyone seriously in years. That was another thing he'd found out from her loquacious little workmate. Alice virtually lived and breathed work. She had no social life to speak of and always made excuses when friends tried to hook her up with potential dates.

He didn't want to admit how pleased he was about that. If he hadn't been happy for the last seven years then why the hell should she be? But then, she was a tetchy little thing. Not many men would put up with her quick temper and acid tongue. But behind that prickly exterior was a warm-hearted person. Some of the time.

Funny, but her sharp tongue had been one of the things he'd most admired about her back then. The fact she didn't kowtow to him because he was super rich. Losing his parents so young had made everyone—even his grandparents at times—tiptoe around him. No one ever said no to him or argued the point with him. He was so used to getting his own way he hadn't factored in anyone else's opinion on things until he'd met Alice. She never ran away from an argument or a difference of view. She didn't cave in to please him. She stood her ground and wouldn't budge if she believed she was in the right.

But what if she had changed? What if those rigidly held opinions on marriage and children had softened? *Too bad.*

Cristiano wasn't going down that road again. Family life was for people who could handle the risk of losing it in the blink of an eye. He had already lost one family. He wasn't going to sign up for a second.

His grandmother's machinations meant he had no choice but to jump through the hoops like an obedient circus dog, but that was as far as it would go. He had considered a register office ceremony but decided if he was going to get married then it would be the old-fashioned way. Besides, his *nonna* would come back to haunt him if he didn't repeat those wedding vows in front of a priest.

But you don't love Alice now.

Cristiano ignored the prod of his conscience. God would have to forgive him for borrowing His house of worship as a means to an end. Over the years he had downgraded his feelings. Told himself he hadn't loved Alice at all. It was too confronting, too painful to admit he had loved her and lost her. Instead he filed it away as nothing but a lust fest. A mad, once-in-a-lifetime passion that had taken him over like a raging fever. Consuming rational thought. Sideswiping common sense.

He was no longer that idealistic young man blinded by lust. He was older, wiser, harder. He could control his passion. He could control his desire. He could control his emotions.

A quiet church wedding with limited guests was the only way to go. There would be no chance of Alice misreading his motivations if he kept things clean and simple. And less complicated when it came time to end it.

For end it he would.

CHAPTER FIVE

ALICE TOLD HERSELF there was no reason she should be cleaning her house like someone with a serious case of obsessive-compulsive disorder but she wasn't going to have Cristiano counting the dust bunnies hiding under the sofa. She had never been able to justify employing someone to clean because she was hardly at home to make much of a mess.

Once she'd sorted the house, she got working on herself. That saying about plumbers with leaky taps equally applied to beauticians. When was the last time she'd waxed her legs? And as for a bikini wax…? It was so overgrown her 'lady land' looked as if Sleeping Beauty had taken up residence.

Well, come to think of it, maybe she had.

It had been about a hundred years since there had been any activity down there.

Alice reached for her perfume and spritzed her wrists and neck. This was probably a good time to ask herself why she was going to all this trouble.

You are so going to sleep with him.

She slammed the door on the thought. No. Not going to happen. She could resist him. Sure she could. He wasn't that irresistible.

Yikes. Yes, he was.

As long as he didn't kiss her it would be okay. Kissing him would be dangerous. Dangerous because his mouth had the amazing power to make her senses spin out of control like bald tyres on an oil spill.

The doorbell sounded and Alice jumped up and smoothed her skinny jeans down her thighs. She'd figured tight jeans might work as a reminder to her self-control. Not so easy to slip out of sprayed-on denim.

Then why did you put on your best bra and knickers?

Alice was getting a little annoyed with her conscience. Nice underwear was standard. So what if she'd put on her most expensive set? Her girls deserved the best support, didn't they? She opened the front door and tried not to swoon when she saw Cristiano standing there dressed in dark blue denim jeans and a crisp white casual shirt that was rolled up over his tanned forearms. His hair was still damp as if he had not long showered and his jaw was cleanly shaven. 'At least you're on time,' she said.

His gaze travelled over her slowly, smoulderingly, until she wondered if her clothes were going to be singed right off her body and left in a smoking heap on the floor at his feet. 'You look beautiful.'

Alice looked at his empty hands and then around him for any sign of the dinner he'd promised to bring. 'I thought you said you were bringing dinner with you?'

'It will be here soon.'

She stepped back and held the door open, breathing in a delectable whiff of his aftershave when he walked past. She closed the door and linked her hands in front of her body, more to keep them away from the temptation of touching him. 'I got the money,' she said. 'I checked my bank account an hour ago.'

'Good to know the lawyer is doing what he's been paid to do.'

Alice unhooked her hands and used one to tuck a strand of her hair back behind her ear. 'Any idea why your grandmother stipulated that clause? I mean, I could end our engagement right now and still be way out in front financially.'

'You could. But you won't.'

She frowned. 'What makes you so sure?'

He was standing close. So close she could see every individual pinpoint of his recently shaven jaw. So close she could feel the magnetic draw of his body. 'Because you're not the sort of girl who'd take money from an old lady without fulfilling the rest of the wishes she expressed.'

'But I hardly knew your grandmother. I only met her a couple of times. We chatted and all that but hardly long enough for her to want to include me in her last will and testament, I would've thought.'

'Maybe, but she liked you and you liked her.' He waited a beat. 'She saw something in you. A quality she warmed to.'

'Stubbornness?'

He gave a soft laugh. 'That and...other things.'

What other things? Alice wanted to ask.

'Would you like a drink? I have wine and soft drinks or—'

'Later.' He slipped a hand into the inside pocket of his dark blue blazer and took out a ring box from a designer jeweller. 'For you.' He flipped the box open and inside was a gorgeous diamond in a classic setting.

Alice took out the ring and watched as the light above their heads brought out the diamond's brilliance. It was so simple and yet so elegant. She slipped it over her finger and it sat there as if it had been made for her. 'It's…'

'If you say "nice" I will not be answerable for the consequences.'

Alice smiled and kept gazing at the ring. 'Perfect. It's perfect, that's what it is. It's exactly what I would have chosen.'

When she glanced up at him he was frowning. 'Would you have preferred that?' he asked. 'To choose it yourself?'

Alice had never seen him look so uncertain before. 'I guess if this was a normal situation then maybe I would have. But it's fine since it's not. Anyway, I'll give this back once we're done.'

'I don't want it back.'

'But it's—'

'It's yours, Alice. You can do what you want with it when we're through.' He released a short breath. 'I'm sorry. I should have consulted you on what you'd like. I didn't think. The old one was so…so inappropriate. I'm annoyed I didn't see that before. It didn't suit your hand at all.'

Alice shifted her lips from side to side. This was a new thing—Cristiano admitting to getting something wrong. 'Just your luck to pick someone so independent she can't even let a guy choose a ring for her.'

'It wasn't just the ring I got wrong, though, was it?'

Alice couldn't hold the sudden intensity of his gaze. She looked at the new ring instead and angled her hand so the light caught the facets of the diamond. 'Thing is, my mother has three rings, all of them ghastly. She pretended to love them when her partners gave them to her. I always wondered why she did that.' She glanced at him again. 'Surely if you're going to marry someone and agree to spend the rest of your life with them you'd be honest with them from the get-go?'

His mouth lifted in a rueful smile. 'That was another quality my grandmother liked in you. Honesty. You didn't filter your opinions. You spoke your mind and to hell with anyone who didn't agree with you.'

Alice couldn't help a tiny cringe at how outspoken she had been back then. She had been very much 'my way or the highway' in her thinking. She'd held strong opinions on issues that, in hindsight, she had not researched well enough to warrant holding such strident views. How many people must she have offended, or even hurt, by expressing such unqualified and oftentimes ignorant opinions? Back then she had considered the notion of compromise or backing down as a weakness, a flaw. But now…now she wondered if being able to give and take, and listen rather than speak, was a more mature and balanced way to approach life.

'I'm surprised your grandmother even remembered me. You and I were only together six weeks. There must've been a lot of women in your life since. I don't suppose she's left each of them—?'

'No. Just you.'

Alice wanted to ask if he had fallen in love with any of them but knew it would make him think she was jealous. Which to her great annoyance she was. It didn't seem fair that he'd moved on with his life so quickly when she had supposedly been his soul mate. What if she had changed her mind in the weeks after their breakup? Too bad, because he'd already partnered up with someone else.

'I know what you're thinking,' Cristiano said. 'You're thinking I didn't take long to replace you, yes?'

Alice hadn't realised her expression was so transparent. Or maybe he really could read her mind. Scary thought. 'You made no secret of your love-life. It was splashed over every gossip magazine.'

His gaze was unwavering. 'And that bothered you?'

Alice frowned. 'Why wouldn't it bother me? You bought me a frightfully expensive ring and told me I was the only woman in the world for you, and yet within a week or two of me ending our relationship, you're off with someone else.'

'Did you change your mind?'

'No, of course not.' Alice knew she had answered too quickly by the way one of his brows rose in an arc. 'I was just annoyed you hadn't…'

'Hadn't what?'

She let out a gusty little breath. 'Missed me.'

He stepped closer and placed his hands on the tops of her shoulders. 'You think I didn't miss you?'

Alice couldn't shift her gaze from his mouth. It was drawn there by a desire she could not override with self-discipline or common sense. The warmth of his hands was burning through her clothes, setting her skin on fire. Making her aware of his male body standing close—so close she could sense the stirring of his blood in tune with her own. She placed her hands flat against his chest, touching him, feeling the heat and strength of him.

Wanting him.

The deep thud-pitty-thud of his heart beneath her

palm reverberated through her body, sounding an erotic echo deep in the centre of her being. She curled her fingers into the fabric of his shirt, not caring that it caused it to crumple and the tiny buttons to strain against the buttonholes. She closed the hair's breadth distance between their bodies, an electric frisson coursing through her at the intimate contact.

What did it matter if she was the one to cave in first? It was what she wanted. What they both wanted. She had missed touching him.

Being held.

Being wanted.

Alice stepped up on tiptoe and pressed a barely touching kiss to the side of his mouth, her lips tingling from the contact with his newly shaven skin. Cristiano's minty fresh breath mingled with hers but he didn't take over the kiss. Was he trying to prove how strong he was compared to her? That he could resist her even if she couldn't resist him? She smiled to herself. She knew just how to get him to weaken. She sent the tip of her tongue out and licked the surface of his bottom lip. A cat-like lick to remind him of how clever she was with her tongue. How she had made him collapse at the knees when she got to work on him.

His hands went from her shoulders to her hips, tugging her so close she could feel the hardened, pulsing ridge of him against her belly. 'Haven't you heard that saying about playing with fire?'

Alice shamelessly stoked the fire by rubbing her pelvis in a circular motion against his. 'You want me.'

'I didn't say I didn't.'

'But you said our marriage won't be—'

'So, that rankled, did it?' A teasing glint danced in his eyes. 'I thought it might.'

So he'd said that deliberately to get a rise out of her? Did he want her or not? Or was he just playing with her? Letting her dangle like a pathetic mouse being tortured by a mean-spirited cat. Alice pursed her lips and tried to pull back but his hands were clamped on her hips. 'Let me go.'

'Is that really what you want?'

'Yes.' She all but spat the word out. But inside her body was screaming. *No-o-o-o!*

'Fine.' He dropped his hands and stepped away, a knowing smile lifting the edges of his mouth. 'No harm done, *si*? But if you change your mind, you know where to find me.'

Alice ground her teeth so hard she thought her molars were going to crack. The only harm done was to her pride. Why had she allowed him to get the upper hand? He'd fooled her into thinking he had changed. He had even expressed his regret—albeit in veiled terms— about the ring he'd bought in the past. But at the heart of it all he wanted to prove was he had moved on from her—that he hadn't got any lingering feelings where she was concerned. He hadn't missed her one little bit. He'd soon found someone else to scratch his itch. He might still desire her, but that was all he wanted from her now. Sex.

How different from what he had offered her in the past. Back then he'd promised her the world—his heart, his soul, his love. Now all he promised was mind-blowing, body-tingling sex. A trashy little affair to pass the time until they could end their relationship once they'd fulfilled the terms of his grandmother's will. How could she agree to something like that when it was so unlike what they'd had before?

Because you still want him, that's why.

Not that much.

Are you sure about that?

Alice wasn't so sure about a lot of things any more. The desire Cristiano stirred in her refused to bank down in spite of all her efforts to control her response to him. It was like simmering coals deep in her body, just waiting to erupt into leaping, quick-licking flames. Could she risk an affair with him and to hell with the consequences? She could keep her feelings separate. That was what men did without any bother. Why couldn't she?

'I'm not going to let you play games with me, Cristiano.'

'Games, *cara*?' His brow rose above one eye. 'Isn't that your specialty?'

Alice pressed her lips together. 'You won't win this. You think you can get me to beg? Think again. I don't want you anything like the way you want me.'

A satirical light entered his gaze. 'There's one simple way to test that little theory of yours. Would you like to try it?'

Alice stepped two more steps back and folded her arms across her body. 'If you come any closer I'll… I'll bite you.'

'Promise?' His sexy half-smile made something deep in her belly turn over.

The doorbell sounded and Cristiano reached past her to answer it. 'That will be our dinner.'

Cristiano carried the meal he'd organised to be delivered from a nearby restaurant through to where Alice had set up the dining table. She was angry with him for not acting on her invitation. He'd wanted to. So much his entire body throbbed with the need to crush his mouth to hers. Still throbbed. He wanted her but on his terms, not hers. What was she playing at anyway? A teasing kiss or two to prove he had no resistance when it came to her?

That he'd *missed* her?

He'd missed her all right. He'd missed her so damn much it had taken him months to sleep with another woman. The women he'd been seen in public with after their breakup were just casual dates, but he had not pursued them any further. A drink or two, a dance, a dinner or a show—that was all. He hadn't been able to stop himself comparing them to Alice. Finding fault with their looks, their clothes, their manners or their conversation—or lack of it. Even when he did start sleeping with partners, he'd felt something wasn't quite right. But he'd put that down to the fact of how different having a hook up or fling was from having a relationship where you truly got to know the person.

But had he known Alice? Truly known her? He hadn't even got her taste right in rings. Not that any ring would have been right given she looked upon marriage as a form of modern-day slavery.

Not that his views back then had helped. It had taken him a few more years than he was proud of to see where Alice had been coming from. His conservative views on marriage had undergone some significant changes. He no longer saw a woman's role in such black and white terms. He understood the need for women to have the opportunity to reach their potential career-wise in the way most men took for granted. Having both a career and a family was something as a young man he had never questioned, and yet for a woman it had so many more implications. Careers and children were hard to juggle if one wanted to do both things well. Even men these days were starting to question the high demands of corporate life and how it impacted on their relationships at home.

But while Cristiano might have changed some of his strong views, he wasn't so sure Alice had changed hers. She seemed even more committed to her career, with expansion plans on the horizon. She hardly ever dated, according to her helpful employee Meghan. Why was that? Alice was a normal healthy young woman in the prime of her life. Why wouldn't she be out there doing what every girl her age did? She didn't even have a housemate. She lived all alone in a gorgeous house that looked as if it could be in a beautiful homes magazine.

But was she happy?

Cristiano didn't think so…but then, maybe that was because he was annoyed she hadn't been as committed to him as he had been to her. Or was it more because she was seemingly happy and he wasn't? He hadn't been happy, not from the moment she'd told him they were over. How had he got it so screwed up? He'd thought she loved him. Her body had if not her heart. She had been his most giving lover, and without doubt the most exciting. He had blithely thought she would accept his proposal with unbounded enthusiasm.

Blithely or arrogantly?

He hadn't expected her to say no because back then he had been the one with the money and status. He was the Prize Catch as the press put it. He had chosen the restaurant that night in which to deliver his proposal, not out of design but eagerness. That was what annoyed him the most. He had been too impatient. He had picked the ring up on the way to meet her after work. That, too, had been more impulse than plan. He had walked past a high-end jeweller's and that had been it. Decision made. No thought had gone into it. It had simply *felt* like the right thing to do.

Which showed how much feelings weren't to be trusted. He had been so excited about his dreams for their future, so focussed on securing her commitment, that he hadn't picked up on her mood. He'd been like a goofy kid unable to contain himself. If he had waited until they got home to his villa in Milan would she have given him a different answer? If he had given her more time? A few days, weeks or even months? Would she have felt less pressured? Less cornered?

So what's changed?

Cristiano winced at the nudge of his conscience. He had cornered her again. Forced her to bend to his will. He had a goal to achieve. He was focussing on the big picture instead of examining the finer detail.

But he had to get those shares back before his cousin blew the lot. And he had to do whatever it took to keep the villa otherwise it would go to some stranger. He didn't have a choice any more than Alice did.

It was marry her or lose a third of his family's company and the villa he knew as home.

As if he were going to allow *that* to happen.

CHAPTER SIX

AFTER DINNER THAT night, Alice didn't see Cristiano again until Friday when he picked her up to take her to the airport for their flight to Italy. Being stressed from having to organise another beauty therapist to cover her for the weekend when her usual girl had to pull out at the last minute, as well as see her own clients and get away on time, hadn't done her mood any favours. She hadn't had time to refresh her make-up or send a brush through her hair. And God only knew what she'd thrown in her overnight bag this morning when she'd missed her alarm and had to pack in a frantic hurry. How dared Cristiano look so damn fresh and clean and smell so divine? Didn't he have to work and sweat like normal people?

Once they were seated on the plane in business class—*of course*—Alice leaned her head back against the headrest and closed her eyes. 'You would not believe the day I've had.'

Cristiano's hand came to rest on top of hers where it was lying on the armrest. 'Want to tell me about it?'

Alice looked at his hand on top of hers. His skin was so tanned and the sprinkle of dark hair so masculine compared to the smooth, pale skin of hers. His fingers curled around her hand, reminding her of the way his strong powerful body gathered her close in the past. His thumb began an idle stroking across the back of her hand, a mesmerising rhythm that stirred her blood. She disguised a little shiver…or at least hoped she did.

'First, I didn't hear my alarm. My phone was on silent last night because I— Well, anyway. Then I had a staffing issue, which is the bane of my life as a small business owner. Suze, the girl I'd organised to come in to do my Saturday clients, caught a stomach virus. To her credit, she was prepared to work but I can't expose my clients to illness. It wouldn't be fair to them if they caught it.'

Alice stopped to draw breath to find him looking at her with an unwavering gaze.

'Am I boring you?'

His lips curved upwards in a slow smile. 'Not a bit. Go on.'

Alice had trouble remembering what she'd been talking about. All she could think of was how delicious his mouth looked when he smiled. Not a mocking smile, but a smile that said: *You're fascinating to me.* His eyes too made her brain scramble. Intensely dark, fringed with thick black eyelashes her clients would have paid a fortune to graft on.

'Erm…so then I worked through my clients and two were late, which is a nightmare because it has a knock-on effect that makes me late for my next client and so on and so on. And then, my last client wanted to talk once I'd done her waxing. Her husband is unwell—he just got diagnosed with cancer. I could hardly rush her out the door, now could I?'

'Of course not.'

She let out a long exhausted-sounding breath. 'Beauty therapists are like hairdressers. No wonder we're called therapists. Half the time I'm more of a psychologist than I am anything else.'

His hand picked up hers and turned it over, his thumb stroking the inside of her palm in a slow circular pattern that made every rigid muscle in her back soften like honey in a heatwave. 'You enjoy your work, though, don't you?'

Alice didn't even have to think about her answer. 'I love it. I love being able to make women—and it's mostly women, but I have male clients too—feel good about themselves. I like the skin-care element too. I've been able to help numerous clients with troubled skin. Nothing lifts self-esteem more than feeling good about how you look.'

'So how did the wedding arm of your business come about?'

Alice couldn't remember talking to anyone this much about her work other than her employees and a couple of girlfriends. Her mother never showed much interest—she was always too worked up about her own issues and only required Alice to listen, not talk.

'Sort of by accident or serendipity. I did the make-up for a bride about five years ago, and then her bridesmaid chose me, and then she told her friends, and everything built up from there. Word of mouth still rules in spite of the digital age.'

Cristiano's thumb was on her pulse now, that same slow stroking motion on the underside of her wrist making her sink even further into the plush leather seat. 'So tell me about your expansion plans.'

'Well…my salon in Chelsea is getting too small

when I do weddings as well as normal clients,' Alice said. 'My regular clients aren't too happy if I book the salon out too many Saturdays in a row for weddings. I have a dream to set up a luxury wedding spa where brides and the wedding party can be the focus of attention. There will be an area for official photos or glamour shoots too. Of course I'll have to move between both salons at first, but ultimately I'd like to concentrate on the wedding side of things.'

'Because you have a thing about weddings?'

Alice gave him a beady look. 'The *money*. Weddings bring in the money, especially high-profile ones.'

His thumb stroked the fleshy pad of hers, making her legs feel as if someone had removed all the bones. 'You don't find it slightly…ironic?'

'Ironic I want to make money?'

He smiled a crooked smile. 'You know what I mean, Alice.'

Aleece.

Oh, dear Lord, how was she supposed to stay sane when he said her name like that?

She gave a little shrug. 'Just because I do a lot of bridal make-up doesn't mean I want to be one myself. You own and operate hotels, does that mean you want to live in one?'

His eyes didn't once leave hers. 'Not all marriages are slave camps. When a good marriage works it can be a wonderful thing.'

Alice gave him a pointed look. 'If you think it's so wonderful then why aren't you married by now?'

His thumb traced over the diamond on her left hand, his eyes still locked on hers. 'If all goes to plan I soon will be.'

Alice concealed a little swallow. 'But it's not like ours is going to be a normal one.'

'It could be if that's what you want.'

She frowned. 'You mean...last for ever?'

'No.'

Did he have to sound so damned emphatic?

'I meant we could have our fun while it lasts.'

Not for ever? Just 'fun' for now. Alice shifted her lips from side to side. 'If I agreed to...to having fun with you, does that mean you'll be having fun with other people at the same time?'

His mouth tilted in another smile. 'From what I remember of the fun we had together, I don't think I'd have the energy for anyone else.'

Alice held his gaze for a long moment. Was this wise? Offering to have an affair with him for the short duration of their engagement and marriage? What kind of arrangement was that? And could she trust him to remain faithful?

Funny, but she felt she could. He might have changed in other ways but she couldn't see him cheating on a partner. He wasn't that sort of man. 'Thing is... I haven't had a lot of fun just lately so you might be disappointed in what I bring to the...erm...game.' It seemed the right choice of word, all things considered.

Cristiano brought her hand up to his mouth, pressing his lips to the tops of her fingers, all the while holding her gaze with the steadiness of his. 'I can bring you up to speed in one session.'

I can well believe it. Alice tried but failed to suppress a frisson-like shiver. 'So...when would you want to...to start having fun?'

He slid a warm hand around the nape of her neck

and drew her inexorably closer, only stopping once her mouth was within a breath of his. 'I'd do you now but I wouldn't want to disturb the other passengers with your screams of pleasure.'

Alice kept her eyes trained on his smiling mouth, her heart leaping in excitement, her whole body trembling with feverish anticipation. Only he could make her sob with pleasure. Sob and scream and shudder from head to foot. How had she resisted him this long? It was crazy to keep denying herself the sensual thrill of his touch. So what if it only lasted a few months? A few months were better than no months. She'd spent the last seven years missing the magic of his lovemaking. Why not enjoy it while it lasted? 'You're not thinking of using one of the bathrooms?'

'No. I'm going to make you wait until we get home.'

Cruel. Cruel. Cruel.

Alice stroked a fingertip over his top lip, following the contours of his vermilion border, his stubble catching on her skin like a thorn on silk. 'I could take things into my own hands...' she said with a suggestive glance.

His eyes glinted and his hand on the back of her neck slid under the curtain of her hair, the slight drag on the roots sending a bolt of fizzing electricity down her spine. 'Hold that thought.'

Alice closed the distance between their mouths, touching hers down on his as softly as a butterfly landing on a petal. She eased back but because his lips were dryer than hers they clung to her softer skin as if they didn't want to let her go. He made a rough sound deep in his throat and brought his lips back to hers in a slow, drugging kiss that made her insides coil and twist and tighten with longing. His tongue entered her mouth in a smooth, deep glide that had a deliciously erotic element to it. It called hers into a sensual dance that made her feminine core contract with need. The kiss went deeper and deeper, drawing from her a response she had never given to anyone else. Shivers coursed through her body—her skin prickling, tingling, and aching for the touch of his hands. Her breasts suddenly felt too small for her bra—they were straining against their lace barrier, desperate to feel the warm, firm possession of his hands. To feel the stroke of his tongue, the hungry suckle of his lips, the sexy scrape of his teeth.

He shifted position, tilting her head to one side as he explored every secret corner of her mouth, the dark shadow of stubble around his mouth and on his chin abrading her softer skin like a fine-grade rasp.

Somehow the thought they were on a crowded plane and couldn't take the kiss any further only heightened the intensity of it. She couldn't remember kissing him in the past without it ending with them making love. Their first kiss had ended in bed. Every kiss of their affair had been the same. It was as if their lips couldn't touch without their bodies being engulfed by raging desire. They hadn't kissed in public other than a quick brush of the lips because she hadn't been comfortable about public displays of affection. Still wasn't, which made it all the more surprising—if not a little shocking—that she was doing it now, within sight and hearing of three hundred fellow passengers.

But every pulse-racing moment of it tantalised her senses until she completely forgot where they were. She spread her fingers through his thick black hair, greedily succouring his mouth as if without it she would die. She made a mewling sound in her throat, her need of him escalating. No one had ever kissed her like this. No one had ever made her feel this way. This madness, this ferocious need that clawed at her core and made every inch of her flesh scream and beg and plead for release.

Cristiano finally pulled back, his hands still cradling her face, his eyes so dark it was impossible to identify his pupils from his irises. He pressed the pad of his thumb to her kiss-swollen lower lip and then to a spot on the middle of her chin. 'I've given you stubble rash.'

Alice traced a fingertip around his mouth, the floor of her stomach giving a kick like a miniature pony when his masculine roughness caught at her skin. 'I'm running an autumn special on lip and chin waxes if you're interested.'

His eyes glinted their amusement. 'Thanks, but I'll pass.'

She stroked a fingertip down the bridge of his nose and then the shallow trench of his philtrum ridge down to where it met his top lip. His lips twitched as if her touch tickled. Then he captured her finger and closed his lips over it, drawing on it while his tongue stroked its underside, his gaze holding hers in a sensual lock that made her insides shudder.

How could it be possible to want any man more than she wanted this one? Was that why she had bolted when he'd pressured her to marry him in the past? Because he was the one man who could make her forget about her promise never to become enslaved to a man. Never to lose her autonomy. Never to need someone so badly they had the power to destroy her. Cristiano had the power to destroy her self-control. He only had to look at her and her self-control folded like a house of cards in a gale-force wind.

Cristiano took one of her hands and threaded his fingers through hers. 'I've been thinking… I don't remember ever kissing you before without it ending in sex.'

Alice ran her tongue over her lips, tasting him. Wanting him. Aching for him. 'I was thinking the same. Freaky, huh?'

His gaze searched hers for a long moment. A small frown tugged at his brow, making a two-pleat fold between his eyes. 'I seem to remember we didn't do a lot of talking back then, either.'

Alice gave him a wry look. 'I don't know about that. I talked but you didn't listen.'

His crooked smile had a faint touch of regret about it. 'We didn't listen to each other.' He released a long sigh and looked at their entwined fingers, his thumb rhythmically stroking the length of hers. 'It was a long time ago, *sì*?'

Alice settled into the seat, resting her head against his shoulder. 'It sure was.'

So much so I feel like a different person now.

CHAPTER SEVEN

IT WAS CLOSE to midnight when they arrived at Cristiano's villa in Milan. Stepping over the threshold was like stepping back through time.

Alice swept her gaze around the stunning entry, taking in the marble floors and the grand staircase that led to the upper floors with its decorative black balustrading. There were priceless chandeliers and wall lights, the marble and bronze statues and artworks that would be the envy of any serious art collector. Some things were the same, and yet others were different. It had been redecorated and repainted but it was still Cristiano's home—the place where he had spent the first eleven years of his life until the tragic death of his family.

The villa had been rented out following his parents' and brother's deaths as Cristiano had lived in Stresa with his grandparents. But Alice knew how much this place meant to him. He had spent the happiest years of his life here.

She had spent the happiest six weeks of her life here.

Cristiano took her hand and drew her to his side. 'Having second thoughts?'

Alice turned in the circle of his arms and linked her arms around his neck. 'No. Why would I? It's just sex.'

His gaze held hers for a long beat. 'You're not worried about the boundaries blurring?'

Worried? Damn straight, I'm worried.

'No,' Alice said. 'But clearly you are. What are you worried about? That you might fall in love with me all over again?'

A steel shutter slammed down at the backs of his eyes. 'I told you before—I wasn't in love with you. I was in lust.' He dropped his hold and stepped away from her. 'I'll take the bags up. You go on ahead. I'll be up in a minute.'

Alice stood without moving. Did he have to make it sound so…so clinical? He was making her feel like someone he'd picked up in a bar and brought home for a quick tumble. Where was the man who had once carried her up those stairs like an old-time Hollywood-movie hero? Who had treated her like a princess instead of a prostitute?

'Are any of your household staff here?'

'No. I gave them the night off. I called them before we left London.'

Alice could sense he was annoyed with her. Every muscle in his face was pulled tight, especially around his mouth, leaving it flat and white-tipped.

'Why don't we go up together?' she said.

'You know where my bedroom is.'

Alice lifted her chin. 'Oh, I get it. You want to play I'm-the-John-and-you're-the-hooker? Fine—I can do that.'

She shrugged off her light coat and let it drop to the floor. Then she unzipped her dress and let it puddle at her feet before she stepped out of it, leaving her in bra and knickers and heels.

His eyes turned black, his mouth compressed until his lips disappeared. 'Don't.'

'Don't what?' Alice said, unhooking her bra and tossing it to the floor near his feet. 'I'm having fun, aren't you?'

He kicked her bra out of the way and came to her before she could remove anything else. He took her by the upper arms, his fingers gripping her so tightly she was sure they would leave marks. 'Why must you always fight me at every turn?' he said.

Alice glared back at him. 'I'll fight you until you start treating me as an equal.'

'Then start behaving like an adult instead of a child.'

She pushed her naked breasts against the hard wall of his chest. 'How's this for acting like a grown-up?' She slid her hand down between their bodies to touch his swollen length. 'And this?'

His mouth came crashing down on hers as if some formerly strong leash of self-control inside him had finally snapped. It wasn't a kiss of tenderness, of exploring and rediscovering, but a kiss of raw, rampant hunger.

Alice kissed him back with the same frantic need, their tongues duelling, fighting—a heated, potent combat that made her senses careen out of control. She tore at his clothes, tugging off his shirt with no concern for the buttons. She barely registered the *plink*, *plink*, *plink* of them hitting the marble floor. Next she unhooked his belt and slipped it from his trouser lugs, letting it drop to the floor at their feet.

His hands shoved her knickers down past her thighs, his fingers stroking her damp heat with devastating expertise. The pleasure came at her from nowhere, ambushing her, throwing her into a whirling tailspin that left her gasping.

But no way was she allowing this to be a one-way affair. She ripped his zipper down and freed him into her hands, massaging him as she fed off his mouth, using her tongue against his to remind him of the sensual assault she had in mind for him. He made a guttural sound—a sound so utterly primal it made her insides quiver in excitement.

He wrenched her hand away with a muttered curse, his mouth coming back down on hers with a fireball of passion. He walked her backwards to the nearest wall, part walk, part stumble, and roughly stepped out of his trousers and shoes.

Alice broke the kiss to peel her knickers the rest of the way down her legs and kick off her heels. Cristiano tugged her by the hips back against him, letting her feel the full force of his arousal. Her hand went to him again, while her eyes met his. She loved watching the waves of pleasure contort his handsome features. It was the only time she had ever seen him lose control.

'Wait,' he said, breathing hard. 'Condom call.'

Alice would have thrown caution to one side like her clothes, but knew it would be irresponsible given their circumstances. Not that she didn't allow herself a tiny moment, while he sourced a condom from his wallet, to wonder what it would be like to carry his child.

Cristiano came back to her, one hand going to the wall next to her head, his mouth pressing a hot kiss to the side of her neck, and then over her collarbone and then to her breasts. His tongue stroked each upper curve before circling the nipple, in ever tightening circles until he took the nipple into his mouth, drawing on it in a sensual suck that made the hairs on Alice's head stand on end as if pulled from above.

He kissed his way back up to her mouth, taking it in a deep, plundering kiss that left her clawing at his body for the release she craved. He moved between her legs, lifting one of her legs up and anchoring it on his hip before entering her with a sure, swift thrust that made her gasp out loud.

It had been so long!

He set a fast rhythm as if he knew the sweet and savage agony her body was going through. He drove into her moist heat with determined purpose, his breathing just as ragged as hers. Alice gripped him by the shoulders, her fingers digging into his muscled flesh as the wave broke over her. A smashing wave that tossed her into a spinning whirlpool that shook and shuddered through her body. And then another and another followed in its wake, leaving her boneless, spent and quivering all over with aftershocks.

He continued to rock against her until he came with a deep groan of release, his body shuddering as it emptied, his breath hot and rapid against the side of her neck.

Alice unlocked her fingers and slid her hands down his arms and back up again. 'You certainly haven't lost your touch. But I guess you've had plenty of practice.'

He pulled away from her and removed the condom. Then he bent to pick up his trousers and stepped back into them. 'I'm not going to apologise for having a life.'

Alice stepped past him and scooped up his shirt and slipped her arms through the sleeves, drawing it around her naked body, figuring it was quicker than fumbling around the floor for her clothes, which seemed to be strewn from one end of the foyer to the other. 'Are you suggesting I haven't got one?'

He gave her a levelling look. 'You haven't dated in over a year. Why?'

Alice pursed her lips, locking her arms even tighter around her body where she was trying to hold his shirt in place. 'I've been busy at work. I'm always too exhausted at the end of the day for trawling around the nightclubs or online for a sex buddy. Thanks to your extremely generous grandmother, I can now indulge myself for the next six months with you. Lucky me.'

A line of tension pulled at his mouth. 'Is that all you want from men? Sex?'

'Not all men,' Alice said. 'Only the ones I can bring myself to sleep with.' She stepped forwards and trailed a fingertip down his bare arm. 'You tick all the boxes. You're rich, good-looking and you know your way around a woman's body. Oh, and you always have a condom handy. That's always a bonus.'

His hand capturing her wrist, he searched her gaze for a long pulsing moment. 'You're twenty-eight years old. Don't you want more for your life now than work and no-strings sex?'

Alice closed her mind to the image it kept throwing up of a tiny dark-haired baby with raisin-black eyes. 'Nope. Do you?'

Cristiano's frown made a roadmap of lines on his forehead. His hand fell away from her arm. 'No.'

Alice bent down and picked up her bra and knickers and bundled them into a ball in her hand. 'Then we've got nothing to worry about, have we? We're both in this for what we can get. You want your company shares and your share of the villa and I want the financial security my share in your grandmother's villa will give me once we fulfil the terms of her will.' She slipped on her heels before adding, 'Although, I'm not sure why you're insisting on having a church wedding. It seems a little over the top given the circumstances.'

'I told you my reasons. I don't want people thinking this is anything but a genuine relationship.'

'All the same, it's going to look pretty bad when we divorce in six months,' Alice said. 'Aren't people going to speculate and wonder how genuine it was then?'

He gave her an unreadable look. 'Perhaps you won't want it to end in six months. You might be enjoying yourself too much.'

Alice laughed. 'Funny man. You're good in bed, but not *that* good.'

He sent a lazy fingertip over the back of her hand where it was holding his shirt in place. 'Speaking of bed… I hope I didn't rush you just then?'

'Did you hear me complaining?'

A small smile lifted one corner of his mouth. He sent the same fingertip down the slope of her cheek, stopping beneath her chin to lift it so her gaze was on a level with his. 'I want you like I've wanted no other woman.'

Alice gave up trying to hold his shirt together and linked her arms around his waist instead. 'I bet you say that to every woman you've brought back here.'

He made a twisted movement of his mouth. 'You might not believe this, but I've never brought anyone back here. For a drink or dinner, yes, but not to have sex. Not since you.'

Alice did find it hard to believe. But why hadn't he brought anyone back here? Did it mean he had loved her after all? That he couldn't bear to have anyone here where he had made such passionate love to her? But he was so adamant now he hadn't been in love with her back then. 'But why not?'

His eyes dipped to her mouth but whether it was because he was thinking of kissing her again or avoiding her gaze she couldn't be sure. 'Every room reminded me of you.' He waited a beat before returning his eyes to hers. 'It was…off-putting.'

'It must have cost you a fortune in hotels,' Alice said.

His crooked smile made her insides shift. 'The upside of owning hotels is I don't get to pay for accommodation.'

'Lucky you.'

His hands went to her hips, holding her against the stiffening of his body. The sensation of him swelling against her stirred her blood, making her aware of the tingling nerve endings deep in her core. His mouth came down and covered hers in a long, slow kiss that ramped up her desire to a new level.

Alice returned his kiss, her tongue tangling with his in a sexy tango that made him tug her harder against him as if he couldn't bear to have any distance between them. She moved her hands up and down his back and shoulders, delighting in the freedom to touch him, to stroke him, to feel his sculpted muscles tense and flex under her caressing touch.

She couldn't get it out of her mind—he hadn't brought anyone back here since her. Not one woman. No one had shared his bed with him but her.

Cristiano's hands went from her hips to scoop her up in his arms. 'Time for bed?'

Alice played with the ends of his hair that brushed

his neck. 'You don't have to carry me. I'm too heavy. You'll herniate a disc or something.'

He pressed a brief hard kiss to her lips. 'You're a lightweight. I lift weights that weigh more than you.'

He had the muscles to prove it. She could feel them bunching and tensing under her knees and her back where his arms were holding her, a heady reminder of how strong he was and how potently male.

He took her to his bedroom, which had been re-decorated since she had last been there. Had he tried to remove every memory of his time with her? Tried and failed? It was now decorated in a soft mushroom grey on a feature wall behind the bedhead, with white walls and ceiling, and white linen on the king-sized bed with a matching grey throw placed neatly on the end. There was a grey velvet linen-box-like seat at the foot of the bed half the height of the mattress. The carpet was a soft cream that threatened to swallow her up to the knees when Cristiano placed her on her feet beside the bed.

Alice kept her arms linked around his neck, pushing her body against the warm, hard frame of his. 'You've redecorated since I was last in here.'

'Yes.' He nibbled at her earlobe, sending a frisson scooting down her spine. 'Not that it worked. I still couldn't bring myself to make love with anyone in here. I spent a veritable fortune for nothing. Like it?'

'It's gorgeous.'

'Like you.' He kept kissing her neck, nipping and licking at the sensitive flesh.

Alice couldn't help a thrill of pleasure at his compliment. She didn't see beauty when she looked in the mirror. What woman did? She only saw the things she wished she could change. But when Cristiano looked at her with his dark eyes glittering with desire, she felt beautiful and desirable in a way she never felt with anyone else.

His mouth came to hers in a searing kiss, his tongue delving between her lips in search of hers. She gave herself up to the kiss, a soft whimper escaping her lips when he peeled his shirt away from her body and took possession of one of her breasts in his hand. The warm expertise of his touch made her skin tingle and her nipples tighten into buds. He rolled his thumb over her nipple, his hand then slipping to the underside of her breast, pushing the globe of flesh upwards for the descent of his mouth. He suckled on her engorged nipples in turn, his tongue hot and moist as it moved over the curve of each breast until her body was trembling with need.

He knelt down in front of her, kissing his way from her breasts, down her sternum and to her belly button. He lingered over the tiny cave, dipping the tip of his tongue into its whorled pool before going lower. Alice sucked in a sharp breath as his tongue skated over her lower abdomen, his warm breath a tantalising caress on her most intimate flesh. He separated her folds with his fingers and then brought his mouth to her, making every swollen nerve ending vibrate with delight. The spiralling waves of sensation pulsed through her body with earth-rocking force.

She tried to hold onto her consciousness but it was impossible to do anything but feel. Aftershocks of pleasure rang through her flesh, like a bell reverberating long after it had been struck.

Cristiano got up and eased her down on the bed, only stopping long enough to dispense with his trousers and access another condom. Alice reached for him as he came down over her on the mattress, her hands running over his muscled biceps and then the back of his neck, lifting her head to meet the descent of his mouth.

His kiss was long and deep, thrumming with a building urgency she could feel in every cell of her flesh where it was touching his. His erection probed her entrance and she opened to him, shifting her hips to accommodate him. It was like resuming a dance choreographed just for them. The fit of their bodies in that intimate embrace felt so right, so fluid and sensual—as unconscious and natural as breathing.

Alice stroked his back from his neck to his lower spine, concentrating in the dip above his taut buttocks. She knew all his erogenous zones and it thrilled her to feel his earthy response to her touch. She cupped his buttocks, holding him, rocking with him as he set a rhythm that was in perfect tune with her needs. The feel of him moving inside her body sent her senses into a frenzy of excitement.

No one filled her the way he did. No one knew her body as he did. No one else understood how much she craved this magic of motion, the friction that ruthlessly teased her sensitive flesh until she thought she would explode.

He turned her over so she was on top, his hands cupping her breasts, his dark gaze consuming her as a starving man did a meal he had long waited for in frustrated agony. Alice bent forward over him, her hands placed either side of his head, her hair falling forward to tickle his chest and shoulders. She moved her body in time with his, finding the extra friction that sent her over the edge. The savage pleasure pulsed through her in ever expanding waves like a boulder dropped in a pond. Every part of her body felt the rippling flow of release, until finally a warm soothing tide of lassitude was left in its wake.

His release was close behind hers, the spasms so powerful she could feel them echoing against the walls of her intimate flesh. She could see, too, the contortion of ecstasy played out on his face, and hear his sexy, breathless grunts that made her skin lift in a shower of goose bumps.

Cristiano rolled her back under him, and, balancing his weight on his elbows, he brushed the damp tendrils of hair back off her forehead. 'You never fail to surprise me.'

Alice teased the curls at the back of his neck with her fingers. 'In what way?'

He outlined her mouth with a lazy fingertip, the top lip and then the bottom one until her lips were tingling, his eyes sexily hooded. 'You respond to me like no one else.'

Alice didn't want to be reminded of all the other women he had slept with since her. Even if he hadn't brought them back here, she knew he had slept with dozens of women elsewhere. All those hook-ups in his hotels. Night after night. Year after year. It was too painful to think about—especially while her body was still thrumming with the magic of his touch.

She knew it was inconsistent of her to be so petty about it since she'd been the one to end their relationship. But the thought of him making love to someone else with the same intensity was nothing short of torture. How many women? Had he looked at them the way he looked at her? Had he touched them the way he had touched her? Was he making comparisons? Finding her a disappointment now he'd revisited their intimacy?

She dropped her hands from his hair and began to push against his chest. 'You'd better take care of that condom before we end up with more than a six-month marriage.'

A frown brought his brows together, his eyes studying hers for a beat or two. But then he rolled away and got off the bed and dealt with the condom. He picked up a bathrobe from the hook behind the door and slipped his arms into it and loosely tied the ties. 'Are you on the pill?'

'Of course.'

He bent to pick up his trousers from the floor and hung them over the back of a chair near the window. His expression had gone back to neutral but Alice couldn't help feeling he was annoyed with her again. She could see it in the way he was restoring order to the room. It was his way of controlling his feelings. A battening down of the emotional hatches, so to speak. Funny, but she hadn't realised he did that until now.

She hugged her knees to her chest and rested her chin on top of them, watching him fold his shirt he'd taken from her body such a short time ago. 'You're angry.'

He tossed the shirt to one side as if it personally offended him, and frowned at her. 'What gives you that idea?'

Alice unlocked her arms from around her knees and got off the bed, taking the bed throw rug with her as a sarong. 'I'm going to take a shower while you play housemaid.'

His hand captured her arm on the way past and he turned her to face him. 'What do you mean by that?'

'You're cleaning up the room as if you want to forget what just happened.' Alice unpeeled his fingers one by one, shooting him a look. 'Of course I'm on the pill. Do you think I'd sleep with you if I wasn't?'

His eyes held hers in a lock. 'Even the pill isn't fool-proof. You could miss a dose or have an absorption problem.'

'True, so that's why we have to be careful.'

Even though every time I think about a baby my ovaries start jumping up and down in excitement.

His gaze continued to bore its way into hers. 'So you're as adamant as ever over not having kids?'

Alice hoped he couldn't hear her eggs jostling and shoving each other and saying, *Let me go first!*

'My business is my baby. It takes all my energy and commitment. I don't have room in my life for a child. Anyway, what's with the inquisition? You're not thinking of making an heir and spare to inherit your millions, are you?'

The skin around his mouth tightened until it was more white than tan. 'No.'

'That's quite a change from the man seven years ago who couldn't wait to start a family.'

'I have different goals now.'

'What did your grandmother think about that?'

Cristiano's expression turned rueful. 'She wasn't happy about it. She only had my father and would've loved more children but it never happened. She had a stillbirth before my father and numerous miscarriages after.' He let out a long slow breath and continued. 'She adored my mother. She treated her as if she were her own daughter. There was none of that mother-in-law angst everyone talks about. My mother loved Nonna as much if not more than her own mother. Family was everything to Nonna.'

Alice had seen that love of family first hand when she'd met Volante Marchetti. Even though the old woman had not long ago lost her husband Enzo, she had been nothing but warm and loving and welcoming towards Alice. And when it came to Cristiano, well, Alice had felt slightly envious to see the depth of love the old woman had for him. There were parents who didn't love their children more than Volante had loved her grandson. 'Why do you think she wanted you to marry me? Surely she must've known it was the last thing either of us would want?'

'I'm not sure...' He dragged a hand down his face, the sound of his palm scraping against his stubbly jaw loud in the silence. 'No, that's not quite true. She was unhappy with how I was living my life. She was quite vocal about it towards the end. She wanted the best for me, and, in her mind, didn't think I was getting it.'

Alice gave a soft little snort. 'I hardly think I'm the best thing that's ever come into your life.'

Cristiano's gaze met hers for a long beat of silence. 'Nonna would disagree.'

'That's very kind of her, but I'm—'

'It's fine, Alice,' he said. 'I'm not going to hold you to our agreement longer than necessary. I'm only allowing it to go this far because I can't allow those shares to get into my cousin Rocco's hands. I'm not going to watch everything my parents worked so hard for go down the mouth of a poker machine or on a gaming table.'

Alice frowned. 'Didn't your grandmother know about his gambling tendencies?'

He shook his head, his look grim. 'I made the decision not to tell her. Stupid, I know now in hindsight. But she was so ill and frail and I didn't want to send her to her grave with that worry on top of everything else. She changed her will a week or two after her diagnosis.'

'Would you have tried to stop her if you'd known at the time what she planned to do?'

He seemed to consider it for a moment. 'I'm not sure… Yes, no, maybe. It was what she wanted so what right did I have to try and change her mind? She wasn't suffering from dementia or any mental impairment brought on by her illness. She had a right to compose a will that reflected her dying wishes, and yet… I wish I'd warned her about Rocco, but, to be honest, I'm not sure I would have even if I'd known what she planned to do. She adored him. He's her late sister's only child and her godson. It would have broken her heart to know he wasn't the golden boy she believed him to be.'

Alice shifted her mouth from side to side, thinking about Volante Marchetti with her razor-sharp mind and intelligent gaze. Not much would have escaped that wise old bird's eye. 'What if she did know?'

Cristiano looked at her blankly. 'Know what? About Rocco?'

'Yes. Maybe she knew you would do anything to save those shares from being frittered away,' Alice said. 'Anything, as in marrying your enemy.'

He gave her a sideways smile and glided a hand down the length of her bare arm, making her skin lift in a veil of goose bumps. 'Is that what we are? Enemies?'

Alice put her hand to his face, sliding it down the raspy skin of his cheek. 'Well, you could say we are, except now we're making love not war.'

He gathered her close, locking his hips against hers,

stirring her senses into overdrive with the heated probe of his body. 'I thought you were going to take a shower?'

She moved against him, her inner core leaping in excitement to find him hard as stone. 'I was. Want to join me?'

He unwrapped her from the throw, his eyes going to her breasts. He bent his head and covered one tightly budded nipple with his mouth, drawing on the puckered flesh until she was restless with clawing need. She worked on his trousers, unzipping them with more haste than finesse. His mouth came down on hers in a scorching kiss, his tongue tangling with hers in a tango of lust that made her blood all but sizzle in her veins. She could feel the swell of her most intimate flesh, the dragging sensation of need that was part pain, part pleasure. His hands gripped her by the hips, holding her to the pulsing heat of his body, his chest crushed against her breasts, the masculine hair tickling and teasing her sensitised skin.

Cristiano took her by the hand and led her to the en suite. He prepared himself with a condom while he waited for the shower to get to the right temperature, and then stepped in with her. The water cascaded over their bodies, heightening Alice's senses as his hands skimmed her wet, naked flesh. She pressed her lips to his chest, kissing her way down to his navel, circling her tongue and then bending down in front of him so she could take him in her mouth. She had never pleasured another partner this way. Had never wanted to. Had made excuses not to. The thought of doing it with someone else was almost repugnant. But with Cristiano it felt like a sacred act, one that was mutually pleasurable, for she loved feeling the potent strength of him against her lips and tongue. She loved hearing his groans, and witnessing his knees buckle when she drew on him. She loved feeling his hands gripping her head to anchor himself against the tumultuous throb of release.

But this time he wouldn't let her take him over the edge. He pulled away from her and brought her back to her feet. Then he bent down so he was between her parted thighs, his mouth working its magic on her feminine folds. He knew exactly what pressure and what speed to trigger the explosion. It rocked through her body like a torpedo, sending ripples of delight through every cell until her thighs tingled as if they were being trickled with fine sand.

Alice tugged him by the hair to get him to stand up, pressing her mouth to his and tasting her own essence on his lips and tongue. He moved from her mouth down to her neck, nudging and nuzzling her while he positioned himself. She guided him with her hand, lifting one leg so it was balanced on his hip, a gasp puffing out of her lips when he surged into her with his own raw groan.

The water falling over them added another sensory delight, the rocking speed of his thrusts ramping up her need until she was on the knife-edge, teetering there but unable to go any further. Cristiano pulled out and, with a sexy glint in his eyes, turned her so that her back was to him. Alice planted her hands on the marble wall of the shower, standing on tiptoes so he could gain the access he wanted.

There was something about this position that had an element of wickedness about it. A primitive wickedness that was as thrilling as it was slightly shocking. He moved between her buttocks, the hot glide of his engorged flesh tantalising her senses until she was breathing hard in excitement. He surged into her wetness, the different angle catching her right where she needed it, the fast-moving friction of his urgent thrusts triggering an orgasm so powerful she felt it move through her like a high-speed missile. The whirlpool of pleasure stole every conscious thought, leaving her spinning in a swirling black sea of magic.

Cristiano gave three more powerful thrusts, his legs quaking against hers, his breathing rough and uneven next to her ear. Alice waited for him to collect himself before she turned in his arms, locking her arms around his neck and pressing a lingering kiss to his mouth. His hands settled on her hips, his mouth moving against hers with slow, heart-tripping deliberation.

After a long moment, he lifted his head, his gaze dark, rich and gleaming with sexual satiation. 'Like old times, *si*?'

Alice licked her tongue over his lower lip, leaning into the hard warmth of his body. 'Better.'

Way, way better.

CHAPTER EIGHT

CRISTIANO WOKE NOT long before dawn to find Alice nestled up against his chest soundly asleep. Her hair was tickling his chin but he didn't have the heart to disturb her. Or maybe it was more because lying here with her was like time travelling back to a time in his life when he'd felt he had ticked all the boxes. Felt complete and satisfied in a way he hadn't since. One of her hands was resting against his chest, right over his heart. Her silken legs were entwined with his in an intimate linkage that made his blood stir.

Would this hunger for her ever be satisfied? How many times had they made love last night? He had been like a randy teenager. He couldn't seem to get enough of her. Was it a case of making up for lost time or... something else?

He didn't want to think about the something else.

He wasn't sure why he'd told Alice about his reluctance to sleep with anyone else here since her. Why should he care if she thought he'd bedded anything in a skirt for the last seven years? But somehow what they'd shared under this roof had meant something to him even if it hadn't to her. He hadn't wanted to dilute those memories with a host of other bodies, other faces, other smiles, and other perfumes. Or maybe it was a form of self-flagellation. A perpetual punishment for being so foolish to believe she had been The One.

No. He was fine with things as they were. What could be better than to make the most of their 'forced' time together? Wasn't that what he'd wanted? A chance to get her out of his system so he could finally move on with his life?

It was a good plan.

An excellent plan.

Why had his *nonna* orchestrated it other than to force him to revisit his relationship with Alice? His grandmother knew his life hadn't been the same since Alice left. She knew he hadn't moved on. Not properly. But to leave half of the Stresa villa to her seemed a bit of an extreme measure. Not that he'd let on to Alice how much the place meant to him. He'd let her think the company shares were his focus. The lakeside villa—like this one in Milan—had been in the Marchetti family for a hundred and fifty years. To lose one pebble, let alone half of the property, to someone outside the family was unthinkable. Even if it was to Alice, with whom he'd had the most passionate affair of his life.

There was nothing to stop her selling her share out from under him when their marriage ended. There was no guarantee she would give him first option. She might not even want to sell her share, which would mean he would have to sell his, or deal with having to share the villa with her on an ongoing basis. He could think of nothing worse than having to negotiate times to visit so he didn't run into her new lover or house-party guests. His family home reduced to a time-share property? Unbearable.

Alice's breathing was soft and even, but every now and again she would release a little purring sigh of contentment and nestle even closer. How many times had he watched her like this in the past? Dreaming of their future together, the life they would live, the children they would have, the happiness they would create together to make up for the tragedy he'd experienced.

He had her back in his bed, but would it be enough?

It would have to be because there was no way he was going to offer her anything else. His days of wearing his heart on his sleeve—or anywhere on his person, for that matter—were well and truly over. His heart was in lockdown. In solitary confinement. No walks in the exercise yard. No day release. No bail. No parole.

This thing between him and Alice was about lust now, not love. A lust that would burn brightly for a while and then gradually fade away just like every other relationship he'd had.

Except with her.

Cristiano sidestepped the thought. He would not allow himself to think like that. This was for now, not for ever. He wasn't a 'for ever' guy now.

He was a 'for the moment' man.

Alice opened her eyes and blinked up at him like a baby owl. 'Is it time to get up?'

Cristiano was already 'up'. His body had been up ten minutes ago when her legs had wrapped around his and her hand had slipped to his abdomen. 'Not yet.' He brushed back her tousled hair. 'There's no hurry.'

She gave him a naughty-girl smile when her hand slid lower and found him fully erect. 'No hurry, huh?'

Cristiano sucked in a breath when her hand started working its wicked magic. She licked her lips and slithered down his body, breathing her sweet hot breath over his abdomen and groin. No one but Alice could reduce him to this—to a quaking wreck of a man without the strength of will to stop her. He barely had time to source a condom before she took him to the stratosphere.

He sank back against the pillows to regain his breath, his arm drawing her close to his side. 'Give me a couple of minutes and I'll be right with you.'

He felt her smile against his chest where her cheek was resting. Her fingers did a piano-playing exercise on his right pectoral muscle. 'Is sex this good with your other partners?' she asked after a moment.

Cristiano had already revealed a little too much in that department. No point giving her more ammunition. 'Fishing, *cara*?'

She made a pouting gesture and went to move away but he held her still. He turned so she was trapped beneath him. She refused to meet his gaze so he inched up her chin so she had no choice. Her blue eyes glittered with resentment but behind that he could see doubt and insecurity moving like shadows. 'I'm not a kiss-and-tell man,' he said. 'I consider it disrespectful.'

Her lashes came down to half-mast over her eyes. After a long moment she released a serrated-sounding breath. 'The last time I had sex I came home and showered for an hour.'

Cristiano's gut clenched as if a steel-studded fist had grabbed his intestines. 'You weren't…?' He couldn't even say the ugly word.

Her lips twisted in a rueful motion. 'No, it was completely consensual, it's just I hated every minute of it. Not that there were too many minutes of it, mind you. Three or four at the most.'

Cristiano brushed back some strands of her tousled hair from her forehead. He hated the thought of her making love with someone else. Hated, hated, *hated* it. For years he'd refused to think about it. He wouldn't allow his mind to torture him with the thought of another man touching her body the way he had touched her, holding her the way he held her. He knew it was arrogant, but he wanted to believe he was the only one who brought that passionate response out of her. *His* body. *His* touch. His need of her triggered the fire in her blood in the same way she triggered his.

'If the chemistry isn't there then the sex will always suffer.'

Her fingertip traced a slow line around his mouth. 'That's something we were never short of, isn't it?' Her words had a faint wistfulness about them.

He captured her finger and kissed the end of it. 'No, that's one thing we had in spades.' In spades and buckets and truck and trailer loads. Still had. He could feel it thrumming between them, the way their bodies meshed as if unable to keep their distance.

Alice linked her arms around his head, her fingers lifting and tugging and releasing the strands of his hair in a way that made every inch of his scalp tingle. 'I've never enjoyed sex with anyone else like I do with you.' Her lips gave a little sideways quirk. 'I should hate you for that. You've ruined my sex life.'

Cristiano gave her a look of mock reproach. 'You haven't done mine any favours, either, young lady.'

Her eyes studied his for a long moment. 'Are you saying it's…better with me?'

He pressed a soft kiss on her forehead. 'It's different.'

Two fine pleats appeared between her eyes. 'How?'

He smoothed away her frown with the pad of his index finger. 'We should get a move on. It will take an hour or so to get to Stresa.'

Her frown snapped back. 'Don't change the subject. Talk to me, Cristiano. Tell me what was different—'

'Look, it just was, okay?' Cristiano rolled away and swung his legs over the edge of the bed. What did she want him to say? That he'd missed her every goddam day since? That every time in the last seven years when he'd touched another woman he'd thought of her? And how much he wished it *were* her? That sex was just sex with anyone else but with her it was making love?

No way was he going to say that.

Even if it was regrettably true.

He heard her sit up on the bed, and then felt her silky hand travel the length of his rigid spine, from his neck to his tailbone, in a soothing caress that made every knob of his vertebrae quiver. She leant her head against his back, her arms going around his waist, the little rush of air from her sigh tickling the skin behind his shoulder blades like the wings of a moth.

'Don't be mad at me,' she said.

Cristiano let out his own sigh and swivelled round to gather her against his side. He dropped a kiss to the top of her head. 'I'm not mad at you, *tesoro.*'

I'm mad at myself.

For still wanting her when he should have been well and truly over her. He wasn't some creepy stalker guy who couldn't let go. There should be no reason he was stuck on her to the point where he couldn't bear to contemplate a future with anyone else. He could have anyone he wanted. He didn't have to fight for dates. If anything, he had to fight them off. But something about

Alice had stayed with him. Like a tune he couldn't get out of his head.

Alice snaked a hand up around his neck, gazing into his eyes with such intensity he wondered if she could sense how much he had missed her. That in spite of all his denials and dissembling she knew—her body knew—he only felt this body-stunning magic with her. Her eyes went to his mouth, her tongue sneaking out to moisten the soft swell of her lips.

'I don't want us to bicker and fight any more. A relationship shouldn't be a competition. It's so…so exhausting.'

Cristiano slid a hand under the curtain of her hair, his mouth coming down to within reach of hers. 'Then we'd better put that energy to much better use, *si*?'

Her eyes shone with anticipation and she lifted her face for his kiss. 'Now you're talking.'

After a quick breakfast, Cristiano drove Alice the ninety-kilometre distance to his grandmother's villa in Stresa situated on the shores of Lake Maggiore. Alice hadn't forgotten how beautiful the lake was with the historic Isola Bella and Isola Superiore a short boat trip from the shore. But seeing it again on a gorgeous autumn morning with the leaves just starting to turn was nothing less than breathtaking.

Cristiano pulled into the driveway of the villa, which had remained empty since his grandmother's death. He'd explained on the journey there that Volante had insisted on dying at home even though he had offered to have her with him in Milan. He had visited as often as he could and Alice was not surprised to hear he had been with Volante when she'd drawn her last breath. But it made her wonder if coming back now his grandmother was gone was far more painful than he was letting on.

Cristiano opened the front door and led the way inside the quiet villa. It was built on a grand scale with dozens of rooms both formal and informal. It was so big it should not have felt like a family home and yet seven years ago it had.

Not now, however.

Now it was a place of ghosts. The furniture was draped in dustsheets and the long corridors and high windows with their curtains drawn were like eyelids closed over tired eyes. Silence crept from every corner. Achingly lonely silence.

Alice slid her hand into Cristiano's, her own eyes suddenly tearing up. 'It must be so hard to come here now. Have you been back since…?'

He squeezed her fingers and turned to look at her. 'No.' His brows came together and he blotted one of her tears with the pad of his thumb. 'She would not want you to cry, *cara*.'

Alice blinked a couple of times and forced a smile to her lips. Their newfound truce was doing strange things to her emotions. Emotions she normally had under the strictest control.

'Sorry. I'm not normally so emotional. I hardly knew her…except I can't help thinking how different this place is without her.' She swiped at her face with the back of her hand. 'I wish I'd written to her. How hard would it have been to send a Christmas card? I just wish I'd let her know I'd never forgotten her, you know?'

He tucked her hand in under his arm. 'You're here now, which is what she wanted.'

Alice still couldn't understand why Volante had left

her a joint share in this villa and with such strange conditions attached. Not only was the villa—even a half-share—worth millions, it was where Cristiano had spent his childhood and adolescence after his family were killed. Surely if anyone deserved the villa it was him? But he had given no indication of being upset about not inheriting it fully. His focus had always been on the shares he stood to lose control of if he didn't fulfil the terms of the will. Even if it meant marrying the woman who had rejected him seven years ago.

'If you'd inherited the villa completely what would you have done with it?' she asked.

He gave a one-shoulder shrug. 'Made it into a hotel.'

'Really? You wouldn't have wanted it as a private retreat?'

He gave her a wry look. 'It's a bit big for one person.'

'Yes, but you might not always be on your own,' Alice said, torturing herself with the thought of who he might spend the rest of his life with. 'You might want to have a family one day. You can become a father at any age so—'

'It's a good location for a hotel,' he said as if she hadn't spoken. 'The gardens too are perfect for weddings and other functions.'

Alice kept her gaze trained on his. 'But doesn't this place mean more to you than that? Don't you have memories you—?'

'What is a house without the people you love inside it?' he said, with a flash of irritation in his gaze. 'It's nothing, that's what it is. It's just bricks and mortar. An empty shell where every room reminds you of someone you've loved and lost.'

Alice swallowed, watching in silence as he tore off

a couple of dustsheets and dropped them to the floor in puddles of white like collapsed sails. She pictured him as a young boy going back to his family's villa after the accident, her heart cramping at the thought of what it had been like for him to walk into that sad vacuum of a place that had once been full of love and laughter.

'I'm so sorry…' Her voice came out little more than a cracked whisper of sound.

He raked a hand through his hair and let out a long rough sigh. 'No, I'm the one who's sorry. I shouldn't have spoken so harshly to you. Forgive me.'

Alice closed the distance between them and slipped her arms around his waist, looking up at his grimly set features. 'It's fine. This is really painful for you.'

After a moment his expression softened a fraction as if her presence calmed him. He gave her a twist of a smile, his hand brushing an imaginary hair away from her face.

'I should have been back here weeks ago. I just couldn't seem to do it. I didn't want to face this place without her in it. It reminded me too much of the trip home after my parents and brother were killed.'

Alice moved her arms from around his waist and took his hands in hers, gently stroking their strong backs with her thumbs. 'I can't imagine how that must have been for you.'

He looked down at their joined hands for a moment before returning his gaze to hers. 'My grandparents tried to spare me the trauma of going back home but I insisted. It was weird…surreal, really. Everything at home looked the same but it was different. It was like the villa was holding its breath or something.'

His gaze got a faraway look and shifted from hers.

'It was like my life had been jammed on pause. I stood there thinking if only I could turn back the clock. Maybe if I hadn't been sick they wouldn't have had to make the detour to my grandparents' place, then they wouldn't have been on that road at that particular time.'

Alice clutched at his hands. 'You mustn't blame yourself. You were a child. Kids get sick all the time. You can't possibly blame yourself for someone else's stupidity. It was that drunk driver's fault, not yours, that your family were killed.'

Cristiano's fingers shifted against hers, his eyes still shadowed.

'I was cautious about expressing my grief because it only made it harder on my grandparents. If I showed how devastated I was then they would have that to deal with along with everything else. They were so strong but it can't have been easy bringing up a child at their stage of life. They'd stepped back from the hotel business to enjoy a quieter life, but of course all that changed. My grandfather had to run things until I was of an age to take over.'

He slipped his hands out of hers and walked over to one of the windows that overlooked the lake.

Alice wanted to follow him but sensed he was gathering himself. She couldn't recall a time when he had spoken with such depth about his loss. He had never seemed to want to talk about it before. Why hadn't she taken the time to encourage him to unburden himself? She had been so immature back then she hadn't seen how the loss of his family was why he over-controlled everything. She had been mulish and opinionated instead of compassionate and understanding. If only she had been less focussed on her own opinions she might have realised how tragic his life had been and how it had coloured everything he did.

Her background had its issues, certainly, but nothing compared to what he'd been through. She looked at his tall frame standing there and pictured the child he had once been. Trying to be strong for his grandparents. Containing his grief to protect them. Hadn't she done the same with her mother? Tried to be strong, becoming the adult instead of the child in order to help her mother through every broken relationship. Ignoring her own needs until she could barely recognise them when they cropped up. 'Oh, Cristiano...'

He turned and looked at her with one of his smiles that wasn't quite a smile. 'You know what's ironic? My brother was the one with his heart set on taking over the business. I had other plans.'

Shock ran through Alice in an icy tide. Plans? What plans? How had she spent six weeks with this man and not once realised he'd had other plans for his life than the hotel business? He was so successful. He owned and operated some of the most luxurious boutique hotels in the Mediterranean. When you thought of boutique hotels you thought of Cristiano Marchetti. But what had *he* wanted to do with his life?

'You mean you didn't want to be in the hotel business? Not at all?'

He picked up a photograph of his grandparents as a young couple that was on the walnut table near the window, his fingers moving over the carved frame as if he were reading Braille.

'No. I wanted to be an architect. But it was impossible once my parents and brother died. I don't think I even mentioned it to my grandparents after that. I knew my fate. The responsibility was ultimately mine otherwise everything my parents and grandparents had worked for would be lost. I had to shelve my plans and immerse myself in the business. But don't feel too sorry for me, *cara*.'

He put the photograph back down and glanced at her.

'I have plenty of opportunity to express my creativity when I'm working on renovating an old building.' His mouth twisted in a self-deprecating manner. 'I make the architect's life hell for a few months but that's life.'

Alice was in a turmoil of regret over not realising any of this until now. She had made so many assumptions about him. She had even playfully mocked him about his wealth on occasion. And not so playfully recently, when she'd made that crack about all the silver spoons hanging out of his mouth.

All the clues were there now she stopped to reflect on their time together. He had been reluctant to talk about his past because he found it so painful. Not just because of the loss of his family but the loss of the life he had mapped out for himself. He had lost control of everything the day his parents and brother were killed.

She thought of all the times she had talked to him about her plans to build her own beauty spa. She had told him how she had wanted to do it since she was a little girl when she went with her mother to a beauty salon when her mother got her nails done for her second wedding. Alice had been captivated by all the lotions and potions and the sense of luxury so unfamiliar in her life back then. She'd made a decision right then and there to own and operate her own beauty salon where women could escape the humdrum of life and spoil themselves with some pampering. She had fought for her dream and achieved it in spite of the disadvantages of her background.

But Cristiano's background—the one she had envied so much—had been the cause of him *not* being able to live his dream.

Alice walked over to where he was standing and placed her hand on his forearm. 'I've always felt jealous of your wealth, that you could buy anything you want, travel anywhere you like, do anything you like. But it's been more of a burden than anything else, hasn't it?'

He placed his hand over hers, bringing it up to his chest. 'It's both a blessing and a burden but I would much rather have the security of wealth than not. Don't get me wrong. I enjoy my work. I didn't for a long time, but I do now.'

'But who will take over from you once you get to retirement age?' Alice asked. 'Your cousin?'

'God no,' he said with a roll of his eyes. 'Rocco has no head for business. His idea of a hotel makeover would be to install slot machines in every room. My parents and grandparents would spin in their graves.' He sighed and released her hand. 'No, I'll probably sell the business outright when the time is right.'

'But if you had a family, a son or daughter, they could take over and—'

'You seem a little hung up on this issue, Alice.' His tone was on the edge of being crisp. 'Does this mean you've changed your mind about having children?'

Alice forced herself to hold his gaze. 'We're not talking about me. We're talking about you. You have so much to offer a child. You have a strong sense of family. You've had great modelling in both your parents and grandparents. Why wouldn't you pass on that wonderful heritage to your own offspring?'

'Let's talk about you, then,' he said, his gaze unwavering. 'Who will you leave your goods and chattels to? A dog's home?'

Alice pursed her lips and then puffed out a sigh. If they were supposed to be working at a truce then why shouldn't she be honest with him?

She shook back her hair and raised her gaze back to his. 'Okay, I'll let you in on a secret. I have thought about having kids. I've thought about it a lot recently.'

'And?'

'And it's something I'd like to do one day. When I find the right man, of course.'

His expression became shuttered. 'What made you change your mind?'

Alice picked up another photo next to the one of his grandparents. It was a family shot of Cristiano with his parents and older brother. She had seen it before without really seeing it. Cristiano was a happy child in that photo, smiling with an open and engaging expression. Nothing like the serious and closed-off man of today. She put the photo back down and looked at him again.

'It was a gradual thing rather than an overnight change of heart,' she said.

Not unlike my feelings for you.

'I realised what I'd be missing out on when I saw my friends and my clients with their babies. It's such a special relationship—unique, really—the love between a mother and child.' She gave him a flutter of a smile. 'My mother drives me completely nuts but deep down I know she loves me more than anyone else on this planet. I want to feel that love. I want to experience that bond.'

His mouth turned up at one side in a rueful angle. 'What a pity my grandmother meddled with your life. You'll have to put your baby plans on hold for another six months.'

Alice shifted her gaze. 'Yes, well, I'm only twenty-eight. I don't have to panic just yet.'

There was an odd little silence.

Alice wondered if he was thinking of the irony of their situation. He had desperately wanted a family seven years ago while she had wanted her freedom. Now he wanted his freedom while she was peering into every pram that went past.

What if she didn't find a man she could love enough to father her children? But who else could she want but Cristiano? Her feelings for him had been on slow burn in her heart. Banked down out of bitterness because he hadn't fought for her in the past. But the more she thought about her future, she couldn't imagine sharing it with anyone other than him. She would rather be alone than be with someone else.

Maybe that was why she had panicked and pushed him away. She had seen him as the one man who could make her sacrifice the dream of owning her own business. It had been too confronting for her as a twenty-one-year-old on the threshold of her life. Too threatening in case he hadn't loved her enough to give her the freedom to pursue her own goals instead of subsuming her life into the powerful engine of his.

But now...now she had established her business. She knew who she was and what she wanted for her life. And that included the things he no longer wanted. Marriage. A family. To love and be loved.

But Cristiano no longer loved her, if he ever had.

The only reason he was with her now was because of the shares that hung in the balance. If it hadn't been for his grandmother's will she would never have heard from him again. She had to remember that. He was only marrying her to get what he wanted. He might still desire her but he was a full-blooded man with a healthy appetite for sex.

This thing they had going on was for now, not for ever.

CHAPTER NINE

CRISTIANO LED ALICE through the villa but his mind was preoccupied.

She wanted a family.

After all those heated arguments in the past over not wanting kids. It had been a sticking point in their relationship. He had thought her selfish for putting her career above having a family. Selfish and unnatural. But now he was the one who was career focussed. He had made himself so busy he couldn't find time for a steady relationship, let alone a family that would need nurturing day by day, week by week, year by year. He didn't want it because the thought of losing it was too terrifying. Too awful to even contemplate.

He knew all too well how it felt to have his world ripped out from under him. Once was enough. More than enough. Loving someone meant you could lose them. You could lose part of yourself and never get it back.

'May I see the garden now?' Alice said, breaking through his reverie.

'Sure.' Cristiano took her hand and led her to the French doors leading out to the terrace. 'This was one of my grandmother's favourite places. She would sit out here for hours watching the birdlife in the garden.'

'It's such a beautiful place.' Alice's voice had a reverent note to it. 'Around every corner is another surprise. It's like a story unfolding.'

Cristiano waited on the terrace while she wandered about the garden. She stopped to smell the roses his grandmother had planted as a young bride, her fingers softly touching the fragrant petals. The sun caught her hair and turned it into a skein of shining silver, and she brushed some strands away from her face that the light breeze had toyed with and tucked them back behind her ear. She caught him looking at her and gave him a smile that made something inside his chest ache.

'This would make a great wedding venue, don't you think?' she said. 'The wisteria walk would be a gorgeous place for the bride to walk towards the groom.'

'Would you like to get married here?' Cristiano asked.

A slight frown creased her smooth brow. 'But I thought you wanted a church wedding?'

He shrugged. 'As long as it's legal who cares where it's conducted?'

She pulled at her lower lip with her teeth and turned slightly to look at the angel fountain his grandmother had installed after the stillborn birth of her first child the year before Cristiano's father had been born. So much of his family's history was embedded in this place. There wasn't a shrub or tree or yew hedge that hadn't witnessed a Marchetti triumph or tragedy.

After a moment Alice turned to look at him. 'To be honest, I'd rather be married here than in a church. It would make it less…' She seemed to be searching for the right word and bit into her lip again.

'Binding?' Cristiano said.

Her mouth went into a flat line. 'Don't you feel the slightest bit uncomfortable about all this? Marriage is a big deal. As the words of the ceremony say: it's not to be entered into lightly.'

Was she having second thoughts? His guts churned. If she didn't marry him he would lose the shares and the villa. He couldn't allow that to happen.

'Look at it this way. We're fulfilling an old lady's dying wishes by getting married. It's not about us. It's about Nonna. And I think she would be thrilled if we had the ceremony here. I'll get working on it straight away.' He held his hand out for hers, drawing her against his side. 'Now, let's make the most of the day here in Stresa.'

It was a lovely day in spite of Alice's misgivings about where things were heading in their relationship. Cristiano organised a private tour of the islands and a gorgeous lunch at a restaurant by the lake. They drove back to Milan late in the afternoon and, after a quick shower and freshen up, he took her to one of the city's premier restaurants, where the maître d' welcomed Cristiano by name and showered them with effusive congratulations and a bottle of champagne on the house.

Alice sat opposite him sipping her champagne and wondered if he was thinking about that other restaurant only a few streets from here where he had proposed to her while the rest of the diners looked on. With the benefit of hindsight, she wished she'd handled it a little better than she had. But the shock of his sudden proposal after only a few weeks of dating had thrown her into a panic.

Surely she could have let him down without publicly humiliating him. Why had she been so crass and immature? How must he have felt to be left in that restaurant with everyone staring at him open-mouthed? The ring he'd chosen thrown onto the table as if it were a cheap fairground trinket. She hadn't even gone back to his villa, because her passport had been in her tote bag, and she'd caught a taxi straight to the airport and got on the first flight she could.

'More champagne?' Cristiano asked into the silence.

Alice put her hand over the top of her glass. 'Better not. I've had too much already.'

'You're not driving so if you want another I don't mind.'

She waited a couple of beats. 'Did you ever meet the person who—?'

'No.' The word was delivered with such finality it sounded like a gavel falling.

Alice moistened her lips. 'Did they express any remorse? Make any effort to contact you or your grandparents?'

His mouth was twisted in an embittered line. 'No. He was the sort of person who blamed everyone but himself for his wrongdoing. He didn't even get jail time. The judge overseeing the case had connections with his influential father. But karma got him in the end. He was killed in a bar fight. A drug deal gone sour.' He shifted his water glass half a centimetre and then did a slow tap of his fingers on the tablecloth. 'I thought it would help to know he'd got his comeuppance, but strangely it didn't.'

Alice reached across the table and grasped his hand. 'That's because you're not at heart a vengeful man.'

His half-smile was a little crooked. 'Am I not?' His fingers toyed with her engagement ring. 'You would not have liked what I was thinking when you stormed out of that restaurant seven years ago.'

She looked at their joined hands rather than meet his gaze. 'I'm sorry I reacted the way I did back then. It was so…so petulant and immature of me to behave like that.'

He gave her hand a quick squeeze before he released it to sit back in his chair. 'I shouldn't have put you under so much pressure. I was in too much of a rush after my grandfather died.' He did that slow tapping thing again next to his glass, his forehead creasing in a frown. 'Funerals can do that to you. Make you realise how fragile life is.'

Alice thought about him attending his family's funerals, the weight of grief he'd had to shoulder so bravely as a child, and then as an adult saying goodbye to each of his grandparents in turn. She had only been to one funeral—an elderly client who had passed away after a short illness. It had been sad but not tragic. Her family had celebrated her long life and sent her off with a party that had gone on until the early hours of the morning. What did Alice know of how it must feel to say that final goodbye to someone so beloved as a parent, grandparent or sibling?

'All the same, I wish I'd been a little kinder to you.' She let out a tiny sigh. 'I guess that's why you didn't contact me.'

Something flickered in his gaze. Surprise? Alarm? Regret? It was hard to distinguish which. 'Did you want me to?'

Alice wasn't sure it served any purpose to admit to how much she'd hoped he would. What was done was done. It was in the past and best left there. 'No. We were over as far as I was concerned.'

His eyes held hers for a long beat or two. 'How soon did you date someone else?'

She gave a little shrug. 'I don't know…six or so months maybe.' She flashed him a brittle glance before she could stop herself. 'Certainly longer than it took you.'

There was a small silence.

'I made sure I was seen with other women within days of us breaking up,' he said. 'But it was eight months before I could bring myself to sleep with anyone.'

Alice flickered her eyelids in shock. He'd waited *that* long? 'Eight months? Really?'

He gave a grim nod. 'It just didn't feel right rushing into another intense relationship.'

'It was pretty intense, wasn't it?'

He gave that sexy half-smile again and reached for her hand. 'It still is.'

The door was barely closed behind them when they returned to Cristiano's villa when he reached for her. The drive home from the restaurant had been a form of foreplay. His looks, his touch on her thigh when he changed the gears, the throb and roar of the engine that reminded Alice of the potent hormones surging through his body. His mouth came down on hers in a scorching kiss, his tongue tangling with hers in a provocative duel that made her tingle with anticipation.

She tore at his clothes with desperate hands, sliding her palms over the warm hard flesh of his chest and abdomen. He shrugged off his shirt and set to work on her dress, ripping down the zipper at the back and sliding his hand down the length of her spine, holding her against his pulsing heat. He brought his mouth to her neck and décolletage, his lips and tongue lighting spot fires beneath her skin. His hands cupped her breasts from below, pushing them upwards for the descent of his mouth.

She gasped out her pleasure when his mouth closed over one tightly budded nipple, his tongue swirling around the sensitive areola until she was sagging at the knees.

Alice sent her hands lower to free him from his trousers and underwear, taking him in her hand and stroking and squeezing him the way she knew he liked. He groaned his approval against her breast, creating a buzzing sensation that made the hairs on her scalp lift in a Mexican wave.

He lifted his mouth from her breast, his voice low and deep and gravelly with desire. *'Ti desidero.'*

'I want you too.'

He lifted her in one effortless swoop and carried her upstairs to his bedroom. He laid her on the mattress and, after dispensing with the rest of his clothes, dealt with the rest of hers. But somewhere along the way he slowed down the mad pace of his lovemaking and subjected her to an exquisite worship of her body from head to foot that made every cell throb and vibrate with need. His lips, his tongue, his hands, even his breath skating over her skin built her desire to fever pitch until she was all but begging for mercy.

'How much do you want me?' he said against her belly, his stubble grazing her skin.

'So much. Oh, please…*please*…' She writhed and twisted, aching for that final push.

He sheathed himself with a condom and entered her in a thick thrust that set off an explosion in her swollen flesh. She arched her spine to keep the contact where she needed it, the rioting sensations shooting through her like fireworks. She had barely recovered from that first orgasm when another one followed, a deeper one that rolled through her in tumultuous waves.

The contractions of her body must have triggered his own for he tensed all over and then surged deeper into her and shuddered and spilled.

Alice flung her head back against the pillows with a blissful sigh. 'Wow. Double wow.'

He propped himself up on his elbows and traced a fingertip down between her breasts. 'Not many women can orgasm like that without direct stimulation.'

She smiled and stroked a hand down his muscled arm. 'So I'm special, am I?'

His gaze intensified. 'You're the most responsive lover I've ever had.'

Alice tiptoed her fingers over his bicep. 'That's really saying something since you've had so many and all.'

He frowned at her tone and moved away to deal with the condom. 'You shouldn't believe everything you read in the press. If I'd bedded even half the women the press said I had, I wouldn't have had time to run my business.'

Alice sat up and reached for the throw on the end of the bed, wrapping it around her body. She was annoyed for broadcasting her jealousy again. How would she be able to walk away from their relationship with any dignity once it was time to go if she kept yammering on about his playboy lifestyle? He had a perfect right to have lovers. Numerous lovers.

No one had stopped her doing the same. No one but her, that was. She should be feeling happy he had at least refrained from bringing anyone back to his villa since her. That was huge. And the fact he had waited eight months surely should make her feel a little mollified, but sadly it didn't. He might not have moved on as quickly as the press had reported but neither had he come after her. He had kept his distance and seven long years had gone past. Seven years they could have had together...

She stood from the bed. 'I'm going to take off my make-up.'

He came to stand in front of her, his expression softening. 'I thought we agreed not to take cheap shots at each other.'

Alice rolled her lips together and then sighed. 'I'm sorry.'

He lifted her chin, brushing his thumb over her lower lip. 'I want us to be friends when this is over. It's what my grandmother would've wanted.'

'You don't think she wanted us to...to make a go of it?'

His hand fell away from her face. 'If she did then that's too bad because it's not going to happen.'

But it could if he wanted it to.

Alice tried to ignore the tight spasm of her heart. He was ruling out any possibility of them being a proper couple. Refusing to contemplate a future with her. A future with all the things she longed for now. What a cruel quirk of fate to have their roles reversed.

'Did I say I wanted it to? I'm just saying she probably had it in mind when she conjured up this scheme. At the very least she would've wanted us to settle our differences.'

Cristiano ran a hand through his hair. 'We've done that.'

'Have we?'

He let out a long breath and stepped close to her again, cupping her cheek in one broad hand, his dark chocolate eyes holding hers. 'You no longer hate me, do you, *cara*?'

I never hated you.

Alice gave him a wobbly smile. 'Do you still hate me?'

He brought his mouth down to within a millimetre of hers. 'Does this feel like hate to you?' And covered her mouth with his.

It felt like heaven.

When Alice got back to work on Monday it was like stepping into controlled chaos.

Meghan greeted her with a beaming smile from behind the reception counter. 'You would not believe the number of clients who want to see you. You're fully booked for months and months. Years probably. Your engagement to Cristiano Marchetti has opened doors. Big doors. Guess which Hollywood superstar wants you to do their make-up for their wedding in November? You'll never ever guess.'

She pulled out a chair and pushed it towards Alice.

'Here, you'd better sit down before I tell you.'

Alice ignored the chair. 'It's all right—I won't faint. Who is it?'

Meghan named a rising-star female actor who was the current toast of Hollywood.

'And that's not all,' she continued in a rush of excitement. 'She's going to fly you, all expenses paid, to the wedding location. It's top secret so as to keep the press away so you won't be told until the very last moment. You'll have to sign a confidentiality agreement.

I bet it's going to be in Bora Bora or maybe at Richard Branson's place, you know, Necker Island. Or maybe St Bart's. Oh, God, imagine if it was in St Bart's. You'll need an assistant, won't you?' She clasped her hands as if in prayer. 'Take me with you? Please, please, please?'

Alice laughed at the exuberant puppy-like look on her young employee's face. 'I'll have to see if the booking comes off first. No point getting too excited. You know what some of those Hollywood celebrities are like. Their weddings are cancelled at a moment's notice.'

Some of Meghan's enthusiasm sagged. 'True, but if it goes ahead things will never be the same around here. You'll be the wedding make-up artist to the stars.'

I have to get through my own 'wedding' first.

Alice's first client of the day a few days later was a bride-to-be who was booked in for a trial make-up session.

Jennifer Preston was the epitome of a woman radiantly in love. She had been coming to Alice for years as a client and somehow over the time their relationship had morphed into friendship. Jennifer had always bemoaned the fact she hadn't been able to find a suitable partner. But now she was happily engaged to a man she had met on a blind date set up by a friend and it truly was a match made in heaven.

Even a hardened cynic like Alice had to admit love at first sight could happen. Jennifer's fiancé, Marcus, dropped her off at her appointment, and the way he looked at Jennifer when he kissed her goodbye made Alice feel like an imposter. Not that Cristiano didn't look at her with affection and tenderness, but it wasn't as if he were truly in love with her as Marcus was with Jennifer and had been from the moment they'd met.

During Jennifer's trial make-up session, she told Alice about her wedding dress and the romantic honeymoon Marcus had planned. 'You know, Alice, a few months ago I was single and hating it,' Jennifer said. 'Now I'm getting married to a man I adore and he adores me. But you know what I'm talking about. That man of yours is a seriously fast worker. Have you chosen your dress?'

'Erm… Not yet, but I plan to duck out between clients this afternoon,' Alice said. 'So much to do, so little time.'

Jennifer rolled her eyes. 'Tell me about it.' She leaned forward to check her make-up. 'Gosh, you've done a brilliant job. I look almost beautiful.'

Alice put her hand on Jennifer's shoulder and gave it a squeeze. 'You *are* beautiful. You're positively glowing.'

Jennifer placed her hand over Alice's, her eyes shimmering with excitement. 'I haven't told anyone else but Marcus yet, but I'm pregnant. Six weeks. Will you be godmother when it's born?'

Alice blinked in surprise. 'Me?'

Jennifer swung the chair around so she was facing Alice instead of talking to her reflection in the mirror. She grasped Alice's hands in hers. 'Why not you? You and I have been banging on about the paucity of good men in London for the last seven years. Now we're both getting married within weeks of each other. And who knows? Maybe you'll get pregnant soon too.'

Alice stretched her mouth into a smile that felt as fake as her upcoming wedding. 'I'd be thrilled to be godmother. Truly honoured.'

Jennifer smiled. 'That's settled, then. Of course, you're bringing Cristiano to my wedding? I'll talk to the wedding planner about changing the seating arrangements. I've put you on a great table.'

'That's very kind,' Alice said. 'I'll have to check with him to see if he's free that weekend.'

'I'm sure he'd do anything for you,' Jennifer said, eyes sparkling. 'He's a man in love, right?'

CHAPTER TEN

ALICE RUSHED OUT between clients to check a couple of wedding boutiques in the area but couldn't see anything that captured her attention. Or maybe it was her mood that was the problem. She'd been fighting a tension headache all afternoon. It didn't feel right trying on dresses for a wedding that wasn't going to last. It wasn't just the expense of a dress, which was astronomical at the top end of town, but more the thought of play-acting at bride and groom when all she wanted was for it to be real.

How different would this shopping trip be if she were a bride like Jennifer Preston? Trying on beautiful gowns and veils, imagining Cristiano's face at the end of the aisle when she appeared at the church.

Maybe even carrying his baby...

Instead, Alice was going through the motions of bridal preparation knowing in her heart that her relationship with Cristiano was doomed for despair. If he'd wanted their relationship to be for ever then surely he would have said something by now?

She had spent every night with him since they'd come back from Italy. Their relationship had settled into a less combative one but was no less exciting. Every time he looked at her, she felt the rush of attraction course through her flesh. The dark glint in his eyes was enough to make her shudder with excitement.

Like this morning, for instance. He had given her that look and she had put aside her breakfast and made mad passionate love with him up against the kitchen bench. His touch was as magical as ever, in some ways even more intensely satisfying than in the past. Or maybe that was because Alice knew his touching of her was only temporary, that within a few months they would part and go their separate ways. The thought of it was heart-wrenching. How had it taken her this long to re-alise she loved him?

Or had she always loved him?

Was that why his proposal had been so threatening? She hadn't been ready to admit to how she felt about him. She'd needed more time. More time to question the opinions she'd formed out of fear, not facts. Loving someone back then had felt like giving up a part of her-self and never getting it back. But true love shouldn't be like that, surely?

True love was supposed to build up, not destroy.

To heal and create harmony, not hurt and dissension.

'Can I help you with anything?' a shop assistant asked in the last bridal boutique Alice wandered into. 'Oh, my goodness! You're Alice Piper, the wedding make-up celebrity. You did my friend's wedding make-up last year. Congratulations, by the way. Gosh, what an honour, you coming in here for your wedding dress. Let me show you around. Did you have a budget in mind?'

'Erm… I'm just looking at the moment,' Alice said, wondering how she could back out of the shop before the woman gave the paparazzi a heads up to boost her business. She wasn't the best shopper under pressure as it was. She needed time to think. Time to reflect. The last thing she needed right now was the press showing up and flashing cameras and microphones in her face.

The woman frowned. 'But aren't you getting married, like, in a couple of weeks?'

Don't remind me how close it is!

'October first,' Alice said, trying to ignore her thumping heartbeat and the beads of perspiration breaking out on her upper lip.

Cristiano had confirmed the details a few days ago. Their flights were booked, the staff notified at his grandmother's villa to get the place ready for a small wedding party. It was all happening so quickly and yet she felt on the perimeter of it all, like an observer on the sidelines.

'We can still get something made in time.' The woman gave Alice an obsequious smile. 'Especially for someone of *your* status. Nothing off the rack for Cristiano Marchetti's bride, hey? How about we look at some designs?' She whipped out a bridal magazine and fanned the pages open. 'White? Cream? Lace? Satin? Organza?'

Alice swallowed a ropey knot of panic. So many dresses… Who knew there were so many shades of white and cream? So many designs. So many decisions to make. So little time. How did brides do this without having a meltdown? No wonder so many of them got the Bridezilla tag.

The boutique was suddenly too hot, too stuffy, as if someone had sucked all the oxygen out of the room. Her head was in a vice, the pressure mounting until it felt as if her brain were going to explode through her skull.

She swayed on her feet, her vision blurring. The walls were buckling, closing in on her. Nausea churned in her stomach and then climbed up her throat on sticky claws.

'Are you all right?' The shop assistant grasped Alice by the arm. 'Here, sit down and put your head between your knees.'

Alice sank to the velvet-covered chair and lowered her head to her lap. She was vaguely aware of the shop assistant talking to someone on the phone and then a glass of water being handed to her. She sat up to take a few sips but the room was still spinning.

The woman took the glass from her. 'I've called an ambulance. They should be here soon.'

Alice looked up at her in alarm, her heart hammering like a drummer on crack. 'I don't need an ambulance.'

There was the sound of a siren screaming out-side. It echoed the silent scream inside Alice's head. *No-o-o-o-o!*

'Too late,' the woman said. 'Here, give me your phone. I'll call your fiancé for you.'

Alice clutched her bag against her body as if it con-tained the Crown Jewels. 'It's all right—I'll call him. I don't want him to panic over nothing.'

The woman tottered away to greet the paramedics coming through the door. 'She's over there. She nearly fainted. She was talking to me as good as anything and then she went as white as that dress in the window. I reckon she's pregnant. I was exactly the same when I had my daughters.'

Shoot me now.

Cristiano had finished with his meeting with the archi-tectural firm he'd employed to do the designs for the makeover of his Chelsea building so decided to call in at Alice's salon to see if she was finished for the day. He could have called or texted her, but he knew she kept her phone on silent when at work and sometimes forgot to unmute it. Besides, he liked seeing her in her work environment. She was always so professional but he got a kick out of knowing that behind that cool and composed façade and that neat little uniform was a feisty and passionate woman who came apart in his arms.

But when he walked into the salon Meghan, her assistant, was in a flustered state.

'Why are you here?' she said. 'Shouldn't you be at the hospital?'

Cristiano's stomach dropped like an anvil hitting concrete. 'Hospital?'

Meghan was wide-eyed with strain. 'Yes, Alice fainted in a shop. I got a call from the owner a few minutes ago. She said Alice has been taken to hospital for observation. I've been in such a state trying to cancel all her clients as well as do my own. Is she all right? What's wrong with her? They wouldn't let me speak to her.'

Cristiano's heart was giving a very good impression of needing urgent medical attention itself.

Alice sick? Taken to hospital?

Panic pounded like thunder in his blood.

No. No. No. Not again.

What if he couldn't get there in time? Things happened in hospitals. Bad things. People went in and didn't always come out. Or they did, but in body bags just like his family. 'Which hospital?'

Meghan told him and then added as he rushed out of the door, 'Oh, my God. You didn't know?'

'My phone's been off all afternoon.' He took it out of his jacket pocket and almost dropped it in his haste. But there were no missed calls from Alice and no text messages, either. What did that mean? She couldn't call because she was too ill? Unconscious? In a coma?

His heart flapped like a blown tyre. His pulse hammered. He was so consumed with dread it felt as if a pineapple were jammed halfway down his throat.

'Tell her I've got everything under control here,' Meghan called after him. 'Well, sort of...'

Cristiano hailed the nearest cab and then spent the entire journey wishing he'd dragged the cabby out of the driver's seat and driven the thing himself. By the time he got to the hospital he was so worked up he could barely speak. He had to draw in a couple of deep breaths when he walked through the door.

The clean antiseptic smell hit him like a slap, instantly transporting him to that dreadful day. After his parents and brother were killed he had gone with his grandparents to the hospital where they had been taken. He still remembered those long corridors with the sound of his trainers squeaking as he walked that agonising walk to where his family were lying lifeless. He remembered the looks from the doctors and nurses—a mixture of compassion, I'm-glad-it's-not-my-loved-ones-lying-in-there, and business-as-usual indifference. He remembered the shock of seeing his mother's and father's and brother's bodies draped in shroud-like sheets. Not being able to grasp the thought of them never coming home, of life never being the same.

It had felt as if he had stepped into a parallel universe—it hadn't been him standing there looking at his family but some other kid. Someone who *could* deal with it. Someone who wouldn't carry the wound of loss around for the rest of his life.

Cristiano found the emergency department and asked a nurse for Alice's whereabouts in a voice that sounded nothing like his own. He was led to a cubicle where Alice was lying with her eyes closed and hooked up to a saline drip. He saw the rise and fall of her chest and a giant wave of relief swept through him. He opened his mouth to say her name but nothing came out. He reached for her hand not attached to the drip and she opened her eyes and gave him a tremulous smile. 'Hi.'

He sank to the chair beside the bed because he was sure his legs were going to fold beneath him.

'What happened? What's wrong, *cara*? Are you unwell? I was so worried I thought you might be…' He swallowed back the word. 'You scared the hell out of me. Are you all right?'

'I'm perfectly fine. I just got a bit dehydrated and almost passed out. I didn't want all this fuss but the lady in the shop I was in was so pushy and—'

'It was a good thing she was,' Cristiano said. 'Why haven't you been drinking enough? Are you not feeling well? You should have said—'

'I was busy, that's all.' She gave him a weary smile. 'Since we got back from Italy I've been run off my feet. I didn't get lunch and I hadn't had anything to drink since breakfast and that was only a sip or two of tea.'

He cradled her hand in both of his. Guilt slammed through him. It was his fault she hadn't had a proper breakfast. He had distracted her with a passionate kiss that had ended with them making love up against the kitchen bench. He couldn't resist her when she was all dressed up for work in that crisp smart uniform. He couldn't resist her, period. He brought her hand up to his mouth and gently pressed a kiss to it.

'How soon before I can take you home or do they want to keep you in overnight?'

She lifted her arm connected to the cannula. 'Just until this runs through.'

Cristiano stroked her fingers. 'You almost gave me a heart attack, young lady.'

She gave him a rueful movement of her lips. 'Sorry.'

'What shop were you in?'

Her gaze fell away from his. 'A bridal boutique.'

Cristiano made a 'that figures' sound. 'Yeah, well, I felt like passing out when I came in here. Bridal boutiques aren't your favourite haunts and hospitals aren't mine.'

Her gaze came back to his, her brow wrinkled in concern. 'I'm so sorry for making you panic. I didn't want anyone to call you. I knew I'd be all right once I got some fluids on board.'

Why hadn't she got someone to call him? Didn't she realise how that made him feel? Didn't she have an inkling of what he'd gone through just then? 'But you should have called me or had someone do it for you.'

Her frown deepened. 'Why should I?'

He gave her a speaking look. 'Come on, Alice, we're engaged to be married, for God's sake. I'm the first person you or someone taking care of you should call when something like this happens.'

Her gaze slipped out of reach of his. 'We're not exactly like a normal couple, though, are we?'

Cristiano tightened his hold on her hand. 'This isn't the time or place to have this conversation. You're not well and I'm in no state to be rational.'

There was a long silence.

'Aren't you going to ask?' Alice said.

'Ask what?'

She turned her head to meet his gaze. 'Whether I'm pregnant.'

Cristiano's heart juddered to a stop and then started again with a sickening jolt. 'Are you?'

'No.'

He was glad...*wasn't he*? Of course he was. A baby was the last thing he wanted. A baby would change everything. He didn't want anything changed. Their marriage was two weeks away and that was all he wanted to think about right now. Get the job done. Mission accomplished. Move on.

'That's good.' He gave her hand a reassuring squeeze. 'I bet you're relieved about that.'

Another weary smile flickered across her mouth. 'Sure am.' She shifted on the bed as if the mattress was uncomfortable. 'I've been asked to be godmother to a client-stroke-friend's baby. I'm going to her wedding after I do her make-up next weekend. She's invited you since we're...you know, supposed to be engaged.'

'Would you like me to go with you?'

Her teeth sank into the pillow of her lip for a moment. 'I guess it'll be a good practice run, huh? See how it's done and all.'

'You've been to a wedding before, surely? Or has your aversion to them stretched that far?'

'I was flower girl at my mother's second marriage,' Alice said. 'I tripped going up the aisle and my stepfather told me off for it afterwards in front of all the guests. I was so mortified I wet my pants.'

Cristiano frowned. 'How old were you?'

'Six. He carried on about it for years and my mother never did anything to stop him.' She gave a little sigh. 'I was glad when he left her for another woman. But for a while after Mum blamed me for jinxing their wedding day.'

'Does she still blame you?'

'No, not now.' Another sigh wafted past her lips. 'But I didn't go to her third wedding on principle.'

'In case you tripped up the aisle?'

She gave him a worldly look. 'No, because her third husband has wandering hands and is a thief.'

Cristiano could see now why she had a thing about marriage. 'What about your father? Did he ever marry again?'

'Yes, and surprisingly it's working,' she said. 'He and Tania haven't had it easy, though. They have a little boy with severe autism. That's why I give Dad money from time to time, to pay for Sam's therapy.'

'That's kind of you.'

She gave a little movement of her lips that could have loosely passed for a smile. 'My dad isn't as bad as my mother always makes out. He just wasn't ready for marriage way back then. He's grown up now. He's taking responsibility for his wife and family. I know he wasn't an angel by any means when he was married to my mother, but he wasn't in love with her. Not the way he is with Tania.'

Her fingers plucked at the hem of the sheet.

'I guess that's what makes or breaks a marriage. Whether the love is strong enough to cope with what life dishes up.'

The nurse came in at that point and Cristiano moved aside so she could detach the drip from Alice's arm. He couldn't help thinking of how little he had known of Alice's background in the past. Why hadn't he asked her more about her childhood? Why hadn't he told her more about his?

They had been two people madly in lust with each other, sharing their bodies but not sharing their hearts and minds. Not communicating other than on a physical level. He had found out more about her in this hospital cubicle than he had in the whole time he had dated her in the past. Would it have made a difference if he'd talked to her? Really talked to her?

'You're good to go,' the nurse said once the drip was out and the paperwork dealt with. 'Take care of yourself, Alice. Keep those fluids up and get plenty of rest, okay?'

'I'll make sure she does,' Cristiano said.

Alice walked out of the hospital with Cristiano's arm around her waist. Her headache had eased and her stomach had stopped its churning. He had looked so undone by her being sick. She had never seen him look so distressed. Did that mean he cared more about her than he let on? Surely it wasn't an act for the sake of appearances?

But then there was a lot hanging in the balance. If she didn't fulfil the terms of the will then he would lose those shares and the home he had grown up in after his family were killed.

Or was that why he had been so rattled? Because hospitals reminded him of the accident that had taken his family from him?

Cristiano hailed a cab and within a short while they were home at her house and she was tucked up in bed with a long cool glass of water with a slice of lemon and ice cubes in it. He sat on the edge of the bed beside her, his hand taking one of hers in a gentle hold. 'How are you feeling?'

'Tired and a bit embarrassed about all the fuss I've caused.'

His fingers stroked the back of her hand. 'Yeah, well, you certainly gave me a bad half an hour or so.' His thumb did a slow brush over each of her tendons as if he were committing them to memory. He looked at her with a strained gaze. 'I thought I was going to lose you a second time.'

Alice squeezed his hand, her heart giving a little flutter at the depth of caring in his eyes. 'I wish I hadn't left the way I did back then. I ended up hurting myself more than you.'

'We hurt each other, *cara*,' he said. 'I can't believe I was so damn stubborn about it. I could've called you in a day or two. I *should've* called you. But I was too proud. Proud and angry. All those years went by. Not a day passed without me thinking of what could have been.'

His fingers tightened on her hand.

'I thought losing my family was bad, but losing you seven years ago was like a lid slamming down on all of my hopes. I decided it was better to be alone than to invite such rejection again. I've kept every relationship since as shallow and temporary as I could. Until now.'

Until now.

What did that mean? Did it mean he wanted their relationship to continue past the six months laid down in his grandmother's will? Alice reached up to stroke his face.

'We've been such stubborn fools—me in particular. I was so determined not to love anyone in case they took control of me, but I think I fell in love with you that first day when you made me laugh about my backpack catching your clothing. I spent the next six weeks denying it, blocking it. Sabotaging it.'

He pressed his lips against her bent fingers. 'We have a second chance to work at our relationship. Nonna has given us that. But let's talk about that when you're not feeling so out of whack.' He leaned forward to drop a kiss to her forehead. 'I'll sleep in one of the spare rooms so you get a good night's sleep.'

Alice hung onto his hand when he rose from the bed. 'No, don't go.'

'Alice, I—'

'Just hold me, okay?'

He gave a sigh and gathered her close, his chin resting on top of her head. 'As long as you need me I'll be here.'

How about for ever?

CHAPTER ELEVEN

ALICE WOKE THE next morning to find Cristiano lying beside her on top of the bedcovers with his legs crossed at the ankles. He was still fully dressed, although his tie was askew and the first three buttons of his shirt undone and his sleeves rolled up his forearms. His hair was rumpled as if he'd raked his fingers through it and his face looked tired and drawn.

She rolled to her side and tiptoed a fingertip down the bridge of his nose. His face gave a twitch or two and then his eyes opened and he sat bolt upright.

'What?' He sucked in a harsh-sounding breath. 'Oh, sorry, *cara*. You okay? Did you say something?'

'No, I was just watching you sleep.'

He dragged a hand down his face. 'Is that what you call it? I feel like I've been awake for a month.' He narrowed his gaze and lifted his arm to peer at his watch. Dropping it back to the bed with a dead arm flop. 'God. Five a.m.'

Alice stroked her fingers down the raspy slope of his cheek. 'Do you realise that's the first night we've spent together without making love?'

He cranked open one eye. 'Why do you think I'm on the outside of these sheets?'

She nestled closer, leaning over him so her breasts were crushed against his chest. 'I'm not sick now. In fact, I'm fighting fit.'

The other darkly glinting eye opened. 'I thought we weren't supposed to be fighting any more?'

Alice slipped a hand down to where he was as hard as stone. 'Feels to me you're already armed and dangerous.'

He gave her a sexy grin and flipped her so she was lying beneath him, his hand cupping her breast. 'If I were a good man I'd insist you have something to eat and drink before I ravish you.'

She trailed a fingertip across his lower lip. 'I'm only hungry and thirsty for you.'

He took her mouth in a long slow kiss that stirred her senses into overdrive. But just when she thought he'd reach for a condom and take things further, he pulled back and got off the bed. Something about his expression alerted her to a change of mood.

'Sorry, *cara*. I must be a better man than I thought.' He leaned down to brush her forehead with a light-as-air kiss, so light it was just shy of being impersonal. 'Stay right where you are. I'm going to give you breakfast in bed.'

Alice lay back against the pillows while she waited. Maybe they'd talk about their future over breakfast. Surely he hadn't forgotten what he'd said last night?

They'd been given a second chance to work at their relationship.

He was being so kind, so solicitous. He was acting exactly like a man in love…wasn't he? Last night he had looked so distraught at the hospital and again when . they'd come home, fussing over her and holding her in his arms all night without getting a wink of sleep himself. Didn't that mean he loved her?

Then why hadn't he said something?

She'd told him last night she loved him…or at least that she had fallen in love with him the first moment they'd met. Why hadn't he said it back? Or hadn't he said it because he didn't feel that way now? Had his tenderness last night just been a reaction to the shock of finding her in hospital?

Alice couldn't stop the panic rising. What if she'd misread their conversation last night? What if he'd just said those words to settle her for the night after her health scare? Was it her imagination or was he withdrawing from her? When had he ever pulled away from a kiss? Was he backing away from a longer relationship?

Had her confession of love made him rethink their involvement?

In two weeks they would be married, but on what terms? Temporary. No future stretching out in front of them. No plans for making a family together and raising them with love and commitment. Their relationship, although it would be formalised with a certificate of marriage, would be nothing more than a transient affair—as he'd stated time and time again he wanted it to be.

How could she agree to that when she wanted the opposite?

Yesterday, when the doctor asked Alice if there was any possibility she could be pregnant, a balloon of hope had risen in her chest. But then she'd realised the futility of harbouring such a hope. Cristiano didn't want a family. He didn't want what she wanted.

The sad irony of their reversed wishes made her realise again how devastated he must have felt when she'd walked out on him that day in that restaurant. When the pregnancy test came back negative she was both relieved and disappointed. She didn't want to force him to stay with her. She wanted him to love her and commit to her, not because of a baby, not because of his well-meaning grandmother's machinations, but because he loved her more than anything else in the world. More than his stupid old shares, more than a luxury villa.

She thought of her friend Jennifer. She and Cristiano and Jennifer and Marcus would be married within a week of each other and yet you couldn't find two different couples. Jennifer and Marcus were deeply in love. They planned to do all the things young couples on the threshold of a life together planned.

What did Alice and Cristiano have? A six-month time limit. He wanted his shares and his family villa and the only way to get them was to marry her. Without his grandmother's will their affair would not have resumed. She would be fooling herself to think otherwise. He'd had seven years to do something about their 'unfinished business' and he had done nothing.

Cristiano came back with a tray with muesli and toast and juice and tea. One bowl. One plate. One cup. 'Here we go.' He balanced the tray on her knees. 'Breakfast in bed.'

Alice picked up the cup of steaming tea. 'Aren't you going to join me?'

'I have a couple of emails to see to. Stuff to do with the wedding and so on. Do you need a hand choosing a dress? I've got some time today if you're—'

'Don't you know it's bad luck for the groom to see the bride's dress before the wedding?'

Something about his slanted smile made her heart

shrivel like a dried-up leaf. 'It's not like we have to worry about that, do we?'

Alice searched his face for a moment, her teeth worrying her bottom lip. He didn't seem at all fazed by the fact their marriage was going to be temporary. Surely if he cared about her he would say something?

Why wasn't he saying something?

Didn't he have a conscience? Marriage was sacred. No one should enter into it without proper commitment and consent. It was a travesty to do otherwise. Didn't he feel the slightest bit conflicted about what they were doing? There was her answer right there. No. He didn't. All he wanted was the terms of the will ticked off. Goal achieved. Problem solved.

She put her cup back down and lifted the tray off her knees.

'What's wrong?' Cristiano took the tray off her, frowning. 'Why are you getting out of bed?'

Alice got to her feet and pushed her hair back behind her shoulders. 'I'm not sure I can do this.'

'It's just breakfast in bed,' he said. 'No one's insisting you take the day off work, although maybe I should. You push yourself way too hard. Meghan told me you never take a holiday.'

She turned and faced him. 'I thought we were going to talk. So let's talk.'

'About what?'

Alice wrapped her arms around her body as if to contain the emotions threatening to burst out of her. What was with his blank expression? Didn't he remember anything about last night? 'About us. About the fact I love you and want to have a future with you. A family.'

His expression locked down, every muscle on his

face freezing as if turned to marble. 'I don't think now's the right time to talk about—'

'When *is* the right time?' Alice said. 'We have two weeks until we get married. You told me last night we would discuss the fact we've been given a second chance at our relationship via your grandmother. So let's discuss it. I'm not unwell now.'

He moved to the other side of the room, straightening objects on her dressing table that didn't need straightening. His back was turned to her but she could see part of his reflection in the mirror. He was shutting her out. Withdrawing from her.

'Can we talk about this some other time? I have a lot on my mind right now.'

Alice wasn't going to be fobbed off. 'If we don't discuss it now, then I'm afraid I can't marry you. It wouldn't be right for me or for you.'

He turned from the dressing table, a flash of irritation firing off at the back of his gaze and a muscle leaping in his jaw. 'What are you talking about? You stand to inherit millions out of this.'

She let out a frustrated breath. 'Life isn't just about money, Cristiano. It's about much more than that. I don't care about the money. Do you really think if I were motivated by money I would've rejected your proposal seven years ago?'

'We're not talking about back then, Alice.' His voice was deep and steady but that muscle near his mouth was speeding up. 'We're talking about now. I've told you what I'm prepared to commit to and having a family is not even on the whiteboard.'

'I want more than a temporary marriage,' Alice said. 'I want a proper one. I want a family. Last night when the doctor told me I wasn't pregnant I realised how much I wished I were having a baby. But you don't want a baby. You don't want what I want at all.'

His eyes were obsidian black, the tension around his mouth making his lips appear white at the corners. 'We agreed on the terms. You're the one who's been on a soapbox for years about how marriage is a domestic prison for women, and now you want the white picket fence and the double pram?'

Alice held his gaze with a resolve she hadn't thought possible even minutes earlier. But she couldn't back down now. *Wouldn't* back down. He'd had plenty of opportunity to tell her he loved her but he hadn't. Even if he said it now, how could she believe it wasn't a ploy to make her agree to the terms of the will?

'I want the fairy tale and I don't want to settle for anything less than absolute commitment,' she said. 'I want my marriage to be for ever, not for six months.'

He stalked to the other side of the bedroom, his hand rubbing at the back of his neck as if something were burning him there. He swung back to face her, his expression going back to cold, hard marble. 'I'm not going to parrot the words you think you want to hear. Why are you doing this—?'

'I wouldn't believe you if you said you loved me now,' Alice said. 'You're completely focussed on getting those shares and keeping your grandmother's villa in your family's hand. That's all you care about. You don't care about me. I don't think you ever did. You care about what *you* want—what I would do for you by being your wife. Our relationship has always been more about you than us as a unit, and if you were honest with yourself you'd admit it.'

'Alice, listen to me.' His voice softened but she got the sense his anger was not far away. 'You're still not well. You're not thinking straight. You have too much to lose to throw this now. Just hop back into bed and I'll—'

'And you'll what?' Alice cast him a frosty glare. 'Seduce me into seeing things your way? That's what you always tried to do in the past. You never listened to me when we had a difference of opinion. You tried to solve everything with sex. But sex won't solve this. I want more from you than great sex. Much, much more.'

He drew in a deep breath and released it in a whoosh. 'So that's it? Marriage or nothing?'

Alice gave him a wry look. 'Your words, not mine, but they'll do.' She took off her engagement ring and handed it to him. 'I think it's best if we don't see each other again.'

He ignored her outstretched palm, his mouth curling up at one corner. 'Keep it. You can pawn it so you can set up your spa or throw it away for all I care.'

Alice closed her hand around the ring, not one bit surprised when it cut into her palm as sharply as his words had into her heart. 'You won't ever be happy, Cristiano, because deep down you don't think you deserve to be. You refuse to love someone in case they withdraw that love or fate takes it away from you.'

He snatched up his jacket from the back of the dressing-table chair. 'Leave your psychoanalysis for someone who gives a damn. You don't know me as well as you think.'

'I know,' Alice said. 'That's why we were doomed from the start. You don't want anyone to get close to you. I can't be in a relationship like that. I want emotional honesty.' *I want you to love me.*

'Oh, and you're the big expert on emotional honesty, aren't you, Alice?' His eyes blazed with bitterness. 'You think I'm going to believe you're suddenly madly in love with me? A few days ago you wanted to gouge my eyes out. What you're doing is manipulating. Trying to get your future sorted by issuing me with an ultimatum. How about a bit of intellectual honesty, hey? Let's try that instead. I can't give you what you want. Simple as that. Take it or leave it.'

'I don't hate you. I never hated you.'

He gave a snort. 'Yeah, well, guess what? I don't give a damn either way.'

Alice winced when the bedroom door snapped shut on his exit. She listened to the tread of his footsteps as he left her house, her breath stalling in the hope he would stop and turn back. Come back up the stairs and swing open her bedroom door and say he was sorry. That he would sweep her into his arms and say of course he loved her and wanted to spend the rest of his life with her.

But the only thing she got was silence.

Cristiano had never felt so flooded with such confusing emotions. Anger. Disappointment. Bitterness. Anger again. A hot cauldron of bubbling feelings was threatening to explode out of his chest. He had to stop to lean over and place his hands on his knees to get control of his breath. In. Out. In. Out. How could she do this to him? Now?

Two weeks.

Two miserable weeks and his shares and the villa would have been secure.

Why? Why? Why?

He'd thought they were fine. He'd thought everything was ticking along just as he'd wanted it. But just like seven years ago she had blindsided him. His guard had been down. He was so thrown by her being taken to hospital he hadn't seen what was right in front of him. That sexy little crawl over his chest to make him feel secure and then *wham*! She wanted to control him. Manipulate him into doing things her way.

No way was he going to be her puppet. He'd told her the terms. He'd been honest about what he was prepared to give. She was the one shifting the goalposts.

Just like you did in the past, dropping that proposal on her.

Cristiano swatted away the thought as if it were an annoying fly. *So?* He'd shifted them right on back. A short-term marriage was all he was prepared to have. And even that was a stretch. He didn't want the responsibility of maintaining a long-term relationship. He didn't want the *emotional honesty* such a relationship demanded.

If he opened up the vault of his heart then that would undo all the work he'd put in since he was that boy of eleven hearing his parents and brother were never coming back. He could not allow himself to be that vulnerable. Not again. Look at what last night had done to him. Rushing into that hospital to see Alice had thrown him into a chest-seizing panic. He'd lain awake most of the night with residual dread still chugging through his veins like jagged cubes of ice. He hadn't trusted her confession of love last night. If she'd loved him way back then, why had she walked out and never looked back?

You did the same to her.

Cristiano didn't want to be reminded of how badly he'd handled things in the past. It was better this way. He couldn't give her what she wanted. He wasn't that person any more. Maybe he'd never been that person. He was too damaged by the loss of his family. He kept people at a distance. He controlled them because it was the only way he could harness the fear. The fear that clawed at him. The fear that reminded him with sharp little jabs of how easily he could lose the ones he dared to love. It was easier not to love. To not even think about the word. To pretend his feelings were something else. Lust, attraction, mild affection.

Anything but love.

By the time Alice got to work she had another headache. But the pain in her head was nothing to the pain in her heart. Cristiano had summed up his feelings about her. He didn't give a damn either way. He could take her or leave her. He had chosen to leave her.

'Hey, where's your engagement ring?' Meghan asked when she came in for the day. 'My first client wants to see it. She read about you and Cristiano on…' She frowned. 'Is something wrong?'

Alice blinked away the moisture in her eyes. 'Cristiano and I are not getting married after all. We've broken—'

'Not getting married?' Meghan gasped. 'Why the hell not? You two are the most in love couple I've ever seen. The air crackles like a power station when you guys are in the same room.'

Alice pressed her lips together to stop them from trembling. 'He doesn't love me. He's…oh, it's too complicated to explain.'

'What do you mean he doesn't love you?' Meghan's eyes were slit-thin with incredulity. 'You should've seen him when he came here yesterday and found out you were in hospital. I thought he was going to pass out on the spot. He was as white as our deluxe collagen face mask.'

Alice wished it were true. Wished he loved her. But if he loved her he wouldn't be baulking at commitment. That was what love was all about. Commitment. Trust. A future, not a time line.

'He doesn't want what I want. He doesn't want kids.'

Meghan's face fell. 'Oh...well then, that's a deal-breaker.' But then she brightened again. 'But maybe he'll change his mind. Lots of men do. They come round to it eventually, when they—'

'He won't,' Alice said. 'He's stubborn like that.'

Meghan waggled her eyebrows. 'Mmm, like some-one else I know.'

Alice frowned. 'Don't you have work to do?'

Meghan gave her a 'kicked puppy' look. 'I'm really sorry about you breaking up with Cristiano. But he's had a lot going on in his life—his gran dying and this big new development. Maybe he needs a bit of time to think things over.'

'Like another seven years?'

Meghan bit her lip. 'He really is stubborn, isn't he?'

Alice gave her a grim look. 'He could open a men-toring academy for mules.'

CHAPTER TWELVE

CRISTIANO WAS PRESSING on with his London development on principle. He wasn't the sort of man to walk away from a business deal because of personal issues. He kept work and his private life separate. Mostly. Although having to visit the Chelsea site with Alice's beauty salon on the ground floor of the building he'd bought was like having molars pulled with bolt cutters. Confronting failure was something he assiduously avoided. Returning to the scene of the crime, so to speak, was anathema to him. He would prefer to be on the other side of the globe right now. Siberia. Outer Mongolia.

Anywhere but here.

Somehow the press had heard the engagement was off. He had refused to comment and apparently so had Alice as the articles were evidently from 'reliable sources close to the couple' whatever the hell that meant. But after a week of being chased to and from his hotel by the paparazzi, things had settled down.

Seven days of living without Alice. Not seeing her. Not touching her. Not making love to her.

Nothing.

A big yawning cavern of emptiness stretched out ahead of him. Just like the last time, only this time it was harder. Much harder. How had he done this before and for seven years? He'd convinced himself he'd done the right thing. Let her be free to live the life he couldn't give her. But the thought of her getting on with her life without him was eating away at him. Gnawing on his nerves until he was all but twitching with restlessness.

Cristiano had to meet with the architect on site to discuss some of the plans he had for the refit of the building. But the whole time he was in the meeting his eyes kept drifting to the window in the hope of seeing Alice coming in or out of her salon.

He was surprised the architect didn't notice, or maybe he did and was too polite to say anything. He'd noticed a wedding ring on the architect's finger and noticed too the screensaver on the guy's phone when he answered a call. It was a photo of his wife and young toddler and newborn baby. All the things Cristiano had convinced himself he didn't want.

But he *did* want them.

The realisation was like a light being switched on, shining on all the dark lonely places in his heart. Illuminating the hopes and dreams he had stashed and hidden away out of fear.

Cristiano finished the meeting and was about to turn left away from Alice's salon when he stopped mid-stride. This was ridiculous. What was he doing? Walking away a second time? Turning his back on the best thing that had ever happened to him? Who was he fooling?

He wasn't in lust with Alice. He was in love. He had always been in love with her. That was why he was so damn terrified. That was why he'd rushed the proposal seven years ago. He'd been so worried he might lose her so he'd made her an offer he'd thought she wouldn't be able to refuse.

But he'd got it all wrong. So horribly wrong.

He'd thought losing the shares and his *nonna*'s villa was the worst thing that could happen to him. But losing Alice was far worse. He couldn't lose her. Not again.

He had to talk to her. He couldn't let another day—another minute—pass without telling her he loved her and wanted the same things she wanted. Why had he left it a week? Seven days of miserable hell. No way was he leaving it a second longer.

He spun on his heel and went back the other way but he'd only taken two strides when he saw Meghan from Alice's beauty salon trotting towards him.

'Hi, Cristiano,' she said. 'Bad news about your breakup with Alice. But don't worry. I've got it all sorted. I've found her a new man. I'm setting up a blind date for her. He's a friend of a friend and he's so keen on having kids he's already got cupboards full of toys. Isn't that sweet?'

Cristiano felt as if he'd been slammed across the head with a plank. 'A blind date?'

'Yup.' Meghan's eyes twinkled. 'It worked a treat for one of our clients. They're getting married this weekend. Jennifer and Marcus. Alice is doing Jennifer's make-up for it.'

Cristiano had trouble speaking past the knot of despair stuck in his throat. 'She can't do that.'

'What?' Meghan's expression was guileless as a child. 'Do Jennifer's make-up? Don't be silly. That's her specialty!'

What Alice's specialty was to make him as mad as a wasp-stung bull. How could she date another man so quickly? What the hell was she doing going on a blind date? What if the guy was a freak? Some stranger who would— He couldn't bear to think about it. Jealousy rose in him like bile. He was choking on it. He could feel it bubbling up his windpipe like an overflowing drain. 'Where is she?' he asked.

Meghan pointed to the salon. 'She's in her office working on accounts. But she doesn't want to be—'

'You can cancel your friend of a friend, okay?' Cristiano said. 'If she's going on a date with anyone it's going to be with me.'

Alice couldn't concentrate on the rows of numbers on her computer screen. Normally seeing all those healthy figures would have made her do a happy dance. But she had never felt more miserable. A week had gone past and no word from Cristiano. Not even a text message. Nothing. A big fat nothing. The press had done their thing for a few days but she'd refused to speak to them. She'd even resorted to using disguises to avoid them when walking to and from her house or the salon.

Her mother had been 'too upset' to talk to her, which was typical. As if it was Alice's fault the marriage wasn't going ahead. Well, it was, but that was beside the point. But how could she go ahead with a marriage that was the opposite of what a marriage should be? What she wanted *her* marriage to be?

Meghan had been a stalwart support, making numerous cups of tea and bringing in a steady supply of cinnamon-covered doughnuts—Alice's weakness when dealing with stress. Sugar and fat were the only pleasures she had in her life now.

There was the sound of bell tinkling as the salon door

opened…although tinkling wasn't the right word. Firm footsteps came striding through the salon and Alice barely had time to get to her feet when her office door slammed back against the wall and Cristiano appeared. 'What the hell do you think you're doing?'

Alice kept her expression cool and composed even though her heart rate was doing its hummingbird impersonation. 'Accounts. It's been a good week for me. One of my best, actually.'

His expression was thunderous, all stormy clouds and dark shadows and lightning flashes in his eyes. 'Meghan tells me you're dating someone else.'

Alice frowned. 'What?'

His mouth was pressed into a chalk-white line. 'Don't do it, Alice.' He released a tight breath. 'Please.'

Alice was starting to join some dots and it was creating an interesting picture indeed. 'When were you speaking to Meghan?'

'Just now, outside.' He jerked his head towards the street. 'She said she was setting you up on a blind date with some friend of a friend who wants kids.'

'I don't know anything about a blind date,' Alice said. 'And you've got a hide storming in here telling me what to do with my private life when it's no concern of yours and nor will it ever—'

'If you want to have kids so badly then you can damn well have them with me.'

Alice opened her mouth to fling back another round of fire but stopped and gaped at him instead. Had she heard him correctly? Kids? He wanted kids? But then she realised what was going on. Jealousy. Not love. The big green-eyed monster was behind his change of heart.

She narrowed her gaze. 'So, let me get this straight.

You're offering to be a sperm donor and a cardboard cut-out husband because you're...*jealous*?' She said the word as if it were some sort of contagion.

Cristiano came around to her side of the desk and grasped her by the upper arms.

'Damn straight I am. Alice, I love you. I've been a stubborn fool all this time refusing to acknowledge it. I can handle the loss of the shares. I can handle the loss of the villa. What I can't handle is the loss of you. I've already lost you once. I don't want to lose you again. I was already coming here when I ran into Meghan. Please believe me, *cara*. Don't let anything else keep us apart. Will you marry me? Not because of Nonna's will, not because I'm jealous but because I love you and want to spend the rest of my life with you.'

Alice looked at him with watering eyes. 'Do you mean it? You're not just saying it because of the deadline?'

His hold tightened as if he were terrified she was going to slip out of his grasp. 'I don't care about the deadline other than I want to do what Nonna wanted. She knew I hadn't got over you. She knew I was too stubborn to see you again so she orchestrated it so I had no choice.'

Alice smiled. 'Like Meghan.'

He frowned. 'Meghan?'

Alice laced her arms around his neck. 'I'm not going on a blind date. Why would I do that when I only have eyes for you?'

Relief washed over his features and he smiled. 'The little meddling minx. She and Nonna must be kindred spirits.' He gathered her tight against his body. 'She saw what Nonna saw, what I refused to see. I love you, *tesoro mio*. I love you desperately. Please say you'll marry me.'

Alice looked into his handsome features so full of love and adoration for her. The softness in his dark brown eyes, the way he looked at her as if she were the most precious thing he could ever hold in his arms—made her feel so happy she could barely speak.

'I will marry you, darling. I can't think of anything I would rather do than be your wife and the mother of your children.'

He crushed her mouth beneath his in a kiss that spoke of the depth of his feelings. He drew back to smile at her, his own eyes suspiciously moist.

'I've spent so much of my life avoiding getting close to people in case I lost them. But I got to thinking I might as well have jumped in my family's coffins with them if I don't live a full and authentic life. I owe it to them to make the most of the time that was snatched away from them.'

Alice touched the track of dampness leaking from his eyes. 'I wish I'd been able to meet them. I'm sure they were wonderful people who loved you so much. They would be thrilled you're embracing life at last. I'm sure of it.'

Cristiano brushed her hair back with his hand. 'I've been thinking about what we can do together. You could have your wedding spa as a feature of my hotel. Here in London but also in Italy and France and Greece. You could have your own franchise. It will be something to build together.'

Alice held his face in her hands and kissed him. 'You are making all my dreams come true. I would love that.

It would be so wonderful to do it together just like your grandparents and parents did.'

He kissed her soundly, only breaking away to gaze down at her with a look of such devotion it made Alice's eyes tear up again.

'We've only got a week to pull off this wedding,' he said. 'Do you think we can do it?'

She stroked his lean jaw, and looked lovingly into his eyes. 'Together we can do anything.'

One year later...

Alice smiled at Cristiano as he came in from bringing in their bags from the car. They were spending their first wedding anniversary at his grandmother's villa where they came every few months to relax and recharge. Yes, *relax.* That word she used not to have in her vocabulary.

Her beauty spa at Cristiano's Chelsea hotel had finally opened a few weeks ago to great fanfare and she had recently appointed Meghan as her business manager and it was working a treat. It meant Alice could have the occasional week off without worrying about her clients not receiving the attention she prided herself on giving them.

And because she intended to take even more time off in a few months' time.

Alice took Cristiano by the hand and led him to the walnut table in the sitting room where the family photos were arranged. Whenever they came back to the villa they stood there and quietly acknowledged his family. Their wedding photo was next to his parents' and grandparents' wedding photos, creating a sense of continuity she knew gave him great comfort. It gave her great comfort too to see him so happy and settled after so much heartache. She hadn't told him yet, but soon there would be photos of the next generation of the Marchetti family.

'I have something to tell you, darling,' Alice said, squeezing his hand in excitement. 'I wanted to wait until we got here so the rest of the family could hear it as well.'

Cristiano's dark brown eyes misted. 'You're... *pregnant*?'

'I did a test this morning. I've been bursting to tell you but then I thought how lovely it would be for you to hear about it here amongst those who loved you so deeply.'

He gathered her close, kissing her tenderly and then holding her with such gentleness she had trouble keeping her own tears in check.

'How far along?' he said. 'Are you okay? Not sick? Feeling faint? Shouldn't you be resting? What about work—?'

Alice put a fingertip to his mouth to stall his speech. 'Meghan is going to cover me while I take maternity leave. And I feel fantastic...well, apart from a tiny bit of squeamishness. I'm six weeks pregnant according to my calculations. It must have been the weekend of the opening of your hotel and my spa.' She gave him a twinkling look. 'I seem to remember we had a lot of fun together that weekend.'

Cristiano cupped her face in his hands, his own eyes gleaming. 'I didn't know the meaning of the word until I met you. You've made me so happy, *cara*.'

Alice smiled and drew his head back down so her lips were within reach of his. 'We make each other happy, which is what your *nonna* recognised right from the start. I can't imagine how miserable I would be now if it hadn't been for her meddling.'

Cristiano grinned. 'Wise woman, my *nonna*. She knew there was only one woman in the world for me.'

He brushed her mouth with his. Once. Twice. Three times.

'You.'

* * * * *

If you enjoyed this story, don't miss these other great reads from Melanie Milburne

UNWRAPPING HIS CONVENIENT FIANCÉE
HIS MISTRESS FOR A WEEK
THE MOST SCANDALOUS RAVENSDALE
ENGAGED TO HER RAVENSDALE ENEMY
AWAKENING THE RAVENSDALE HEIRESS
RAVENSDALE'S DEFIANT CAPTIVE

Available now!

MILLS & BOON®
MODERN™

POWER, PASSION AND IRRESISTIBLE TEMPTATION

0317/19

MILLS & BOON®

EXCLUSIVE EXTRACT

Stefano Moretti wants only revenge from his wife, Anna. When she reappears after leaving him, with no memory of their marriage, he realizes that this is his chance…for a red-hot private seduction, followed by a public humiliation! Until Stefano realizes there's something he wants more than vengeance—Anna, back in his bed for good!

Read on for a sneak preview of
ONCE A MORETTI WIFE

Stefano pressed his thumb to her chin and gently stroked it. 'When your memories come back you will know the truth. I will help you find them.'

Her heart thudding, her skin alive with the sensation of his touch, Anna swallowed the moisture that had filled her mouth.

When had she given in to the chemistry that had always been there between them, always pulling her to him? She'd fought against it right from the beginning, having no intention of joining the throng of women Stefano enjoyed such a legendary sex life with. To be fair, she didn't have any evidence of what he actually got up to under the bedsheets; indeed it was something she'd been resolute in *not* thinking about, but the steady flow of glamorous, sexy women in and out of his life had been pretty damning.

When had she gone from liking and hugely admiring

him but with an absolute determination to never get into bed with him, to marrying him overnight? She'd heard of whirlwind marriages before but from employee to wife in twenty-four hours? Her head hurt just trying to wrap itself around it.

Had Stefano looked at her with the same glimmer in his green eyes then as he was now? Had he pressed his lips to hers or had she been the one…?

'How will you help me remember us?' she asked in a whisper.

His thumb moved to caress her cheek and his voice dropped to a murmur. 'I will help you find again the pleasure you had in my bed. I will teach you to become a woman again.'

Mortification suffused her, every part of her anatomy turning red.

I will teach you to be a woman again?

His meaning was clear. He knew she was a virgin.

Anna's virginity was not something she'd ever discussed with anyone. Why would she? Twenty-three-year-old virgins were rarer than the lesser-spotted unicorn. For Stefano to know that…

Dear God, it was *true*.

All the denial she'd been storing up fell away.

She really had married him.

Don't miss
ONCE A MORETTI WIFE
By Michelle Smart

Available April 2017
www.millsandboon.co.uk

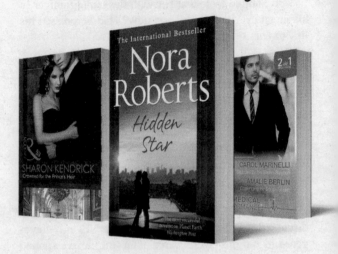

MILLS & BOON®

Read on for an exclusive extract

How did she walk away? Lydia wondered.

How did she go over and kiss that sulky mouth and say goodbye when really she wanted to climb back into bed?

But rather than reveal her thoughts she flicked that internal default switch which had been permanently set to 'polite'.

'Thank you so much for last night.'

'I haven't finished being your tour guide yet.'

He stretched out his arm and held out his hand but Lydia didn't go over. She did not want to let in hope, so she just stood there as Raul spoke.

'It would be remiss of me to let you go home without seeing Venice as it should be seen.'

'Venice?'

'I'm heading there today. Why don't you come with me? Fly home tomorrow instead.'

There was another night between now and then, and Lydia knew that even while he offered her an extension he made it clear there was a cut-off.

Time added on for good behaviour.

And Raul's version of 'good behaviour' was that there would

be no tears or drama as she walked away. Lydia knew that. If she were to accept his offer then she had to remember that.

'I'd like that.' The calm of her voice belied the trembling she felt inside. 'It sounds wonderful.'

'Only if you're sure?' Raul added.

'Of course.'

But how could she be sure of anything now she had set foot in Raul's world?

He made her dizzy.

Disorientated.

Not just her head, but every cell in her body seemed to be spinning as he hauled himself from the bed and unlike Lydia, with her sheet-covered dash to the bathroom, his body was hers to view.

And that blasted default switch was stuck, because Lydia did the right thing and averted her eyes.

Yet he didn't walk past. Instead Raul walked right over to her and stood in front of her.

She could feel the heat—not just from his naked body but her own—and it felt as if her dress might disintegrate.

He put his fingers on her chin, tilted her head so that she met his eyes, and it killed that he did not kiss her, nor drag her back to his bed. Instead he checked again. 'Are you sure?'

'Of course,' Lydia said, and tried to make light of it. 'I never say no to a free trip.'

It was a joke but it put her in an unflattering light. She was about to correct herself, to say that it hadn't come out as she had meant, but then she saw his slight smile and it spelt approval.

A gold-digger he could handle, Lydia realised.

Her emerging feelings for him—perhaps not.

At every turn her world changed, and she fought for a semblance of control. Fought to convince not just Raul but herself that she could handle this.

Don't miss
THE INNOCENT'S SECRET BABY
by Carol Marinelli
OUT NOW

BUY YOUR COPY TODAY
www.millsandboon.co.uk

Join Britain's BIGGEST Romance Book Club

50% OFF your first parcel

- **EXCLUSIVE offers** every month

- **FREE delivery direct** to your door

- **NEVER MISS a title**

- **EARN Bonus Book** points

Call Customer Services
0844 844 1358*

or visit
millsandboon.co.uk/subscriptions

* This call will cost you 7 pence per minute plus your phone company's price per minute access charge.